P9-BZJ-163

THE TEMPLAR BROTHERHOOD

A Lost Treasure of the Templars Novel

JAMES BECKER

BERKLEY
New York

BERKLEY

An imprint of Penguin Random House LLC

375 Hudson Street, New York, New York 10014

Copyright © 2017 by Peter Smith

Penguin Random House supports copyright. Copyright fuels creativity, encourages diverse voices, promotes free speech, and creates a vibrant culture. Thank you for buying an authorized edition of this book and for complying with copyright laws by not reproducing, scanning, or distributing any part of it in any form without permission. You are supporting writers and allowing Penguin Random House to continue to publish books for every reader.

BERKLEY is a registered trademark and the B colophon is a trademark of Penguin Random House LLC.

ISBN 9780451473974

First Edition: October 2017

Printed in the United States of America

1   3   5   7   9   10   8   6   4   2

Cover photos: man standing in cave © Paul Gooney/Arcangel; human skull © freedomnaruk/Shutterstock; note written in Latin © Le Panda/Shutterstock

This is a work of fiction. Names, characters, places, and incidents either are the product of the author's imagination or are used fictitiously, and any resemblance to actual persons, living or dead, business establishments, events, or locales is entirely coincidental.

If you purchased this book without a cover, you should be aware that this book is stolen property. It was reported as "unsold and destroyed" to the publisher, and neither the author nor the publisher has received any payment for this "stripped book."

PRAISE FOR THE NOVELS
OF JAMES BECKER

The Lost Testament

"Extremely satisfying and ridiculously exciting! I was glued to *The Lost Testament*. . . . Let the fast pace, the exciting plot, the likable leads, and the spot-on prose carry you away."
—For Winter Nights

Echo of the Reich

"Amazingly good."
—Fresh Fiction

"It deserves the widest possible audience."
—Reviewing the Evidence

"Clever and imaginative twists . . . highly recommended."
—Euro Crime

The First Apostle

"Fast-paced action propels the imaginative and controversial plot."
—*Publishers Weekly*

"This is an utterly spellbinding book . . . stunning and breathtaking. . . . I was left shattered and stunned."
—Euro Crime

The Messiah Secret

"An entertaining hunt-and-chase thriller . . . appealing and clever protagonists coupled with intriguing history."
—*Publishers Weekly*

"Superbly crafted . . . it breaks new ground . . . a tightly worded, sharply written thriller."
—CrimeSquad.com

"Exciting and gripping . . . gets your adrenaline racing."
—Euro Crime

ALSO BY JAMES BECKER

The First Apostle
The Moses Stone
The Messiah Secret
The Nosferatu Scroll
Echo of the Reich
The Lost Testament
The Lost Treasure of the Templars
The Templar Archive

Writing a novel is a lonely occupation, and I would like to thank both my British literary agent, Luigi Bonomi of LBA, and his American counterpart, George Lucas of Inkwell Management, for their continued support and encouragement. And, of course, my thanks go to Brent Howard and the dedicated team at Penguin Random House in America, who manage to weed out the bits that don't work and give a good polish to what I always hope is a diamond in the rough.

And, finally, and as always, my profound thanks to Sally, for her patience and recognition that although I might be in the same house as her, and even in the same room, I'm not always actually there, my mind transporting me to all sorts of unfamiliar locations, back and forth across the centuries and around the world.

THE TEMPLAR
BROTHERHOOD

Prologue

He had endured with fortitude. That, nobody could deny.

They'd started relatively gently, placing rods between his fingers and squeezing his hands in a kind of vise to break the bones in his fingers one by one, but he'd said nothing in answer to their repeated questions. Then they'd subjected him to the searing agony of the strappado, tying his hands together behind his back, attaching weights to his feet, and then jerking him off the ground by a rope secured to his bound wrists. But still he'd remained silent, even when they'd used the red-hot iron to burn deep furrows in the flesh of his naked body, but when they lost patience and put him on the bed, he knew he would finally break.

They tied his body down, lashing his arms and legs

with ropes so that he couldn't move at all, his feet projecting over the end of the iron frame. Then they coated his
feet in oil, stoked the charcoal brazier, added more fuel,
and positioned it just inches away from the soles of his
naked feet. Almost instantly, a wave of unbearable agony
swept through his body as he felt—and could even smell—
his own flesh start to cook.

And then he screamed. A scream that cut through the
dark and gloomy silence of the makeshift torture chamber
located in the cellars under the Paris preceptory of the
Knights Templar. A scream that sounded as if it could
echo for a thousand years, or imprint itself forever on the
dank stone walls of the chamber. A scream that sounded
as if it might never end.

But it did. As the last of his breath was forced out of
his lungs, the man jerked twice against his bonds and
then lay still and silent, his ruined body limp.

"Insert the screen," the inquisitor ordered.

The two torturers stepped forward and slid a thick and
heavy plank of wood between the brazier and the feet of
the heretic, feet from which smoke was rising and from
which most of the skin had already been burned away,
the flesh beneath blackened from the heat, blood dripping
steadily onto the unyielding and stained stone floor.

For a few seconds the inquisitor said nothing more,
just stared at the body lying in front of him. Then he
seemed to come to a decision.

"Try him."

One of the torturers stepped over to the brazier,
wrapped a length of heavy cloth around the end of an

iron bar that projected from the side of it, pulled it out, and moved across to stand beside the body on the metal bed. He looked across at the tall wooden chair in which the black-robed inquisitor was sitting, awaiting final confirmation. Then he lowered the glowing end of the bar onto the stomach of the heretic and simply left it there.

Again, the smell of burning flesh rose from the bed as the red-hot iron seared its way through skin and flesh, but the body of the man remained silent and motionless.

The inquisitor made an impatient gesture, and the two torturers began loosening the bonds from the dead body, preparing to drag the corpse out of the chamber.

"If we go on at this rate, Brother Guillaume," the second inquisitor said, "we will have none left to subject to the cleansing flames. How many is that now?"

Guillaume Humbert, better known as Guillaume of Paris, the Grand Inquisitor of France and Confessor of the King, and the man given the task of extirpating the heresy of the Knights Templar, shook his head.

"Do not be concerned. He is the twenty-third soul we have failed to save, another suicide prompted by our gentle and righteous questioning. There are plenty of others still awaiting our attentions."

The rules governing the use of torture by inquisitors were based upon a papal bull issued on 15 May 1252 by Pope Innocent IV and entitled *Ad extirpanda*, and were comparatively rigid. But, like all rules, they were subject to discussion and interpretation. No individual, for example, could be tortured more than once, but the inquisitors simply regarded each new session as nothing more than a continuation of the first or the previous interrogation, and would continue indefinitely, until they'd either got what they wanted from the subject or he or she—because with regard to the appalling danger of heresy the church made no special allowances for women—was dead.

They were also forbidden to spill blood, to cause mutilation or death. This meant that no cutting instruments such as knives or pincers could be used, but crushing devices such as thumbscrews or iron boots that shattered the bones of the feet were felt to be entirely acceptable, and any mutilation that resulted was simply seen as an accidental by-product of the process, merely collateral damage. One favored technique was to extract the teeth, one by one and ignoring the comparatively small volume of blood that resulted as each tooth was pulled out, and to ask a question before each extraction. Then they'd probe the fresh cavity with a slim but red-hot spike if the answers failed to satisfy the inquisitors.

Death, when it occurred, was considered to be either an accident caused by the overenthusiastic application of a particular technique or instrument, or a deliberate act of suicide by an unreformed heretic, unable to speak the truth to his inquisitors. In fairness, as the task of the inquisitor was to save souls, torturing an individual to death was generally seen to be counterproductive, because of the certain knowledge that the soul of a suicide would be immediately and permanently consigned to the devil and the flames of hell. It would be an obvious and unfortunate failure of their task.

When Guillaume of Paris had begun his work, there

were 138 members of the *Pauperes commilitones Christi Templique Solomonici*, or the Poor Fellow-Soldiers of Christ and of the Temple of Solomon, more commonly known as the Knights Templar, languishing in the dungeons of their own preceptory, located just outside the city walls on the northern side of Paris. Thanks to the range of tortures applied, only 115 still remained among the living after exactly one month of questioning, and many of those would clearly not emerge from the building alive. And if Guillaume of Paris had his way, those that did survive would only be permitted to walk the short distance from the preceptory to the heavy wooden stake where they would end their days in the flames that would consume their bodies but ultimately, if the teachings of the church were to be believed, save their immortal souls.

The men chosen to extract detailed confessions of the heresies perpetrated by members of the Knights Templar were friars of the *Ordo Praedicatorum*, or Order of Preachers, the religious order approved by Pope Honorius III on 22 December 1216. They had become known as the "Black Friars" because of the black cappa, or cloak, they wore over their white habit, and from the fifteenth century onward they were commonly referred to as the Dominicans, after the name of their founder, Saint Dominic of Guzmán. A more irreverent Latin name that would later be given to them was *Domini canes*, meaning "Hounds of the Lord," a play on the name *Dominican*.

The order was founded to preach the gospel and combat heresy—meaning anything that the church did not agree with—and its motto was *Laudare, Benedicere, Praedicare*, which translated as "To Praise, to Bless, to Preach." But there was little evidence of any such noble and intellectual paths being followed in the dungeons of the Villeneuve du Temple. Instead, the two black-robed friars spent their days sitting on their elevated wooden seats, watching with total impassivity as a seemingly endless number of men were dragged into the chamber and their bodies progressively broken in front of them as the questioning, and the tortures, grew more intense.

The inquisitors knew, of course, that there was not the slightest possibility that any of the members of the Knights Templar were innocent of the charges laid before them. That would imply that the pope, Clement V, and the king of France, Philip IV, better known as Philippe le Bel or Philip the Fair—the men who, on Friday 13 October 1307, had orchestrated the arrest of every member of the Templar order they could lay their hands on—were both wrong. That could obviously not be the case, as Clement V, as the occupant of the Throne of Saint Peter, was relaying the word of God, with Philip acting as his secular confederate. The guilt of the Templars, therefore, was undeniable, well-established and common knowledge, and all the inquisitors were doing was trying to extract signed confessions for the crimes and heresies that they were certain the knights had perpetrated.

Because their guilt was certain, no witnesses for the defense would ever be called, no denials of the charges accepted, and of course there was no possibility of counterarguments. Anything the accused men said apart from a confession was clearly intended as nothing more than a devious way of excusing their very obvious guilt, so it could be—and invariably was—disregarded.

And up to that point in the interrogations, most of the Templars had admitted to at least some of their crimes after only the mildest of torture techniques had been applied to them. Most, for example, had admitted denying Christ upon their reception into the order, and even more that they had spat upon a crucifix during some of their secret ceremonies. Because it was known that members of the Knights Templar were forbidden to enjoy carnal relations with women, it was widely believed that they engaged in homosexual activities, but this charge, perhaps unexpectedly, bearing in mind what they were suffering, was admitted by almost none of the imprisoned knights. On the other hand, most agreed that they had been required to indecently kiss their superiors in the order, usually on the navel or at the base of the spine. In truth, and a fact that was certainly known but totally ignored by the inquisitors, according to the established rules of the Knights Templar, sodomy was regarded as an entirely sufficient reason for a knight to be expelled from the order, an offense that was considered just as serious as the murder of a Christian or desertion on the battlefield. And those knights who had admitted to this crime against nature had only done so when the agony of their tortures reached levels that almost no human being could endure.

Some other members of the order had admitted virtually everything the inquisitors suggested, in some cases even before they'd received their first wound from the glowing iron bar or had any of their fingers broken, but others stubbornly refused to say anything no matter what persuasion was applied to them, and even after having been shown a forged letter purporting to have been written by the Grand Master of the Knights Templar, Jacques de Molay, in which he confessed to every crime and practice suggested by the inquisitors and urged his subordinates to promptly do the same.

And although Guillaume of Paris was satisfied with most of the answers he was extracting from the rank-and-file members of the order, there was one question about which he had been specifically ordered by King Philip to obtain an answer. So far every knight he'd questioned had either denied any knowledge of this matter or had simply refused to reply. To make matters worse, it was not a question that directly related to what Guillaume privately regarded as the "Templar heresy," but concerned an entirely different matter, definitively secular rather than religious.

In fact, it was a question that he did not feel was appropriate to ask in the circumstances, though he knew he had no choice in the matter. If he disobeyed the king, he knew he could easily find himself back in that selfsame torture chamber, but this time as a victim rather than as an interrogator. And he would do anything to avoid that happening.

Having disposed of the broken body of the last victim, the two torturers returned to the chamber and stood before the pair of inquisitors, awaiting further instructions.

"Whom do you wish to question next, Guillaume?"

For a few moments, the Grand Inquisitor did not reply to his fellow friar, considering the strategy he would use for the next interrogation. The problem he had was that he was certain very few members of the Knights Templar order would know the answer to the question he'd been told to ask, and that those high-ranking knights would probably be prepared to endure any torture, and even go to their deaths, rather than reveal that particular piece of knowledge. But he was certain that the Grand Master, the knight in charge of all the other Templar Masters around the world, would know the information he sought. The two other men likely to have had access to the information were Hugues de Pairaud, the Visitor of the Temple, and Geoffroi de Charney, the Preceptor of Normandy. A third possible knight was Geoffroi de Gonneville, the Preceptor of Aquitaine. None of these four men, all of whom were just yards away from the torture chamber, chained to the walls of the dungeons, would be likely to talk easily, and he dared not run the risk of any of them dying under interrogation. Those four were destined to publicly burn, or never emerge from prison again. His instructions in that regard had been most explicit.

But perhaps there was an alternative, a way of persuading them to give up the information without running the risk of permanently damaging them. They were, after all, four comparatively elderly men who would never be able to withstand the kind of tortures that a man in his twenties could tolerate.

Guillaume of Paris made his decision.

"Bring in Jacques de Molay," he ordered.

Minutes later, the two torturers reappeared, half carrying and half dragging a bearded man with long white hair, barefoot and wearing a stained and filthy gray robe, who had clearly already suffered from the attentions of the inquisitors.

Against one wall of the chamber was a metal chair that was used to support a victim while his feet were being crushed in the iron boot, and Guillaume of Paris pointed at it.

"Tie him to the chair," he ordered.

As soon as de Molay had been immobilized, one of the torturers seized the metal boot and placed it in front of the chair, and started to make it ready for use, but the inquisitor stopped him with a single command.

"No," he said, "go back and bring another one of the prisoners. One who has not yet been questioned, and who is young and strong and able to last the rest of the day."

The torturers nodded almost simultaneously, turned, and left the chamber. They were paid to use their strength and ability to inflict the maximum possible level of pain on their victims, and to work under the specific instructions of the inquisitors. In short, they were paid to listen and to obey, and not to talk.

"Until today we have only questioned one man at a time," the second inquisitor said. "Why are you involving a second heretic?"

"I have received the most detailed orders from my master, the king," Guillaume of Paris said. "There is one matter which concerns him deeply and which I have been instructed to resolve if I am able. I believe that the information the king seeks is known to de Molay, but I also believe that he will not divulge it without extreme persuasion. I therefore intend to make him watch as the torturers practice their dark arts on a younger member of his order. Perhaps he may be induced to give the answers that I need, knowing that if he does not, the young man will suffer unbearable agonies in front of his eyes, agonies that I will make clear de Molay can end with a single word."

The second inquisitor nodded, clearly recognizing the logic of the older man's argument.

"If the matter is confidential," he said, "perhaps I should leave you."

Guillaume looked up as the door opened and the two burly torturers reappeared, dragging a third man, struggling ineffectually in their grip, between them.

"Yes," Guillaume said. "Perhaps you should."

He waited until the other friar had left the chamber, then stepped down from his seat and walked across to where Jacques de Molay was secured to the metal chair, looking at him with hostile, frightened eyes.

"You know the information that I want from you, old man," Guillaume said, his voice soft but laced with menace. "But it will not be you who suffers if you fail to give it to me. Now, will you answer the question I asked you before?"

De Molay shook his head, and then very deliberately spat, his spittle landing squarely on Guillaume of Paris's cloak and sliding slowly down the material.

The inquisitor looked down at the spittle for a moment, then back at the man in front of him.

"Very well," he said. "When you are ready to talk, nod your head. I will be watching both you and the suffering of this young knight, who I believe is a recent recruit to your godless order."

Then he turned and walked back to his chair, seated himself comfortably, and looked across at the two torturers, the young Templar knight still writhing in their grasp.

"Prepare him," he instructed. "We will begin with the strappado."

1

"What we have here," David Mallory said, looking carefully at the ancient piece of vellum and running his fingers through his slightly untidy blond hair, "is yet another puzzle. And I don't mind telling you that this is getting a bit tiresome."

Robin Jessop looked from the vellum—a piece of fine calfskin used in the medieval period for only the most important of documents—to the three sheets of paper upon which, a few minutes earlier, Betty Howarth had transcribed the ancient text, letter by letter, under Robin's direction. She glanced at Mallory and then again at the vellum. It had been folded about the midline, the outer surface darkened with age, while the other, inner surface was much lighter in color, having been protected by the fold and the narrow confines of its hiding place under the false bottom of the wooden chest. The writing on this inner surface was clearly legible, the ink still a solid black. Not that they could read it, of course, because the author of the text had done his best to make sure that that would not be possible. Or at least, not possible without a lot of effort and, more importantly, knowledge.

The three of them were sitting at two of the small circular tables Robin had positioned at the rear of her small antiquarian bookshop in the old coastal harbor town of Dartmouth in Devon. Behind the tables was a long counter on which stood a cutlery tray and a pile of assorted side plates, plus two covered glass cake stands, one bearing the remaining third of a Victoria sponge and on the other a couple of slices of walnut cake. At one end stood a till, and beside that a basic Windows laptop connected to a laser printer. Behind the counter was another long shelf on which stood a professional coffeemaker, cups and mugs and bags of beans on the shelves above it, and a large kettle next to half a dozen boxes of tea bags of different types.

The idea of the tables and the catering equipment was simple enough: the lady who actually ran the bookshop, Betty Howarth, was a very accomplished cook, with a particular talent that leaned toward the production of delicious cakes. Antiquarian books were not popular purchases with casual browsers, much of Robin's business being conducted through her specialist website and by e-mail, but the allure of coffee or tea and carrot cake or whatever sweet delicacy Betty had prepared the previous evening was more than many of the people who stepped through the door could resist. It was slightly galling to Robin that on some days her bookshop made far more money from providing refreshments to the passing trade, many of whom had no discernible interest in any kind of printed publication, ancient or modern, than from any books that Betty managed to sell.

But there were no customers in the shop that afternoon. The sign on the door had been turned around so that the word CLOSED was prominently displayed, and underneath that Robin had taped a single sheet of paper on which the slightly more informative message CLOSED FOR STOCKTAKING. OPEN TOMORROW AS USUAL had been printed using the laser printer at the end of the counter.

In reality, they weren't stocktaking. For an antiquarian bookshop, where the goods on offer are obtained as job lots from private buyers or purchased, often in bulk, at auction, the very idea of stocktaking is not simply redundant but largely meaningless. The products that the establishment sold were the books displayed on the shelves, and that really was the end of it. The only items individually recorded by Robin were those few books that each had a significant value—her threshold figure was one hundred pounds—and those she kept in a couple of locked glass-fronted bookcases near the back of the shop. They were on display, but not accessible to casual browsers, just in case.

No, the reason the shop was closed was because Robin had received a delivery of books and a number of ancient pieces of parchment and vellum. These much older documents had not been specified on the bill of lading produced by the bookseller in Switzerland who had sold her the bound volumes, simply because Robin and Mallory had added the undeclared ancient deeds and other records to the shipment before dispatch, and nobody had known about it apart from the two of them. Those documents comprised the long-lost and much sought-after Templar Archive, the detailed records of properties and other assets owned by the order as a part of their estate holdings. Houses, castles, manors, extensive tracts of land, and in some cases entire villages, all of which had been bequeathed or handed over to the order in the centuries before the Knights Templar were purged by King Philip the Fair of France in October 1307.

They had managed to locate the Archive among several chests of documents hidden away for over half a millennium in a complex cave system they'd found at the end of a valley in Switzerland, caves that extended in a network below the nearby hills. In some ways, that had been the easy bit, but they had also managed to convince both the Swiss authorities and a group of armed Italian thugs that the Archive had been destroyed. These men were enforcers employed by a militant arm of the *Ordo Praedicatorum*, the Dominican order whose members had emerged to become the pope's personal torturers and assassins in the medieval period.

And that wasn't all. They had also been able to get a courier company to send the medieval box that had originally contained the Archive, complete with a sophisticated antitheft device built into the lid, from Switzerland to Dartmouth, where it had arrived at more or less the same time as the books and parchments.

Robin still had to make a decision about what to do with the documents they had recovered, because in many cases the medieval records showed clearly that hundreds of acres of real estate in many European countries didn't actually belong to the people and organizations that claimed ownership of them. In fact, the documents unambiguously stated that these now extremely valuable properties had been given to the Order of the Knights Templar in perpetuity, often with a caveat that should the order be disbanded for any reason, the ownership should pass to the then Grand Master of the Templars, and from him to his heirs and assignees. It was entirely likely that there were hundreds or even thousands of ordinary citizens living in Europe and descended from high-ranking Templars who were the proper legal owners of these pieces of land and, more importantly, the documents Mallory and Robin had found in the Archive could prove this beyond the slightest doubt.

To say that the deeds and records were dangerous was a huge understatement; *explosive* was much closer to the mark. Certain important families and organizations throughout Europe could end up with many of their assets seized from them if these documents were made public, and would no doubt take any measures they could to ensure that the deeds never saw the light of day. Exactly what they were going to do with the Archive was a question that Robin and Mallory still had to address.

"It's not just a puzzle," Robin said, pointing at the piece of medieval vellum. "If what we transcribed on that first piece of parchment is correct—and you know as well as I do that it almost certainly is—then what we have here is most probably a solid clue. Something that could lead us to the third trial or trail that Jacques de Molay put in place over seven hundred years ago. What we're looking at could be the first tangible evidence to show what really happened to the Templar treasure before the order was purged."

Mallory nodded, his gaze still fixed on the vellum in front of him, a relic that neither he nor Robin had any idea existed until the faintest of anomalies had struck him about the medieval chest that they had recovered from the cave system. There was a tiny, but noticeable, mismatch in its dimensions: the interior depth was slightly less than the outside measurement suggested, a discrepancy that he had verified using a ruler. From that point, finding the hidden compartment in the base of the chest had taken just a few minutes. He'd used a knife to lever out the false bottom of the chest and, inside the space that this action had revealed, they'd found the vellum.

"So you think we should go for it?" Mallory asked, looking up at Robin, his blue eyes searching her face.

She nodded.

"We've come a long way already," she said, "but those bloody Dominicans grabbed the chests we found in Cyprus and pretty nearly killed us—"

She broke off for a moment as she saw the expression on Betty's face.

"I didn't tell you that bit, Betty," she said, "but you know that we came out of it completely unscathed."

"Despite the grenades," Mallory added mischievously, the fingertips of his left hand unconsciously running down the faint white mark of a jagged scar on his left cheek, an old healed injury that had become more visible as his face had acquired a tan.

"Grenades?" Betty said, her voice carrying the barest twinge of incipient hysteria.

"Actually," Robin chimed in, giving Mallory a hostile glance, "it was only one grenade, and when it went off it wasn't anywhere near us, so stop trying to frighten Betty. I grant you that this time we definitely came out on top, because we've still got the chest and the most important single bit of the Templar Archive, but realistically that's not a huge amount to show for all our efforts. The Archive has the potential to make a lot of people a lot of money, especially the lawyers, but that doesn't really include us, unless we're going to sell the individual property deeds either to the people who presently think they own particular bits of real estate, or to the people who actually own those same bits. And I think either option would be difficult to achieve successfully, and might be extremely dangerous. And we can't even really sell the medieval chest, because of the booby trap built into the lid. I've no doubt the local woodentops would class it as a lethal weapon and confiscate it, because those two sword blades are like a kind of giant flick-knife. So our total financial benefit from everything we've done so far amounts to precisely zero. And a lot less than zero if we add up what it's cost us in airline tickets, hotels, and hire cars to get to where we are right now."

Mallory pointed at the piece of vellum.

"But there's no guarantee," he said, "that this piece of encrypted Latin text is actually going to take us any closer to the lost treasure of the Templars. And even if we can work out how to decipher it and follow whatever clues are hidden within the text, realistically it's quite possible that the contents of the treasure chambers of the order were broken up and dispersed hundreds of years ago by the surviving knights. There may quite literally be no treasure left to find."

"I fully accept that," Robin said, "but I absolutely feel that it's worth a try. We might just as well decode this—if we can—and then follow the trail to see where it leads us. At the very least, then we'll have explored every possibility. And don't forget the Dominicans. They aren't going to give up the quest they've been committed to for the last seven hundred years, and we're still right in their sights. That bastard Toscanelli, in particular, is almost certain to come after us at some time, just looking for revenge, so getting to the end of the trail first could be extremely beneficial to our health."

"I thought you might say that. I was really just checking to make sure that you know what we're letting ourselves in for—again. But before we make a start doing that, there are another couple of decisions we need to make."

Robin nodded, her serious expression a contrast to her

normally cheerful disposition. She had quite short black hair, large dark brown eyes that Mallory always felt he could lose himself in, and a slightly bent nose above full lips. Not a classically beautiful face, perhaps, but enormously and compellingly attractive, certainly as far as Mallory was concerned.

"I know," she replied. "The chest and the Archive. What do we do with them?"

"I think the Archive is probably the easier of the two to sort out. At least for the moment, we can't let anybody know that it didn't go up in flames on that hillside in Switzerland, because if word of that gets out I can pretty much guarantee that all sorts of extremely unpleasant people will come out of the woodwork and do their level best to inflict severe harm on us and either recover or destroy all the documents. So the easiest thing to do, in my opinion, is to put it all in a cardboard box, walk it round to your bank, or preferably to an entirely different bank where you're not a customer, and stick it in a safe-deposit box. And then more or less forget about it."

Robin considered what he'd said for a few moments, then nodded agreement.

"That makes sense," she said. "And the chest? I presume you think that putting it on display in the window of the bookshop would be a pretty bad idea."

"It would. I'm quite certain that we've not seen the last of those murderous Dominicans and I wouldn't be surprised if they mounted a surveillance operation against you and against this shop. I know they probably think at the moment that the Archive and the box it was hidden in have both been destroyed, but putting that medieval chest on display anywhere would certainly give them second thoughts. So I think you need to hide that away as well. But in that case, I think you could just leave it upstairs in your apartment, tucked away somewhere in your office."

"Right," Robin said briskly, "then that's exactly what we'll do."

Packing the Archive away took about twenty minutes, because Robin was determined that the fragile old documents should not deteriorate any further while they were in her possession. So she used a number of sheets of special packing paper designed to be used to wrap ancient books and parchments, paper that was mechanically and chemically stable, and packed the entire collection into a cardboard box that met the same specifications. The last thing she wanted was for the parchments in particular to be damaged by chemicals leaching out of the packing material. Once she was happy, she sealed the box, made a brief phone call to the bank that was the actual owner of both her bookshop and the apartment she lived in above it, and arranged for a safe-deposit box to be leased to her. Then she and Mallory walked around to the bank, Mallory carrying the box, and saw it locked safely away in part of the vault after completing the required paperwork.

When they walked back into the bookshop, Betty was already busy with the coffee machine, and when they sat down she placed a slice of Victoria sponge on a side plate in front of each of them, and followed that with a mug of coffee.

"We'll take the chest upstairs later," Robin said. She pointed at the slice of cake on the plate in front of Mallory. "Now you can throw that down your throat, wash it down with the coffee, and then put on your Latin decryption hat, because that's probably what we're going to be doing for the rest of the day."

2

Dartmouth, Devon

Gary Marsh selected a radio station that was playing middle-of-the-road music, turned the volume down until the sound was barely audible, and then reclined the driver's seat of his car a couple of notches to give himself a bit more comfort for what might turn out to be a very long day indeed. The car was unremarkable, a characteristic that was also embodied by the driver. Middle-aged, appearing to be somewhere between about thirty and fifty, but with one of those faces that's hard to age, short grayish hair, and no features that made him stand out in the memory of most people who saw him. Which of course was the point. A surveillance specialist who people would remember for some reason was unlikely to ever prove good at his job. And Marsh was very good at what he did. Even his long-suffering wife, Ginny, who frequently wished he'd take up some other, more conventional employment because of the time he inevitably spent out on the road and often incommunicado, had to admit that.

His mobile phone—a somewhat larger unit than most people carried, with an extended-life battery fitted as well as a number of unusual and in some cases technically illegal apps—was clipped to a holder on the dashboard, the charging lead snaking down to a power socket on the center console. A copy of the *Daily Mail* newspaper was propped on the steering wheel, and he gave every impression of a man waiting for his wife or somebody, and reading the paper just to pass the time.

In fact, Marsh never read newspapers of any type, simply choosing one by size for whatever job he was contracted to perform. In this case, he'd wanted a paper he could hide behind whilst in the car, but not one so large that it would be cumbersome to carry when he left the vehicle.

He had found a parking place in Dartmouth—no mean achievement on its own—but also one that gave him a distant but uninterrupted view of Robin Jessop's antiquarian bookshop, which he frankly hadn't expected. He'd anticipated that he would have to park the car somewhere and then walk the streets of the town until he found a suitable vantage point from which he could watch the target premises. The space he had found was in one of those free-parking-for-two-hours-but-no-return-within-one-hour zones, but that didn't bother him.

He owned two virtually identical vehicles, the same make, model, and color, and tucked away in the trunk of each of them was a spare set of number plates applicable to the other vehicle. They were fitted with slim but powerful magnets, and it would be the work of only a few seconds for him to replace the existing number plates with the spare set. If a traffic warden or police officer walked past, a check on the vehicle details, whichever plates were visible, would confirm that it was properly licensed and insured. The practical upshot of this technique was that he could change the identity of the car at a moment's notice and so remain in the same parking place all day if he wished, and if it proved necessary to do so.

As he stared down the road toward the bookshop, he reflected again at his surprise at being where he was and doing the surveillance that he was being paid to perform. About two weeks earlier, he had been contracted to mount a surveillance operation against Robin Jessop by a man that he remained convinced was a senior police officer, and probably up to no good. But surveillance, while not the kind of activity that most men would boast about in their local bar, was at least fundamentally harmless, and he had been paid a substantial sum of money for his time and expertise.

The operation had proceeded smoothly enough until he had witnessed another two-man team also targeting Robin Jessop, and he had seen that at least one of these men had been carrying a pistol. That changed the entire thrust of his tasking, at least in his own mind, and after a certain amount of soul-searching he had breached the unwritten terms of his contract and told Jessop what he had been hired to do, and had at the same time also told her about the armed man who was on her trail. Surveillance was one thing, but the only reason anyone carried a gun was to use it, and Marsh had no intention of getting involved in anything like that.

Within a remarkably short period of time his principal—the anonymous police officer who had hired him—had ended the contract and paid him the balance of the agreed fee. But the previous day he had been contacted once again by the same man and told to resume his surveillance. Same target, same briefing. The payment he had been offered was again substantially more than he would normally expect from a job of that type, but he had accepted it immediately, canceling another less interesting and much less lucrative assignment in order to do so.

He told himself that his decision was entirely financial, but in reality it was much more complex than that. Although he had never met Robin Jessop or David Mallory, the man who seemed to be almost permanently by her side, they seemed to be a fairly decent couple, and Marsh rationalized his assignment as being as much about keeping them safe as about watching what they did. For some reason, he felt somewhat protective toward them, a feeling that would certainly not be shared by whatever new surveillance operative would be hired if he declined the job.

That day, almost exactly nothing had happened. There had been two deliveries of reasonably large cardboard boxes by a couple of different courier companies early that afternoon—presumably boxes of books, bearing in mind the profession Robin Jessop had chosen—and Mallory and Jessop had arrived at the shop separately a short time later. They had left the shop only once since then, when the two of them had walked down the street, Mallory carrying a cardboard box that didn't appear to be particularly heavy.

Marsh had followed at a discreet distance, using his digital camera at intervals, and watched as they entered a nearby bank. A couple of minutes later, he'd walked into the building himself and perused a handful of the brochures extolling in the most favorable terms possible the niggardly interest rates that were on offer. He'd seen Jessop talking to a bank official in a quiet area away from the main counter, watched her complete a number of forms, and then all three of them—the official, Jessop, and Mallory—had disappeared through a door controlled by a keypad and a swipe-card reader, Mallory still carrying the cardboard box. His tiny digital camera, a piece of equipment that fitted comfortably into the palm of his hand, had recorded the various steps in the transaction. They'd reappeared about five minutes later, just as Marsh was fending off the attention of a junior employee apparently eager to make some kind of a sale, and the cardboard box was no longer in evidence. The conclusion was simple enough: Jessop had obviously been depositing something of value in one of the bank's safe-deposit boxes.

He'd followed the two targets at a distance back to the shop and continued up the street to where his car was parked. And since then, there'd been no movement whatsoever from either of them.

He decided that he would watch for another hour, and if neither of them had emerged from the building in that time, he would walk the fifty or so yards down the street toward the bookshop and visit the convenience store he had spotted earlier and buy himself a handful of packets— sandwiches, if they had any, and if not cookies and chocolate bars—plus a couple of small bottles of water. They would keep him going until Mallory and Jessop settled down somewhere for the night, when he would be able to make his own arrangements and find a place offering suitable—meaning cheap and convenient—accommodation in the town.

And at that point, he would also contact his principal and provide him with a short verbal report on the activities, or more accurately the lack of activities, he had witnessed during the day, and that would include the transfer of the cardboard box to the vault of the local bank. His brief had been to watch Robin Jessop as the main target, and although the fact that she had deposited something at the bank didn't seem directly relevant to his instructions, he knew his principal would wish to know about it, if only for the sake of completeness.

3

Via di Sant'Alessio, Aventine Hill, Rome, Italy

Livio Fabrini looked up in some surprise as the door of his office swung open and Silvio Vitale stepped inside.

To say the man was an autocratic boss was to severely understate the case. Within the confines of the electronically shielded and highly secure belowground basement area of the building on the Aventine Hill, Vitale ruled with what amounted to a mailed fist. He almost never visited any of his subordinates. He issued orders, and the men—no women were employed by that section of the order—under his command obeyed them. Immediately and without question. If he wanted to talk to any of them, he would make a call and that person would report to him in his office.

"Silvio?" Fabrini said, a question in his voice. "Can I help you?"

"I certainly hope so," Vitale snapped. He was not an

imposing figure, with a slim build, unremarkable features distinguished only by a thin mustache that covered the length of his upper lip. He had a generally friendly appearance that was, as Fabrini and everyone else in the building knew only too well, extremely deceptive. He was capable of switching in an instant from apparent bonhomie to incandescent rage, episodes of seething anger that were usually characterized by both calculated brutality and extreme violence directed against anyone who offended him.

"Is it these documents?" Fabrini asked, gesturing toward a pile of ancient parchments, some still folded neatly, others opened up, that virtually covered his wide oak desk. Stacked against the wall of his office in two stacks were six large metal-bound and obviously ancient wooden chests.

"Of course it's those documents. Why else would I bother coming all the way over here to talk to you?"

Fabrini nodded. Like Vitale, he was a long-term employee of the order and, also like the man in charge, he invariably wore a black suit that had become a kind of unofficial uniform for those individuals who worked in the basement of the building. In fact, he was one of the longest-serving members of the order, now in his seventies, with an encyclopedic knowledge of almost everything to do with the *Ordo Praedicatorum*, and especially of the quest on which the order had embarked the better part of one millennium earlier, and which even today was its single most important and overriding priority. Like Vitale, he was slim—perhaps *thin* would be a more accurate description—with dark hair, a hunched posture, and somewhat gaunt features dominated by a large and bladelike nose that from certain angles gave him an uncanny resemblance to a resting bird of prey.

Vitale picked up a couple of the pieces of parchment and scanned the handwritten words and sentences with a somewhat distracted gaze, but nodded when he noted on each document the unmistakable symbol of the Knights Templar at both the top and bottom of the text.

"So, are these what we thought they were?" Vitale demanded.

"I can tell you that they are a part of the lost Archive of the Knights Templar," Fabrini replied, "though as you can see I have barely begun to scratch the surface of the total number of documents that Toscanelli and his men recovered from Switzerland. In my estimation, to properly study this huge collection of parchments could take years and would require the services of quite a large number of our members to process, collate, and assess the information."

Vitale shook his head, as always somewhat frustrated by Fabrini's apparent inability to give a short and straight answer to a short and straight question. He respected the old man's depth of knowledge, dedication, and commitment to the order, but just wished he would get to the point a hell of a lot quicker than he usually did.

"So are you telling me that we *have* recovered the documents relating to the assets of the order of the heretics? Because that's not what Toscanelli told me he'd found."

Fabrini nodded.

"I don't believe that Marco Toscanelli is necessarily the best person to offer an expert opinion on documents such as these," he said. "His abilities seem to lie more obviously in the physical plane, as an enforcer or perhaps as an assassin. Cerebral activities, such as thinking about anything more complex than interesting methods of killing people, do not seem to me to be his strong suit."

"Forget about Toscanelli," Vitale snapped. "Just tell me what we have here."

"As I said when I looked at the very first parchment to be taken out of these chests," Fabrini said, "these are vitally important documents, and they are undoubtedly genuine. Every one that I have studied so far has been related to a kind of a financial transaction, sometimes involving portable assets such as bullion or jewelry, but an almost equal number of them have involved real estate, property holdings of one sort or another. So without a doubt, what Toscanelli managed to recover, in his unique blundering fashion, is the Templar Archive. But what these documents don't refer to are the deeds of gift and assignment that we were expecting to find."

"So, the short version of what you're trying to say is?"

"Unless one of these boxes contains something very different to the documents I have already examined, what we have recovered is the less important part of the Templar Archive. These pieces of parchment refer to short-term financial transactions, normally involving the deposit of a physical asset, or the assignment of a piece of real property, in exchange for which a person would be extended a line of credit or a cash sum so that he could complete a matter of business. But what these documents do not refer to are the vast real estate holdings that the heretics accumulated over the centuries. I would expect that those documents would be far fewer in number than those I am examining, and might well have been kept for safekeeping in a different location to these chests."

It wasn't exactly a short answer, and it certainly wasn't the answer that Vitale had been hoping to hear.

"Right," he said. "You'd better keep on checking what's here. Let me know immediately if you find any documents that could relate to the Templar real estate holdings."

Without waiting for Fabrini to respond, Vitale turned on his heel and stalked out of the office. It looked to him as if Toscanelli's assessment of the situation had—perhaps surprisingly—been correct. And that meant that there was one important question that needed answering, as a matter of some urgency.

Vitale strode back to his own office and pushed his way in through the open door. Marco Toscanelli was sitting in the chair in front of Vitale's desk, exactly where he had been when the other man walked out of the office.

"Fabrini thinks the same as you do," Vitale said, sitting down and facing Toscanelli. "What you brought back from Switzerland was the working part of the Archive, the records of the financial transactions that took place on a daily basis in the Templar preceptories and commanderies throughout Europe. He thinks that the other part of the Archive, the one containing details of the order's real estate holdings, might even have been stored in an entirely different location to the one where you recovered the chests."

Vitale stared at his subordinate for a few moments before he said anything else.

Toscanelli remained silent. He knew far better than to ever try to interrupt Vitale, especially when he was obviously annoyed, as he was at that moment.

"So we need answers to a few questions," Vitale said. "First, is Fabrini right? Did the Templars separate the records of their day-to-day transactions from the documents that we are interested in, the deeds relating to their real estate holdings?"

That, at least, was a question that Toscanelli felt qualified to answer.

"I think they would have kept them in the same place," he said, "but obviously I can't prove it. That cave system under the mountainside in Switzerland was so well hidden, and so well protected by those booby traps, that I would have thought they would have felt entirely safe in keeping all their records in that one place. And I suppose the other side of the coin is that if they did have a second hiding place, we have absolutely no idea where to even start looking for it."

Vitale nodded noncommittally, but didn't reply immediately, just stared across his desk at Toscanelli. Even looked at through the eyes of a normal heterosexual adult male, the man was obviously attractive. He was tall, well-built, and with movie-star good looks, deep brown eyes, his features tanned and regular under a thick mop of curly black hair. But he was a long way from being the sharpest tool in the shed, and Vitale suddenly remembered an ir-reverent remark somebody had passed about Toscanelli years earlier. "He has the body of a Greek god, and the brain of a Greek goat." It was perhaps a little harsh, but Vitale knew there was more than a grain of truth in it.

What Toscanelli was good at—usually—was taking care of problems where the answer to the difficulty lay primarily in the application of violence, and particularly the application of terminal violence. Though when it came to taking care of the English couple—Robin Jessop and David Mallory—in this way, he had proved to be singularly inept. Maybe, Vitale wondered for a moment, Toscanelli was past his sell-by date and would need to be retired, most probably on a permanent basis, when it was clear that his usefulness was entirely at an end.

On the other hand, his assessment of the events in Switzerland seemed particularly astute, and what they had found under the mountain might prove to be valuable. So maybe he wasn't quite over-the-hill yet.

"Talking of clues," Vitale said, deciding to explore another avenue first, "how, exactly, did Jessop and Mallory manage to locate the entrance to the cave behind the waterfall, bearing in mind that the only possible lead they could have had was the photographs they'd taken of the outsides of those two chests you recovered from Cyprus?"

Toscanelli spread his hands in the universal gesture that translated as a total lack of knowledge.

"I know our experts checked every inch of those chests," he said, "and to the best of my knowledge they found nothing. But somehow Jessop—because she seems to be the brains of the outfit—must have found something. Some pattern or some clue that sent her and Mallory to Chartres Cathedral. But we don't know what it was that she saw, or even what other information the two of them found during their visit to France. I've talked to Roman Benelli, who seems to know more about encryption systems than anyone else here, and his best guess is that there might have been an inscription on an old tombstone, thirteenth century or earlier, that might have been the code word they needed to decipher the last part of that original manuscript that Jessop found."

Toscanelli again spread his hands.

"But what tombstone they looked at, and what inscription they recorded, we have absolutely no idea. And now, because we picked up their trail and followed them into the cave in Switzerland, the exact clue they found doesn't really matter. That particular lead is now a dead end."

"And you are quite sure," Vitale asked, "that there was no sign in that cave system of the Templar assets or their sacred treasure?"

Toscanelli shook his head.

"We covered every inch of that network of caves, and I'm quite certain that there's nothing else there. That complex was intended to keep the Templar Archive safe until the order could regroup and emerge again to spread their heresy throughout Europe. No, in my opinion, and for what it's worth, the Templars hid their assets and the treasure somewhere else. Possibly, even probably, in another country."

Vitale nodded. On this particular occasion, Toscanelli's take on the situation exactly matched his own.

"That's something else we have to think about. Right now I'm more interested in the other bit of the Archive. Tell me again exactly what happened when you confronted Mallory and Jessop in that dead-end cavern."

Toscanelli nodded and once more explained to Vitale what had taken place and what they had seen: the English couple they had been pursuing trapped in the cave with no way out, the possibility that they had a small box or chest with them, and then the echoing thunder as Mallory and Jessop used a length of rope to trigger the final Templar booby trap, dropping hundreds of tons of stone from the roof of the cave to form an impenetrable barrier between themselves and their pursuers.

"And you believed that they had trapped themselves by doing that?"

"As far as we could tell at the time," Toscanelli said, "that was the obvious conclusion. What we hadn't anticipated was that the Templars had managed to design the booby trap so that as well as blocking the way through the cave, it opened up an escape route through a hole in the roof or maybe in a side passage. But as soon as we saw that their car had gone, I knew that they had somehow managed to get out of the cavern."

"With the rest of the Archive?" Vitale asked.

"We didn't know that at the time, but when we finally caught up with them, they certainly had an old wooden box with them. A box full of documents of some sort, but we never got close enough to see the documents or examine the box. And then of course Mallory poured petrol over it and set it on fire."

"So do you think that what you saw him destroying was the Templar Archive?"

Again Toscanelli spread his hands wide and shrugged.

"As I said, we couldn't get close enough to see properly. All I do know is that he poured petrol over what looked like a small medieval wooden chest that contained documents of some sort. So either that *was* the Archive, and they decided that the only way they were going to get out of Switzerland was by destroying it in front of that senior government official, or they somehow or other managed to find a duplicate chest, and the whole thing was just a trick."

"You told me you went back to the hillside after everyone else had gone. What did you find?"

"We went back, yes, because I wanted to examine what was left, which wasn't much. The chest had been completely destroyed by fire, and all that remained were the metal fittings, a few slivers of wood, and some fragments of parchment. I picked up the biggest pieces I could find, and I sent them all for radiocarbon dating the moment we got back to Rome."

"And the result was?"

"The laboratory complained about having to do a rush job and then added all sorts of caveats about inaccuracies caused by the fire that had destroyed the chest, and a number of other factors, but the consensus date for the wood was 1327, with a margin of error of fifty years either way, and the piece of parchment I supplied dated from forty years earlier."

"So the dates fit pretty well," Vitale said. "Obviously we have no idea when the Archive was placed in the chest, but sometime in the early part of the fourteenth century has to be about right. And you also found several pieces of parchment?"

Toscanelli nodded.

"Yes, about a couple dozen bits, the biggest roughly half the size of the palm of my hand. There are fragments of text written on most of them, letters and a few words. As far as Fabrini was able to determine from his analysis, the wording is consistent with medieval Latin and most probably refers to transactions of various kinds. He told me that the fragments I found were not dissimilar to the other documents we recovered in the six big chests."

"You would expect it to be similar," Vitale pointed out, "because it would be the same age, written on the same kind of material and referring to the same kind of transactions. On the other hand," he went on, "if Mallory somehow managed to find a medieval chest somewhere, stuffed a few dozen of the records of normal Templar transactions inside it, and then set fire to it, what you found would be a perfect match for that as well."

Vitale paused for a moment and stared at Toscanelli.

"You've had more contact with these people than anyone else. What do you think happened on that hillside in Switzerland?"

Toscanelli didn't reply immediately but paused for a few seconds, mentally analyzing what he had seen and what he knew about Jessop and Mallory.

"Despite what I saw," he said eventually, "my instinct tells me that it was a trick. A good trick, certainly good enough to fool that Swiss government official."

"Explain."

"It's Jessop more than Mallory, in my opinion. She's an antiquarian bookseller, and that must mean she has a huge interest in ancient documents of all kinds. That's her business. We know they managed to get out of that cave, and were almost certainly carrying the lost Templar Archive with them when they left. What I can't believe is that Jessop would then allow Mallory to set fire to documents of such tremendous historical importance, especially because of the implications of the information that is contained within those documents. I think they somehow managed to smuggle the Archive out of the country, and probably just burned up a handful of unimportant parchments, very likely inside the chest in which the Archive had been stored."

"So you think her personality and profession were the determining features?" Vitale asked.

"If you put it like that, yes."

Vitale was silent for a few moments; then he nodded briskly.

"We don't always see eye to eye, Toscanelli," he said, "but in this case we do. I have already ordered inquiries to be initiated in Switzerland to see if any shipments were made from antique shops and book dealers to Jessop's store, and through one of our tertiaries I have ordered surveillance to be resumed on her in England. If they did manage to get away with the Archive, I promise you that we'll find out about it."

Toscanelli nodded.

"If you want, I can go—"

"You're not going anywhere, Toscanelli. Because of what happened on Cyprus, when you let Mallory and Jessop slip through your fingers, and your incompetent bungling later in Britain, you're now compromised in England, so that's one place that you can't go to in the immediate future, unless we decide to give you a different identity and another diplomatic passport."

Vitale paused for a few moments, considering.

"In fact," he went on, "it might be worth altering your appearance, just in case we do decide you need to travel to Britain."

"You mean plastic surgery?" Toscanelli sounded quite alarmed at the prospect of going under the knife.

Vitale shook his head.

"You're not valuable enough to the order to justify spending that kind of money on changing your face. No, from now on you just don't shave. A full beard is by far the easiest way of giving you an entirely different look."

"I understand." Toscanelli sounded relieved. "Is that everything?"

"Of course not. The original parchment, the *Ipse Dixit* text that started this hare running, stated clearly that there were three trails that would have to be followed in sequence. The first part of the quest took you to Cyprus and to that cave below the old castle, and the second part ended in that complex of caves under the Swiss mountain. We still don't know how, but something Mallory and Jessop saw in the metallic decoration on the two chests buried in Cyprus led them to Switzerland. The problem we now have is that presumably they know what the final clue is, and have some idea about where to start following the trail that will take them to the last remaining part of the Templar treasury."

"You mean the treasure itself? All the assets that vanished from Templar strongholds in the last days before the order was purged?"

"That's exactly what I mean. The vast quantities of gold and silver, jewelry and precious stones, and all the rest of it. Everything of value that the order possessed at the end of its existence. That treasure is the only thing left, the only thing that we have not so far been able to find or account for. We now know—or at least I believe—that the Archive has finally been recovered, and we will be taking steps to get our hands on the documents that compose it.

"But far more important than that is the contents of the Templar treasury, and of course the sacred relic worshipped by them. The probability is that the chest that Mallory and Jessop recovered from the Swiss cave system didn't just hold the lost Archive, but also a document or an inscription or something that will allow them to continue with the third and final part of the quest. And that means that the end of our task is in sight. We watch them, we follow them, and when the trail comes to an end, we'll take the treasure and the relic from them."

"And what about Mallory and Jessop?" Toscanelli asked. "What happens to them?"

"Then you can kill them, of course. In fact, if the circumstances permit, I'll even let you take your time. You can have a little fun with them before they die. I'm sure you'll enjoy that, almost as much as they won't."

4

Dartmouth, Devon

"Are you getting anywhere?" Betty asked.

She was slightly overweight, dark haired, middle-aged, and perpetually cheerful. And, at least in Mallory's supremely unqualified opinion, she probably looked on Robin as the daughter she'd never had.

Her short marriage had ended very abruptly when her husband, a professional fisherman, had set out on his boat with two other local men for a five-day fishing voyage, and had simply vanished. No sign of him, his two companions, or his fishing boat had been seen since, though a section of the hull of what was clearly a very similar vessel had washed up a couple months later dozens of miles farther down the coast in Cornwall. It was never confirmed that this wreckage had come from his boat, because of the absence of any positive identifying marks, but the paintwork was approximately the right color.

The shipping lanes off the southern coast of England are among the busiest in the world, and it was conjectured that the fishing boat might have been run down in the dark by a much larger vessel, perhaps one on which a proper radar watch was not being kept. Or perhaps the fishing boat's radar reflector had been lost overboard and nobody on the ship had noted the faint return on the radar or seen the boat's lights.

As was always the case with any kind of a maritime disaster, there were a number of possible explanations, any one of which could have been correct, but none offered more than a few crumbs of comfort to Betty, who had instantly lost her soul mate and the man she had hoped to grow old with. But at least she had been left financially secure, the insurance policy clearing the mortgage on her cottage, and her husband's life insurance had been enough to provide her with an adequate, if not comfortable, income for the rest of her life.

But she would have gladly swapped all that just to have him back.

"I think the expression 'not really' more or less covers it," Robin said, gesturing with her pencil toward a haphazard collection of sheets of paper, each covered with successive and unsuccessful attempts at working out what the text on the piece of vellum meant.

Sitting at the table beside her, Mallory nodded agreement.

"About the only thing we know for sure," he said, "is that the text is encrypted. And we knew that before we even started. But everything we've tried up to now to decipher it has just turned one piece of gibberish into another, slightly different piece of gibberish."

"I'll make some more coffee," Betty said, standing up and walking around the counter toward the coffee machine, "and perhaps another slice of cake might help stimulate your thought processes."

"Thanks," Robin said, tossing down her pencil in irritation. "I'm not quite sure how much improvement an injection of caffeine is likely to make to our performance, but it will certainly be very welcome."

The very first clue that Robin had encountered in what had become an all-consuming quest, what seemed like a lifetime earlier but had in fact been only a few weeks, was a piece of ancient parchment rolled up and secreted away inside a book safe, a leather-bound box that looked exactly like a book until you tried to open it. More by luck than by judgment, she had used a long-bladed screwdriver to release the catch holding the box closed, and in doing so had triggered a functional antitheft device that comprised two rows of needle-sharp spikes that were forced out of the box by powerful springs. Luckily, none of the spikes had been driven through her hands, but the brutal efficiency of the device had set the tone for almost everything that she and Mallory had subsequently experienced.

Opening the book safe incautiously would inevitably have resulted in serious damage to a person's hands, but opening the two chests they had found under the floor of the cave on Cyprus would have been lethal. Lifting the lid released a pair of razor-sharp blades, easily capable of disemboweling anyone standing in front of the chest, and even the small wooden chest they had recovered from Switzerland contained a simpler, but still very effective antitheft device: two spring-loaded blades that were released the moment the lid was lifted. And the cave system itself, a warren of tunnels and caverns that ran below a mountain in the canton of Schwyz, had contained at least three separate booby traps, one of which had resulted in the death of one of the pursuing Dominican enforcers. The other two had been potentially even more dangerous, consisting of carefully planned and prepared rockfalls that had been triggered by simple release mechanisms that were still fully operational some seven hundred years after they had been constructed.

That first piece of parchment had been covered with an encrypted text, and in trying to decipher it, Robin had enlisted the aid of David Mallory, an IT specialist who was the only man she had ever encountered with an interest in codes and ciphers. Working together, they had cracked the code on the first part of the text written on the parchment, and later further sections of text had yielded their secrets when the two of them had solved additional clues.

But the text written on the piece of vellum had, so far, not succumbed to any of their attempts at analysis. Mallory had been hoping—and expecting—that the anonymous compiler of the text had used some kind of a substitution code in its preparation, and most probably Atbash or a variant of it. Plain vanilla Atbash was the simplest possible letter-substitution code, created simply by writing out the alphabet in a horizontal line with the reversed alphabet written underneath it. Simple enough to do, and simple enough to decode, a fact that had clearly been well understood by people in medieval times. Variants had been introduced, typically involving displacing the reversed alphabet so that, for example, instead of the letter *Z* occurring underneath *A*, it would be under an entirely different letter of the alphabet, with all the other letters shifted accordingly.

A further refinement was the replacement of the reversed alphabet with one or more code words or, in some cases, the addition of code words to the beginning and end of the alphabet, which greatly increased the security of the encrypted text and hence the degree of difficulty in trying to decipher it.

"About the only thing I am completely sure of," Mallory said, his frustration evidenced in his voice and on his face, "is that we're definitely not looking at basic Atbash. Whoever encrypted this used something much more complex than that, and almost certainly replaced the alphabet with code words."

"And if you don't know what those code words are," Betty suggested, "then you may not be able to decipher the text."

"Exactly," Robin said. "We've tried all the obvious words that we can think of. Things like the names of the Templar grand masters, the places where they had their most imposing and important fortifications, and even things like the names of the symbols that were most commonly associated with the order. Things like the Templar battle flag, the beauséant, and the red cross, the *croix pattée*, that they wore on their surcoats and was emblazoned on their shields. But as David said, nothing we've tried produces anything like the plaintext we're hoping for."

Mallory picked up a fork and cut the end off the slice of Victoria sponge that Betty had just placed in front of him.

"One definition of insanity," he said, swallowing the cake, "is doing the same thing over and over again and expecting a different result each time. I know that's not exactly what we're doing here, because we are trying different words, but I do get the feeling that we're wasting our time. The problem is, Betty, that if the correct code words that we need to use are, for example, *Temple Mount* and *Jacques de Molay*, we not only need to know that, but also which one comes first, are they written forward or backward, do they come at each end of the alphabet, or are they used by themselves? There are just so many permutations that we could end up doing this not just for hours but for days or weeks. And there's no guarantee that we'd crack it in the end."

"So have you got any other ideas?" Robin asked.

Mallory took a sip of coffee before he answered.

"That is good coffee," he said. "Well, I have been kicking a few possibilities around. I think we can fairly definitely eliminate the more complex types of encryption, things like double substitution or double transposition ciphers, where you use one code word or words to encrypt the original message, and then use a second code word or words to encrypt the encrypted text, if you see what I mean. That's basically quite a simple technique, but if you don't know both the code words that have been used, it's also virtually impossible to crack. Unless of course you got access to something like a Cray supercomputer that can mount a brute-force attack and perform tens of millions of calculations every second. My laptop is quite powerful, but it's several orders of magnitude too slow to try anything like that.

"In fact," he went on, "you can even add an extra layer of complication to this technique. Some messages encrypted using double transposition contain a very short piece of plaintext right at the beginning, sometimes just six numbers or occasionally six numbers split into two groups of three and preceded by the letters *P*, *L*, and *W*. Those refer to the page, line, and word, which is a way of telling the recipient of the message exactly what words are being used as code words for the two stages of encryption. The only thing that requires is that both the sender and the recipient must have copies of precisely the same book, and precisely the same edition, so that the particular word referred to will be the same in both volumes. But with the millions of books that have been published over the centuries, it wouldn't be at all surprising if two people possessed copies of precisely the same book. And, of course, from a counterespionage point of view, there is nothing even faintly incriminating about just another book, so that particular technique has been in use for quite some time. But I really don't think that what we're looking at here is anything like as complicated as that."

"So what can you do?" Betty asked. "In fact, is there *anything* that you can do to solve it?"

"In the absence of any better ideas," Mallory said, "I think the only thing we can do is just rely on frequency analysis. That will take some time, but unless I'm missing something, eventually it should start to produce results."

"I have no idea what you're talking about," Betty said. "It is something to do with radios?"

Mallory gave her a smile, and shook his head.

"No, nothing like that," he said. "You can produce a frequency analysis table for any language, and what that will do is list the most commonly used letters in the alphabet for that language. For example, in English the six commonest letters found in most pieces of text are *E, T, A, O, I, N*, which is what you'd expect because four of the five vowels are in that list. Of course, the frequency does depend upon the type of text being analyzed, because obviously a romantic novel, say, might throw up a slightly different set of letters to a property conveyance or a vicar's sermon, but as a general rule that list works. So, maybe what we should be doing now is applying that same technique to the text we have in front of us."

"I'm on it," Robin said, opening up her laptop, selecting a search engine, and rapidly typing a phrase into the field at the top of the screen. Within about a second the results were displayed, and she tracked down the list of sites before choosing one that hopefully would give her what she wanted.

"This might do the trick," she said. "It's a website containing the results of an analysis that was performed on a collection of mixed-genre Latin texts, texts that amounted to well over a quarter of a million words. Interestingly, the result is not that dissimilar to English, with the six commonest letters in the Latin alphabet being *I, E, A, U, T, S,* so again four of the five vowels are in the list. In fact, those six letters weren't just the commonest that the researchers identified in the text, but actually amounted to well over half of the letters used, and the first three letters—*I, E,* and *A*—accounted for almost one-third of the total. Luckily," she added, "this particular analysis also lists all of the letters in the Latin alphabet and their frequencies."

Betty looked at her slightly doubtfully.

"I think you told me a long time ago that the Latin alphabet changed over time, so how do you know that this list of letters will work for the text that we're looking at?"

"You're quite right," Robin agreed, "and that may prove to be a problem. We'll just have to wait and see. I suppose the good news is that the present twenty-six letters of the Latin alphabet became established during the Middle Ages, which is more or less the period that this piece of vellum has to date from. Before that time, in classical Latin there were only twenty-three letters, all but two of which were derived from a much earlier, Etruscan alphabet. The missing letters were *J, U,* and *W,* which of course isn't a double *U* at all, but a double *V.* Today those twenty-six letters form the English alphabet and are also the most important part of the character set of most other European languages."

"So if you want to be pedantic about it," Mallory

chimed in, "that Roman chap who turned up and proclaimed, *Veni vidi vici*—'I came, I saw, I conquered'—wasn't actually called Julius Caesar at all, but Iulius Caesar, because when he was around the letter *J* hadn't been invented."

"That sounds like a typical nitpicking objection," Robin said. "The kind of thing you get on a pub quiz night when the bloke who came second is arguing the toss over the answer to one question."

"Just trying to get things right. Anyway, let's see if we get anywhere with frequency analysis."

Robin took a fresh piece of paper and wrote out the complete frequency table that she had found on the website.

"If you think this is going to work," Betty said, "why didn't you try this right from the start?"

Mallory shook his head.

"We could have done," he agreed, "but it's a bit of a hit-and-miss process, not to mention pretty dull and boring, and Robin and I both thought that if we could guess the words the medieval scribe had used to encrypt the text, we'd get a result a lot faster. What we have to do now is go through the entire encrypted piece of Latin, letter by letter, and count the frequency of each one. Then we have to apply the frequency analysis table and write out the whole thing again, this time with the letters that we think are the plaintext versions of the encrypted Latin, and just see if it makes any better sense."

"And we might have to do that more than once," Robin

said, "because although we might well end up identifying the vowels fairly accurately, it's the consonants that give the language its shape, and frequency analysis gets less and less accurate the further down the alphabet you get. So we'll probably have to try a number of different letters in particular spaces in the text before we can identify exactly what each word is. And the other problem we have," she added, pointing at the folded piece of vellum, "is that the author of that text used what's known as *scriptio continua*, or continuous script. That means there are no gaps between words, because to include gaps would obviously make decryption a lot easier, and the whole point of this message is that it should not be easy to decipher."

Before starting, Robin placed each of the three sheets of paper containing Betty's transcription of the text on the laser printer, and made half a dozen copies of each sheet using the photocopier function. Then she took a clean sheet of paper, checked that the pencil she'd picked up had a decent point, and waited for Mallory to start.

He took the first of the photocopied sheets and read out the first letter on the top line, which was the letter *M*. Robin noted that on her sheet, and then began recording every time that letter appeared in the ciphertext as Mallory read it out, using the simple and classic notation of four vertical lines and crossing them with a diagonal bar to make five as he identified each occurrence of the letter. While she did that, he drew a diagonal line through each letter *M* on the transcription as well, so ensuring that he didn't miss any.

When he'd finished the first sheet, he repeated the same process, with the same letter, on the second sheet and then again on the third. And once he'd done that, he went back to the first sheet of the transcribed text again, read out the second letter, and began the process all over again.

It was, by any standard, an almost terminally boring occupation, and by five thirty that afternoon, with perhaps one-third of the transcription analyzed, Robin and Mallory both decided, at virtually the same moment, that enough was enough. At least for one day.

Betty shut down the catering facilities at the back of the shop, pulled on her coat, picked up her handbag, and left the premises, heading for the ferry that would take her to her small and comfortable terraced cottage on the opposite side of the river Dart.

Mallory and Robin left the building a couple minutes later, Mallory carrying the wooden chest, inside of which were both the piece of ancient vellum and all their notes. They walked around the back of the bookshop and up the spiral staircase to Robin's apartment, where she placed the vellum in her safe while Mallory tucked away the medieval chest in an alcove. They knew they were going to spend a bit more time looking at the transcription and their notes when they returned to the apartment, so Mallory slid the papers into his computer bag, which he had decided to leave in the study while they ate their meal. It was peculiar, but since meeting Robin he had become noticeably less paranoid about always having his laptop computer with him. Though he still had some way to go: his most up-to-date backup hard drive was tucked away securely in the inside pocket of his jacket.

A few minutes after that, they retraced their steps and headed down toward the river frontage and one of the restaurants where they could enjoy an early dinner.

5

Dartmouth, Devon

Gary Marsh watched as the middle-aged and slightly plump woman left the bookshop, and he tracked her with his binoculars as she headed toward the ferry terminal. When Jessop and Mallory appeared, he abandoned the binoculars in the car and headed down the street toward them—Jessop, after all, was his primary target.

He watched them walk around the side of the building, Mallory carrying an old wooden chest, and guessed that they were making their way toward the apartment he knew was located directly above the shop. He didn't make any attempt to follow them, just loitered on the main road waiting either for them to reappear or, if they intended to remain in the apartment for some time, for them to stay out of sight. Seven or eight minutes later, they stepped back onto the pavement from the side alley and headed for the center of the town, apparently oblivious to his presence.

He followed them on the opposite side of the road until they entered one of the many restaurants located near the water's edge in Dartmouth. Once he was certain that they would be in the building for long enough to eat a meal—he'd seen them seated near one of the bay windows, the waiter handing each of them a large menu once they had sat down—he retreated about a hundred yards to a convenient low wall that was just the right height to sit on, and a vantage point that allowed him to still see the front entrance of the restaurant. Then he took out his phone to call his principal.

"Nothing much is happening now," he began, "and that's been pretty much the pattern for the entire day. They were in the bookshop for most of the afternoon, and right now they're sitting down to a meal in a local restaurant that will be a hell of a lot better than the crisps and sandwiches that I'm just about to eat."

"Okay. We're interested in any deliveries Jessop might have received, especially any that might have come from abroad."

Marsh thought for a moment or two before he replied. For some reason, he didn't like the way the conversation was heading. He had a strong suspicion that if he told his principal about the two largish boxes that had arrived at the shop late that morning, the next step in the operation might well be a request for him to break in and find out what, exactly, had been delivered. But he also knew that he really had very little option.

"You do know that she sells books for a living, don't you?" he asked. "She's had about five packages arrive at the shop today, some of which I presume were books. In fact," he added, embellishing the story somewhat, "I'm pretty sure that the last couple came from Amazon. Is that the kind of delivery you're interested in?"

"Of course not. The shipments we're watching out for will probably be quite large boxes, probably delivered by courier, and most likely with a Swiss address for the sender."

"I pride myself on being largely invisible in most circumstances," Marsh said, "but I promise you that if you want me to get close enough to the shop to read the information displayed on a delivery note, somebody is going to notice me. Binoculars and a parked car won't do it. The best I can do for you is give a rough estimate of the size of anything that arrives at the shop. Don't you have any other information, like the expected delivery time or what the package is supposed to look like?"

This time, the principal paused. Perhaps, Marsh wondered, he was taking instructions from whoever was pulling his strings, because he was quite certain that although the anonymous senior police officer was the man issuing orders and paying the bill, his every action was being directed by somebody else, somebody who remained even deeper in the shadows.

"We have no definite information about any of that. There is a possibility that Jessop may be sent a number of ancient documents that would probably fit inside a heavy-duty cardboard box with a capacity of perhaps two or three cubic feet or thereabouts. It is also possible that she might be sent a small wooden box or chest which would probably also be the same sort of size as the cardboard box. It would probably be packed inside protective covering, but if by any chance the box were visible, it would be clearly ancient and almost certainly bound with metallic reinforcing bands or decoration."

"There were two deliveries late this morning that were similar in size to that," Marsh said, thinking back to what he had observed. He had seen the delivery of two large packages that almost precisely matched the description that had just been supplied by his principal, and he had later seen Mallory leaving the bookshop carrying an ancient wooden chest with prominent metal reinforcing.

"You should have told me immediately that they were delivered."

"I'm not a mind reader," Marsh snapped. "I wasn't aware that you were looking out for packages as well. My briefing from you told me I was to make the woman Robin Jessop my primary target for surveillance, with David Mallory as the secondary. And that's what I did. You're lucky I even bothered noting what was in her mail delivery."

"Are they still in the restaurant?" the principal asked.

Marsh brought the pair of compact binoculars up to his eyes, focused the instrument on the front wall of the restaurant, and quickly located Robin Jessop. Mallory was partially out of sight behind a curtain, but Marsh had no doubt that the man was still there.

"Yes. It looks like their starters have just arrived."

"Good. What we'd like you to do is to go to Jessop's shop and apartment, right now, while they are out of the picture, get inside, and find that chest and the contents of that large cardboard box that was delivered this morning. And a word of warning. If you do find the chest, you may well also find that there's some kind of an antitheft device, spring-loaded hidden sword blades or something of that sort, most likely concealed in the lid. So don't just open it up and hope for the best."

"That's helpful, I suppose. So, how do I get the lid open to check what's inside?"

"The information I have," the principal said, "is that the booby trap, if there is one, is designed to target somebody opening the chest from the front, which is what you would usually do. So our advice is to use some kind of a tool to lift the lid, and stand behind the chest while you're doing so."

"You're full of good news tonight," Marsh said, "and just so you know, breaking and entering is not what you might call a specialty of mine. I can get a Yale lock open without too much trouble, but if she's got deadlocks and stuff on her doors, the only way I'll be able to get in is if I force them open or break a window or something. And that really falls outside my remit. If you want that done, you're going to have to find somebody else. I value my freedom and my independence too much to commit an openly criminal act, no matter what fee you offer me."

"Well, at least get over there and take a look. That's not illegal, as far as I know."

"You should know," Marsh pointed out, "because you're a copper. And something else you should know," he added, "is that I'm calling you on my mobile and one of the apps I have running on the phone is a recorder, so everything you've said to me and everything I've said to you is now recorded on the data card. And another thing is that whenever I finish one of my telephone calls, the phone automatically uploads the audio file to the cloud, so there's a permanent record of what we've said. Just thought you might like to bear that in mind."

"There's no need for that."

"There is in my world. I've been shafted too often to start taking chances."

The principal sounded substantially less than impressed by what he'd just heard, but Marsh didn't care. Ever since he had begun in the business, he had done everything possible to make sure that he was never implicated in any form of criminal activity, and as a matter of routine he had always recorded all telephone calls that related in any way to his employment.

Then another thought struck him, as he turned and began retracing his steps toward Jessop's antiquarian bookshop.

"You didn't ask about Jessop's other activities today," he said, "and if you want my guess, whatever arrived this morning in that large cardboard box is now well beyond your reach."

"What do you mean?"

"After that box was delivered, Mallory and Jessop walked out of the shop carrying a different cardboard box, but still quite a big one, and went to the local bank with it. I followed them inside, and I'm certain that they deposited the box in the bank's vault. So if you want to get it out of there, you're going to have to hire a team of experts who specialize in hacking their way into the safety-deposit boxes held inside banks. Alternatively, you'll have to use that other impressively effective blunt instrument you have access to that would let you get inside."

"What blunt instrument?" the principal asked.

"I thought you'd know, if anyone did," Marsh replied. "A search warrant, of course. No need for bulky men in balaclavas wielding thermic lances, plastic explosives, or oxyacetylene cutters in the middle of the night. All you have to do is just turn up one bright and sunny morning, wave the warrant in front of you, and wait for the bank manager to lead you downstairs into the vault, unlocking the doors as he goes. Of course, I have no idea which safety-deposit box you need to look inside, and I have no clue what reason you could give to persuade some legal eagle to issue the warrant in the first place. But those are your problems, not mine."

"Hopefully it won't come to that," the principal said. "While you're in the apartment, assuming you get the door open, see if you can find the chest and take some pictures of it, especially any metallic decoration on the outside. If there are any words written on the inside or anywhere else on the chest, photograph those as well. The other thing we're interested in is any kind of ancient parchment, so if you see anything of that sort, get some decent pictures of it. Also, if you see anything written down that looks like a code, or any photocopies or written copies of old texts, take plenty of pictures that show the text clearly. Ideally, don't remove anything from the apartment, because we don't want Jessop to know that anyone has been in there. You should try to leave everything exactly the same when you leave as it was when you arrived."

By that time, Marsh had almost reached Robin's shop, and he glanced up and down the street to check for passersby before he did anything else.

"Right. I'm outside her place now," he said, "so I'll call you in a few minutes, whether or not I get inside."

6

Via di Sant'Alessio, Aventine Hill, Rome, Italy

Vitale was fluent in a number of languages, and when his telephone rang he looked first at the caller identification on the small screen before he answered the call. The double-four prefix was unmistakable, and even before glancing at the rest of the number that was displayed, he knew precisely who was calling and in which language he should speak.

"Good evening, my friend," Vitale said in perfect English. "Have you any news?"

Not far from the center of Exeter, sitting on a public bench made from cast iron and wood, and dedicated to the eternal memory of some local worthy he doubted that anyone had ever heard of, Gary Marsh's principal pressed his disposable mobile phone—a burner, in the language of the criminal world, and purchased sometime previously specifically for this operation—closer to his ear before he replied. He was a tertiary, a lay brother of the order, and one of several thousand unacknowledged supporters of the Dominicans around the world. Chosen for their dedication to the cause and at least in part for their own specific knowledge, assets, and—especially—access to government and commercial organizations, they were tasked with smoothing the way for any operations that the order might become involved in, and with providing covert assistance whenever necessary.

"The private inquiry agent we discussed is about to enter the target premises. I have given him specific instructions about the chest, as you requested, and provided him with information about what we are seeking in the most general terms. I have also ordered him to disturb nothing, and to rely on photographs of anything he sees of interest within the building. If at all possible, I'm hoping that he will be able to gain entrance to the property and leave it again without the target having any idea he was ever there. Do you have any other instructions at the moment?"

In his office on the Aventine Hill, Vitale shook his head.

"Not at the moment, my brother. Please contact me again once your operative has completed his assignment."

7

Marsh checked the street again, then walked quickly through the alleyway that led to the rear of the building and the spiral staircase that gave access to Robin Jessop's small apartment. He didn't feel comfortable with what he was doing, but he rationalized his actions because until he actually walked inside the building, uninvited, he wasn't breaking any laws. And he expected to be in and out of the apartment in less than five minutes, no matter what he found or didn't find.

He hadn't mentioned to his principal that he'd actually seen Mallory carrying the case out of the shop and down the alley and, presumably, up to Jessop's apartment, so he was reasonably confident that he would at least find that ancient relic there. The medieval booby trap sounded intriguing, in a kind of lethally dangerous way, but hopefully he would avoid triggering the device when he looked at the old chest. Or at least not be directly in the firing line if he inadvertently actuated whatever it contained.

At the top of the stairs he paused again and adjusted his watch. Then he glanced down at the street below, checking for any potential witnesses, but it was empty of pedestrians, and he couldn't see anyone sitting in a parked car nearby, the way he himself had observed an unidentified man breaking into the building less than two weeks earlier. Quite apart from anything else, Robin Jessop clearly attracted a lot of attention from the criminal elements—in which category, at least at that moment, he included himself—which was puzzling, bearing in mind her profession.

For an instant, he wondered if the whole bookselling business was just some kind of a front, and that she was actually a spy or secret agent, or followed some entirely different profession. But then he rejected the notion. The idea of a spy in the sleepy town of Dartmouth really didn't make sense, and not even the looming presence of the Royal Navy officer training college, the concrete battleship that was HMS *Britannia*, suggested otherwise.

Marsh knocked on the door in a somewhat perfunctory fashion, knowing beyond doubt that both Jessop and Mallory were still feeding their faces in the nearby restaurant, and when he got no reply he took a lockpick gun from his pocket, inserted the end into the Yale lock that secured the door, applied gentle turning force, and squeezed the trigger rapidly several times. The lockpick gun turned, and the door opened silently inward, Marsh immediately stepping inside. Before he did anything else, he pulled a packet from his jacket pocket, extracted a pair of latex medical gloves from it, and pulled them on, replacing the empty packet in his pocket before moving on.

It wasn't a big apartment, as was quite obvious from the size of the building, and it took him less than thirty seconds to look into every room. But it was immediately apparent that the only room he needed to bother with was the study, which had presumably originally been a small second bedroom.

The moment he stepped inside that room, he saw a clearly very old wooden chest on the floor in a kind of alcove almost opposite the door, which just confirmed what he had seen earlier: Mallory had obviously carried the chest from the bookshop up to the apartment. He walked over to it, lifted the chest out of the alcove, and placed it on the floor. Then he stood behind it, reached over the top of the ancient relic, seized the front of the lid, and opened the chest. Almost disappointingly, nothing happened, but when Marsh looked inside the lid, the mechanism that composed the booby trap was clearly visible, and it only took him a few moments to locate the metal pins that somebody—presumably Mallory—had inserted through holes in the lid to safely lock the device.

The chest was empty, but when he looked inside it he saw that there was a false bottom, because the piece of wood that formed the base was standing on its side instead of having been pushed flat. He made a quick estimate of the space that would be available if the base was in place, and guessed at around three-quarters of an inch. That would have been enough to hold a few documents, but nothing more substantial than that. Marsh took half a dozen pictures of the inside and the outside of the chest with the camera on his smartphone before closing the lid and replacing the relic where he'd found it.

Then he turned his attention to the rest of the small study. He walked across to the opposite wall and looked at the safe, and even tried turning the T-shaped handle on the door, but it was locked. Safecracking was a skill he certainly didn't possess, so he just took a couple of pictures of the safe, including the name on the front, and a close-up photograph of the keyhole, then turned away. There were a few papers lying on the desk, one of which he photographed because he thought the information on it might be useful to him personally, rather than to his principal, later. He quickly checked the others but found nothing of obvious interest.

But beside the desk was a leather computer bag, which he picked up and opened. He ignored the laptop, power adapters, and other cabling that occupied one side of it, and instead inspected the three narrow slots on the opposite side that were intended to hold documents. As they were in fact doing. There were perhaps a couple dozen sheets of paper tucked away inside these.

Marsh pulled the wad of papers out of one slot, fanned them slightly so that a part of each one was visible, then placed them on the floor and took three photographs. That would ensure that when he replaced them in the computer bag they would be in exactly the same order as when he took them out. Then he looked at them more carefully, realized that they were all handwritten but that many were duplicates, presumably photocopies, and quickly took close-up pictures of each one that seemed unique. Some sheets were covered in apparently random patterns of letters, and he took a series of photographs of those as well.

He quickly collected all the papers, making sure they were in the same order as they had been before, and slid them back inside the leather computer case, which he replaced exactly where he had found it, but turned round the other way. Despite his briefing, he had decided that leaving a couple of fairly obvious clues in the apartment might give Mallory and Jessop a warning that they were again under surveillance.

Then the watch on his left wrist emitted a muted beeping tone, which he immediately silenced by pressing a button with his thumb. He had set the alarm on the watch for exactly seven minutes, which was all the time he was prepared to allow himself to spend inside the property, and that time was now up.

The very last thing he did was to glance around the office at floor level, checking the handful of electrical outlets. Older buildings in Britain are almost invariably ill-equipped with power sockets, because when they were constructed people genuinely didn't need more than perhaps two or three in every room except the kitchen. But the demands of modern technology, which required power supplies for computers, printers, and photocopiers, and charging stations or docks for mobile phones and tablets, meant that almost everybody used either extension leads or mains adapters, or both, because they had to.

Tucked away more or less out of sight was exactly what he was looking for: a single power socket in the wall, into which a white mains adapter was plugged. From it, two electrical leads snaked away, one obviously supplying power to a printer. It took Marsh less than six seconds to remove the adapter from the socket and replace it with one he had been carrying in his pocket, and to attach the two power leads to it.

Moments later, he was standing at the door of the apartment and looking through the fish-eye peephole to make sure there was nobody outside the door. Then he opened the door, pulled it closed behind him, making sure that the Yale lock clicked into place, and walked down the spiral staircase.

He retraced his earlier steps, his path taking him in front of the restaurant where he had seen Jessop and Mallory sitting down to their dinner. He glanced to his right and saw that they were still in exactly the same place, talking animatedly together and with almost empty main-course plates in front of them. Marsh guessed that he could probably have spent another five or ten minutes in the apartment before there was any chance of them arriving, but that would have cut it far too fine for his own peace of mind. And, he hoped, he had probably got whatever it was that his principal was looking for.

He found another convenient spot to sit while he made a phone call. Or, to be exact, to send one text message and then make a phone call.

Marsh took a small spiral-bound notebook out of his pocket and flicked through it until he found the page that he needed. On it was a mobile phone number—though the SIM card it was linked with was not and had never been fitted in a mobile—and a coded instruction.

In fact, the mains power adapter that he had installed in the target apartment was rather more than it seemed. It would function exactly like any other adapter, but tucked away inside it, safe from prying eyes, was a microphone attached to an extremely nonstandard piece of circuitry. The device was actually a mains-powered bug that was designed to monitor any sounds within about thirty feet of its location.

In his professional capacity, Gary Marsh employed surveillance devices of many different types, but he always preferred to use equipment that operated from the mains supply in the target premises, because that meant he only needed to access the property once. Battery-powered devices fitted with adhesive pads or magnets were easy enough to attach under a desk or some other convenient place, and were usually small enough to be missed unless a thorough search was undertaken, but they normally had a battery life measured in days, or at best a couple weeks, and changing or charging the battery obviously required continued and frequent access to the device, something that was only very rarely possible. Marsh did use them when only short-term surveillance was needed, but he didn't really like them.

Of course, the microphone inside the adapter was only a part of the story. The bug also contained a SIM card, and that was the clever bit. The built-in circuitry had both incoming and outgoing call functionality, which meant he could dial the number of the embedded SIM card from any phone in the world, and that would allow him to listen to whatever the microphone was picking up at that moment. In a target environment such as an office, where there would be activity between set hours, that was a useful option, but it really wouldn't work in Robin Jessop's apartment. She and Mallory might be out all day doing other stuff, and then work in the office late in the evening. Knowing that was one reason why he had installed that particular bug, which included a further refinement.

Marsh opened the messaging app on his mobile and entered the number of the SIM card as the recipient. Then he typed the coded instruction that had been supplied by the manufacturer as the text of the message, and sent it. That programmed the bug to call Marsh's mobile phone as soon as the microphone detected any sounds in its vicinity, which meant that he could listen in to whatever was happening in Robin Jessop's office, just as if he were sitting invisibly in a corner of the room.

That message sent, Marsh dialed the mobile number of the man he was working for.

"I'm out," he said when his call was answered. "There was an old wooden chest in the apartment, and there was some kind of complicated steel mechanism hidden in the lid. It looked like a couple of sword blades attached to powerful springs, but somebody had fashioned a pair of steel pins and slid them through holes in the decoration on the outside of the lid to stop it working. Like a couple of safety catches, I suppose."

"Good work. That will please my—er—associates."

Marsh didn't miss the slight hesitation in the sentence, and not for the first time he wondered exactly whom he was dealing with, because it clearly wasn't just one senior police officer involved in a kind of covert surveillance operation. There had to be a number of other people giving him his instructions.

"Did you find anything else?"

"There's a biggish safe in the study. It looks as if it's bolted to the wall, and I don't have the skill to even try and get it open, but I've taken shots of it so if you do decide to get someone else to pay a visit, at least he'll know what he's facing. There were a few papers on the desk, but nothing of any obvious interest. But I did find a computer bag and there were papers inside it that seemed to be the kind of things you were looking for. I didn't take them, but I did photograph them, and if you let me have a confirmed e-mail address, I'll send them to you."

"That's good," his principal said. "Use the same e-mail address as before. Do you still have the details?"

"Yes. Once I've done that, what do you want me to do next?"

There was a brief pause while the man at the other end of the line apparently considered his response. Then he obviously came to a decision.

"We may want you to take further action over this, but I'll need to see the photographs and discuss what you've found with my colleagues, so stay in Dartmouth or somewhere nearby tonight and expect a call from me in the morning."

*   *   *

Robin and Mallory finished their meal some fifteen minutes later, but didn't linger over coffee in the restaurant. Instead, they decided to return to Robin's apartment and perhaps do a little more work on trying to decipher the encrypted Latin text. They walked back, following the same route that they had taken earlier, while Gary Marsh dogged their footsteps about one hundred yards back and on the opposite side of the road, effectively invisible on the streets of the town, which were now getting busy as people emerged from their houses and apartments in search of food and drink and evening entertainment.

When Robin and Mallory turned into the alley that gave access to the rear of the building, Marsh abandoned his covert surveillance of the two targets and continued along the road toward his car. In the trunk of the vehicle he had, as he always had when on a job, an overnight bag containing a light sweater, two clean shirts, four changes of underwear and socks, pajamas, a washing kit, an alarm clock, a couple of paperback novels, and a handful of other bits and pieces that in his experience would make his night in a strange bed in a strange hotel in a strange town as comfortable as possible.

When he reached the vehicle, he glanced at his watch. With a bit of luck, as long as the hotel he chose wasn't too far away, he might even be in time for dinner, which was a far more attractive prospect than the snack meal he had expected to have to eat, probably sitting in his car with only some fatuous DJ on a radio station for company.

Before he decided where to go, he checked his satnav,

which showed that what was probably the main hotel in Dartmouth was a fairly short walk away, and it was the work of only a few seconds to dial the number and book a room.

Twenty minutes later, having unpacked and hung up his meager possessions in the small double overlooking the river, Marsh walked down the staircase to the dining room and sat down at a table for one with a satisfied sigh.

8

Dartmouth, Devon

Robin opened the door of her apartment and stepped inside, Mallory right behind her. She headed for the kitchenette to turn on the kettle, while he slipped off his jacket and hung it on one of the hooks in the hallway. Then he stopped and just stared at the carpet right in front of him.

"What is it?" Robin asked, peering around the corner from the kitchenette and looking right at him.

"It might be nothing," he said, "but there's a kind of a whitish discoloration on this carpet, just inside the door, and I don't remember seeing it when we went out."

"I don't really do housewife stuff," Robin said. "So if you're having a pop at me for not wielding the Hoover properly, then you're wasting your time."

Mallory shook his head.

"I wasn't, I promise you." He dropped down to his knees and bent forward to examine the faint mark more carefully. He extended his hand to the whitish discoloration, touched it, and then rubbed his thumb and forefinger together. "It's like a very fine white powder," he said. "In fact, I think it's talcum powder."

Robin walked out of the kitchenette and squatted beside him. She repeated his action, examining the slight trace of powder on her fingertips, and then smelling it.

"There's a small tin of talcum powder in the bathroom," she said, "but that's where it lives. I'll only bring the tin out of there when it's empty and I need to throw it away. And that powder has very faint perfume. This stuff, whatever it is, doesn't smell of anything."

Mallory looked at her, his expression serious.

"I think we might have had a visitor," he said. "A visitor who's either not very competent as a burglar, or who's trying to send us a message."

"Message? What message?"

"This looks to me like the powder you get in a packet of latex gloves, but if he had stood outside your front door and put the gloves on there, the wind would have dispersed the powder in a matter of minutes, and we'd have been none the wiser. But by waiting until he stepped inside, he left a fairly obvious trace. That's what I mean by saying he's either not very good or very good indeed, and he wants us to know that he's been here."

Robin nodded, the puzzled expression on her face giving way to irritation.

"I'll check the place out," she said.

Mallory walked into the study and looked round. Everything appeared to be as he had left it, until he looked at his computer bag. He had left it with the back of the bag leaning against the wall, the natural thing to do so that the front pockets were easily accessible. But now it had been turned around so that the back of the bag faced the room. He didn't touch it, but just called out to Robin.

"I didn't leave this bag in that position," he said, "so somebody has definitely been in while we were out at the restaurant."

"Did they take anything?" she asked.

"I don't know yet. I'll just check."

He opened the computer bag and took out his laptop. He placed it on the desk, opened the lid, and watched as the opening routine ran. It went as far as his password prompt and then came to a stop, waiting for his input.

"That seems to be okay," he said. "Cracking my password would almost certainly have taken a lot longer than the length of time that we were away, and even if the burglar had his own boot disk and tried to get in along that route, I don't think he could have accessed my system that quickly."

He opened up the document pockets in the computer case and pulled out the papers that the two of them had been working on down in the shop. He scanned them quickly, making sure that none was missing.

"These all seem to be here," he said. "As far as I can tell, anyway."

"But someone has definitely looked in your bag?"

Mallory nodded.

"Yes. And what that means, I think, is that this wasn't some opportunistic burglary by a lowlife looking for something to steal so that he could sell it to buy drugs, because if it was, then for sure my computer wouldn't still be here."

"So you mean it might have been the Dominicans again, still dogging our footsteps?"

"I think this is perhaps a bit too subtle for them," Mallory said, "bearing in mind that the last time we entertained them—using that word in its loosest possible sense—here in Dartmouth, they more or less came in with all guns blazing. My guess is that the Dominicans are behind it, yes, but I think that they've probably recruited some expert local help, and what we're seeing is his footprints, if you like."

"So you mean that we probably didn't throw them off the trail in Switzerland when we burned up that other chest and the documents?"

"Perhaps not. Or maybe this is just a kind of belt-and-braces thing. We know for a fact that they translated most of that first piece of parchment that you found in the book safe, and that specifically said that there were three trails that had to be followed. And they've been behind us all the way, first on Cyprus, and then in Switzerland. Maybe what they're doing is trying to find out if we have any idea where the third trail is going to take us, and that's why this was a low-key nonburglary burglary: they just wanted to see what we've got. And if that is the case, whoever came in here will certainly have seen that medieval chest."

"But that doesn't prove anything," Robin objected.

"No, but if I was running their operation, I'd be very

suspicious if I found that the people I was following had a medieval chest complete with a booby trap in the lid, a chest that was virtually identical in appearance to another chest that I had just seen burned and reduced to dust in the middle of Switzerland. Even if I was particularly stupid and obtuse, I think I would definitely suspect that a switch had been pulled. And I don't think those Dominicans are either stupid or obtuse."

"So, if you're right," Robin said, "the Dominicans or whoever these people are will have copies of our transcriptions of the encrypted Latin text."

Mallory nodded.

"We have to assume that, yes. Whoever broke in here will either have photographed the sheets of paper we were working on, or might even have had the cheek to duplicate them using your photocopier. My guess is that he'd have used the camera on his phone, if it had a high enough resolution, or maybe a small high-spec pocket camera, because then he could transfer the pictures onto a computer or, more likely, send them electronically to somebody with an e-mail address in Rome. Whoever did this," he finished, "almost certainly wasn't the principal. He was probably somebody recruited locally who was just following orders."

"You mean it wasn't one of those Dominican thugs?"

"It might have been, but I doubt it. This was a very clean and unobtrusive entry to the property, and that probably means whoever did it was a specialist, somebody with the right tools to get in and out undetected. If it had been one of the Dominicans, I would have expected the door to be broken down, or at least forced open, and both the wooden chest and my computer would probably be missing."

Robin looked puzzled.

"So, why the clues, I suppose you could call them? The talcum powder and your computer case turned the wrong way round? Are you sure they weren't just accidental? The result of clumsy searching, maybe?"

"They could be, but in my opinion they weren't. I think we're probably again under surveillance by that guy who called himself John, the one who rang your mobile in the hotel in Okehampton and basically told us to get out of Dodge. I know he's working for the other side, but for some reason he also seems to have our best interests at heart. At the very least, if it is him, he has told us exactly what the situation is."

At his corner table in the dining room at the hotel a few hundred yards away from where Robin Jessop and David Mallory were analyzing the situation, Gary Marsh ended the call he had received, a call that had been initiated by the bug in the adapter a few seconds after the targets had entered the apartment, and allowed himself a brief smile before turning his attention again to his meal.

"Message delivered," he murmured to himself, picking up his knife and fork.

9

Via di Sant'Alessio, Aventine Hill, Rome, Italy

The communication system in the secure basement of the anonymous property on the Via di Sant'Alessio possessed a number of unusual features, including an online spam checker that analyzed the contents of any e-mail from an unknown address before downloading the message, and automatically bounced any confirmed spam message straight back to the sender. In fact, this rarely happened, because the e-mail addresses used by the organization were far from being either obvious or intuitive. But occasionally some Internet marketing company managed to harvest one of the e-mail addresses and for about a week or so a few entirely unwanted messages were handled in this way.

Most of the traffic comprised routine reports from the organization's agents, and these were usually machine-encrypted and automatically decrypted on arrival, the embedded routing indicators ensuring that the correct officer in the building received the messages. Each e-mail also included an embedded priority code, and whenever the building fielded only a skeleton staff—which was mainly overnight and on Sundays—the on-watch communications officer was alerted every time a message with a priority of "Urgent" or higher was received. He was tasked with inspecting the contents of each such message and deciding whether or not the designated recipient should be called in to deal with it.

By far the smallest number of messages were those sent by the tertiaries, the lay brothers who unofficially and covertly assisted the organization for short periods of time and for very specific matters. For security reasons, these men—and they were invariably male—were never privy to any of the encryption systems in use, and accordingly all their messages arrived as plaintext e-mails. But precisely because these messages involved matters of considerable importance to the organization—otherwise there would have been no need to request the services of a tertiary in the first place—they were always automatically accorded the highest possible priority.

So when a plaintext e-mail arrived in the early hours of the morning from a Web-based e-mail address that had been allocated to a tertiary based in Devon, in the United Kingdom, the communications officer didn't even bother glancing at the text or the attachments. He simply made a note of the routing and then dialed the mobile telephone number of the officer who had been nominated to deal with this particular matter.

His conversation with the man was short and to the

point, and less than twenty minutes later Roman Benelli used the external keypad to unlock the steel door giving access to the basement, and walked into the communication suite.

"Where is it?" he asked.

The communications officer looked up and nodded at the new arrival. The man was wearing a black suit that appeared to be at least two sizes too small for his somewhat chunky frame, and his round face displayed what looked far more substantial than designer stubble. It was common knowledge that Benelli had to shave at least twice a day, and it was popularly believed that his entire body under his clothing was covered by a thick pelt of black hair. Not that anybody in the organization had ever seen him naked, of course. Or wanted to.

"I've routed it to your computer and I've printed one copy of the message and two copies of each of the attachments. They're on your desk."

"Thanks," Benelli said, and walked down the corridor to his office.

While he waited for his computer to load the operating system, he read the hard copy of the message. Before he even looked at the attachments, he guessed he was probably already out of his depth. His specialty was the translation of dead or obscure languages, particularly Coptic and Aramaic and of course Latin, into modern Italian, but he was also the only person in the building who had any knowledge at all of codes and ciphers, and inevitably anything involving encrypted text from any period and in any language landed on his desk.

The attachments were obviously photographs, possibly taken by a high-resolution camera in a mobile phone, and the images displayed excellent clarity, every letter on the handwritten sheets being sharply in focus. That was the good news. The bad news was that the context was somewhat uncertain.

He read the text of the e-mail again—his spoken English was far from fluent, but he had no trouble in reading and understanding the language—but that didn't particularly help. According to the tertiary, the photographs had been taken of a number of sheets of paper removed from a briefcase believed to belong to David Mallory, one half of the English couple who had proved to be such a thorn in the side of the organization so far.

Benelli was well aware of the shambolic events in Switzerland, when Marco Toscanelli had apparently been outwitted by them for a second time, and had let the long-lost and immensely valuable Templar Archive slip through his fingers. He also knew, because Silvio Vitale had told him, that the organization had again mounted surveillance against them in England. This was both in an attempt to confirm that they had somehow managed to get out of Switzerland with the Templar Archive intact and, much more important, to find out if they had also discovered any clues as to the whereabouts of the Templars' sacred relic and their lost assets, the vast hoard of bullion, jewels, and other enduring and enormously valuable treasure that had simply vanished from the pages of history at almost the same moment that the Templar order had been purged.

Benelli looked again at the printed copies of the photographs, trying to make sense of them. Most of them seemed to be pictures of sheets of paper covered in capital letters, clearly handwritten. On a couple of pages it looked as if the writer had been performing frequency analysis on a piece of text, with individual letters being written on the left side of the page and each occurrence then being recorded. All of which was interesting, if not immediately helpful.

Then he looked at the e-mail sent by the tertiary working for them in the United Kingdom, and realized that all the pieces of the puzzle were actually in front of him, though the communications officer hadn't bothered printing all of the photographs that had accompanied the e-mail. In particular, he had failed to print the images of the ironbound medieval box that had been spotted in the woman's flat by the surveillance specialist tasked with entering the premises. And when Benelli looked closely at the interior shots of the box, he could clearly see that the false bottom of the chest had been removed, and could even make an estimate as to the likely size of the revealed hidden cavity.

"Perhaps two centimeters in depth," he murmured to himself, then glanced back at the printouts showing the handwritten letters. "Deep enough for several pieces of parchment or vellum."

There was a knock on his office door, and a moment later the communications officer walked in, carrying a small cup of espresso.

"I hope it was worth your while coming in for that," the communications specialist said, gesturing at the printed sheets on the desk in front of Benelli. "But you looked as if you needed something to keep you awake."

"Thanks for the coffee. I'll probably need several cups, from the looks of this."

"Are you getting anywhere?"

Benelli looked again at each of the images, then compared them to the e-mail attachments, making sure that he had hard copies of everything, and at the same time hoping to find a photograph of whatever the original document or documents had been. But in that, he was disappointed, though unsurprised.

"There obviously isn't a photograph of the original document," he said, pointing at the printed pages. "It was probably a piece, or maybe even several pieces, of parchment or vellum. They probably took it out of the secret compartment at the bottom of the chest and simply transcribed it," he rationalized. "Perhaps it was far too big, or too awkward a shape, to photocopy."

"So, what's on this sheet? Just single letters followed by a basic numbering system?"

"That's exactly what it is," Benelli replied. "It looks to me as if they got nowhere with trying to crack the encryption using plain Atbash or word substitution, and this is their stab at frequency analysis."

"At bash? What's that?"

"Don't worry about it. It's just a basic letter-substitution code that was quite often used during the medieval period. The other pieces of encrypted text relating to this quest all used variants of Atbash, and this probably does as well. It's just a matter of working out the code words that were used to encipher it in the first place, and that's why the English couple seems to have been trying frequency analysis. You calculate the most frequently used letters in the ciphertext and then substitute the commonest letters in use in Latin—and I'm quite sure that this *is* Latin, at this period of the Middle Ages."

The communications officer didn't look any the wiser, but just nodded and then left Benelli's office.

It was late, and he was already tired, but the espresso helped, at least a little. For the moment, he put the frequency-analysis sheets to one side and concentrated instead on what was clearly the transcription of the hidden document or documents, the parchment or whatever the English couple had found. Maybe he could try some different possible code words, the names of people or places most intimately associated with the Knights Templar, names that might not be familiar to Mallory or Jessop. Without the slightest shadow of doubt, the Dominican order knew far more about the order of heretics than anyone else—after all, they had been on the trail of the Templar treasure for over seven centuries—so this seemed to Benelli to be a reasonable idea. And even if it didn't work out, he could still go the frequency-analysis route.

Just before three o'clock in the morning, he gave up. He was so tired that the letters on the sheets of paper seemed to be blurring and running into one another, and he was constantly making mistakes as his concentration slipped. He knew that he had not achieved anything, and wasn't likely to until he had managed to get some sleep.

But there seemed little point in returning to his apartment in Rome. He was so tired that driving himself was probably not a good idea, and trying to get a taxi to take him back there at that time of night would probably prove futile. There was a very basic bedroom located in the basement of the building that was intended for exactly this kind of situation, and at that moment the thought of the monastic solitude, bare walls, and hard mattress on the single bed in the room that awaited him seemed infinitely appealing.

Benelli shut down his computer, locked the printed sheets of paper away in his personal safe, went into the communications suite, and told the officer what he intended to do. He also asked the officer to make sure he was awake by seven thirty so that he would be able to brief Silvio Vitale when he arrived at about eight.

He walked into the bedroom, took off all his clothes apart from his underpants, and slid between the sheets, not even bothering to wash or clean his teeth. Less than two minutes after he put out the light, he was sound asleep.

10

Dartmouth, Devon

Things hadn't gone much better in Devon. Robin and Mallory had continued working on the frequency-analysis sheets until late in the evening, when Robin had virtually lost patience with the tedious process.

"There has got to be an easier way of doing it than this," she snapped, tossing her pencil down and leaning back in her chair. "Isn't there some blasted computer program that you can use?"

Mallory stared at her for a few moments.

"Oddly enough," he admitted somewhat sheepishly, "bearing in mind what I do for a living, I never thought of that. I'll have a look."

While Robin went out into the small kitchenette to make yet another coffee, Mallory performed a quick Internet search, and by the time she came back carrying two mugs, he'd downloaded three fairly small and quite simple programs.

"I'm not entirely sure how much help these three programs will actually be," he said, "but we can certainly give them a try. One of them is specifically designed for cracking a single transposition monoalphabetic substitution cipher, which is just a fancy way of describing a Caesar or Atbash cipher. The second one is a frequency-analysis cracker, and that might be slightly more useful, because although we're almost certainly looking at a substitution cipher, as I said right at the beginning, it certainly isn't a plain vanilla Caesar cipher. We've already tried every possible shift, with the alphabet reversed as well, and made no progress whatsoever."

He pointed at the sheaf of papers in front of him.

"Just like before," he added, "whoever encrypted this text didn't use the straight alphabet for the decryption code words, but instead picked a combination of words, probably with at least fifty-two letters in total, so there would be at least two solutions to every possible letter in the ciphertext. And that increases the number of possible decodes enormously."

Robin nodded.

"I know, and that's what's been really irritating me. Just pick out any three letters from this lot," she said, pointing, "like these, for example. *G, C, D*. Because the letter *C* occurs quite frequently in the encrypted text— we've already established that through the frequency analysis we've done so far—it's most likely to be one of the vowels, which in the Latin alphabet means it's most probably *I* or *E*. If it was a word in the English language, that could decode as almost anything from *FIG* through to *SEX*, and until we could work out one or both of the other letters, we'd be going nowhere."

"You're right. It's really frustrating."

"You said there were three."

"Sorry?"

"Three programs. You said you'd downloaded three programs. What does the third one do?"

"Oh, yes," Mallory replied. "That's something a bit different. It's a word-pattern analyzer. If you're trying to break a monoalphabetic ciphertext, and you know a couple of the letters in a particular word, it will do a dictionary search and bring up all the words in the chosen language that match the shape of that word."

"You've kind of lost me now."

"I'll give you an example. Suppose you have an encrypted word like *KPCCRRF*, and you believe that the letter *P* decodes as *A*. You feed the encrypted word into the program, which converts it into a numerical equivalent, in this case 1233445, so you have two unique letters, followed by two sets of two repeated letters, and then another unique letter. So, numerically, that is the shape of the word. Then you replace the number 2 with the letter that you believe was represented by the encrypted letter *P*, and then just look up the result. What the program does is check every possible word in the selected language where the second letter is *A* and that's followed by two pairs of letters. In English, there are only four possibilities: *BALLOON*, *BARROOM*, *BASSOON*, and *RACCOON*, and in this case using that software would have positively confirmed that the ciphertext *R* is the plaintext *O*, and given only two possible plaintext decodes for the first and last letters of the word."

"I see what you mean," Robin said, "and that's really rather clever. But it would only be any use to us if it works with languages other than English."

"That's not a problem. You can upload a word list or dictionary for almost any language, including Latin. And you're right: it is clever, but we've got two obvious limitations. First, we don't yet have a single confirmed plaintext letter and, second, and just as important, because the original text is written without any breaks—the *scriptio continua* that was used—at the moment we have no idea where any of the words start or end. So we'll need to do quite a bit more work before this clever program will be any use to us. But now that I've downloaded these programs, we might as well give the frequency-analysis calculator a try. The good news is that it'll produce the results a hell of a lot faster than we'd be able to do using a pencil and paper."

"And the bad news?" Robin asked. "I assume there is some bad news?"

Mallory nodded.

"Kind of, yes. To get the program to work, I'll have to type the original ciphertext into my laptop. The handwritten sheets aren't going to be good enough to scan in and then use an OCR—optical character recognition—program to read them."

"I do know what *OCR* stands for, thank you. You'd better get started, then. I'm going to finish this coffee, make sure the outside door's locked, and have a shower.

I feel dusty and grubby. Then I'm going to bed. I expect you to follow me there before too long."

"Trust me," he said, "I'll be as quick as I can."

Transcribing the ciphertext wasn't difficult, but it was extremely tedious, because Mallory knew that he had to check every single letter that he typed to make sure that he didn't miss any out or press the wrong letter on the keyboard. When he heard the shower switch off, he was only about halfway down the first of the three sheets that they had prepared.

He glanced at his watch, saved the document he was working onto the hard drive, and made a separate backup copy on a memory stick, then closed the lid of the computer and headed for the bathroom himself. He'd finish the transcription in the morning.

11

Via di Sant'Alessio, Aventine Hill, Rome, Italy

Roman Benelli was up, washed, shaved, and dressed, albeit in precisely the same set of clothes he'd been wearing the previous evening, by a quarter to seven, and was back at his desk and looking again at the printed images in front of him five minutes later.

As dawn broke gloriously—and invisibly, to Benelli in his underground office—over Rome, the pages didn't look any better or more hopeful to him than they had before. None of the Templar-specific names and words he had tried had worked, and after inputting another dozen or so as code words and then trying an Atbash decode of the first line of the text—all of which achieved precisely nothing—he came to the reluctant conclusion that the only way he was going to solve the decryption would be to apply frequency analysis, tiresome and time-consuming though that exercise would be.

When Silvio Vitale pushed his way into the office without knocking—as usual—just after eight, Benelli was already hard at it.

"This is the data sent by the tertiary in England?" Vitale asked, as Benelli stood up to greet him.

"Yes. I told the communication section to send a copy to your computer as well."

"I know. I saw that when I arrived, but I've not looked at it yet. What I want to know is what you're doing about it."

Benelli explained that he had tried a large number of different code words that were directly relevant to the Knights Templar, but without any success at all.

"There appears to be no indication within the document about how to decode the text. Sometimes a person carrying out an encryption will include a hint in plaintext, or possibly a series of initials that suggests what the decryption key might be."

"You mean like the letters *P, C, C, T, S* could mean *Pauperes commilitones Christi Templique Salomonici*, the original Latin name of the order of heretics? And those could be the code words needed?"

"Exactly," Benelli replied. "It's clear from the pictures obtained by the tertiary—or rather by the agent he used— that there was a concealed space inside the wooden chest." He picked up one of the photographs. "This piece of wood obviously concealed a cavity at the bottom of the chest, which looks to me as if it's about two centimeters deep. I assume that whatever the British pair found was inside it."

Vitale nodded.

"But there's no picture of whatever they recovered from it? Or have I missed that?"

"No, there's no photograph of it, so we don't know for sure what it was, but it was most likely a piece of either parchment or vellum—probably vellum, as it was an important document."

"What's the difference?"

Benelli looked slightly surprised by the question.

"Very little," he replied. "In fact, they're essentially the same thing. The word *parchment* refers to an animal skin that's been prepared for writing on, and vellum was the highest-quality skin available. The word is derived from the Latin *vitulus*, meaning a calf, or more likely *vitulinum*, which literally translates as 'made from a calf.' And the finest-quality vellum of all was uterine vellum, made from the skin of calf fetuses, though there's some doubt about whether that was ever used during the medieval period. Parchment and vellum were both prepared in the same way. First the skin was flayed. Then the hair was removed with a kind of lime solution, often made from rotting vegetable matter. That part of the process usually took a few days, but the people doing it had to take care with it because if they left the skin for too long in the liquid it would end up being too soft to be usable. Once that dehairing phase had been completed, the skin was washed, mounted on a stretching frame, and left to dry in the open air."

"Interesting, but not helpful, Benelli. I'm not interested in the mechanics of the process, only in the result, in what was actually on the vellum or parchment or whatever it was. So, you haven't got a picture of it, but you have got a transcription?"

"Yes. That was what I showed you first."

"And nothing you've tried—none of the possible code words, I mean—has so far cracked the encryption?"

"Exactly," Benelli said. "But at least we know that English couple is in the same position. They don't know how to decrypt this, either."

"How can you be sure of that?"

Benelli pointed at another of the sheets of paper on the desk in front of him.

"Because if they knew or had deduced the code words, there would be no need for them to be doing frequency analysis, and that's obviously what these pages of letters are. They're trying to work out which encrypted letters occur most frequently in the text so that they can use a Latin letter-frequency table to work out what the plaintext equivalent might be."

"I know the theory, Benelli. And that's what you're doing as well?"

"Yes. I've tried everything else, so as far as I can see it's the only possible way forward."

Vitale looked at the pages.

"It'll be quicker if you split the work. I'll send in three or four other people to help you. Give each of them one section of the transcription and tell them exactly what you want them to do and how to do it. Any problems, let me know."

Benelli nodded, and Vitale noticed the look on his face.

"What?"

"Frequency analysis may not provide the information we need, or not immediately."

"Explain."

"Looking at the analysis that I've done already has not produced the results I would have expected. Even in a small piece of encrypted text, just a couple of sentences, frequency analysis should quickly identify at least half a dozen of the commonest letters, and in Latin there should be two that are far more common than any of the others, the letters *I* and *E*. And that isn't what I see here."

Vitale leaned forward and looked at the page and the analysis that Benelli had completed on the first section of the text.

"There are two ways of doing this. The English couple obviously decided to analyze the entire piece of text. Noting the first letter of the first word, and then counting every subsequent recurrence of it. That works, but it means that until they reach the end of the text the analysis remains incomplete. The quicker way to work is to take a much smaller piece of text and carry out the same analysis on that. Then you take the results and apply them to the rest of the ciphertext, and that often works. It may need refining to positively identify every single encrypted letter, but it will certainly generate most of the plaintext alphabet."

"Presumably not in this case," Vitale suggested.

"Not unless the section I picked is very different to the rest of it, no. I'm not seeing two letters appearing more commonly than any others. Instead, there are eight letters that seem to be dominating the table. And the most likely explanation for that is that we're looking at a very complex Atbash cipher, where there weren't just twenty-three or twenty-six letters in the code word or words corresponding to the Latin alphabet—depending on the period—but more like seventy. Maybe even a hundred. Let me show you what I mean."

Benelli took a fresh sheet of paper, wrote out the normal alphabet in a single horizontal line, then wrote three horizontal lines of random letters below it.

"Now, if you look at the letter *E*," he explained, "instead of there just being one equivalent letter in a single code word below it, you have a choice of three. That obviously increases the possible permutations for each letter, but to make it worse those three letters in the vertical line below the *E* also occur elsewhere in the code words. They have to, because there are only twenty-six letters in the alphabet and to have code words totaling seventy-eight letters inevitably means that there will be repeats. In this example I've made up, the three letters below the *E* are *P*, *G*, and *R*, and *G* can also represent the letters *K* and *S*. So if you look at the letter *G* in the ciphertext, the plaintext equivalent could be *E*, but it could also be *K* or *S*."

"So what you're telling me is that for every single word there could be three or four possible plaintext equivalents for each letter in the ciphertext."

Benelli nodded.

"That's exactly what I mean, so the number of possible permutations is huge. The related problem is that the transcription of the encrypted text has no spaces in it, and

I'm quite sure that if there had been breaks in the original, whoever did this transcription—Mallory or Jessop— would have included them. So the encrypted text must have been written in *scriptio continua*, and that means we have no idea where each word starts or finishes, which will make interpreting the text even more difficult."

Vitale stared at Benelli for a few moments before speaking again.

"So are you telling me that you *can't* decrypt it?"

"No," Benelli said hurriedly. "I'm not saying that at all, but even with the assistance of some other people to help with the frequency analysis, because of the amount of trial and error we will have to do to make any sense of the text, it's probably going to take us a long time to complete the task."

"Define 'a long time,'" Vitale instructed. "Hours? Days? What timescale do you actually mean?"

"Certainly several days. Perhaps some weeks. And if it proves to be particularly intractable, it might even be months. At the moment, I simply don't know."

Even Vitale's silences could seem threatening, and not for the first time Benelli wished that the task of decrypting the ancient text had been given to somebody else.

"We need this done as soon as possible," Vitale said. "You'll get your extra men to complete the frequency analysis. Then I want you and anybody else in this organization who has even the slightest experience of cipher systems to work on this, to the exclusion of everything else. From now on, until this matter is resolved, that is to be your highest priority."

"Suppose the English couple cracks it first?"

A humorless smile appeared on Vitale's face.

"It would be quite convenient if they did," he said, "because that would save us—or rather you—a lot of work. They are already being watched, and the moment we are certain that they have decrypted the text, our men will move in and seize the information. I will probably have them killed at the same time to tie off that loose end. And that would at least stop them embarrassing Marco Toscanelli every time he encounters them."

12

Dartmouth, Devon

Mallory set his mental alarm for seven, but woke up just after six. Careful not to wake Robin, he eased out of the double bed, picked up his clothes from the chair, pulled the bedroom door closed behind him, and walked back into the study. He opened up his computer, made a mug of instant coffee in the kitchenette, then settled down to work.

Robin emerged from the bedroom at half past eight, wearing a nightdress that was so short it barely covered the interesting bits, her hair tousled and her face sleepy but infinitely appealing.

"And you got up when?" she demanded.

"About six," Mallory replied, leaning back in his chair.

"Well, I hope you haven't just been sitting there, staring into space or checking out porn sites," she said.

"I've said it before," Mallory objected, "that with you around, looking at porn is the furthest thing from my mind. I've finished the transcription, and the program is now chuntering away doing the number crunching. Can I make you a coffee or something?"

"I'll do my own. Thank you. I've got a much more important job for you to do."

He looked at her inquiringly.

"You can go out and buy my breakfast. There's a baker about a hundred yards down the street, and I'd like one large *pain au raisin* or two small ones if the big ones have all gone. Do not bring me back a croissant, because I really don't like them."

"Understood," Mallory said, "and by the time I'm back we should have the results of the frequency analysis."

He was back in just over ten minutes, Robin's breakfast order fulfilled to the letter, and immediately checked the information displayed on the screen of his laptop.

"It's worked," he said, "and it's pretty much what I was expecting."

"Which is what?" Robin asked, taking a bite out of her pastry.

"I remember you telling me about the frequency analysis of that piece of mixed-genre Latin text that was posted on the Internet, but I couldn't remember the order of the letters, so I looked it up again."

"It's *I, E, A, U, T, S*," Robin reminded him, "or those are the first six letters anyway, and the *I* and the *E* between them represented nearly a quarter of the letters used."

"Got it. In fact, I guessed that I would need the full list of all the letters to really make any kind of sense of the transcription, so I saved the result. I found a couple

of different lists with minor differences, but nothing significant. What we've ended up with isn't exactly clear-cut,
but I think we can probably work with it."

"Let me guess. You didn't find two letters that occurred more often than any others and that might be *I*
and *E*. You probably found four of them."

But Mallory shook his head.

"No. I found a total of nine, and that suggests we're
looking at an Atbash cipher where the code words used
probably contain over seventy letters in all, giving the
man who encrypted the plaintext three possible choices
every time he used the letter *I* or *E*."

"But surely if he had three letters he could choose, that
would imply that there should be six letters that would
occur more frequently than the others?"

"You're quite right, but inevitably each of the code
words would contain more than one occurrence of the
letter that represented an *I* or *E*, so the letter *M* may be at
the top of the popularity list, and may well decode the
letter *I*, but it could also decode any other letter in the
alphabet."

Robin looked surprised, then shook her head.

"That's going to make deciphering it bloody difficult,
or at least take a hell of a long time. There are so many
possible permutations that even if we do manage to make
sense of it, I wouldn't be entirely convinced that we were
making the *correct* sense of it. As I understand it, decrypting using frequency analysis pretty much relies on being
able to identify the dozen or so most common letters with
a fair degree of certainty. If there are three possible op-

tions for each one, that's really going to increase the degree of difficulty."

"You're right as usual, but I don't see any other way of doing it."

"Neither do I," Robin agreed, then paused for a moment.

"What?" Mallory asked.

"I was just thinking it through, trying to look at it logically. Whatever that encrypted text says, the Templars must have intended that it could be read at some time in the future."

"That makes sense. As we know, when Philip the Fair's men swooped on the Templar strongholds in France in October 1307, they not only found the treasuries virtually empty, but also couldn't find most of the knights to arrest them. That virtually confirms that the order knew what the king of France was intending to do, and made sure that his plan wouldn't succeed. The knights dispersed, taking the treasure with them, and almost certainly planned to revive the order once the danger passed.

"Don't forget, the Knights Templar owed allegiance to one man, and only one man: the pope. He was the most powerful man in Europe, arguably the most powerful man in the world, and in matters relating to the Templars, the king of France, like every other European ruler, was subordinate to him. It would make sense for the Templars to expect the pope to countermand the wishes of Philip the Fair and restore the order. What they perhaps didn't expect was that the incumbent pope—the misnamed Clement V, because there was no clemency in him—was so weak and pliable that he simply did exactly what Philip told him to do and abandoned the Knights Templar to the torture chambers of the Dominicans and the flames of the stake."

Robin nodded.

"Exactly. And very poetic. So, my point is, if the Templars thought the order could be revived, then they must also have expected somebody, at some time, to recover the Archive and find that piece of vellum. We also know that most of the knights, despite their noble origins, were borderline illiterate at best and some were completely illiterate, so it would make sense to include some kind of a clue or hint to help with the decryption. I think there must be something we've missed, either on the vellum or on the chest itself."

While Robin opened the safe to recover the piece of vellum, Mallory cleared an area on the desk and placed the ironbound wooden box on it.

"We found clues in the metalwork on those other two chests," he said, "but I don't think that's what we've got here. There are metal bands around this box to reinforce the wood, but there's nothing like the ornate scrollwork we saw on the others."

Mallory ran the tips of his fingers over the metal straps on the lid, then opened the chest and removed the false bottom, below which the vellum had been concealed. He checked the piece of wood that he had removed, but it appeared to be devoid of any markings. The only unusual feature was that the underside of it had apparently been given a coat of very dark brown paint, virtually the same color as the wood itself.

"That's odd," Mallory said, showing Robin the painted surface. "I wonder why they did that."

"Maybe they intended it to act as a barrier between the vellum, because that's pretty fragile, and the wood itself. But I really don't know."

"Yes, but if they did that for some sort of protection, why didn't they also paint the inside of the chest, or at least the bottom of it? Because the base of the chest, where the vellum was hidden, is just bare wood."

Robin used her powerful desk lamp to illuminate the interior of the box, and together they scanned every square inch of it.

"I don't see anything," Mallory said. "Do you?"

"No. No scratches or marks on the wood, apart from those left by the carpenter who made the box seven hundred or so years ago. What about the exterior?"

"If they were going to record any important information, I would have expected it to be inside the box, where it would be safe from damage." Mallory closed the lid and pointed at the metalwork that reinforced it. "These are just strengthening bands, nothing like the ornamental scrollwork we found on those other chests. And as far as I can see, there are no marks on any of the metalwork that could help us decode this text."

He and Robin examined every part of the chest but found nothing significant. Then Mallory put the box back on the floor and they turned their attention to the vellum. Robin placed it carefully on the desk and, again using her desk light, they checked the entire object, inspecting both sides of it. They also confirmed again that their transcription of the ciphertext was accurate, without mistakes, omissions, or additions; they found absolutely nothing that could possibly provide the clue that they needed.

"So, I suppose that's that," Robin said, sounding completely fed up. "Back to the bloody frequency analysis."

Mallory nodded, and while Robin returned the vellum to her safe, he moved his laptop back toward the center of the desk. But he didn't start work immediately, just sat there staring at the scattered sheets of paper that covered much of the surface of the desk, apparently lost in thought.

And when Robin turned back from the safe and looked at him, there was a broad smile on his face.

"What?" she demanded, sounding irritated.

"I think," Mallory began, "that I know where we should be looking. And if I'm right, the answer has been more or less staring at us right from the start."

13

Dartmouth, Devon

"Well, don't keep me in suspense," Robin said. "What are you talking about?"

But for a moment, Mallory didn't reply because another, largely unrelated and fairly unpleasant thought had just crossed his mind. He frowned, then glanced up at Robin and smiled.

"I will tell you," he said, "but I think we deserve a small celebration first. Get dressed, and I'll take you out and buy you a coffee."

"What?"

"You know. Coffee. Hot brown liquid, comes in a cup."

"I do know what coffee is, you idiot. But why do we have to go out?"

"Because I'd like to," Mallory replied, and at the same time wrote "JUST AGREE WITH ME" in pencil on one of the pieces of paper on the desk.

Robin looked at what he'd written and nodded.

"Oh, very well," she said. "I could do with a breath of fresh air."

Less than ten minutes later—Mallory having already got used to Robin's almost masculine ability to simply pull on clothes and be immediately ready without any of the usual prolonged fannying about that had been a part of all of his previous experiences with members of the female sex—they walked down the metal spiral staircase from Robin's apartment and headed off down the street.

"What's going on?" Robin asked.

"Something's been niggling at me ever since last night," Mallory said.

"You mean about the nonburglary burglary, I suppose?"

"Yes. I know we assumed that it was simply an attempt to find out what we had, to take pictures or copies of the transcription we were working on, and to photograph the chest as well. But it suddenly occurred to me that there might have been more to it than that. If it was organized by the Dominicans, their aim is obviously to decipher the text and beat us to the prize. But at the moment we have no idea what the text says, and we won't have an idea until we manage to work out a way of deciphering it, and they must have exactly the same problem. So it suddenly dawned on me that while we were sitting there in your office discussing the frequency analysis and the ways we could do the decryption, it was entirely possible that somebody working for the Dominicans was listening in."

Robin stopped dead on the pavement.

"You mean, somebody's bugged me?"

"Probably not you personally, because that would be too difficult for a whole number of reasons, but I think it's at least likely that there might be a bug somewhere in your office."

"That's disgusting."

"It may be, but that's also probably the reality of the situation. You know how high the stakes are in this. We've been involved with these Dominican enforcers up close and personal, and we absolutely know that they're prepared to kill anyone who gets in their way. So invading your privacy by sticking a bug in your apartment isn't going to bother them at all."

Robin took a few more steps along the pavement, then stopped again.

"If you're right," she said, coloring slightly, "where would they have put the microphone?"

"Not in the bedroom," Mallory assured her, immediately guessing at her concern. "They're not interested in what you get up to in bed."

"That's a relief, I suppose."

"If there is a bug, it'll be in your office, and it'll probably be voice activated. There'll be a recorder somewhere within a hundred yards or so, and every day, probably, someone will turn up at that location to change the tapes. In fact, these days, they'll probably be using some kind of digital recorder because they're a lot smaller and the recording time is much longer."

They walked on and Mallory opened the door of the

café to let Robin step inside. While she chose a table near the window, with a view over toward the river Dart, Mallory bought two cups of coffee and a couple of allegedly homemade chocolate muffins and carried his purchases on a tray over to the table.

"So, what can we do about it?" Robin asked, using a knife to cut her muffin into bite-sized chunks. "You know far more about this sort of thing than I do. If there is a bug, can you find it and remove it?"

Mallory nodded.

"I've not been involved in spying, obviously," he replied, "but many businesses these days are worried about industrial and commercial espionage, and on a couple of occasions I've been asked to sweep a room to make sure there aren't any hidden microphones in it as a part of my IT work. So if there is a bug, I can certainly find it and I can also remove it. What I'm not quite sure about is whether that's a good idea."

"I don't want people listening to me in my own apartment," Robin said firmly. "I'd never feel able to fart again," she added with a smile.

"I'm not thinking about leaving it in place permanently," Mallory explained. "But I was wondering if we could use it to our own advantage."

"For misdirection, you mean? Now, that's not a bad idea. We could try to convince the listeners that the ciphertext is insoluble, and that we've given up. Or try and send them off in the wrong direction, perhaps."

"That's exactly what I mean, and that's why I needed to get you out of the flat, because I couldn't explain all this if the Dominicans were earwigging on what we were talking about."

"So, what do we do next? Go back to the apartment, obviously, but what then?"

"This time," Mallory said, "I do have a kind of plan."

14

Via di Sant'Alessio, Aventine Hill, Rome, Italy

To say that Silvio Vitale was annoyed would have been something of an understatement. He had left Bellini's office in a cold fury, as he once again realized that the hidden hoard of the Knights Templar, the vast wealth and the even more important treasure for which the Dominicans had been searching for over seven centuries, was potentially slipping from his grasp.

When he had seen the handwritten transcription on his computer screen that morning, he had assumed that, although the decryption process might take some time, it would certainly be achievable. But if Benelli's assessment of the degree of difficulty was anything like accurate, it was in fact entirely conceivable that they would never be able to decipher the entire piece of text. And that was not good news. In fact, Vitale had been impressed with himself, and pleased that he had refrained from abusing the man responsible for trying to solve the riddle. Cursing him would have achieved nothing except alienating him, and as Benelli was the only person likely to be able to decrypt the cipher, Vitale knew that he couldn't afford to do that.

He had allocated additional resources in the shape of three other men to assist in the process of frequency analysis, but he was under no illusions about how successful that part of the process might be, in view of what Benelli had already discovered. But if the text prepared by the Knights Templar—the text written on vellum or parchment and then concealed by them in the wooden chest that had served as a repository for the most valuable documents that composed the Templar Archive—could not be deciphered, then the quest that the Dominicans had been tasked with completing over seven hundred years earlier would finally fail. And Vitale was not prepared to let that happen. Not, as the saying goes, on his watch.

He sat at his desk, considering his options. The one thing he dared not do was seek outside assistance with the decryption. He was well aware that he could call on the services of experts in cipher technology, but the risk of one of those experts realizing the true nature of the search, and of the prize that might still lie at the end of the trail, was too great to be contemplated. In fact, it wasn't the prize itself that was so dangerous, but the implications—the appalling worldwide implications—if knowledge of its true nature were ever to be made public.

For a few minutes he thought about the possibility of dividing up the encrypted text, of separating it into a number of much smaller documents that could perhaps be handled by outside experts without compromising the full meaning of the text and hence the quest. But even doing that would still pose a risk, because it was more than possible that almost any part of the ancient text might provide some specific information about the prize, as well as its location. And unless Benelli's assessment of the text was completely wrong, it was entirely probable that even an expert would be unable to resolve the cipher unless he had access to the whole document, so it would be a fruitless attempt. And Vitale had already decided that he could never allow that.

So, apart from waiting for any results that Benelli might obtain from the transcription, the only other way forward that Vitale could see working was to dog the footsteps of the English couple. After all, they clearly had possession of whatever the transcription had been written on, and if some hint relating to the decoding method was present on the parchment or inside the box, then presumably they would be able to use it, produce the plaintext version of the message, and then follow whatever clues it provided.

At present, through the tertiary working in the British police force, he had ordered only discreet surveillance, but it was clear that he would have to change this, to increase the intensity and the number of watchers, and have a team of men in Britain ready to move at a moment's notice to follow the English couple wherever they went. Or possibly to do what he'd ordered when the whole thing had started: send a team into Jessop's apartment with instructions to recover the ancient box, and the parchment, and kill them both.

But before he could even start to formulate his new orders, two things happened virtually simultaneously. His e-mail client was set up to check for messages every fifteen minutes, and at that moment the speakers attached to his desktop computer emitted a musical double tone to indicate that new mail had arrived. It was only one message, and as he glanced at the address of the sender, he realized it had been sent by the tertiary in Devon he had been thinking about only seconds before.

He clicked on the message to open it, but as he did so, his mobile phone rang. He checked the number before he swiped his finger across the screen of his phone to answer the call.

"Yes?" he said briefly and in English, recognizing the 44 country code.

"Do you know who I am?" the caller asked.

"Yes. I've just received your e-mail, though I haven't read it yet."

"That's what I wanted to talk to you about. This morning I heard from the surveillance specialist I hired. As you ordered, he concealed a microphone in the target premises, and earlier today he listened to a very interesting conversation between the two subjects."

"When was this?" Vitale demanded. "When did this conversation take place?"

"A little over an hour ago."

"Then why did you not call me immediately?"

"I wanted to be sure of my facts before I spoke to you.

The recording he made was uploaded to the cloud, so I had to download it before I could play it back. I think you'll find it interesting, and I've attached it to the e-mail you now have. It's the very last section that's important."

Vitale nodded, though this obviously conveyed nothing to the caller.

"Very well," he said. "I'll listen to the recording immediately. Kindly call me back in exactly fifteen minutes, when I'll probably have some further orders for you."

He opened the message, looked quickly at the text, and then double-clicked on the attachment, a single audio file. Because of what the tertiary had just told him, he ignored the first part of it and skipped through until he reached about the eighty percent mark. Then he pulled on a set of headphones and started listening.

After a few seconds, he pressed the fast-forward control to move more quickly through the recording, pausing to listen to the odd sentence every few moments. And then he reached one section of the audio file that he listened to in its entirety. And when he'd done so, he moved the cursor back and listened to it again. And then played it once more, just in case he'd missed anything.

When his mobile phone rang for the second time that morning, he took off the headphones to answer it.

"Have you heard anything further?" he demanded.

"Nothing yet," the tertiary replied. "The operative conducting the surveillance is waiting for them to return to the apartment, so we shouldn't have too long to wait."

"Call me the moment you hear anything," Vitale instructed, and then ended the call.

15

"You said it would be easier to show me than tell me," Robin said, walking into her office and flicking on the light. "So show me."

"I will," Mallory replied, picking up his computer bag and opening one of the side pockets. "Just give me a couple of minutes to sort myself out first."

"I'll give you more than that. I'll go and make us some sandwiches. Ham and pickle okay for you?"

"Perfect," Mallory said, producing what looked something like a chunky and old-fashioned mobile phone and a pair of lightweight headphones, which he put on, plugging the minijack into the device.

Across the room, Robin gave him a quick thumbs-up, then turned and left.

Mallory switched on the multifunction detector, chose silent operation so that he could find any bug in the room without anyone listening in through it being any the wiser, and made a quick circuit.

Immediately, the screen on the device illuminated, confirming his suspicion. Narrowing down the location took only a matter of seconds in the small room. He crouched down beside Robin's printer and identified the location of the bug in the mains adapter plugged into the wall socket.

Then he stood up again, leaving the adapter in place. Before he did anything to it, he needed to confirm that it was the only bug in the property. Without saying a word, he walked around every room in the small apartment, then returned to the office.

To maintain the pretense that neither he nor Robin had any idea the conversation was being monitored, he moved about the room, probably generating enough noise to trigger the device, assuming that it was a voice-activated bug, then stepped over to the doorway.

"How are you doing out there?" he asked.

"Nearly ready."

"We can eat in there. That'll save getting bread crumbs all over the office."

Mallory walked into the small kitchenette, where Robin was leaning against the counter and waiting for him, and closed the door softly behind him.

"One bug," he said quietly. "There's a suspiciously clean and new-looking mains adapter plugged into one of your wall sockets, the one that feeds your printer."

"You have no idea how irritating I find that," Robin said. "The thought of some sleazy little git listening in to everything I say—that we say—in the office is terminally annoying. So, now you've found it, what are you going to do about it?"

"What we discussed, I think. That still seems to me to be the best option." Mallory glanced around the kitchenette. "Did you make any sandwiches?"

"Of course not," Robin snapped. "You've spent the morning filling your fat face with pastries and cakes and coffee, so the last thing I'm going to do is make you any more food, because you don't need it. That conversation we had was just to let you check the office while I was out of the way."

"Right. Okay, so we'll give it a few minutes and then go back in and try to sow a few seeds of disinformation that will hopefully get the opposition chasing their tails somewhere that we aren't."

Five minutes later, they returned to the office.

"I've been really patient up to now," Robin said, "so this had better be good. What have you found?"

"What I haven't found," Mallory replied, "is any way of deciphering the stuff that was written on that piece of vellum. There are just too many possible permutations and options. In fact," he added, "I'm even wondering if that text is a complete red herring, just a piece of gibberish that doesn't actually mean anything at all."

"That makes no sense to me," Robin said, ad-libbing her way through the basic script that Mallory had asked her to follow. "Why would they go to all the trouble of preparing a piece of text like that, hiding it in a wooden chest with the rest of the Templar Archive, and then burying it underneath a mountain in Switzerland?"

"Well, I suppose it may mean something, but there's not much chance of our being able to decrypt it. But I think the important thing isn't the vellum, but the wooden chest. And, in fact, not even the wooden chest itself but just the false bottom, because what I found on the underside of that looks to me remarkably like a map."

"Are you serious? A map of what? Of where?"

"Right now, I'm not sure. It's only a very basic illustration, just a series of lines cut into the wood of the false bottom of the chest. But I'm actually wondering if it might be Rome, because right in the center of the carving are what look like seven hills, with a castle or a tower drawn on top of them."

"I didn't think that the Templars had anything much to do with Rome," Robin objected. "Apart from their connection to the pope and the Vatican, of course."

"That's true, but it still— Hang on a minute." Mallory let his voice rise in obvious excitement. "I've been stupid. Of course it's not Rome. But there's another city that was really important to the Templars, especially after 1307, and that was also supposed to have been built on seven hills."

"Where?"

"Tomar, in Portugal. I'm amazed I didn't make the connection straightaway. It's pretty much in the middle of the country, and was originally a Roman city called Sellium. The Templars were granted the land in the middle of the twelfth century and built a castle there that became their headquarters for the entire country. When the order was purged, Portugal was one of the nations that didn't join in the campaign against the Templars and offered the remaining knights a safe haven. Then, in 1317 the Portuguese king created the Order of Christ, which was basically exactly the same as the Knights Templar but with a new name, a new uniform, a new flag, and immunity from persecution. The new order had a different symbol as well, but it was actually just the old Templar *croix pattée* with a plain white cross set into it as a kind of insert. And from what I've read, the repackaged Templars hadn't lost their magic financial touch. The new order was later heavily involved with Henry the Navigator, and became immensely wealthy during the Portuguese age of exploration."

"So, what you're saying is that it would make very good sense for the Templars to have smuggled the contents of their various treasuries down to Portugal. I assume they would have known they would be safe in Portugal even before Philip's men began their campaign of mass arrests throughout France?" Robin asked.

"I think the evidence is overwhelming," Mallory said, nodding, "that the Templars knew about his plan well in advance. If they didn't, it was a hell of a coincidence that most of the members of the order were nowhere to be found on that day in October 1307, and also that the majority of the treasuries were virtually bare. Don't forget that the Templar strongholds were literally surrounded by potential enemies in every country in Western Europe, and I'm quite certain that they would have been well aware of what was going on all around them. And you're right. The order would also have been making covert inquiries with any country that could have provided it with a safe haven, and that would certainly have included Portugal and probably England and Scotland as well."

"So, do you think we're now on the right track, that the Templar treasure is lying hidden somewhere near Tomar?" Robin asked, really getting into the spirit of the deception.

"This isn't much of a map," Mallory replied, "but that is what I think it means. The trouble is that there's almost no detail, so I have no idea where we should start looking. But I think a good first step would certainly be to get out to Tomar and see what we can find there. And we'll still keep trying to decipher the encrypted text on the parchment because, if it isn't a red herring, it will hopefully provide more information about exactly where we should start looking."

"Good idea. I really think we might be on the last lap of this quest now. So, what are you doing now?"

"My phone's battery is starting to give me trouble, so I've got this external power pack thing that I carry around with me, but that's flat as well, so I need to charge it up. Is it okay if I plug it in here?"

"Yes. Just pull the adapter out of the socket."

"What about these two leads that are plugged into it?" Mallory asked.

"Don't worry about them. One's for the printer, and the other's for the fan next to the desk, and I'm not using either at the moment."

And with that, Mallory pulled the bugged adapter out of the socket. He was still holding his detector, and turned it on, pointing the aerial at the adapter in his hand. The screen of the detector remained completely blank, and he altered the way he was holding it so that Robin could see it well.

"Is that it?" she asked.

"That's it. It's obviously only mains powered—no backup battery—so we're no longer broadcasting. I just hope we sounded natural, and that they take the bait."

"I don't know about the Dominicans, but all that stuff you said about the Templars setting up a new base in Portugal after 1307 and probably taking their treasure with them was really convincing. I almost believed it myself."

Mallory grinned at her.

"It sounded believable because it's true," he said. "Obviously I have no idea whether or not that's where the Templar treasure ended up, but it's certainly one very real possibility. And it would be a bit ironic if it turned out we were right and the trail actually did lead us to Tomar. That would probably count as shooting ourselves in the foot, sending the Dominicans to a place that we have to go ourselves, and before we get there. But it was the best idea I could come up with at short notice."

Mallory walked over to the desk, put the mains adapter on it, and began examining it.

"This is quite a sophisticated piece of kit," he said after a couple minutes, "but I was wrong about it sending the output to a recording device somewhere nearby. There's no radio transmitter built into the circuitry."

He extracted a small piece of plastic from within the adapter and showed it to Robin.

"Do you recognize this?" he asked.

"It looks like a SIM card from a phone."

"That's exactly what it is. This bug includes a cut-down circuit board from a mobile, allowing it to dial a specific number, most likely a mobile phone, obviously, the moment the microphone detects any sound. So as soon as we walked into the apartment, the bug would have called whoever had positioned it in here, and he would then have been able to listen to everything we said inside this room."

"So you mean he could listen to our conversation, but not record it?"

Mallory shook his head.

"I'd be very surprised if he didn't do both. It's not that difficult to set up a mobile phone to record every conversation on it, and that would include an incoming call from a device like this. My guess is that the man doing the surveillance listened to what we said, recording it on his mobile at the same time, and then probably immediately uploaded it to a secure cloud storage somewhere so that whoever he's working for could download it and listen to it themselves. And because we're talking mobile phone technology, the man who planted this bug could be anywhere in the world, as long as he had a signal on his mobile phone and this SIM card had sufficient credit to make the call. It's a clever device."

"So, what are you going to do with it? Smash it up?"

"Certainly not. Because of the way we disabled this, there's a good chance that the listeners will assume we did it entirely accidentally, literally unplugging their device to plug something else in. That means that if we want to pass them another message, to try a bit more misdirection, we can simply plug it back in and have another artificial conversation. So for the moment we should definitely keep it."

"So?"

"So what?"

"So, what did you find? Obviously it wasn't a carving on the inside of that box, so what was it? What have you really got?"

"Something very different," Mallory said, "and after all this, I just hope I'm right."

He walked around the desk and picked up the iron-bound chest that they had recovered from inside the Swiss mountain. He put it on the desk and opened the lid.

"We've looked inside and outside this box several times," he said, "and unless we've missed it there's not a single deliberate mark anywhere on it. There's nothing on the wood that I can see, and the metalwork is simply functional, not ornamental, and there's no sign of anything that could be construed as a clue or message. But there is one thing about this chest that did strike me as being unusual. And it was this."

He reached inside the box and took out the piece of ancient wood that had concealed the compartment at the bottom of the chest. It was blackened with age, but as he turned it in his hand, Robin could see that one side of it had been painted a dark brown color.

"You told me that it's been painted," she said. "So what? We thought that might have been done just to protect the piece of vellum."

"That's what I thought when I saw it," Mallory replied,

"until I realized that it didn't make sense. As I said before, if it was genuinely intended to provide protection, then why wasn't the same paint used on the rest of the hidden compartment? If you look in the chest you'll see that all the other wood is unmarked and in its natural state. And I don't know all that much about parchment or vellum, but I would assume that maintaining the ambient temperature and relative humidity of the place where it was stored would be far more important than painting the inside of the box they put it in. And one thing I do know about caves and caverns is that both the temperature and the humidity are usually stable."

"You're right about that. Vellum needs to be stored at a reasonably constant temperature and humidity. If the humidity is too low, it will get brittle and fragile, and if it's too high then it may well develop mold or fungus. But painting one part of the storage compartment would have no effect at all on either factor. So the obvious question is, why did they do it?"

Mallory turned over the piece of wood in his hands, and then ran his fingernail along the edge of the painted area. Then he looked up at Robin and smiled.

"I was wrong about the paint," he said, "because this isn't paint at all."

"Then what is it?"

"I think it's a kind of wax, and to me that makes far more sense. Have you ever heard of a technique called steganography?"

16

"Sit down, Toscanelli," Vitale instructed as his subordinate entered his office. "Then listen to this."

Moments later, the sound of Robin Jessop and David Mallory talking together filled the room. The moment Toscanelli recognized their voices, his face clouded with anger and he visibly tensed, wondering what was coming next.

"I want to—" he began.

Vitale stopped the playback and glared across the desk at him.

"You've had more contact with these two than anyone else in the organization. I know all you want to do is kill them, but for the moment just sit there, shut up, and pay attention to their conversation. I want your opinion about something."

Toscanelli relaxed slightly, and as the playback of the recording resumed he gave it his full attention.

Vitale played it all the way through to the end, the volume level of Mallory's voice increasing markedly in the last few seconds before the recording abruptly ended.

"The tertiary who is coordinating the surveillance of the English couple sent that a few minutes ago. What do you think about it?"

Toscanelli wasn't quite sure what Vitale was driving at.

"Tomar is an obvious possibility," he ventured. "It's well established that the order of heretics did seek shelter in Portugal."

The exasperation in Vitale's voice was unmistakable.

"I know that. We all know that. I didn't ask you here for your opinion on the established and confirmed history of the Knights Templar. What I want is your opinion of the conversation between Mallory and Jessop. Do you think that it was genuine, or was it in some way scripted and intended to throw us off the scent? Listen to the important section one more time."

Vitale used the controls on his computer to rewind the playback, cued it, and then started it again. Both men listened intently as the sounds of the English voices filled the room once more.

"So, what do you think?" Vitale asked.

"I really don't know."

"Now, why does that not surprise me? Do you think it's possible that Mallory somehow or other found out the apartment was bugged and then he and Jessop performed that little scene so that we would send a team racing off to Tomar to start looking for the Templar treasure? Or was that a genuine conversation that accidentally ended up with Mallory disabling the bug? Because the bug has been off-line since he apparently pulled the mains adapter out of the socket. According to the tertiary, the surveillance operative tried to remotely reactivate the device a few minutes after that recording ended, but was unable to do so. He has been told to keep checking it, and if it comes back online we will be informed immediately. So let me ask you again. Do you think that was a genuine conversation or a setup?"

Toscanelli spread his hands in a gesture that clearly conveyed both his frustration and indecision. But before he could reply, there was a brisk double tap on the door, and moments later another member of the organization— short and stocky with black hair and a tanned complexion dominated by a nose that appeared to be badly broken and equally badly reset—walked into the office, carrying a laptop.

Vitale gestured to the other chair in front of his desk, and the man sat down, lifting the lid of his laptop as he did so and glancing at the display that sprang to life on the screen.

"So, Alessandro, what is your opinion, as Toscanelli here seems to have no idea at all?"

"It will be better and easier if I can show you."

The new arrival stood up and placed the laptop on the end of Vitale's desk, angling the screen so that it could be easily seen.

"You can look at this as well, Toscanelli," Vitale instructed. "Get up and come round to this side of the desk."

"As you instructed when you sent me the recording,"

Alessandro said, "I've analyzed it using two different specialist software packages, both intended to be used to assess the results of polygraphs. Both gave broadly the same result, but it is perhaps easier to see on this one."

The screen of the laptop showed a horizontal voiceprint-analysis display, and below that three further horizontal bands labeled—in English—"Stress," "Hesitation," and "Excitement" and at the bottom of the display a smaller box labeled "Analysis."

"This is an audio-spectrum analyzer that uses a technique known as Layered Voice Analysis and samples over one hundred different parameters present in speech. It displays the three most important types of analysis as percentages in these three bands and then produces a single result, which is displayed in the box at the bottom of the screen. Basically the analysis program is designed to detect deception of any sort, and the result will be color-coded, green meaning no deception, amber possible deception, and red definite deception."

He pressed one of the laptop keys and the display sprang to life, the sounds of the voices coming out of the speakers while the constantly moving audio spectrograph visually showed the sounds as a series of peaks and troughs. At the same time, the readings in the three horizontal bars flickered from left to right and back again as the software attempted to analyze the different parameters.

"This is the part of the conversation where the Englishman is talking about Tomar and its importance to the Knights Templar. Note that the analysis box is displaying a solid green color, which means that no deception has been detected. This, of course, is exactly what we would expect, because what he is saying is established fact. I used this part of the conversation to provide a baseline for the analysis, a section where I could be sure he was telling the truth.

"A polygraph examiner," Alessandro explained, "will begin a session by asking the subject a number of simple questions where there is no doubt about the answers to establish the range of responses. Things like the subject's name, birthday, and job, which will all produce truthful responses, and then he or she will be told to tell lies in reply to a number of other questions. I didn't have that luxury, obviously, so this was the best I could do."

He stopped the playback and cued another section of the recording.

"When Mallory deduces that the carving he is describing is most probably a reference to Tomar, I would expect the level of excitement in his voice to increase, which it does, but notice that the level of stress has also risen, which indicates possible deception."

Alessandro played that part of the recording and Vitale and Toscanelli watched as the analysis box on-screen flickered and then turned amber.

"But this is the most significant section," Alessandro said, cuing another part of the recording. "This is right at the start of the conversation, where Mallory tells the woman that he has found a carving inside the wooden chest. You will see that the levels of stress and hesitation in his voice have both increased, and look at the analysis box."

He played back the relevant part of the audio file, and immediately after Mallory described the carving of the map, the analysis box turned solid red and stayed that way for the next few seconds, until Alessandro stopped the playback.

"That shows definite deception," he said.

"So, your conclusion is?" Vitale asked.

"It's only a fairly short conversation, but to me the results are clear. Mallory probably did find something inside that chest, but whatever it was, it was not a carved map, and it almost certainly had nothing whatsoever to do with Tomar. In my opinion, this was a partially scripted conversation deliberately intended to throw us off the scent, and if that is correct, then the other conclusion is obvious."

Vitale nodded.

"Exactly. Mallory must have known about the bug," he said. "Thank you, Alessandro. We'll take it from here."

Vitale waited until the technician had left the room before he continued.

"Right, the first thing we'll do is continue trying to decrypt the text Mallory and Jessop helpfully transcribed from the vellum, but we obviously do not have the clue that Mallory referred to in his previous conversation."

"Are you sure that wasn't just another piece of misdirection?"

"Yes. Alessandro checked that recording as well, and it showed no deception. We have no idea what Mallory found, but it is clear that he found something, and logically that something has to be related to the vellum. Presumably a way of decrypting the text, or at least some kind of hint that would allow him to start doing so."

"So, what do you want me to do?" Toscanelli asked.

"At this precise moment, nothing," Vitale said, "but you will be on a plane to London today, or tomorrow at the latest. The delay is because I don't know how long it will take to get a diplomatic passport issued to you in a new name. Obviously you can't use the name on your previous passport, because that will certainly be on the British government's watch list."

"We used a private jet before."

"I know. I authorized it. But because of the shambles that that mission turned into, I'm not prepared to do that again. You'll have a team of six men under you, but to keep a low profile two of them will fly out of Milan and two more out of Naples. Those four are already on the way to those two airports. You and the final pair will fly from Rome. All of you will have diplomatic passports, and each of you will have a loaded automatic pistol and two spare magazines, both fully loaded, in your carry-on bags. I do not expect these weapons to be used except as a last resort."

Toscanelli looked markedly more cheerful at the prospect of getting up close and personal with Mallory and Jessop again. "And what are your orders?" he asked.

"I would have thought that was quite obvious," Vitale said. "The two audio recordings obtained for us by the tertiary clearly show that the English couple has discovered something. They also show that Mallory was aware that he was under surveillance. I have no doubt that he and Jessop will move somewhere out of the town of Dartmouth very soon to start following whatever clue they have uncovered. We cannot afford to lose them. So you and your team are to get to Dartmouth as quickly as possible, get inside Jessop's apartment, and recover whatever it is that Mallory has found, using whatever force you think is necessary."

"And Mallory and Jessop themselves?" Toscanelli asked. "What about them?"

"As I believe the English sometimes say," Vitale replied, "they are surplus to requirements once you have recovered the object or clue that they have found. So you can dispose of them—permanently—however you wish. The only criterion is that both you and whatever method or weapon you decide to use must under no circumstances be traceable back to us.

"Apart from that," he added with a bleak smile, "you are free to enjoy yourself for as long as you like with either or both of them. Just remember that this time we must not fail. And they both must die."

17

Dartmouth, Devon

"Steganography today is amazingly complex. The technique involves concealing a piece of classified information within something else that is clearly not in any way sensitive and normally appears to be quite innocent. One typical method is to take a classified document and reduce it enormously in size until it can be fitted within a single pixel in a photograph, an image that can then be sent or displayed quite openly. That's just a development of a slightly older technique, pretty much Cold War stuff, that allowed a document to be concealed within a full stop at the end of a sentence. That was known as a microdot."

"Yes," Robin said, somewhat impatiently, "and I do know a bit about steganography. But whatever the Templars did, it was clearly nothing like that."

"No," Mallory agreed, "but the principle—the idea of basically hiding something in plain sight—goes way back into antiquity. Probably the most famous example involved a slave who was used to carry a crucial message from one place to another. He couldn't be given a written message, because there was too much danger of him being intercepted, and the information was too important for him to try to memorize it. So his master ordered his head shaved, had the message tattooed on his scalp, and then sent the slave off to his destination once his hair had grown again. When he got there, he told the person he had been instructed to contact to shave his head so the message could be read. That's pretty much classic steganography, the secret—the message—hidden in plain sight on the innocent carrier, the slave."

"So, what steganographic technique do you think was used here? I presume it's something to do with the paint—or the wax, I should say—on that piece of wood?"

"That's what I'm hoping. Like you, I assumed that brown stain was paint until I ran my fingernail over it. Paint would have provided a hard and solid surface, but that was soft and my nail just dug into it. As soon as I did that, I remembered another ancient steganography technique."

"And now I know where you're going with that," Robin said, interrupting him.

"You do?"

"Yes. Stop me when I go wrong. In the days before paper—or even papyrus—and ink, it was common for temporary messages, stuff that was important but only in the short term, to be written on wax tablets. They were flat pieces of wood with a shallow depression cut out and filled with wax. A stylus was used to write down the information, and when they'd finished, when the message was no longer important or they'd done whatever they were supposed to do, they could simply wipe a flat blade across the wax to erase the old message. The steganography bit was when an important message needed to be sent, and somebody realized they could use a wax tablet to do it, not on the wax but under it. They carved the message into the wood in the depression, then filled it with wax and wrote something innocuous on it that would arouse nobody's suspicion. When the courier reached the person he was supposed to give the message to, he simply melted the wax off the tablet, allowing the concealed message to be read."

Robin paused for breath and pointed at the length of wood that Mallory was still holding.

"So, is that what you think you've got there?" she asked. "Not a message hidden under another message written on wax, but just something carved into the wood and then hidden by a layer of wax?"

"Spot-on," Mallory said. "Let's see if I'm right."

The ancient wood had darkened with age and felt immensely strong and solid, but even so they proceeded with caution. Mallory tried using a round-ended kitchen knife to lift off the layer of wax but quickly decided that this was not the best way to do it, because the blade could scratch the wood, and perhaps even damage whatever was concealed beneath the wax, possibly making the message indecipherable.

"I can't think of anything that dissolves wax," he said after a few minutes, "but if we can heat it, that will probably work. I don't suppose you've got one of those blowtorch

jobs in your kitchen cupboards, the ones chefs use to cara-
melize their creations?"

Robin shook her head.

"I'm certainly not a chef, and not even much of a cook,
and I definitely don't own anything like that. But I have
got something that would be even better."

"What's that?" Mallory asked.

"What every girl has in her bedroom or bathroom,
dumbo. A hair dryer, obviously. Concentrated heat, focused on one spot, with no danger of a naked flame damaging the wood or even setting fire to it."

"Excellent. I should have thought of that," Mallory
admitted.

A couple minutes later, with the top of Robin's desk
cleared and covered in sheets of newspaper, Mallory held
the piece of wood steady while she moved the nozzle of
the hair dryer over one small area of the wax, heating it
gently. A faintly sweet and not-unpleasant odor filled the
room as the wax started to warm up. They watched as the
surface changed color, the dark brown, almost black, of
the solid wax turning to a reddish brown shade as it
heated up and began to melt.

"That seems to be doing it," Mallory said as the first
drops of wax ran down the wood, Robin chasing them
with the nozzle of the hair dryer to reveal wood of a much
lighter color underneath.

It wasn't a quick process, because the moment Robin
moved the hair dryer, the wax that was no longer directly
receiving the heat from the device began to harden. After
a few trial runs, they decided that the best way to do it

was for Mallory to hold the wood horizontal while Robin eased the dryer's nozzle vertically downward, moving slowly over the wax. That melted the top layer reasonably quickly, and by repeating the operation she ended up clearing a vertical strip about an inch wide every four or five minutes. Even so, it took well over half an hour before the vast majority of the wax was cleared from the ancient wooden board. But still, on the matrix of carved letters that slowly emerged as the wax was removed, a few final traces remained, requiring further gentle heating before every tiny patch of wax was melted off and the individual characters could be clearly seen.

Then Robin unplugged the hair dryer and put it on the floor to cool, and they both looked carefully at what had been hidden beneath the layer of ancient wax.

"That's interesting," Mallory said, "but I'm not entirely sure that it's much help."

"Well, it must be. If it doesn't provide some kind of a key to decode the encrypted text, what was the point of carving it into the wood and then hiding it in the chest?" Robin sounded quite indignant. "That doesn't make any sense at all."

What they were looking at was a virtual block of letters, thirteen characters wide and six deep. The list began with *S, E, U* at the left-hand side of the top line and ended with *N, I, S* on the right of the bottom line. No sequence of letters seemed to form a word, apart from a handful that coincidentally formed short English words such as *FOE* and *MET* and *RAN*, and the one thing they were both certain about was that if any words were included in the sequence, they would be in Latin. And there appeared to be no indication as to how these letters could help decode the information written on the sheet of vellum.

But Robin had to be right. That really didn't make sense, not least because the wood had actually formed one part of the hiding place for the vellum, and it was simply inconceivable that what they had just found and the encrypted text weren't linked in some way. They would just have to work out what that way was.

"You're right," Mallory said, "so let's look at what we've got. I'll do a quick analysis of the letters and see if that helps."

He took a pencil and a fresh piece of paper and copied the block of letters onto it. Then he counted all the occurrences of each letter—a basic frequency analysis—and showed Robin the result.

"There are twenty different letters in that block of text, and the commonest is *E*, which occurs nine times. And that is right in accordance with that frequency table I downloaded from the Internet, and the one you've been using as well. The letter most frequently found in Latin is *E*. Then it all starts going a bit odd, because the next commonest letters are *R* and *A*, both appearing eight times, and they're followed by *O*, with seven. All the other letters in the list occur five times or less."

"Interesting, I suppose," Robin said. "Of course, that's a really small sample, and the one thing it obviously isn't is plaintext, so frequency analysis is most unlikely to work anyway. Though it might be indicative that the commonest letter turned out to be *E*."

"I wonder if the layout is in some way important. There are thirteen columns of letters, and the purging of the Templar order began on the thirteenth of October 1307."

"I think that's a bit of a stretch," Robin said dismissively. "Let me have a look at that."

She took the paper Mallory had been working on and studied it for a few moments. Then she passed it back to him and drew an oval ring around the last nine letters.

"Two things," she said. "First, that is a plaintext Latin word, but spelled backward. *SINOMOLOS* is *SOLOMONIS* backward, and that translates as 'of Solomon.' Of course, that could just be a coincidence, like these apparent short English words that we saw in the block of letters when we first looked at it, but as it's nine letters long that's a lot less likely. Second, I know about the number thirteen and the Templars, but I think there's a more practical reason for the layout of these letters. Thirteen is half of twenty-six, and there are twenty-six letters in the alphabet, so I think that what we're looking at is a series of code words that we can use to decipher the encrypted text. It's just a really rather complicated Atbash cipher. What we need to do is write out the alphabet as usual and then copy these letters underneath it, in three lines of twenty-six letters each rather than six lines of thirteen letters. Why don't you try it?"

"*SOLOMONIS*," Mallory repeated, looking at the word Robin had found. "That's a really obvious link to the Templars, because when they were based in Jerusalem they were given quarters in what is now the Al-Aqsa Mosque. And that building had been erected on what everyone then believed—and in fact many still do believe— to be the site of the ancient Temple of Solomon, the *Templum Solomonis* in Latin. And that was not only their physical base in Jerusalem but also the building that gave its name to the order: officially the *Pauperes commilitones Christi Templique Salomonici*, or the Poor Fellow-Soldiers of Christ and of the Temple of Solomon. The order's full proper name also included the Latin word *Hierosolymi-tanis* at the end, which translates as 'of Jerusalem,' but that's normally ignored. And I've just noticed that to the left of the word *SINOMOLOS* or *SOLOMONIS* is *PMET*. Those are the first four letters of the word *Templum*, but spelled backward."

He looked at Robin and smiled.

"I think you may have cracked this," he said.

18

Heathrow Airport, London

The orders Vitale had issued had been clear and simple. When the first two of his men arrived at London's Heathrow Airport after the flight from Milan had landed, they walked through customs and immigration with barely even a pause, thanks to their diplomatic passports, and went immediately, and separately, to two of the car hire desks in the terminal. Each man hired a fast and expensive sedan, one a BMW and the other an Audi, and then they bought a drink each and sat together at a table in one of the cafés to wait for the arrival of the next scheduled flight from Naples.

A few minutes after that aircraft touched down, the man who had hired the BMW shook hands with his colleague and then went down to the arrivals hall to wait. Just like the other two, the pair of Dominicans on that flight cleared the formalities very rapidly and were the first passengers from it to emerge into the hall, each with only a carry-on bag. The two new arrivals were met by their colleague, paused only to buy takeaway coffees in Styrofoam mugs, and then all three of them made their way to the car park and the vehicle they had hired.

Fifteen minutes later, they were heading west away from Heathrow in the BMW 5 Series toward the M25 orbital motorway. That would take them south to the M3, the road they would use to reach the West Country. The driver was following the map display on the satnav and the verbal instructions delivered—in Italian, thanks to the front-seat passenger spending a few minutes fiddling about with the settings on the device as they found their way out of the airport—by the young woman who apparently lived inside it.

While they headed toward their destination, the two passengers removed shoulder holsters from their carry-on bags and put them on under their jackets, took out their pistols, loaded them, and fitted the weapons in the holsters. The men also had suppressors for their Berettas, but those were too big to fit on the pistol whilst it was in the holster, so they put them in their pockets. There would be plenty of time to attach them to the weapons when they reached their destination.

Back at Heathrow, sitting in the café in the terminal building, the other Dominican enforcer placed his carry-on bag on the table, where he could keep an eye on it, and walked over to the counter to order a meal and another drink. He was waiting for a call or message from Rome to tell him when Marco Toscanelli and the other two men would be boarding their aircraft to London Heathrow at Leonardo da Vinci–Fiumicino Airport, but so far he'd heard nothing.

It looked as if it could be a very long day.

19

Dartmouth, Devon

Mallory took a clean sheet of paper and quickly wrote out the full twenty-six-letter alphabet in a horizontal line across the top, putting in horizontal and vertical grid lines to keep each letter separate. Then he copied out the thirteen letters of the first line of the text block underneath it, ending at the letter *M*, and then added the thirteen letters from the second line, placing them below the letters from *N* to *Z*. He repeated the process with the remaining four lines, to produce an alphabet with a vertical line of three letters underneath each plaintext letter.

A	B	C	D	E	F	G	H	I	J	K	L	M	N	O	P	Q	R	S	T	U	V	W	X	Y	Z
S	E	U	G	U	H	Y	E	R	F	D	O	G	D	U	A	B	M	A	H	C	R	A	Y	E	R
F	F	O	E	G	L	A	S	S	O	R	E	N	Y	A	P	E	R	D	N	A	R	E	M	A	D
N	O	G	D	R	A	N	R	E	B	M	U	L	P	M	E	T	S	I	N	O	M	O	L	O	S

"That's good," Robin said, looking over his shoulder, "and it definitely works, because of what you spotted. Just to the left of the reversed *SOLOMONIS* is *MULPMET*, which is obviously *TEMPLUM* spelled backward."

"I'll do the same thing with the rest of it," Mallory said. "See if anything else makes sense if I reverse the order of the letters."

It didn't take long, and the result was impressive, at least to Mallory.

"These are all names written backward," he said triumphantly, "and all the names are directly related to the Templars. The founders of the order were Hugues de Payens and another eight French noblemen. Knights, in fact. Two of them were brothers and all nine were related to one another either by blood or by marriage. The first six letters of this block of text spell *HUGUES* backward. The other founding members were Godfrey de Saint-Omer, Archambaud de Saint Agnan, Geoffrey Bison, a knight called Rossal, Payne de Monteverdi, André de Montbard, and another knight, named Gondamer. And the other names written backward in this piece of text are *GODFREY, ARCHAMBAUD, GEOFFREY, ROSSAL, PAYNE, ANDRE*, and *GONDAMER*."

Mallory paused and tapped the piece of paper with his finger.

"Nobody knows the identity of the ninth founding knight," he continued, "or at least, they didn't until now. Some writers have pushed the idea that it might have been Count Hugh of Champagne, though the historical record shows that he didn't join the order until his third visit to the Holy Land, in 1125, six years after it was formed. But this last word spelled backward is *BERNARD*, so either that was the name of the ninth knight or, just possibly, it's a reference to Bernard of Clairvaux, who was the nephew of André de Montbard and the most important clergyman of the time to the Templars, because he was orchestrating a campaign to allow for the acceptance of the order by the Catholic Church."

"That seems pretty conclusive," Robin agreed, "and I think it's interesting that the alphabet the writer of this was using contained all twenty-six letters, rather than the twenty-three that were in use until the Middle Ages. Nobody actually knows when the number of letters in the alphabet was fixed, but certainly it had happened by the end of the fifteenth century. Later on, it might be worth getting a piece of the vellum radiocarbon-dated, because that would help clarify when the change took place."

Mallory was still studying the grid of letters that they had uncovered and he had written out. After a few seconds, he tossed the paper back onto the desk and looked at Robin.

"Believe it or not," he said, "I'm not sure how this helps us. We could probably have deduced most of this just by applying frequency analysis to the encrypted text, and we still have the problem of working out which plaintext letter is represented by which letter or letters in the ciphertext. Take the plaintext *E*, for example. According to this table, that could be represented by the letters *U*, *G*, or *R*. The problem is that those three letters also represent a lot of other plaintext letters because of all the duplications in the code words, in the proper names, that they chose. So as well as decoding as *E*, the ciphertext letter *U* can mean *C*, *L*, or *O*. *G* can also mean *C*, *D*, or *M*, and *R* is potentially the most confusing, because that can stand for a total of seven different letters. As well as *E*, it can mean *H*, *I*, *K*, *R* itself, *V*, or *Z*. We can still do this, but it's going to take us a hell of a long time."

He took another piece of paper and wrote out the word *MESSAGE*.

"Let me show you what I mean. If I encrypt that using this ciphertext, and just taking the first option from the code words each time, I end up with *GUAASYU*. But because of all the duplicates in the ciphertext, when I try to decode it, that produces *C*, *D*, *E*, and *M* for the letter *G*, and *C*, *E*, *L*, and *O* for the *U*. Assuming that we're looking for an English word, we might guess that it begins with *CL*, like *CLOUD*, or maybe *EL*, like *ELF* or *ELEPHANT*. Alternatively we could deduce that the second letter is a vowel, the *E* or the *O*, so the decode could be *CE*, *DE*, *ME*, *CO*, *DO*, or *MO*, giving us eight different possibilities in just those two letters. Factoring in the additional complications, such as the fact that the encryptor had at least two and usually three different ciphertext choices for each letter of every word, and that the plaintext was written in archaic Latin, not English, I think it could easily take months to make any kind of sense of this."

"So, what you're saying is that we've achieved nothing," Robin said.

"Not exactly. We have achieved something, just not very much, and certainly not as much as I'd hoped. I can't help feeling that we're missing something fairly obvious."

"Like what?"

"If I knew that," Mallory replied, "we wouldn't be missing it."

For two or three minutes, neither of them spoke, Mallory again examining the grid of letters carved into the ancient wooden plank, while Robin studied the alphabet and code words he had transcribed on the paper, and the results of the frequency analysis that the computer program had produced.

"I don't know if this is significant," she began hesitantly, "but there is a kind of mismatch between the frequency analysis and this grid of code words."

"There is? What?"

"It's in the number of letters. The frequency-analysis program produced results for only eighteen letters, but there's a total of twenty different letters in this grid."

Mallory looked at the sheets of paper she was studying and nodded agreement.

"You're right," he said, "but that really doesn't make sense. I mean, it would be reasonable to assume that there would be very few occurrences of the letter Z in the plaintext Latin document, but the ciphertext equivalents are D, R, and S, and they're duplicated several times." He thought for a moment, then nodded again. "There's only one way that that can work. Whoever did the encryption must only have used eighteen of the letters in the code words, not the full twenty, but I have no idea how or why they did that."

"I agree with you about the 'how,' but the 'why' seems

fairly obvious. As you've just shown, there are so many duplicates that deciphering any word is going to be very difficult. Whoever encrypted this must have done it with the intention that a Templar or some member of the order could later decipher it, so they must have done something to simplify the encryption, though right now we can't see what it was."

Together, they looked carefully at the wooden plank, but apart from the grid of letters it was devoid of any kind of marking. Then Robin retrieved the vellum from her safe and put that on the desk. Mallory reached out to unfold it so that they could look at the original text, but Robin stopped him with a gesture.

"Hang on a minute," she said. "What's that symbol on the front of it? It looks like a checkerboard design."

Mallory looked at the faint and faded image she was indicating and shook his head.

"I think it's just a form of decoration," he said. "I've seen it before in Templar buildings, and it's a repeating pattern of black and white squares. The most likely explanation is that it's a representation of the beauséant, the Templar *vexillum belli*, their battle flag, which in its simplest form was just a black square above a white square."

"You could be right, but don't you notice anything else about that pattern?"

"It's like a small checkerboard, that's all."

"It is," Robin agreed, "but can you see that it's got three horizontal lines containing the black and white squares, but also a top line that has no black squares at all?"

"It's faint, but I can see that, yes. So what?"

"Just a wild idea, but suppose that's a kind of aide-mémoire to show which letters should be used in the ciphertext. Imagine that you write the alphabet along the top line, and then only use those letters that correspond to the black squares. Or just the white squares. I don't know."

"I see what you mean," Mallory said. "So, the letter *A* would be encoded by *S* or *N*, *B* only by *F*, and so on. Let's try that."

He drew another alphabet, and this time he only put the checkerboard pattern of letters into the squares below it.

A	B	C	D	E	F	G	H	I	J	K	L	M	N	O	P	Q	R	S	T	U	V	W	X	Y	Z
S		U		U		Y		R		D		G		U		B		A		C		A		E	
	F		E		L		S		O		E		Y		P		R		N		R		M		D
N		G		R		N		E		M		L		M		T		I		O		O		O	

Then he counted the letters in the grid—thirty-nine—and eliminated all of the duplicates from the total.

"I think you're definitely onto something," he said. "That gives us eighteen unique letters, the same number that the frequency-analysis program came up with. And I've just tried it the other way round, as it were, only using the letters that corresponded to the white squares on the checkerboard. But that only gives us a total of sixteen, so you were right the first time. Brilliant stuff."

"Let's hope it works," Robin said.

It wasn't easy, because of the number of duplicate letters that were still present, even in the reduced number of code words they were using, but eventually the text they had transcribed from the vellum began to yield its secrets. Robin produced a final copy of the Latin text and then spent another hour translating it into fairly readable English.

"So, what have we got?" Mallory asked when she finally put down her pencil and eraser and scanned what she'd written.

"This isn't exactly what I'd been expecting," Robin replied. "It starts off with a kind of summary or justification of the events before and after October 1307."

And at that moment, her phone started to ring.

20

Marco Toscanelli, uncomfortably conscious of the weight of the Beretta pistol in his carry-on bag, suffered a brief moment of panic as he approached the immigration official at Heathrow. But after the briefest of glances at the document that he had proffered, the uniformed man, who appeared to be an Indian, simply nodded and waved him on his way.

Getting the diplomatic passport, which now bore a bad photograph of his unshaven face and the name Marco—because sticking to the same first name was always a good idea—Mancini, the alias that Vitale had given him, had been something of a rush.

The first version that the officials at the Sovereign Military Order of Malta, the SMOM, had provided had been rejected by Vitale because its validity date had been that very day, and he was concerned that questions might be asked of an alleged diplomat traveling internationally with a brand-new passport. Instead, he had returned it to the Palazzo Malta, the SMOM's Rome headquarters, with a request that they backdate it at least a year and include a scattering of immigration stamps within its pages.

All that had taken time, but the SMOM had never had any trouble in taking orders from, or fulfilling tasks for, the Dominicans, with whom they were inextricably linked. The *Supremus Ordo Militaris Hospitalis Sancti Ioannis Hierosolymitani Rhodius et Melitensis*, the Sovereign Military Hospitaller Order of Saint John of Jerusalem of Rhodes and of Malta, commonly known as the Sovereign Military Order of Malta or just the Order of Malta, is the oldest surviving chivalric order in the world, having been founded in Jerusalem in about 1099.

It had then been known as the Knights Hospitaller, and had been chosen as the official beneficiary order to receive all of the confiscated assets of the Knights Templar, a transfer that had been widely expected to be of immense value, and that was to have been supervised by the Dominicans, the militant order that had functioned since the Middle Ages as the pope's personal torturers and enforcers. The transfer had indeed taken place, but because the Templars had clearly anticipated the actions orchestrated by King Philip the Fair of France, virtually all of the movable assets of the Templars had been spirited away before the mass arrests in 1307 that had signaled the end of the order.

But the Dominicans had always taken their instructions seriously, and for the previous seven hundred years they had been actively trying to track down and recover every Templar asset they could lay their hands on. They hadn't achieved very much, but what they had found in the early years had been passed on to the Hospitallers, and in more recent times to the renamed Sovereign Military Order of Malta.

And that was why the two very different organizations enjoyed such a close and mutually beneficial relationship. The issue of diplomatic passports to members of the Dominican order involved in sensitive operations was just one of the many services that the SMOM very willingly provided.

The two men who had been traveling with Toscanelli also walked through passport control and immigration without any problems, and within minutes they had all linked up with their colleague who had flown there from Milan, and who had already hired the vehicle they would be using.

Less than twenty minutes after the aircraft from Rome had landed, the four-man team was in the Audi, checking and loading their weapons and heading toward the town of Dartmouth in Devon.

21

Dartmouth, Devon

"It's a private number," Robin said, swiping her finger across the screen of the mobile to answer the call. "Hullo?"

"Hi, Robin," a male voice replied. "Actually, I was hoping to talk to David as well. Is he there?"

"Yes. Who is this?"

The voice was faintly familiar to her, but she didn't recognize the caller. "It's John."

That was definitive information, but not helpful, because she still didn't know who he was. "John who?"

"Just John."

Then she remembered, and the expression on her face changed. She glanced at Mallory and put the phone on speaker.

"I think it's that spy bloke who bugged us before," she said. "The one who called himself John because he was too ashamed to tell us his real name."

"Well remembered," the voice from the speaker replied. "And it's less about shame than security. A real name isn't that much to go on, but it would be an obvious chink in my armor, so I'm quite happy to stick with something nicely anonymous. Something like 'John,' in fact."

"Hi, John," Mallory said.

"Hang on a minute," Robin interjected. "How did you get this number? I bought a new phone and had a new mobile number issued after that last fiasco."

"Ways and means, my dear, ways and means," Gary Marsh responded. "Nothing very clever about it. You left your mobile phone bill on the desk. It was there in plain sight when I popped in the other evening to see what the two of you were up to."

"I'm glad you find it funny," Robin snapped. "I'd have thought that spying on people was actually a bit sick."

"Actually, I don't find it funny at all. It's just a job, and it pays pretty well, but you are kind of right. There are times when I wish I did something else for a living. This is one of them."

"Go on," Mallory said. "By the way, thanks for leaving those clues to show you'd been in the apartment, that little patch of talcum powder and the briefcase turned around the wrong way."

"I thought you might notice those, and I'm glad you did," Marsh said. "I know we've never met, but I quite like you two and I have the definite feeling that you've got yourselves involved in something much bigger than you think, and that's why I'm being somewhat economical with the truth as far as my employer is concerned, whenever I can. And that's also why I've been giving you the occasional hint. And well-done finding the mains-powered bug, though I'm not sure that the performance the two of you gave before you unplugged it was entirely convincing."

"I suppose you recorded that and sent it to whoever is paying your fee," Mallory suggested. "And would that be an Italian gentleman?"

"I don't actually know. The man I'm dealing with is certainly English—an English policeman, in fact—but I'm equally certain that he's taking his orders from somebody else. And that, really, is why I'm talking to you now, because I don't like the way this seems to be panning out."

Mallory was all attention.

"What do you mean by that, exactly?"

"I mean the last set of instructions I was given about you two bothers me. Listen, usually I just do routine, non-invasive surveillance. I'm given details of the target and an overview of my tasking, which is usually what the man who's paying my bill is expecting the target to do. I don't do matrimonial, because I think that's a bit sleazy—"

"That's something we agree on," Robin interrupted, "and I'm pleased you have some standards and scruples."

"Quite," Gary Marsh said. "I've done a bit of industrial counterespionage, where a company is afraid that its trade secrets or details of its marketing processes or whatever is being leaked to a rival, usually by one of the company's own employees. But as I said, most of the time I end up doing this kind of thing: nonspecific short-term surveillance. Right from the start, with you two, a few things have bothered me."

"So what are you, then?" Robin asked waspishly. "A spook with a conscience? Is that it?"

"If you want to put it that way, then I suppose I am, yes."

"Carry on, John," Mallory said placatingly, holding up a calming hand toward Robin. "What was it that bothered you?"

"First of all, it was the money. The fee I was offered was far too much, given the obvious simplicity of the job. I won't tell you what I was paid per day, but it was quite a bit more than I normally charge per week. Then the tasking didn't really make sense, either. Initially all I was supposed to do was follow you, Robin, and keep my employer informed about your movements. Usually, I'm told to monitor and ideally record conversations and identify anyone the target has any meaningful contact with, but in your case he only seemed interested in knowing where you were at all times. But that changed very recently, when I was told to get inside your apartment. My employer, or perhaps more likely the principal, the man who's been pulling his strings, suddenly became very interested in deliveries to your shop. He wanted to know the size of any packages that you received, and if there was any indication that you were taking those deliveries anywhere else. To a vault in your bank in Dartmouth, for example."

"John" paused briefly, and Mallory responded.

"I suppose you were dogging our footsteps, then, weren't you?"

"All part of the job, yes. And of course I had to tell my employer what I had seen, and that seemed to get him very excited. That was when he told me to get inside

Robin's apartment and try to locate a medieval wooden chest. If I found it, I was to photograph it, concentrating on anything that looked like a pattern in the metalwork or a carving in the woodwork. I was also told to photograph or copy any paperwork or documents that could in any way relate to a medieval manuscript. Anything in Latin, for example. He also instructed me to position a bug in the apartment and to record and then upload your conversations to the cloud."

"Let me guess," Mallory said. "After you recorded those two conversations I had with Robin—when I thought I'd spotted something that would let us decode a particular encrypted manuscript, and the second one, where I suggested we should head for Tomar in Portugal—your orders changed again."

"They did. I was told to keep my distance, but at the same time to maintain my surveillance. Specifically, I was told to contact my employer immediately if the two of you left the apartment, either to go somewhere else in the town or if you went further afield by car. He was most insistent that he should know exactly where both of you were at all times. In my opinion, the implication of that was fairly obvious, but the other thing that concerned me was that he also told me not to react to any incidents that involved either or both of you, and very specifically told me that I was under no circumstances to contact the police, no matter what happened. I've been in this business a long time, and to me that's a clear warning that somebody, maybe more than one person, is going to come looking for you. And reading between the lines, I think they probably aren't going to be the kind of people that you would actually want to meet."

"We've met them already," Mallory said flatly, "or some of their colleagues, and you're right about that. Getting involved with these people is potentially extremely bad for our health. So thanks for the warning. Is there anything else?"

"I do have a sense of the timing involved. In his last call, a few minutes ago, my employer let slip that it was particularly important to know your whereabouts from five o'clock this evening, and that's less than an hour from now. So, in my opinion, you need to move pretty soon, and to be long gone from Dartmouth by five, before your unwelcome visitors turn up."

"Thanks," Mallory said again. "I presume you'll be telling your employer the moment we get on the road?"

"Well, that's the thing. One of the advantages of being down here on the coast is that the seafood is usually excellent."

Robin looked at Mallory and shrugged. Neither of them had any idea where this particular conversational thread was heading.

"And?" Robin prompted.

"And I have a sneaking suspicion that the prawns I had for lunch weren't quite as fresh as I had expected."

"Did you have prawns for lunch?" Mallory asked.

"Is that strictly relevant?"

"Probably not."

"Anyway," "John" continued, "I think it's almost certain that sometime within the next five minutes or so those prawns are going to come back to bite me, and I'm going to be confined to a white porcelain throne for quite some time. And the trouble with being a one-man band is that I'm a one-man band. There's nobody I can get to take over my duties if I can't perform. So, unfortunately, when you do decide to leave I don't think I'm going to be in a fit state to see you go, and so I obviously won't be able to tell my employer that you're on the move."

"Thanks, John. That's a big help."

"The other odd thing about these prawns, though, is that I'll probably recover fairly quickly, and so I should be back in position when whoever is being sent here to find you eventually turns up. If Robin can overcome her natural revulsion to actually speaking to someone like me, I can give you a bell and let you know what the opposition consists of. Numbers of people, brief descriptions, the cars they're driving, all that kind of thing. After all, surveillance is what I do for a living."

"Thank you, John," Robin said. "And I mean that. No bullshit. Thanks very much. We really do appreciate it."

"I'll call you later."

For a couple of seconds both Mallory and Robin stared at the now-silent mobile phone on the desk in front of them.

"Do you think he's on the level?" Robin asked.

"I hope so. But if he isn't, I don't know what he's trying to achieve by warning us. We know that the Dominicans are probably still on our trail, so all he's doing is giving us the specifics of the situation from his perspective, from the point of view of the opposition. And that can only help us."

"So we get back on the road?" Robin asked.

"We get back on the road," Mallory confirmed, "though right now I have no idea where we should be heading, or where this quest is taking us."

"I might be able to help you with that," Robin said.

22

Dartmouth, Devon

The man driving the BMW 5 Series had made much better time than either he or the woman who lived in the satnav had expected. For some reason, most of the roads were virtually empty of traffic, and he'd held the Beamer at well above the limit for most of the way, at least until he reached the narrow and twisting lanes of Devon and had to haul the speed right down. So the estimate of five o'clock that the front-seat passenger had telephoned to Silvio Vitale, which Vitale had in turn relayed to the tertiary, and which he had then passed on to Gary Marsh, turned out to be somewhat pessimistic.

And that meant that when the driver steered the BMW sedan into the street that ran behind Robin's bookshop and stopped in the road right beside the metal spiral staircase that led to her apartment, Mallory and Robin hadn't actually left. Robin was in the bookshop chatting to Betty, the woman who actually ran the place on her behalf, and Mallory had just loaded his computer bag into the trunk in the front of his Porsche Cayman, parked about seventy yards up the road, the closest to the apartment he'd been able to park. The apartment itself was still unlocked, and Robin's overnight bag was sitting on the desk, the top open and waiting for her to add whatever final items she decided she needed.

As Mallory pushed down on the front trunk lid to close it, he looked straight back down the street and immediately noticed the BMW. It wasn't the car that attracted his attention but the sight of the three heavily built men, each with black hair and wearing a black suit, who were climbing out of it. He didn't react for a few seconds, just watched where they were going and what they were doing. But when the leader of the trio reached inside his jacket and extracted what looked to Mallory remarkably like a pistol as he stepped over to the spiral staircase, he knew he had to do something, and quickly.

He had Robin's mobile number on speed dial, and he called it as he dropped into the driving seat of the Porsche. She answered almost immediately.

"We've got company," Mallory said urgently. "If you're still in the shop, leave right now. Turn left and walk toward the river. I'm in the car and I'll pick you up at the end of the street."

"Got it," Robin said.

As he started the engine of the Cayman, Mallory thanked his lucky stars that Robin was not a typical woman. When things got sticky, she didn't hesitate, she didn't ask stupid questions, and she didn't dither. She just acted, and right then, that was more important than anything else.

There was only one problem with the Porsche: when the key was turned in the ignition switch and the engine started, the sound was difficult to ignore. The roar of the 3.4-liter flat-six echoed off the surrounding buildings before settling down to a dull rumble. For a couple of seconds, Mallory took his eyes off the instrument panel to check the rearview mirrors. One of the men who had climbed out of the BMW was standing in the middle of the street, staring toward the Cayman. But there was nothing he could do about that.

Outside the building that housed Robin's small apartment, the leader of the group noticed that one of his men had stopped and was staring down the street.

"What is it?" he demanded in his native Italian.

The third man pointed urgently down the road.

"We were told that the man Mallory owns a Porsche Cayman. I've just seen a car that matches that description pulling out from the side of the street."

The leader hesitated for just a few seconds, considering his options. Then he made his decision.

"Both of you, get back in the car. Follow him and stop him in the town if you can and bring him to me. If you can't, and if it looks as if he's getting away, shoot him or shoot out the tires on the car. Now go."

The two men ran back across the street, climbed into the BMW, and with a brisk squeal of tires drove off in the same direction the Porsche was heading.

Mallory pulled out of the parking space and accelerated briskly along the street, turning right at the end, and then eased the car over to the pavement on the left-hand side and stopped as Robin walked quickly over toward him. Mallory left the engine running but opened the driver's door and climbed out as she approached.

"You drive," he said, walking around to the passenger door and opening it. "One of them spotted the car as I drove away, so they might come after us, and you'll get much more out of this car than I ever will."

The Cayman was Mallory's pride and joy, a treat that he had bought for himself a year or so earlier, but Robin held a competition racing license, and he knew perfectly well that with her at the wheel they could leave the BMW in the dust. He'd seen her in action once before, when she'd been at the wheel of a standard Ford saloon and outdriven a very determined bad guy trying to catch them in that same car, Mallory's Porsche.

"What am I looking for?" Robin asked as she pulled her seat belt tight. "In the rearview mirror, I mean. What are they driving?"

"A silver BMW 5 Series. Probably a hire car, so you shouldn't have any trouble losing it. It might even be a diesel."

"On these roads, that depends on the traffic as much

as anything else." She checked her mirrors briefly, then pulled away. "So, what did you see?"

"Three men wearing black suits who climbed out of the Beamer and headed straight toward the staircase to your apartment. I'm pretty sure that at least one of them was armed, maybe all three."

"So it looks as if John's estimate was a bit out. And we've got another problem as well."

"Don't worry about your bag. We can buy the clothes and stuff you need once we get clear. You've got your handbag and your phone, and that's all that matters."

"I wasn't thinking about my bag," Robin replied, dropping down into second gear to overtake three cars moving very slowly and apparently in convoy in the one-way system along the Quay. "I was going to put that piece of wood from the medieval chest in my safe, if it fitted, or somewhere else where it would be out of sight of prying eyes. But I didn't get around to it, so it's still on the desk in the study. And so is that piece of vellum, because I hadn't put that back in the safe, either."

Mallory nodded.

"I'd forgotten about that," he admitted. "So the bloody Dominicans will now know exactly what we know, so they'll be able to follow the same trail. This is about to turn into a real race."

"And that's not the only race we're in," Robin said crisply. "A silver BMW, two up, is now about half a dozen cars behind us, and there's not much I can do about that until we get clear of the town."

Mallory turned around in his seat and looked behind the Porsche. They'd just swung right onto Mayor's Avenue, and the German sedan was only visible intermittently in the stream of traffic driving through Dartmouth, but he could see enough to confirm Robin's suspicion.

"That's the car I saw," he said after about half a minute. "You will be able to lose them," he added, more of a statement than a question.

"On the open road, no problem. Once we get to Coronation Park I can turn onto College Way, and I'll lose them going up the hill. The real trick is going to be figuring out where we go from there."

Robin's mobile rang, and the Bluetooth system in the Porsche automatically answered it and fed the call through the speakers.

"It's John again," the voice said. "You might know this already, but a silver BMW stopped outside your apartment a few minutes ago. One man went into the building and the other two got back in the car and left in a hurry, so they might well be following you."

"Thanks, John," Mallory said. "We know that, and they're about fifty yards behind us right now."

"Good luck, then. You might need it."

"And thanks for that, as well."

As the call ended, Robin steered the Porsche around the virtually right-angle bend beside Coronation Park, essentially a large roundabout, turning the car away from the waterfront and toward the looming bulk of HMS *Britannia*, the Royal Navy training college that dominated that part of the town. Because they were now heading away from the center of Dartmouth, the traffic began to thin out, which allowed the driver of the BMW to get significantly closer, moving into position only two cars behind.

Robin was boxed in behind a white Transit van that was moving uncharacteristically slowly, White Van Man in Britain usually driving with excessive speed and a total disregard for all other road users.

And then everything changed.

Two round holes suddenly appeared, just a couple of seconds apart, in the left-hand rear door of the Transit van at about head height, paint flaking off around the points of impact.

23

The van driver immediately indicated and began pulling over to the left-hand side of the road. Obviously he had heard or felt the impact of the bullets, and probably assumed that another vehicle had hit him.

"They're shooting at us," Mallory said, unnecessarily.

"Shit hot, Sherlock. I'd never have guessed."

The driver of the car directly behind the Porsche had clearly seen what had happened and for some reason decided to brake, rather than accelerate out of danger. That meant the BMW driver also had to brake, and then swerve around the sudden obstruction, and that upset the passenger's aim. He was firing his silenced automatic pistol through the open side window, and the violent maneuvering of the car meant that his next shot hit the side of the Transit van, but his fourth shot missed completely.

The moment she'd seen the first two shots hit the van,

Robin had been jinking the car left and right, but the van driver's action cleared the way, opening up a space on the right of the vehicle, and Robin instantly took advantage of it, again dropping down into second gear and employing the full power of the Porsche.

The noise of the flat-six engine rose to a roar, and both Mallory and Robin were forced back in their seats by the brutal acceleration. The Cayman screamed up the hill that led out of Dartmouth, the sight of the BMW shrinking almost comically in the rearview mirrors. In seconds, the Porsche was doing over eighty miles an hour, ludicrously fast for that part of the town, but essential to get out of danger.

"The Beamer can't match our acceleration," Robin commented, her voice absolutely calm and relaxed, "but it's still a fast car, and losing it isn't going to be easy. It's already doing maybe sixty miles an hour coming up that hill, so we're drawing away from it but not that quickly."

"At least we're well out of pistol range now," Mallory said, again turning to look behind the accelerating Cayman. "Where are you going to go?"

Robin paused for a moment or two before replying, obviously weighing up her options.

"I don't want to take the obvious route out of Dartmouth, because that's probably where they'd guess we were heading, and the danger in doing that is that we could get held up by traffic or roadworks or something, they could get right up behind us again, and then it would pretty much be game over. I think we should do exactly the same thing as we did last time."

"You mean cross to the other side of the river?"

"Exactly. We can double back into Dartmouth and use the Floating Bridge ferry to get over to the Kingswear side of the estuary. That's the best way to put some distance between them and us."

Just beyond the Church Road junction on the left, the main road bent around to the south. The Porsche was doing well over ninety when Robin straightened it out again, but then she immediately hit the brakes and started slowing down for the Y junction ahead of them.

"The main road goes right," she said, "past Norton and over to Halwell, and if I was planning on getting out of Dartmouth in a hurry, and didn't want to take the ferry, that's the route I would pick."

"You know the area, and I don't," Mallory replied, "but I guess we're not going that way."

"Nope."

At the mini roundabout by the Y junction, she dropped down two gears, flicked the steering wheel to the left, and accelerated hard down Yorke Road, cutting directly in front of a gray-haired lady driving a conspicuously battered white Nissan Micra. The angry bleat of the Nissan's horn followed them distantly as they headed south.

"There are several roads we can take to get back to Dartmouth," Robin said, "but I think this is one of those occasions when time really is of the essence, and we need to get back to the town and get across the river as quickly as possible. I would hate to be waiting in the queue for the Floating Bridge if those two comedians in the Beamer spotted us, then drove up and blasted the hell out of us and this car."

"Amen to that."

Robin continued accelerating for a few seconds, then hit the brakes, hauling the speed right down to make the turn onto Waterpool Road, a narrow, twisting country lane that ran almost due east from their present position and that would get them back into Dartmouth as quickly as possible.

The Porsche slid a few feet sideways as she turned off Yorke Road, but she corrected it effortlessly and continued accelerating, moving the steering wheel left and right as the car reached each bend in the road.

"I'm glad you opted for a Cayman rather than a 911," she said, as she corrected another power slide on a sharpish left-hand bend.

"Why?" Mallory responded, his eyes fixed on the blur of scenery in front of them as hard and rocky pieces of the Devon landscape raced toward the car at ridiculous speed.

"This is midengined, and that means the center of gravity is pretty much in the center of the car. And because of that you can really throw it around."

"I can see that," Mallory said briefly.

"In the dry, a well-driven 911 could lose us, because it has got more power. But the problem with the Cayman's big brother is that it's a triumph of engineering over design, and no matter what the engineers at Stuttgart do, the 911 has a massive and heavy lump of metal hanging right out at the back, behind the rear wheels, and that means it's inherently unstable. In the wet, or on a bad road surface, if you give it the smaller quarter of rather less than half a chance, a 911 will do its best to kill you. Unless you really like living dangerously, and are happy being overtaken by old ladies on bicycles during a rainstorm, the Cayman is a much better choice."

"Right," Mallory muttered, as another bend appeared in front of them, the distance to go before the inevitable impact diminishing with suicidal speed.

And then, almost as a kind of anticlimax, on a gentle right-hand bend, the Porsche reentered the built-up area, and Robin quickly brought the speed down to just over thirty miles an hour, because of the obvious danger of hitting a wandering pedestrian or somebody incautiously stepping off the pavement somewhere. She drove down Crowther's Hill, and after a few more bends and junctions she turned left onto the Embankment, the road that followed the west bank of the river Dart, and which she then followed all the way to Coronation Park. She joined the one-way system, turning into Coombe Road, and then pulled off at the northern end into the waiting area for the Floating Bridge ferry across to Kingswear.

And all the way through the town, both Robin and Mallory had watched everything and everyone, just in case the two men in the BMW had somehow guessed their intentions and had doubled back to lie in wait for them. But they saw nothing to arouse their suspicions.

24

Although Marco Toscanelli wasn't yet in Dartmouth—he was still traveling as quickly as the road and traffic conditions permitted in the hired Audi toward the West Country—he was making his presence, and his displeasure, known to the three Dominicans who were already on the scene. Specifically, he was profoundly irritated that the English couple had managed to slip away from the town, and even more annoyed that a large number of British police officers had now been deployed there because of the unsuccessful attempt to stop them by using their pistols, a very public event that had been witnessed by dozens of passersby and possibly even filmed by some of them using the cameras in their mobile phones.

The only good thing about that incident was that the BMW had followed the Porsche out of Dartmouth, away from the scene. When the front-seat passenger had called

Toscanelli on his mobile, as soon as it was obvious that the Porsche had managed to evade pursuit, he had ordered the driver not to return to the seaside town. Instead, he had told him to drive up to Exeter, dump the BMW in some side street, telephone the hire company and report it stolen, then hire another vehicle and drive back to Dartmouth. Although their diplomatic passports would ensure their freedom if they were stopped by the police, Toscanelli and his men needed to do their work unmolested, and the risk of driving back to the town in the BMW was too great.

But there had been some good news. The third man of the trio that had been the first to arrive had walked into Robin Jessop's apartment, because the door had been left unlocked, and on her desk he had found a piece of obviously ancient vellum bearing a chunk of encrypted text. That had fairly clearly been concealed in the false bottom of the medieval wooden chest that he had also found in the office. And the bonus was that sitting on the desk beside the vellum was the piece of wood that had formed the false bottom of the chest, and on it, in an area that looked newer and fresher than the rest of the timber, and that had presumably been covered by something, was a grid of letters. That, very obviously, was the key that they would need to decipher the text.

When the Dominican had telephoned Toscanelli with this news, the Italian enforcer had been delighted. Although Mallory and Jessop had escaped the net—at least for the moment—he knew that the order now had in its possession all the information necessary to continue with the quest.

As soon as he reached Dartmouth, Toscanelli would photograph everything, check everywhere in Robin Jessop's apartment and not just in the office, then relay the information to Silvio Vitale back in Rome and send him copies of all the images by encrypted e-mail.

The race to follow the third trail of clues that the Templars had left seven centuries earlier was now on. And Toscanelli had no doubt whatsoever about who would be the victor.

25

Devon

The queue for the ferry was fairly short, and just under twenty minutes later the vessel moved away from the jetty and began the short crossing over to the other side of the river.

"It'll be too little, too late, of course," Robin said, fishing in her handbag and taking out her mobile phone, "but I suppose I should tell our wonderful police force that somebody might well be burgling my apartment even as we speak. And if there isn't anything more interesting happening somewhere else, they might send a uniformed constable around sometime this week. Or maybe next week."

"That's very cynical," Mallory replied, "but probably more accurate than you realize. My guess is that the shooting we were involved in will attract quite a large contingent of the Thin Blue Line, and I very much doubt if they'll want to do anything as mundane as investigating a possible break-in. But you should probably do it, and tell Betty to lock up the apartment for you, because I left the door open while I ferried stuff to the car."

But before she could dial the number, the phone rang and the Bluetooth system in the Porsche automatically answered the call.

"Hello?" Robin said.

"Are you okay? It's John."

"We're fine," Mallory replied. "We managed to get away just as the bad guys arrived. Your heads-up was a good call, but the timing sucked. They got here a hell of a lot quicker than we expected."

"They were quicker than I'd been told as well, so we were all caught out. Don't tell me where you are, just in case anyone is listening in, but did you get away from Dartmouth?"

"We're doing that right now, and as far as Robin and I can tell, we've lost our pursuers. In fact, as we're safe where we are at the moment, we were just about to call the local police to tell them that her apartment has been burgled."

"I wouldn't bother, if I were you," John said. "I called them about two minutes after you sped off in that rather nice Porsche to tell them I'd just seen a man force the apartment door. In fact, he just walked in, because it was unlocked, but never mind. I still have eyes on the place, and so far nobody resembling a policeman has appeared. But the burglar—he was the third man who'd arrived in that BMW—left the building about ten minutes after he walked up the staircase. He was carrying the old wooden box that you had in your study, which I presume was what he was looking for."

"I'm sure it was," Robin said, "and that isn't good news, but it was what we expected. Anyway, thanks for keeping us in the picture, and thanks for making that call."

"No problem. Good luck with whatever you're doing and wherever you're going. Keep your eyes open and stay safe."

"So, where are we going?" Mallory asked, as Robin ended the call. He was fully relaxed now that the ferry was moving and they were—at least for the moment—out of immediate danger. "Not Tomar, I hope. There might be a blight of Dominicans there already."

"No," Robin assured him. "As far as I can see, Portugal doesn't actually get a mention in that piece of text."

"Good. You didn't get around to telling me anything about your translation. So, what did it tell you?"

"Rather less than I was hoping, actually. Unless I've missed something, most of it is another explanation of what happened when the order's spies discovered what Philip the Fair was planning. When Jacques de Molay received word of the king's intentions, he apparently thought long and hard about what to do. Right from the start he knew that resisting the king would be impossible. The Templars were powerful, as we both know, but their numbers were small and they would have been unable to combat the massed military forces of the French ruler, simply because all of their French properties were by definition surrounded by the rest of France. De Molay knew that if they refused to allow Philip's men inside when they knocked on the gates, that would only delay the inevitable. The king could order the strongholds to be besieged, and simply starve them out.

"The Templars also couldn't flee the country, because there wasn't enough time for all the knights to leave France before the intended arrests, and de Molay knew that as the leader he would certainly have to stay, along with many of the most senior members. He was sure the king's spies would be watching him and his officers closely and would move against them the moment they tried to leave Paris."

"A hell of a situation to be in," Mallory commented. "They were damned if they stayed, and damned if they tried to leave."

"Exactly. According to the text on the vellum, de Molay held a kind of council of war with his senior officers in the Paris preceptory in about the third week of August, but they all knew only too well that they were in a situation from which virtually none of them was going to be able to escape. They knew that the execution fires of the Dominicans would be where they were likely to end their lives, and they also realized that after what they were probably going to suffer for hours or days in the torture chambers, dying by fire, which would be absolutely indescribable agony but would at least be fairly quick, might even come as a relief.

"But de Molay did what he could. He ordered most of the rank-and-file knights, the younger members of the order, to leave Paris, sending them on apparently legitimate business across France to the other scattered Templar strongholds, carrying specific instructions that would ensure that only a skeleton staff would remain at each location when Philip the Fair's men arrived. It's the next bit of the text that's definitely the most interesting, at least from our point of view."

"What did he do with the Templar treasure?"

"Exactly," Robin agreed. "According to this, de Molay was so appalled at Philip's duplicity—you remember that the two men were supposed to be friends, and de Molay actually took part in a funeral for one of Philip's relatives, an honor that proved their close relationship—that he was absolutely determined to keep the treasure out of the hands of the king. But removing the wealth of the order from the various strongholds in the country was only a part of the problem. He had the men and resources to do it, but what concerned him wasn't the transportation of the treasure, or even hiding it. His big worry was what would happen to it afterward. Again, according to the text we've deciphered, the information de Molay had been given suggested that Philip was determined to exterminate the Knights Templar order in its entirety, and that meant there would be no members left to pick up the pieces once the purge was over. So de Molay was worried about what would happen to the wealth, to the treasure, and to the order's most sacred relic."

"Relic?" Mallory asked. "What relic?"

The Floating Bridge ferry was just about to arrive on the Kingswear side of the river, and Robin clicked her seat belt into place and started the engine of the Porsche before she replied.

"Frankly, I don't know. The text is clear but not specific, if you see what I mean. There are distinctly separate references to the treasure and to this sacred object, which appears to have been almost more important to the Templars than the wealth they possessed. Certainly, Jacques de Molay wanted to transport this relic somewhere safe, as well as hiding the treasure. The text on the vellum makes that very clear, but nowhere does it say what the object actually was."

Robin steered the Cayman off the ferry and accelerated gently around the bend and up Bridge Road, the A379, which would take them north to Paignton, and on to the faster roads leading toward Exeter.

"Maybe this relic is what they found in the hidden chambers of the Temple Mount," Mallory suggested. "The historical record says that the original nine knights spent almost ten years excavating underneath the Al-Aqsa Mosque, apparently looking for something. And most people believe that they did recover some object, simply because of what happened to them next. Once they stopped their digging and stepped back into the pages of the history books, the order was immediately recognized and approved by the Catholic Church, and only a decade later Pope Innocent II issued the *Omne Datum Optimum* papal bull that exempted the Templar order from obedience to all local laws.

"That was an astonishing document, because it meant that the Templars could cross any border without let or hindrance, were not required to pay taxes to anyone or obey any national laws of any sort, and they were to owe allegiance to only one person, the pope himself. No other order or group of men, before or after the Knights Templar, was ever granted such sweeping powers or given such an exemption, and there appears to be no obvious reason why the pope should have issued the document, unless he was effectively forced into it. One of the popular theories is that the Templars stopped their excavations on the Temple Mount because they found what they were looking for, and whatever it was so impressed, or perhaps so terrified, the pope that he was prepared to grant them whatever they wanted as long as the existence of this object remained a secret. That is at least a possible and logical explanation for what happened nearly nine hundred years ago."

Robin nodded thoughtfully as she steered the car along the twisting section of road near the Noss on Dart Marina and then accelerated along the straighter stretch that led to Hillhead.

"There must be theories about what they found, if that idea is correct," she said. "Are we back to the Ark of the Covenant or something like that?"

"Maybe we are. I really don't know. But don't forget that carving we saw at Chartres Cathedral. That building was constructed when the Templars were at the height of their power, and there's a strong chance that they were largely responsible for financing it. The carving very clearly showed the Ark, and one of the interpretations of the inscription is that it was actually hidden somewhere in the cathedral. If that's correct, then the Ark of the Covenant must still have been in existence in the thirteenth century, and was then most likely in the possession of the Knights Templar order. And to go back a step or two, if the Templars had pitched up in Rome and convinced the pope that they were in possession of the Ark, he would almost certainly have done precisely what they told him to do. That was, and arguably still is, the most important lost relic in religious history. It's been described as a machine for talking to God, and if you believe the stuff in the Old Testament, it was also an impressive battlefield weapon. The knowledge that it had been found would have terrified the pope because it would effectively have proved that the Jews were God's chosen people, and that the occupant of the Throne of Saint Peter in Rome was not God's representative on earth but just a usurper and of no consequence whatsoever. The Ark of the Covenant had, and I suppose it still has, depending on who owns it, the potential to destroy the Roman Catholic Church completely."

"But could it have lasted that long? I thought it was only a wooden box—made of acacia wood, I think—covered in gold leaf. An important wooden box, granted, and one that would have been hidden and protected at all cost because of its significance, but just something made out of wood thousands of years ago."

"I really have no idea," Mallory replied. "I know about codes and ciphers, and a fair amount about the Templars, but I don't know very much about religious artifacts of any sort. Okay, so the Templars had both their treasure—their assets, if you like—and this sacred relic. Do we know what they did with them? With either of them?"

"The text wasn't entirely clear, at least the way I translated the Latin into English, but it appears that at the end of this meeting de Molay spent some time alone trying to decide what he should do next. Then he had another meeting, but this time he only summoned four people to his chamber. Three of them were important and trusted knights of the order, men that de Molay knew he could rely on, but not of such senior rank that Philip's men would be likely to stop and arrest them if they were seen leaving the Paris preceptory."

"So, who was the fourth person?" Mallory asked.

"That isn't very clear. The word used to describe him in Latin was *puer*, and that translates as a servant or a young man, so my best guess is that he was some kind of a trusted retainer, perhaps a lay member of the order."

"That's possible. It's worth remembering that only about one in ten of the members of the Knights Templar were actual knights," Mallory pointed out. "Below the knights were the sergeants, who didn't come from noble families and were usually skilled craftsmen. They were the order's blacksmiths, armorers, builders, and other essential tradesmen, but they were also able to hold important ranks, and many of them rose high enough to become some of the most senior members of the Knights Templar. For example, we know that the order had a substantial fleet of ships, mainly based in the Mediterranean, and the man in charge of this fleet, the admiral, if you like, was actually a sergeant. His official title was Commander of the Vault of Acre. The order also had chaplains, who were ordained priests, obviously, and who were tasked with providing spiritual help and guidance to the Templars.

"At the other end of the scale were the visitors general. These were knights of the order who had been personally selected by the Grand Master to act as a kind of roving police force. They were responsible for visiting Templar establishments in the various provinces and countries to inspect the way the affairs of the order were being conducted, to introduce new rules or laws, resolve disputes, and generally act as the eyes and ears of the Grand Master himself. They had substantial powers. They could remove a knight from the order if he had seriously transgressed, and even suspend a local Master if there were problems or malpractices in the way he was conducting himself."

"You told me some time ago there were also squires in the Templar order."

"That's right, though the squires weren't actually in the order, or not always, anyway. Usually they were recruited to serve a particular knight for a specific period of time, after which they would leave and revert to their normal civilian status. Each Templar knight would have at least two, and sometimes three or four, warhorses assigned to him, and the squires would be responsible for the care and preparation of the animals as well as assisting the knight with his own preparations for battle. Just a thought, but if this anonymous fourth person summoned by de Molay had been a sergeant or a chaplain, I would have expected the author of the text to say that. So perhaps the man was actually one of the Grand Master's personal squires, someone not a part of the Templar order, but a person that de Molay obviously trusted implicitly."

"That makes sense," Robin agreed. "Anyway, whoever this person was, he was given instructions, along with the three unnamed knights, about the removal of the contents of the vaults of the Paris preceptory. And the text on the vellum states that it wasn't just the assets held in Paris that were being transported elsewhere. Again, the translation is not entirely specific, but it says something along the lines of "together with those containers gathered severally," which certainly implies to me that it's referring to the assets held by other Templar strongholds in France, and perhaps in other countries as well."

"So, what happened to the treasure?"

"I'll get to that in a moment. The slightly odd thing is that, according to the translation, the fourth man was not personally involved in the transport of the Templar assets, but was just being told what was going to happen to them, almost as if he was overseeing the removal, which doesn't entirely make sense if he was only a squire, even a trusted squire, because the men doing the work were noblemen, knights. He was also given a specific document by de Molay, and charged with keeping it safe. The Latin phrase used was *conservare et salvare in perpetuum*, which translates as something like 'protect and save for all eternity,' but there is no indication as to what this document might be. Clearly, it must have been something to do with the assets being removed, but exactly what it was, I have no idea. The text does then say where the Templar treasure was taken."

"At last," Mallory muttered.

Robin grinned at him.

"It does, but it's not very much help."

"Now, why am I not surprised about that? Ever since we started this, we've found misdirection, confusion, and all the rest of it. So, go on, tell me what vague hint the text provides."

Robin shook her head.

"It's not vague at all, actually," she said. "As I said, it tells us exactly where all the boxes of treasure were taken from the Paris preceptory, and by implication at least where all the other assets from the Templar strongholds in France ended up." She paused for a moment, savoring the expression of almost terminal irritation on Mallory's face. "They were all taken," she said, "to Honfleur."

"Honfleur? Honfleur in France?"

"Unless you know of another Honfleur somewhere, yes."

"Whereabouts in Honfleur?"

"That's what I meant when I said it was specific, but not helpful. All the wagonloads of goods were taken to the port at Honfleur, where they were loaded onto the ships of the Templar fleet that were waiting, ships that sailed with the tide on the following day. And as I'm sure you've probably guessed by now, the text does not say specifically what the destination of all these vessels was."

"Not even a hint?"

"There is a hint, yes, but like almost everything else, it's nonspecific. The text states that the ships sailed to a location described as *pro salute*, which means a place of safety, in the *insulae ad aquilonem*, the islands of the north, and that could mean almost anywhere, but obviously Scandinavia is a strong possibility. I mean, it would make sense for the Templars to choose to hide their assets in a country where they didn't already have a strong presence, somewhere that Philip the Fair would find it difficult to mount a campaign against them, and as far as I know they had never set up shop that far north."

"They didn't," Mallory agreed. "Most of their important strongholds were in the Mediterranean or in the countries that surrounded it, because that's where the action was, though they were also quite well established in England, and I suppose they could possibly describe the British Isles as 'the islands of the north,' so maybe we're closer to the treasure than we realize."

"Or maybe we're not," Robin replied. "Anyway, let's find somewhere to stay for the night. Then we can go through the translation again, just in case there's something we've missed."

26

Toscanelli instructed the driver to keep the speed well down as the car entered the built-up area. He had already seen far more police officers and police vehicles than he thought was normal for the quiet coastal town, and he could not afford to draw any attention to his men or to their mission. Part of the road near the area named on the satnav as Coronation Park had been closed, with three marked police cars, their roof lights flashing, stationed there to block off the traffic. A number of other vehicles, including a white Transit van, were parked in the area, uniformed policemen apparently interviewing their drivers and passengers.

The Italian muttered a curse as they drove past the scene.

"Pietro will suffer for this," he vowed. "He was never told to open fire on them in a public place. That was the last thing we wanted to happen. When we kill them, it will be somewhere quiet and private, because they will both take a long time to die, the woman especially."

He directed the driver into the road that ran at the rear of Robin Jessop's shop, but before the car reached her apartment building, a black-clad figure stepped off the pavement just as the Audi approached him. The man was carrying an ancient ironbound chest in both hands.

The car stopped a few feet farther on, and in a matter of moments the chest was concealed in the trunk of the vehicle, and the man himself was sitting in the rear seat.

"I know you told me to stay in the apartment, Marco," the man said, "but I was worried that the woman might have called the police and told them a burglary was in progress. So I collected what we needed and waited out here on the street for your arrival."

"That was good thinking," Toscanelli conceded. "Have you seen any sign of the police?"

"Not yet, though I did hear the sirens from several police cars in the area, which was really why I left the apartment."

"I'm not surprised nobody has appeared yet. Thanks to that idiot Pietro, they are fully occupied elsewhere in the town. So, what did you take out of the apartment?"

"You told us to find a medieval chest, any ancient documents, and anything that might be a transcription or a decryption of a piece of encrypted text. In the chest there's a piece of parchment or vellum that's in good condition, with a very clear text written on it, and a piece of wood that appears to have formed a false bottom in the chest, and which also has a block of letters carved into it. I also picked up a handful of papers covered in handwritten letters and words, which I think are part of the transcription they did. I couldn't see anything else that seemed useful in the room, and I did check every other room in the apartment. It didn't take long, because it's not very big."

Toscanelli nodded.

"That's good, because I think you found everything we need, everything that our experts back in Rome will require."

"So, where to now?" the driver asked.

"We need to send everything to Rome as quickly as possible, so find somewhere quiet where we can park the car and take the photographs we need."

"According to the satnav, there's a castle down at the southern end of the town. Will that do?"

"Listen to me," Toscanelli snapped. "I don't care where we go. Just find somewhere quiet."

Without another word, the driver moved the car away from the curb, navigated his way around the complex one-way system of narrow streets that get jammed with visitors to the town every summer, and then headed south, following the road beside the river. A quarter of an hour later, he stopped the car in the parking area close to the castle itself. There was only a handful of other vehicles there, all empty, and he chose a spot at one end, where they could open the trunk of the Audi and not be overlooked by anybody.

The area was dominated not by the castle, but by the impressive bulk of the Saint Petrox Church, which loomed up above and behind the fortification. Dating from about the twelfth century, when it possibly began life as a monastery dedicated to Saint Peter, the huge gray stone tower of the church, topped by crenellated battlements, was an imposing sight. The castle itself was a comparatively small structure, but in a good state of repair, perched on the rocks that marked the end of the headland and, strategically, on one of the narrowest points of the river. Control of that location would dominate the river and would imply control of all the traffic on that waterway. Built at the end of the fourteenth century to defend against a possible attack by the French, the fortress had been equipped with muzzle-loading cannon, including one heavy cannon capable of sinking a ship, possibly the first time this particular kind of weapon had been installed in a British castle. As a further refinement, the entrance to the river could be blocked in time of war by a heavy chain that ran between the castle and the opposite side of the river, an indication of the importance of the town and harbor.

Not that Marco Toscanelli had the slightest interest in his surroundings, except as a private place where he could take the photographs he needed. Within a few seconds of the vehicle stopping, his men had lifted the medieval chest out of the trunk and placed it on the ground, where Toscanelli snapped half a dozen pictures with a small but high-specification digital camera. Then he opened the chest up, took out the papers, the sheet of vellum, and the piece of wood, and photographed all of them several times from multiple angles to ensure that all the text on the vellum and the block of letters—which he presumed were code words of some sort—had been clearly recorded.

Then he opened his computer bag, took out a laptop and pressed the START button, removed the data card from the camera, and placed it in the slot on the computer to transfer all the images to the laptop. Once he'd done that, he checked each image to ensure that the transfer had been flawless and the images themselves were perfectly clear.

Once he was satisfied with the photographs, he selected the best and clearest images from the fifty or so pictures he had taken, attached the first of them to an e-mail, and then wrote a short message to Silvio Vitale explaining briefly what had happened. Then, aware of the limitations of all e-mail systems in terms of message size, he prepared half a dozen additional e-mails that each contained only some of the photographs. He encrypted all the messages using one of the standard ciphers employed by the Dominicans, then glanced around the car park.

"You, Cesare," he said. "There's a café just over there near the castle. Go and see if they have Wi-Fi."

The heavily built Italian strode quickly across the car park, looked at the handful of signs on the windows and doors of the establishment, then turned round and walked back.

"They have," he said. "For customer use only."

"Then we'll be customers," Toscanelli decided. "There are five of us," he added, "so I'll go in there with Cesare, and you three can follow in a couple of minutes."

Toscanelli picked a table well away from the other clients

of the establishment, took a seat, and opened up his laptop while Cesare stood at the counter, ordering drinks and something to eat. The Wi-Fi was fast, and although the size of all the messages was large because of the photographs attached to them, they were all transmitted pretty quickly.

"They've gone," Toscanelli said, and closed the lid of the computer before reaching across to pick up the coffee that Cesare had bought.

"So, now what do we do?" the other man asked.

"We've no idea where Mallory and Jessop are right now, so there's nothing we can do about finding them for the moment. Vitale will have to get one of our tertiaries to track them, using the traffic cameras that seem to infest Britain. That will tell us where they've been, but not necessarily where they are, and obviously they don't need to produce identification to stay in a hotel in this country. Our best bet is to trace them through credit card transactions, but even that will be slow and unreliable. Until we get some kind of a positive lead, we'll have to forget about them."

"You mean, we'll just have to sit around and wait?"

"Yes, but hopefully our experts will work out what that encrypted message on the vellum means very quickly, and once they do, then we should be ahead of the game and be able to get to wherever the first clue is located quicker than Mallory and Jessop. And if we can do that, then all we have to do is wait for them to walk into whatever building or site the clues lead them to. Once we've disposed of them, we can take our time in following the rest of the trail."

"You've had dealings with them before, haven't you?" Cesare said.

Toscanelli's expression changed markedly.

"I have," he said, "and up to now they've been lucky. But this time luck won't come into it. We have all the information that they have, and far more expertise back in Rome than the two of them have between them. This time we will beat them to the prize, and they will die. And that is a promise."

27

Bristol, Somerset

Putting some distance between themselves and any possible pursuit seemed like a really good idea, so as the daylight faded with the approach of evening, Robin switched on the headlights and drove on, keeping her speed just a fraction below the legal limit, and with both her and Mallory watching with total concentration for any indication that the Dominicans might have picked up their trail again.

They turned onto the M5 motorway just outside Exeter and drove north until they reached Portishead, just outside Bristol. That looked like a good enough location to go to ground, close to a city with a population of around half a million people, and with fast and easy access to the motorway network. From there, motorways ran west into South Wales, east to London, and north up to the Midlands, and the normal trunk roads provided a huge number of other routes they could take. Finding them in that area would have been next to impossible, or so they hoped.

Robin picked a hotel that offered secure underground parking, and half an hour after they'd left the motorway they were sitting side by side on a large double bed in the hotel room, both of them studying the translation that Robin had produced.

"I see what you mean," Mallory said. "Plenty of information, and that stuff about de Molay and what he did when he learned about Philip the Fair's plot is fascinating from a historical perspective, because it proves beyond any doubt that the Templars did know about the mass arrests in advance. As I said, there's plenty of information, but not much in the way of specifics that would be of any use to us."

"Well, we can't just fly up to Bergen or Copenhagen or somewhere and start wandering about, looking for buried treasure, with a couple of shovels and a pickax. That obviously isn't going to work. So what are we going to do?"

"I don't believe that the author of this text would be so vague that there would be no indication where we should be looking. There must be some kind of clue embedded in it, and it's just something we haven't seen yet. Or perhaps it's something we haven't understood properly. And I was just wondering about that 'islands of the north' reference. There is one enduring mystery that's been linked with the Templars by some researchers, but I really hope that it's nothing to do with our quest, because if it is, then we've already failed. Have you ever heard of Oak Island?"

"I don't think so," Robin replied. "Where is it? And what is it? Apart from being an island, I mean."

"Obviously it's an island—the clue is in the name. It's located off the shore of Nova Scotia in Mahone Bay in Canada, and ever since the end of the eighteenth century people have been digging there, looking for buried treasure. That's not unusual, of course. There are reputed sites of buried treasure all over the world, but what makes Oak Island different are the defenses that some unidentified group of people put in place there to make sure that whatever they'd buried stayed safe and undisturbed. You'll find sites all over the Internet devoted to the island and the so-called Money Pit, and there are all sorts of theories about who constructed it and what may be hidden there, but the reality is that nobody actually knows.

"Briefly, in the summer of 1795 a teenager named Daniel McGinnis landed on Oak Island and found a shallow circular depression in the ground and a tree right next to it with a branch on it that either had a pulley attached—according to some stories—or looked as if it could have been used to mount a pulley, because of the way the other branches had been cut back. There were rumors of pirate treasure being buried in the area, and so McGinnis returned home and then went back to the island with some friends to excavate the depression. The truly bizarre aspects of this story concern what they found when they started digging.

"Without going into too much detail, they found a layer of flagstones about two feet down and immediately assumed that they were on the verge of making a fabulous discovery. They kept on digging, and about ten feet below the surface they hit a layer of oak logs. They dug further still, but didn't find any treasure. What they did find was another oak platform at about twenty feet down and another one at thirty feet down. At that stage they abandoned the excavation, but they came back nearly a decade later with more men and better equipment to continue the dig. And they found the same thing. Oak platforms every ten feet all the way down to ninety feet, plus three other anomalous layers: charcoal at forty feet, putty at fifty feet, and coconut fiber at sixty feet."

"Hang on a minute," Robin interrupted. "That doesn't make sense. You don't get coconut trees in Nova Scotia. They only grow in the tropics, so where did the coconut fiber come from?"

"Nobody knows. And that's not the only thing about the Money Pit that doesn't make sense. Also at the ninety-foot mark, or maybe at eighty feet down because accounts vary, the searchers recovered a stone bearing strange inscriptions. There are drawings and replicas of the inscriptions on various websites, but as far as I'm aware there's no way of telling whether or not these images are accurate. If they are, they really don't make any sense. They're mainly what look like mathematical symbols, drawings of geometric shapes—most of them triangles—and about half a dozen shapes that could be letters. There have been some attempts to translate the inscription, including one that read, 'Forty feet below, two million pounds lie buried.' But the results aren't checkable because nothing has actually been found there, so nobody has any idea whether or not this decrypted message is accurate. There's also some doubt as to whether the message that was apparently decrypted was the one carved on the stone. And there's another problem with it as well."

"This is beginning to sound ridiculously similar to what we've been involved in, although we have had some tangible successes," Robin said. "So, what was the other problem with the stone?"

"One reason for the confusion over the translation is that the first mention of the stone is in a newspaper article from 1862—that's over half a century after the date it was supposed to have been discovered—but in another article published the following year the reporter stated that the stone had been built into the chimney of an old house located near the site of the pit. Sometime later in the nineteenth century, the stone was apparently removed and taken to Halifax, where another expert deciphered the inscription as reading, 'Ten feet below are two million pounds buried.' Exactly who these two unnamed men were or what fields they were supposed to be experts in has never been established.

"At the beginning of the twentieth century, what was claimed to be the same stone was in the possession of a bookbinding company in Halifax, and it was described as being a type of very hard basalt. One complication was that by this time there were apparently no characters visible on the stone, and the unlikely explanation given was that the bookbinder had used the stone for many years as a firm base on which to beat leather. Most people are very doubtful that this process would be sufficiently damaging to the stone to eliminate all the characters. When the bookbinder's business closed, this stone apparently vanished. So the actual whereabouts of this stone can't be established, nobody knows if it was actually the original stone, and there is no proof that the inscription displayed on replicas and in drawings is what was on the original piece of rock."

"It sounds to me as if the stone might have been a bit of a red herring—if any stone can acquire such fishy characteristics. So, what happened to the excavation? The people doing the excavation had got down to ninety feet, but what happened then?"

"Basically, they triggered a booby trap. They carried on digging below ninety feet, but water started to enter the pit, and when the diggers returned the following day the water level in the excavation was only thirty-three feet below the top. They tried pumping, but that didn't work. In fact, it had no effect at all on the level of water in the pit, and that turned out to be a very big clue. They tried digging a parallel tunnel a short distance away from the original. They excavated down to about one hundred feet, and then decided to dig a horizontal tunnel to link up with the original, apparently not realizing what was likely to happen. The moment they broke through, the new tunnel flooded to the same level as the original excavation. With no obvious way of getting rid of the water, they abandoned the digging for some forty-five years."

"Interesting stuff," Robin commented, "but I don't really see how it relates to the Knights Templar. Unless I'm missing something."

"It doesn't, or not directly, anyway. I mentioned a booby trap. Later investigation revealed that there were hidden tunnels linking the Money Pit with a bay known as Smith's Cove, and that was why pumping had no effect, because the water filling the pit came directly from the sea. But that wasn't all. Whoever constructed the Money Pit had built an artificial beach at the cove and constructed a drainage system that covered almost fifty yards of that beach with a series of channels dug into the clay subsoil. These channels had been filled with rocks and covered in eel grass and coconut fiber, all of which acted as a filtration system that allowed the channels to remain clear of debris and silt and so allowed water to flow freely. These channels met inland from the beach and all of them fed into a sloping stone-lined channel that led from that point to the Money Pit, which was about five hundred feet away, and joined it at about one hundred feet below ground level.

"It was an extremely impressive feat of engineering, way beyond anything that any pirate could have achieved, and it would have taken weeks, perhaps even months, to construct. And that's one reason why some people have suggested that the site might be where the last remnants of the Knights Templar order buried their huge treasure. Either that, or it must have been designed and constructed by a whole team of engineers and workmen, and that in turn suggests the probable involvement of a government. But that doesn't really make sense. Why would any government decide to bury something hundreds of feet down underneath an uninhabited island, when they could more easily construct a vault on some piece of land they owned and lock away whatever they were trying to hide in that? At least the Templar theory makes sense if it was their vast reserves of assets, their treasure, that they were concealing."

"Well, we do know that the Templars had impressive engineering skills. That's quite true, and we've had personal experience of some of those. But is there any evidence that they knew the North America continent even existed? After all, we're talking about a period well over a century before Columbus set out to find his route to the East Indies, and kind of stumbled across America on the way."

"To be pedantic about it," Mallory pointed out, "Columbus never saw any part of North America. On all three voyages he bounced around various Caribbean islands, and remained convinced until the day he died that he was actually sailing around previously undiscovered islands of the East Indies. But even if he had stepped ashore in what is now North America, he was a long way from being the first European to set foot there. The Vikings reached the area in the tenth century, and established a colony in Greenland that lasted for almost half a millennium, and another one at a place called L'Anse aux Meadows at the northern end of Newfoundland. That was discovered in 1960, and it's the most important Viking settlement so far discovered in North America. But there is some evidence that the Vikings weren't the first, either, and that it was actually the Irish who discovered America, but until now that's not been proven beyond any doubt."

"I didn't know that," Robin said. "But we seem to have rather drifted away from the Money Pit. What happened next?"

"Oh, yes. After that, the story turns into a bit of a bugger's muddle. Numerous groups, each convinced that they knew exactly what they were doing and how to do it, got involved in the act. The whole area filled up with half-dug tunnels and new pits, to the extent that it became almost impossible to pinpoint where the original Money Pit was located. Then a second flood tunnel, taking water from the South Shore Cove, was discovered in 1899, and that new discovery lent obvious weight to the belief that something of huge value or crucial importance simply had to be buried somewhere underneath Oak Island. Whoever had constructed the pit and its defenses wouldn't have gone to all that trouble unless the value of the buried object justified it.

"The excavations have continued, right up to the present day, but the people who are there now are employing modern machinery of various sorts and, because of the problems of actually digging down into the pit, several boreholes have also been drilled. One of them, drilled at the end of the nineteenth century, went down quite deep. At a depth of about two hundred feet, it apparently penetrated the roof of a concrete vault made from walls over six inches thick and with a height of about seven feet. Analysis of the substances the drill bit cut through included wood, soft metal of various sorts, and what was rather coyly referred to as an unknown substance, whatever that means. Allegedly, the drill bit also brought up a tiny piece of parchment, possibly sheepskin, on which two letters were written, the first one being a *V, U,* or *W,* and the second one the letter *I.*

"It's often difficult to separate fact from fiction in this kind of case, but far more recently a company called the Triton Alliance drilled a borehole known as 10-X in 1976. This went down over two hundred feet and entered some kind of a cavity. A camera was lowered down into the borehole, and according to some reports, images of a severed human hand, a human body—number of hands unknown—some discarded tools, and three alleged treasure chests were seen. Divers were sent down, but saw nothing because of poor visibility, and later the roof of the cavern or whatever they were exploring collapsed. But as far as I know, at least one team of treasure hunters is still out there, still digging away hopefully."

"So, what do you think? Is Oak Island genuinely the last resting place of the Templar treasure? And does that mean we're just wasting our time here?"

"As I said, I really hope not, because even if we could get to the island, there'd be no chance that the two of us would somehow magically be able to get down to the bottom of the flooded Money Pit and find what's down there. Not if all these other teams, with all their equipment, have so far failed. And although they've not found anything in terms of treasure—apart from three links of a gold chain that were supposed to have been recovered back in 1849 and that subsequently vanished—they have recovered a few artifacts that could help date the construction. Some of the worked wood found on the island and presumably used by the original builders was carbon-dated and returned an age of about two hundred and fifty years; a few handwrought nails have been found, and also a pair of wrought iron scissors. These were identified as being Spanish American, and had most likely been made in Mexico about three hundred years ago.

"None of that's conclusive, obviously, because they could be contaminants, objects left at the site at a much later date, but the commonality in the ages of the finds that could be dated does at least suggest that the Money Pit was most probably built about three hundred years ago, roughly at the beginning of the eighteenth century, and only about one hundred years before McGinnis stumbled across the shallow depression in the ground that started this treasure hunt."

"And that's realistically about four hundred years too late for it to be the Knights Templar who constructed it," Robin said. "Right. So it's an intriguing mystery that might never be solved, if what you're telling me is correct, simply because there's a good chance that whatever was buried there will never be recovered. So, with that out of the way, let's try and work out where we need to go and what we need to do."

Mallory looked at her in some surprise.

"I thought you said—or at least you implied—that there was nothing in the text on the vellum that told us where to go. Or did I miss something?"

"Yes and no, really. There is what I think is a kind of clue. In fact, there are three phrases that might well be clues, but none of them really makes sense to me."

She took a pencil and drew a kind of circle around each of the phrases she had identified in her translation of the decrypted Latin as potential clues and pointed the three of them out to him.

Mallory stared at the few words in each part of the translation and then shook his head.

"I absolutely agree with you there," he said. "Not one of them makes any sense to me, either."

28

When his mobile phone rang, Toscanelli answered it immediately.

"Toscanelli."

"Just for a change, Toscanelli, you and your team seem to have done a reasonably competent job." Silvio Vitale's tone was unusually warm.

"Thank you."

"I'm not, of course, referring to the gunplay in Dartmouth. That was utterly stupid and achieved absolutely nothing, and I can assure you that as soon as Pietro gets back to Rome he will be sorry that he gave the order to open fire. Do not, by the way, tell him that. I am keen to interview him personally."

Toscanelli shivered slightly, because he knew precisely what Vitale meant by that.

"Where are you now? And what are you doing?" Vitale asked.

"We had no idea where the next phase of this quest would take us, so we've checked into a hotel in Exeter, in Devon, where we have good access to the British motorway system. We've been here about two hours, and Pietro and his colleague arrived thirty minutes ago after getting rid of the hire car—which the British police are probably already looking for—and obtaining another vehicle. We are now awaiting your further orders, and we can move out at a moment's notice."

"Good. Remain where you are tonight, unless I call you again. I have a team working on the information you sent back to me, and according to Benelli the decryption has already begun. It will probably take longer than you would expect, because there are a large number of duplicates and so even with knowledge of the block of code words the process involves a fair degree of trial and error. But we are getting there, and he is confident that we will be able to read the entire decrypted text tonight, or tomorrow at the latest. Keep your mobile phone with you at all times, switched on and fully charged, because you may well have to act extremely quickly once we know what the text says. Don't forget that Mallory and Jessop"— Vitale almost spat the names—"have had access to this information for significantly longer than we have, so they may already be well ahead of you."

Toscanelli opened his mouth to reply, but immediately realized that Vitale had ended the call. He shrugged, put the phone on the bedside table, and plugged in the charging lead.

Then he turned his attention back to the packet of largely flavorless sandwiches and alarmingly colored crisps that composed his evening meal, along with a mug of instant coffee he'd made at the so-called hospitality station on the other side of the hotel bedroom.

It was an almost entirely inadequate meal, but it had the undeniable advantage that if Vitale called again to tell them to get on the road, he could either shove it in the nearest waste bin—which was realistically the best place for it—or take it with him, as could the other members of his team who were eating their way through largely identical combinations of snack foods in their own rooms.

Toscanelli had vetoed the idea of sitting down to a restaurant meal precisely for this reason, though as he cautiously lifted off the bread from one half of the next sandwich to inspect the contents, he wondered if that had actually been the right decision.

29

Bristol, Somerset

"I can read what the words say," Mallory elaborated, "but I really don't know what they mean. And we're not going to be able to work that out without some context, without first deciding exactly where we should be looking."

He pointed at the first of the decrypted and translated phrases.

"That just seems obvious and completely unhelpful," he said. "Wherever the treasure is hidden, it's bound to be 'where no eyes may regard it'. Otherwise, somebody would almost certainly have already found it. What that probably means is that it's buried, or in a cave or an underground vault or something like that. That second phrase, which states that the prize—not the treasure, I notice—is 'beneath the stone which is not as it seems,' is just a fraction more useful, but it won't help us until we know that we're standing in the right place. Hopefully we'll then be able to see some kind of stone or rock and recognize that it's in the wrong place or whatever that phrase means. Is there any chance that either the decryption or your translation could be wrong, or could some of the words have a different meaning? Anything like that?"

Robin appeared to bristle slightly at Mallory's implication.

"Of course that's possible," she said somewhat snappily, "not least because like any other language, Latin evolved through the centuries, and so the meaning of a word in the colloquial Latin of the early to mid-fourteenth century—which is probably when this was written—might be somewhat different to the entry in a twenty-first-century Latin-English dictionary pulled off the Web. But as far as I can see, the translation we've ended up with should be reasonably accurate, because at least the sentences do make sense. They may not be very helpful, but that's a different problem."

"Even that third phrase, which seems really obscure?"

"Even the third phrase," Robin agreed. "And you're quite right. It does appear to be completely unhelpful, but I played around with every possible alternative meaning, or shade of meaning, that I could find, and that is the most accurate translation I managed to come up with."

Mallory nodded, and then read the translation aloud.

"'In the settlement named for itself, seek behind the eyes,'" he read. "That really and truly means absolutely nothing to me, and if you're right about the rest of the sentence, it doesn't even refer to the actual location of the treasure but to something completely different."

"Exactly. And the word in the phrase that follows that one, the word which definitely doesn't make sense to me, is this one: *licentiam*. Even without a dictionary, it wouldn't be too big a jump to guess that the closest equivalent in English is a 'license' or a 'permit' or possibly even 'permission.' But just like you, I have no idea what the relevance of that is. If we do ever manage to end up locating this treasure, we might well have to organize picks and shovels and buckets, or even a backhoe, to get it out of the ground, but absolutely the last thing we're going to need is a seven-hundred-year-old permit written in Latin."

Mallory nodded slowly, then again read that particular section of the text. Then he grinned and tapped the piece of paper he was holding.

"What?" Robin asked. "Don't tell me you found something I missed. That would be almost terminally irritating."

"No, not really. It's not so much something you missed as applying a bit of a different interpretation to that word *licentiam*."

"What different interpretation?" Her voice was low and almost dangerous.

"We—or at least I—have been assuming that the word *license* or whatever translation you prefer means some kind of permission, but maybe that's not quite right. Perhaps it's not so much an authorization to recover the treasure as an explanation of where it is. It could even be the information we need to locate it."

"You mean like a modern license to excavate gives the appropriate permission to break ground, but also specifies the area as well as the terms and conditions and any limitations? Yes, that's not a bad thought. So all we have to do now is find out exactly where 'the settlement named for itself' is. And I don't think that's going to be exactly a walk in the park."

They both stared at the translation for a few seconds; then Robin uttered a short and not particularly ladylike expression, and picked up the other pages containing the transcription of the encrypted text and the notes she'd made while she'd been working on them.

"You've thought of something?" Mallory asked.

"Yes," she replied, staring at what she'd written. "At least I think I have. That phrase we've been looking at really doesn't make sense, because if that was an accurate translation it should read something like 'the settlement that takes its name from the king or the lord or the river,' not 'for itself.' As it stands, it's senseless, unless for some bizarre reason somebody created a settlement and then named it 'settlement,' which seems really unlikely. But if we make just one tiny change to it, that part of the phrase makes perfect sense."

"It does? What change?"

"This one," Robin said briskly, taking up her pencil, drawing a line through *itself*, and substituting *us* in its place. "One of the possible alternative translations for the word we took to mean 'itself' was 'ourselves,' or just 'us.' Now it reads 'the settlement named for us.' I think we're looking for somewhere that was named after the Templars, and which had had that name bestowed on it well before the middle of the fourteenth century."

"That should help narrow the search," Mallory agreed,

"but there are a lot of place-names in England—probably at least a dozen—that include the word *Templar* or *Temple* and have some connection to the order, and far more than that in other countries. If we have to visit all of them, we're going to be racking up a lot of frequent-flier points and spending days or weeks on the road."

Robin shook her head.

"Not necessarily," she said, "because I think our search is going to keep us much closer to home. Not just keep us in England, but take us to a part of the country not far from where we are right now."

"Where?"

"I'll get to that. It's all to do with that strange phrase about looking 'behind the eyes.' I think that's just a slightly convoluted way of referring to a face, or a head, and if I'm right, then that narrows our search down immediately to just one place. A place that was definitely Templar in origin, that includes the word *Temple* in its name, and which possesses a face."

She stopped talking and looked inquiringly at Mallory.

"This is supposed to be more your field than mine," she said. "Any idea where I'm talking about?"

"Oh yes," Mallory replied with a grin. "I know exactly where you mean now you've laid it out like that. You're talking about Templecombe and the Templecombe Head."

30

Exeter, Devon

The information Toscanelli needed—or at least a part of it—had been sent to his mobile as a message rather than as a call, and the alert tone when it arrived had awoken him at a little after three thirty in the morning.

It wasn't the decryption he'd been expecting, but it was something almost as useful, and had been sent by the duty officer at the Rome headquarters of the order. The ciphertext, according to the first sentence of the text message, was still being worked on, and he—Toscanelli—could expect to receive an abstract of the data soon, whatever that last word actually meant.

But what information the text contained was helpful. Silvio Vitale had again requested assistance from the tertiary who was a senior officer in the local police force, and the man had delivered. He was obviously of a sufficiently high rank that he could request data from the all-pervasive network of roadside traffic and ANPR—Automatic Number Plate Recognition—cameras that covered Britain's motorways and major trunk roads, and his request had borne fruit. The Porsche had been caught on several such cameras, not exceeding the speed limit or doing anything illegal, but just driving away from Dartmouth and north toward Exeter.

When he saw that, Toscanelli smiled grimly to himself, his decision to move his men up to Exeter immediately being vindicated. Unfortunately, the picture produced by the traffic cameras was far from complete. The distinctive Porsche Cayman had driven past Exeter and continued north on the motorway, but it had later vanished. The last sighting of the vehicle had been on the motorway a few miles south of Bristol, when it had still been heading north, but since that moment there had been no sign of it.

The obvious conclusion, the duty officer had suggested, was that their quarry had probably left the motorway near that city and found somewhere to stay out of sight. That, Toscanelli mentally agreed, was the most likely scenario, but it was nothing like specific enough for him to do anything about it. He quickly opened up a Web browser to check the basic data for Bristol, and immediately realized that it would be pointless going there. The place was just too big and he would need something else—another traffic camera sighting or a definite lead based on a transcription of the text—before he could initiate any kind of a search.

Or, at least, it would be pointless and completely counterproductive to head up there that night. He and the rest of his men needed their sleep, and checking out of the hotel at that hour would be so unusual that the night staff would remember it happening, and the whole point of their mission was that it be covert. So they would move closer to Bristol, but only at a sensible hour later that morning, after breakfast.

Satisfied with that decision, he sent a brief text in reply to the duty officer—with a request that he advise Vitale accordingly when he arrived in the building—put his phone back on charge, and went back to sleep.

31

Somerset

"Mind you," Mallory said thoughtfully as he steered the Porsche at an entirely legal speed toward the village of Templecombe, "I do see a couple of potential problems in finding this license or whatever it is."

It had been too late to drive there the previous evening, so they'd set off immediately after breakfast that morning.

Robin looked across at him and nodded for him to continue. He'd offered her the keys to the car at the hotel that morning, but—as he had expected—she'd shaken her head in refusal. If any vehicle she was in was going to be driven in a sensible and responsible manner, then she was never particularly interested in getting behind the wheel, because that kind of driving simply bored her, and she'd much rather be a passenger.

"We do know that Templecombe existed as a settlement before the Knights Templar arrived and built a preceptory there at the end of the twelfth century—that was when they were given the land by a man called Serlo Fitz Odo— and we also know that the name of the village came from the Latin *Combe Templariorum*. But the origins of the Templecombe Head are much more mysterious."

"I know," Robin replied, "because I did a bit more research this morning while you were snoring like a bull with chronic asthma on your side of the bed. Reading the decrypted text suggests, at least to me, that whatever we are supposed to find is somewhere behind the Templecombe Head. That's the obvious interpretation of the phrase 'behind the eyes,' and that's also the problem. As you know, the Head itself is a painting done on wooden boards that depicts the face of a human male, but experts can't agree on whose face it is."

"One account I read said that Jesus Christ was a contender."

Robin nodded.

"He is, but the problem is that artistic convention in the early Middle Ages decreed that paintings of Christ should show him with a halo, as a mark of divinity, and the Templecombe Head has no halo. The counterargument is that the Templars were known to use images of Christ without a halo, which might imply that it was a painting owned or commissioned by the Templars. The other option is that it might be intended to show the face of John the Baptist, who was obviously a very important character in the early Christian Church, but not considered to be divine. So, the short, snappy summary is that it could be either of these two men, or neither of them, and it could even be somebody entirely unknown to history but of some importance to the painter or to the society in which he was working. In short, nobody knows. But what we do know, because of radiocarbon dating, is that the wood on which the painting was done dates from about the thirteenth century, so it is more or less contemporary with the presence of the Knights Templar in and around the village, and the style of the painting suggests that it dates from roughly the same period, so we're probably not looking at a nineteenth-century painting on a piece of thirteenth-century wood, for example."

"I do know that the Head is now on display in the local church, the Church of Saint Mary, at Templecombe," Mallory said, dredging a possibly unrelated fact from his memory vault, "but as far as I remember it hasn't always been inside the building."

"Spot-on. In fact, nobody knows where the painting was originally displayed, or even if it was ever on display at all. It was only found by accident back in 1945, when a local woman found it in an outhouse, where a part of the ceiling had fallen down. She was either trying to do some kind of repairs to it, or possibly collecting wood— the surviving accounts vary—when she looked up and saw a painted face staring down at her from the ceiling, which must have been a slightly surreal moment. Apparently the painted panel had been put in the roof to keep it out of sight years earlier, because it was wired to the inside of the roof, and then the ceiling had been plastered over. We also don't know why this was done, unless it was simply for safekeeping. Maybe it was because of fears of a German invasion of Britain in either the First or the Second World War, and then the person who'd hidden it either died or perhaps just forgot about it.

"After that, the painting had a bit of a hard life, because the local vicar decided to clean it in his bath using scouring powder, which had the effect of removing most of the color. It was restored in the late 1950s before being given to the church in 1956, and was restored a second time in the 1980s. It occasionally gets taken out of the church to be exhibited elsewhere, but most of the time the Church of Saint Mary is its home."

"That's pretty much the story as I remember it," Mallory said, "and you're right about that creating a problem. If we knew for a fact that the Templecombe Head had always hung in the church, then there would be a reasonable chance that whatever we're looking for would be carved into the wall behind it, or something like that. But because of the history of the painting, the way it's been treated, and the peculiar sequence of events that ended up with it being given to the church, the one place we can be pretty sure we can forget about is the wall where it's hanging. After all, we don't know for certain that that painting ever had anything to do with the church, though my guess is that it did, because the way the face was painted suggests to most people that it was a kind of sacred art."

"So where *do* we start looking?"

"At the picture, if we can get access to it, because the other possible meaning of the phrase is better, just about. The alternative explanation of 'behind the eyes' is really simple and obvious. Maybe it refers to the back of the painting itself, to the wooden panel on which it's painted. But you know what the downside of that is."

"Yes. That idiot vicar scrubbing at it in his bath and then the two later restorations. They would obviously have been working on the painting, on the face painted on the wood. They probably wouldn't have bothered even looking at the reverse, unless there was some clearly written text or message, and even if there had been, they'd most likely have ignored it unless it helped establish when the picture was painted, or who either the artist or the subject was. But I don't recall reading about a text on the reverse."

"That's because there isn't anything there, at least as far as I know. Did your researches tell you anything else about the Head?" Mallory asked.

"No. That was pretty much as far as I got."

"It might be worth checking up on this once we get to Templecombe, but I remember reading somewhere that the painting had probably been used as a door at some point in its history, because on one side there are, or perhaps there were, hinges and on the other side a keyhole. As far as I can see, the only thing we've got going for us is that we're pretty sure that the painting is important and can lead us to what we're looking for. So what we really need to find is a space that the painting could be used to secure as a door, and if we can track down something like that, we might just crack this.

"The other thing in our favor is that some parts of the church are original, and date back to the twelfth century, and I suppose it would be reasonable to assume that whatever the Templars hid, they might well have concealed in the church, on the basis that the secular buildings in the village and even the preceptory itself might well be torn down, modified, or rebuilt, but the church was likely to remain in its original state, apart from necessary repairs and perhaps extensions, purely because of its religious significance. Oh," he added as another thought struck him, "the other obvious problem we have is that after the order was purged, the village and all the Templar properties there were given to the Hospitallers. They had no reason to like the Templars, and so it's certainly possible that they might have found whatever was hidden and either used it or destroyed it. And if that *is* what happened, we'll be wasting our time even going to the village."

"Then let's hope that didn't happen. So, the church should be our first stop?" Robin asked.

"I think so, yes. And if we find nothing at the church, we'll just have to think again."

Ten minutes later Mallory braked the Porsche to a halt on the outskirts of Templecombe, selecting a quiet street— and there were plenty of those—more or less at random.

"It's probably better to leave the car here," he said, "away from prying eyes, just in case we've got unwelcome company. It's too distinctive to park in a more obvious place."

"Makes sense. So, where's the church?"

Mallory pointed to a sign at the end of the road they'd just driven down.

"I think that will tell us which direction to go," he said.

The signpost did, and minutes later they were standing outside the churchyard and looking at the ancient gray stone building.

English country churches are often elegant structures, the old walls penetrated by delicate stone tracery studded with the rich glowing colors of stained glass, and frequently topped by a soaring tower that seems to be almost literally reaching up toward the heavens. They are usually calm, peaceful, gracious, and welcoming buildings, whatever your religious persuasion or lack of one.

The Church of Saint Mary at Templecombe was different from that description in almost every respect.

"It looks more like a fort or a castle than a church," Robin commented, when they stopped on the road outside the substantial wall that enclosed the church and the grassy area that composed the churchyard.

"I know exactly what you mean. Even if I didn't know anything about the history of the place, I think I'd probably guess that it was originally a Templar chapel. It just has that solid and uncompromising look about it that was so characteristic of a lot of their architecture."

For a few seconds they stood there in silence, staring at the building in front of them.

They were looking at the face of the tower, but there was no elegant spire reaching up toward the salvation of God in heaven. Instead, the tower was squat, square, and solid, and looked more as if it was getting ready to withstand an attack or a siege than to welcome a group of worshippers.

Massively constructed of gray stone—probably ham-stone, Mallory thought, bearing in mind where they were—it dominated that part of the building. In the center, at ground level, was a Gothic arch, seemingly too small, almost out of proportion with the tower above it. Recessed a short distance inside the arch was an equally small door, the ancient solid wood glowing a dark gray-brown in the sunlight. The reason for that part of the design was obvious: a large door would have offered a bigger target and potential way of getting inside for any attackers, so the Templars invariably made their entrances as small as reasonably possible, to provide a more effective defense.

And that philosophy was continued in the rest of the structure. Perhaps a dozen feet above the arch was a window, an opening filled with diamond-shaped panes of leaded glass, but so narrow that it did not appear to have been constructed to allow light inside the building. What it looked like more than anything else was a large arrow slit, a break in the solid wall that would allow a couple of bowmen to stand side by side and engage an approaching enemy, and possibly also wide enough for the defenders to pour boiling oil or other noxious substances over a group of people trying to break down the main door and so repel them.

Directly above that was a clock, and a little higher was another, larger window, this one without glass but barred with slabs of horizontal worked stone separated by gaps, presumably intended to allow fresh air into the building. The top of the tower was marked by a line of crenellated battlements, and they looked like the real thing, not any form of decoration. They had clearly been built to permit a defending force to engage an enemy from the roof of the building whilst themselves still being protected by the thick stone. At each of the four corners, prominent gargoyles jutted out to allow water to drain off the flat roof, and the whole structure was supported by solid stone buttresses at each corner at ground level.

Behind the tower, a more conventional church building extended to both the left and the right, complete with windows of a more normal size.

"According to what I read this morning," Robin said, "this place was given a major Victorian renovation in the nineteenth century, which was probably when most of what we're looking at now was modified. But the tower most likely hasn't been touched since it was built in the twelfth century. And it stands on Saxon foundations, so there's been something—some religious building, I mean—on this spot for a hell of a long time."

"And it looks like it, too," Mallory agreed. "Well, standing here looking at it butters no crumpets, as they say, so let's get inside."

32

"How accurate is this information?" Toscanelli asked.

The voice at the other end of the call, that of the duty officer in Rome, was slightly distorted by the scrambling system he was using, his words interspersed with anomalous squelching sounds and occasional breaks. In reality, it wasn't that unlike a normal mobile-to-mobile call, when both phones were at the very edges of their respective cells, and what he was saying was clearly understandable.

"Very. The tertiary has reported two sightings of the target vehicle from traffic cameras, one near the center of a town called Portishead, which is near Bristol—"

"I see it," Toscanelli interrupted, looking at the local area map spread out on the table in front of him and placing his right forefinger firmly on the town the duty officer had just identified. He and his men were sitting at adjoining tables in a café on the east side of Bristol, having driven up there in their two hire cars first thing that morning to await further orders or information from Rome, information that would let them hunt down their quarry.

"Good. The second camera was on one of the roads leading out of the town, down toward the south, and that ties up with the transcription of the ancient text. There is a small settlement named Templecombe that lies in that direction, and we believe that Mallory and Jessop are making their way there. Our experts here have now decrypted most of the text. The statements are obviously subject to interpretation, but they believe that one section refers to that village and to an ancient painting found there years ago. It's known as the Templecombe Head and it's on display in the local church. We think that is what the two of them are trying to examine."

"Understood," Toscanelli said, looking again at the map. "I see where this place Templecombe is. We can be there in less than an hour."

"There's something else. The next part of the text tells us to 'seek behind the eyes,' and we think that means there's something written or carved into the back of the painting, because it was done on wood, not canvas. That means you have to get hold of the painting so we can examine it."

"Understood. Anything else?"

"Yes. I have a message for you from Silvio Vitale."

"Oh, yes?" Toscanelli replied cautiously. Any message from the head of the enforcement arm of the Dominican order was not necessarily good news.

"He said," the duty officer continued, "that now we have the decryption almost complete, Mallory and Jessop are of no further interest or use to us. We have all the information needed to complete the quest. You are to find them and kill them, as a matter of urgency."

"It will be a pleasure," Toscanelli said, his voice a dangerously soft purr.

33

"So, that's it?"

Robin's remark was framed as a question, but as they were both standing in the church and looking up at the enigmatic features of the Templecombe Head, Mallory took it as no more than a statement of fact and didn't respond to her comment. Instead, he glanced over toward the altar, where the rector was explaining something about the history of the building to a tour group of about a dozen people. The tourists had already spent a few minutes in front of the Templecombe Head and had then moved elsewhere in the building, allowing Robin and Mallory to step forward and examine it.

"We're lucky we arrived at about the same time they did," he said. "I didn't realize the church was usually kept locked for security. For the security of this painting, actually."

It was positioned on the south wall of the church at a

little over head height, so looking at the image was easy for both of them. Even without the knowledge they had of the history of the painting, it would have been quite obvious that it was old. Everything about it—the style, the way the features were painted, and even the borders and layout of the picture—looked medieval.

Staring back at them was the face of a bearded man with long hair of a light brown shade that almost verged on ginger. His eyes and mouth were open, and although his face was largely expressionless, the emotion conveyed in it by the painter was, if anything, surprise. The head appeared disembodied, with no sign of even a neck below the face, though the colors were so faded that the paint strokes depicting the figure's neck and shoulders might simply no longer be visible. Surrounding the image was a geometric pattern, a shape that looked almost like a painted stone border that could possibly have been intended to represent an ornate window, or perhaps a kind of frame within the painting to emphasize the importance of the subject. The upper part of the painting was cut off at about the level of the top of the head, which suggested that originally the panel might have been slightly larger.

Attached to both sides of the design and to the bottom center were three identical shapes with a distinctly floral appearance, almost like stylized leaves. The one to the left of the face was far clearer than the other two. Mallory pointed to that one.

"Those remind me of a kind of expanded fleur-de-lis design," he said. "You know, the Prince of Wales's feathers and all that."

"Does that help?" Robin asked.

"No. Of course not. I was just pointing it out."

"Apart from that possibly suspect observation, do you notice anything else about it?"

Mallory stared at the painting for about half a minute, then shook his head.

"One very obvious problem for us is that it's stuck inside a heavy sealed wood-and-glass frame that looks to me as if it's screwed to the wall. That means our chances of getting a look at the back of it are virtually nil, at least without lifting it off the wall and taking the frame to pieces, which we'd probably be stopped from doing pretty quickly. Oh, and the shape of the entire image is a bit lopsided, as if the wood panel was originally slightly bigger than we see here today. Apart from those two pretty obvious points, nothing really leaps out at me. So, what have you seen that I haven't?"

"It's not something I've actually seen," Robin said, almost hesitantly. "It's more a sort of impression I've formed. A couple of impressions, actually."

"Go on."

"Tell me what you think he's feeling. That man in the painting, I mean."

Mallory stared intently at the image, then shook his head.

"I'm no art historian," he said, "and the style of the painting is really quite primitive, but if you wanted a one-word answer—"

"That would be good," Robin said.

"Then I suppose I'd have to say he looks surprised."

"Bravo. That's exactly what I mean. Most portraits, even in the days when this was probably painted—the twelfth or thirteenth century, something like that—were posed. The subject would look composed. More to the point, he or she would definitely have their mouth closed, not least because dental hygiene in those days was virtually nonexistent, and a lot of people had probably lost most or all of their teeth by the time they reached adulthood. An open mouth was definitely not a good look."

"So why hasn't he got his mouth closed?"

"There's one obvious reason that occurs to me, and I'll tell you my idea in a minute. And it ties up with the surprised expression on his face. It looks almost as if someone's just stabbed him unexpectedly in the back. In fact, it's almost more a look of shock than one of surprise. But there's something else that's odd about it, and that's his eyes."

Mallory looked back at the painted image and then shook his head.

"They look normal enough to me," he said, "apart from being half-closed. In fact," he added, "I suppose that's a bit odd. If he'd been surprised by something, surely you would expect him to have his eyes wide open?"

"That wasn't what I meant," Robin said, "but you do have a point. No, what I was looking at was where the man in the painting was looking. Which is straight at the two of us, and that's unusual."

Mallory looked uncomprehending.

"I don't follow."

"Artistic tradition and unwritten rules. That's what I mean. Over a quarter of a millennium after the likely date of this image, in about the middle of the sixteenth century, Titian was working in Venice. While he was there, he painted a famous picture of Venus, a nude, that appalled the Catholic Church."

"I thought nudes were a common subject for artists and sculptors, and had been since way back in the time of the ancient Greeks. The men in most of the early statues wore a fig leaf or nothing at all, and the women usually had a bit of cloth, some part of a garment, covering their interesting bits."

"They were," Robin agreed, "and they did, but that wasn't the point. What really incensed the Vatican was the fact that in Titian's work the nude model was looking straight out of the painting at the viewer. That established an obvious connection between the viewer and the model. She was lying naked on a couch in a pose that was certainly provocative for its time, and she was looking at you. That's what the church couldn't handle. Up till then, both women and men had been painted naked, but they were always doing other things and not looking at the viewer of the painting. So with those works it was as if the viewer was just watching a scene, only acting as a spectator and taking no part in what was happening. Titian's painting changed all that. It was almost as if the woman in the picture was inviting you inside, in both senses of that word."

"So, you mean this is anomalous, a piece of art that's out of place in terms of its content because of the date it was probably painted. Is that what you're saying?"

Robin nodded.

"It's definitely anomalous, but there is one possible

reason that would explain what we're looking at, the face with the open mouth and half-closed eyes. I think the artist of this work painted exactly what he saw, and what he was looking at wasn't the figure of a man posing for a painting. In fact, it wasn't a figure at all, which explains why there's no sign of the subject's neck or shoulders, or any other part of his body. I think he was painting the head of a man who had just been decapitated. When you die, your eyes don't close and your mouth could well drop open, because all muscle control is instantly lost. He just painted what he saw in front of him."

That stunned Mallory.

"I'd never thought of that," he admitted after a few moments, "but that does makes sense. And it would certainly explain the surprised look on his face. He's surprised because he's dead. That also means that whoever this painting represents, he had to have been an important man."

"An important man to the Templars, certainly," Robin said, "and that does at least suggest who it might be. Though there is one particular problem with that."

"You're right. There is. You're obviously talking about John the Baptist," Mallory replied. "Perhaps the most important man ever to be beheaded, or at least the one that almost everybody knows about. According to the legends, John had criticized Herod Antipas for marrying Herodias, the former wife of his—Herod's—brother, and had been imprisoned as a result. Herodias was furious about this rebuke, and demanded John's execution, but Herod refused. Then her daughter, Salome, danced in front of Herod and so entranced him that he offered her anything she wanted as a reward. Salome asked her mother, Herodias, what she should request, and Herodias told her to demand the head of the Baptist on a silver platter. Herod reluctantly agreed.

"Like most of the stuff in the Bible, there are a lot of problems and contradictions with this, and there are several different versions of the story. But it's been quite well established that the Templars were Johannite in their beliefs: they worshipped John the Baptist, not Jesus Christ. In fact, one of the accusations leveled at the Templars by their Dominican inquisitors was that they were forced to deny Christ, and spit and trample on the cross as a part of their initiation ceremony when they joined the order.

"According to a few of the surviving testimonies from those dark days, some of the Templars agreed that they did do this, but they claimed this was so that they would be prepared and able to exhibit virulent anti-Christian behavior in front of their Muslim enemies if they were ever captured and endure it with their faith still intact, and there may well have been some truth in that. Verbally or physically denying Christ wouldn't have been easy for anyone in those days, and particularly not for a member of an order of warrior knights dedicated to Christianity, so it could have been a kind of preparation for what could happen to them. On the other hand, because they were Johannites, Christ would definitely not have been a religious figure of any particular importance to them."

"I didn't know they worshipped the Baptist. Why did they?"

"Possibly because of something else that's an obvious and unresolved anomaly. If Jesus Christ genuinely was the son of God, by definition He would have been the most important man ever to walk on the surface of this planet. But if that were the case, how could John have baptized Him? That would mean that John was morally and religiously His superior. Logically, Christ should have been the one administering the baptism to John. And it's not just the Templars who thought that. The Mandaeans of southern Iraq believed exactly the same thing for a slightly different reason. They revered John and condemned Jesus as a false prophet, a person who was entrusted with certain religious teachings by John and then perverted them for his own ends. And I think there are a handful of other groups scattered about the world that believe something similar as well."

"So, do you really think that this is a painting of the severed head of John the Baptist?" Robin asked. "Done from life—or rather from death—I mean?"

Mallory grinned at her.

"As you hinted a couple of minutes ago, there's a very obvious date problem if it is. John the Baptist, assuming he was a real historical figure at all, which is by no means certain, died in the first half of the first century AD. This picture dates from well over a thousand years after that, if the radiocarbon dating of the wood is accurate, and it almost certainly is, because it's such a well-established technique. So the short answer has to be no. But what it could be is an accurate copy of an original painting that was done at the time of John's death. Maybe the Templars held the original artwork somewhere, and just had copies of it painted for each of their commanderies and preceptories, where it could be revered and even worshipped, just as in a Christian church the congregation worships the crucified Christ. They're both icons or idols, just different people.

"In fact," he went on, warming to the idea, "that could tie up with what little we think we know about Templar ceremonies. They were supposed to worship a disembodied head, an idol they called Baphomet, and that's a name that doesn't sound all that different to Baptist, actually, at least in English. So perhaps that is what this image displays. Maybe this is the Baphomet image for the Templar establishment here in Templecombe. This could be what they worshipped, in which case it would certainly have originally been on display here in the church, probably somewhere near the altar. It's come home, so to speak, after about seven hundred years. It's just in the wrong position in the building, and now it's an unusual piece of decorative art, not an object of veneration."

"In that case," Robin said, "we definitely need to see the back of the wooden panel, just in case there *is* something written on it."

34

Templecombe, Somerset

Mallory glanced over toward the altar, where the group of obvious tourists appeared to be preparing to leave, some members already starting to drift away toward the door. A couple of minutes later, the last of them left the building, and as they did so, the rector walked over to where Robin and Mallory were standing.

He was a tall, spare man, wearing a dark suit that hung loosely from his narrow shoulders. The black shirt and clerical collar both looked several sizes too big for him, and his neck protruded from the shirt in a manner somewhat reminiscent of a tortoise's head extending from its shell, an impression somehow reinforced by his prominent Adam's apple. His thin face was topped with a sparse thatch of graying hair, his forehead underlined by a pair of impressively bushy gray eyebrows.

"I really need to close up quite soon," he said, "because

I have other appointments elsewhere today. Do you have any questions I can help you with?"

"It's not so much a question," Robin said, giving him the full benefit of her disarming smile, "more like a request."

"Try me," he replied. "My name's George Unwin, and I'm the rector here. And you are?"

"I'm Robin Jessop. I buy and sell old books, not that I'm here to do that today. And this is David Mallory, a good friend."

"Welcome to my church, both of you. A request, you said?"

Robin nodded.

"I know it's slightly unusual, but we're both very interested in this old painting and we wondered if it would be possible to lift it off the wall so that we could examine its reverse, the back of the wooden panel."

The rector's eyebrows rose in perfect synchronization, and a look of bemusement crossed his face.

"I've been asked a lot of questions about the Head over the years," he replied, "and there are a couple of things that have always interested me about it. Things that suggest that perhaps the painting was originally on display somewhere, most probably even here in the church, though I can't prove that, obviously. And I've had a few odd requests from visitors, as you'd expect, but never that. May I ask why you would possibly want to do such a thing?"

"We think there could be an inscription or something on the back of the wood panel that could help date it, and perhaps even give a clue to the identity of the subject."

Unwin glanced at Mallory, who so far hadn't said a word to him, then shifted his gaze back to Robin.

"No," he said simply. "I'm sorry, but you can't do that. The painting is fragile enough as it is, and I can't allow anything to be done to it that would jeopardize it in any way. And, besides, it would be pointless."

"Why pointless?" Mallory asked.

Unwin shook his head.

"The Head wasn't just stuck in that frame and hung on the wall," he said. "Obviously it was examined very carefully before that was done, and I can assure you that the reverse of the panel is absolutely unmarked."

Robin's face fell, but Mallory just looked irritated.

"I don't know where this theory of yours came from," Unwin went on, "but I can assure you that it's completely wrong. And I can prove it."

"How?" Robin asked the obvious question.

"I have high-resolution photographs of both sides of the panel that were taken before it was placed in the case. In fact, I keep a set of those pictures here in the church to show people who want to study the Head. Getting decent photographs of it is difficult because of reflections on the glass in front of it. Mind you, most visitors are usually only interested in the face itself, not the back of the panel. But if you follow me I'll show you."

"Hang on a minute," Mallory interrupted. "You said you thought the Head might at one time have been displayed here in the church. What made you think that?"

"It's not the actual Head per se," Unwin replied,

"more the condition of the wood and what the marks on it might suggest."

"You mean the keyhole and the marks left by hinges?" Robin suggested.

Unwin looked slightly surprised.

"You *have* done your research," he said. "Yes, exactly that. One popular theory is that the wooden panel might just have been cobbled into use as the door of some domestic cupboard, in a house somewhere here in the village, but to me that seems pretty unlikely. I'm quite certain that even the most uneducated and uncultured person would have been able to recognize the painting as something special, even if they had no idea of its history or purpose. Not that we actually know anything very much about it, either, even today, but you know what I mean."

"So, what do you think happened to it?" Mallory asked.

"This is only my opinion"—Unwin sounded almost embarrassed—"and not one that's shared by many—or even any—of my ecclesiastical colleagues, iconography still being something of a controversial subject in the Church. But I've never quite understood why it's considered perfectly normal to have a picture or a statue of Christ dying in agony on the cross but not an image of Him as he would have appeared in life. And there's another factor that reinforces my opinion. This church was constructed by the Knights Templar, as I'm sure you already know, and it's quite well established that their tradition was to not display a halo in paintings of Jesus, so it's most probably a Templar image."

"So, you think this is a picture of Jesus?" Robin asked. "It doesn't look much like the conventional images of Him that we've got used to."

"Obviously I can't know for sure, but I believe it's at least a possibility, though the absence of a halo is a potential problem if the painting wasn't owned or commissioned by the Templars. Don't forget that the classic image of Jesus, a handsome bearded man with long hair, that we now have is a fairly late development, probably dating from the medieval period or thereabouts. The earliest paintings were based on the handful of contemporary verbal descriptions of Christ, as a man with an entirely different appearance— short, squat, and almost ugly—and they are much closer in appearance to this portrait. So, to answer your question, yes, I think this could quite easily be a medieval copy, probably Templar, of a very early portrait of Jesus."

"But what about the hinges and the lock—or the keyhole, I should say?"

Unwin smiled at Robin.

"This might sound a bit unusual, but I suspect that at one point the painting was mounted in this church, probably somewhere near the altar, where it could be seen by the congregation, and most likely covering a shallow cupboard where items of some value were stored, perhaps some of the church silver, for example. That would explain both the hinges and the lock. While the cupboard was closed it would display the face of our savior, perhaps as a more authentic representation than most of the other images we have become familiar with. And that would also seem to me to be a far more likely location for the painted panel than the front of some villager's pot cupboard or something similar. Whatever its history, and whoever it's supposed to represent, I think the painting is very obviously religious rather than secular in concept and execution."

That certainly piqued Mallory's interest.

"That does make sense," he said. "Have you any idea where that cupboard might have been located? And why the painting then ended up in the roof of a village outhouse?"

The rector shook his head.

"No to both, I'm afraid. The church was extensively renovated during the Victorian period, and my guess is that if there ever was such a cupboard, it was probably removed when that work was being done. And over the years tastes and customs change, so perhaps the painting was thought unnecessary or even vulgar or inappropriate by the church authorities and disposed of. Or maybe it was removed when most of this parish was confiscated from the Templars after the order was purged in the early part of the fourteenth century and their properties handed to the Hospitallers. Or it could have been lost much more recently. Perhaps it was even stolen from the church. I really have no idea, and neither has anyone else. Unfortunately both the church and the village archives are noticeably silent on the subject of the painting."

And that seemed to be more or less the end of that. It looked to Mallory as if the trail that had started with the discovery of an ancient lost manuscript inside a booby-trapped book safe had come to a sudden, unexpected, and final end in a little-used country church in a tiny village deep in rural England.

Mallory glanced at Robin and shook his head. If they'd read the clues correctly, whatever the next link had been in the chain they were following, it was now lost and gone forever, probably swept away unnoticed during the Victorian renovation of the building.

"Come with me," Unwin said, recognizing their mood change, "and I'll show you those photographs. Just to satisfy your curiosity."

He led the way to a narrow side door and opened it.

They followed him into a small white-painted room that clearly served various different purposes. On one wall were several coat pegs on which a number of garments were hanging, from their appearance presumably used during church services of one sort or another, while most of the floor was occupied by anonymous cardboard boxes piled one on top of another. At one end was a small wooden desk and a single padded swivel chair, the surface of the desk covered in papers, and a small wooden crucifix mounted on the wall a short distance above it, where anyone sitting at the desk would be able to see it at eye level.

"This is my robing room and occasional office," Unwin explained. "I visit a number of different churches in this area, and it's often helpful to leave clothes and other things here."

He stepped over to the desk, pulled open one of the drawers on the right-hand side, and pulled out a large brown photographic envelope, the backing stiffened with cardboard. He opened it and extracted the contents.

"Here we are," he said, clearing a space on the desk and fanning out the photographs. "These show the Head itself, and these are what most people want to look at. These other half dozen images just show the reverse, and, as you can see, the wood is unmarked, nothing carved on it, and no sign there was ever anything written in ink or painted on it."

Robin and Mallory bent forward over the desk and stared at the pictures. As they did so, the muffled sound of conversation from the main part of the church gradually became audible. Unwin turned around and headed for the door.

"More visitors," he said. "Excuse me while I tell them I'm shutting the church in a few minutes."

The door closed behind the rector as he left the room.

"He's right," Robin said, staring down at the photographs and sounding utterly dispirited. "There's nothing at all on any of these photographs, apart from the usual blemishes you get on any piece of wood. I really thought we'd cracked it with that 'behind the eyes' clue. We've obviously missed something, or misinterpreted it. I hate to say it, but this really could be the end of the trail."

"Quiet," Mallory said urgently. "Listen."

Robin glanced up at his face, but Mallory was giving all his attention to what he was hearing from outside the room.

Voices raised in anger, or making threats. It was impossible to tell which. But something was very obviously wrong.

And then they both heard a loud and echoing bang that could only be one thing.

35

"That was a gunshot," Mallory said. "It must be those bloody Dominicans. I mean, who else could it be?"

He reached around to the small of his back, pulled out the Browning Hi-Power pistol he'd acquired from one of the hired assassins who'd tried to take them down on the road outside Okehampton what felt like half a lifetime ago. He racked the slide back to chamber a round and set the safety catch.

"I didn't know you had that with you," Robin said.

"Just as well I did. You wait here. There's a phone on the wall over there. Dial triple nine and get the cops and the medical people heading this way. Tell them there's been a shooting."

"We don't know what's happened yet."

"I think I can guess. Those Italians don't fire warning

shots. Unwin's dead or at least wounded, and the Head has probably gone by now."

Mallory eased the door open silently and peered outside. He saw nothing. He glanced back at Robin, who was already reaching for the wall-mounted phone, then slipped out of the room.

He ran as quickly and quietly as he could across to the opposite wall, from the corner of which he would be able to see the main part of the church, including the wall upon which the Templecombe Head was hanging.

Or, as he realized immediately when he took a quick glance around the corner, where the Templecombe Head had previously been hanging, because it was no longer there. The wall was bare, and a few feet away, lying curled in a ball on the old stone floor of the church, was a black-clad figure. But there was no sign of the Dominicans whom Mallory had expected to be there.

He again checked that the safety catch was engaged on the Browning, then slid the pistol back into the rear waistband of his trousers and ran forward.

Mallory knelt beside the rector. He had no need to feel for a pulse, because the man was audibly groaning, and clearly still alive. His hands were clutched to his stomach, his whole body seeming to be folded in on itself, as if the bullet that had wounded him had tripped some kind of internal hinge. A spreading deep red stain on the floor attested to the seriousness of his injury. Mallory could see at once that Unwin had been shot in the stomach, one of the most painful of all gunshot wounds. Excruciatingly painful, but not necessarily fatal if expert medical treatment was available quickly.

"Who did this?" Mallory asked urgently.

But the rector didn't respond, his eyes closed and his mouth clamped shut as his mind and body struggled to come to terms with the incredible pain he was experiencing.

Mallory knew there was nothing he could do for him, there being no first aid he could render for that kind of injury. Or, rather, he had already done all that he could by getting Robin to scramble a medical team. He stood up, took out the pistol again, and ran over to the open door of the old church.

Not knowing how far away the Dominicans would be, he slammed to a halt inside the doorway and looked cautiously outside.

About thirty or forty yards away, two bulky men wearing dark clothes were struggling under the weight of the large wooden box that obviously contained the Templecombe Head, another man, similarly garbed, walking briskly beside them.

As Mallory edged forward to get a better view, the man apparently acting as an escort looked back and saw him.

The recognition was instant. Mallory had last seen the Italian on the side of a hill in Switzerland, standing alongside Toscanelli, the psychopathic leader of the group, the Dominicans temporarily rendered harmless by the Swiss authorities. And the Italian equally obviously recognized him.

The Dominican enforcer turned on his heel, immediately pulled out a pistol and aimed it in one fluid movement, then squeezed the trigger twice. The first nine-millimeter bullet crashed into the old stone a couple of feet to Mallory's left as he ducked back inside; the second hit higher and slightly farther away.

Then the Dominican started running back toward the church, obviously intending to finish the job.

For Mallory, it wasn't a difficult decision. These men had just shot down the rector—an entirely innocent man—in cold blood as he'd presumably tried to stop them from robbing his church, and had basically left him for dead. And Mallory had no doubt that the enforcer would do his best to kill both him and Robin if he got the chance.

So he decided not to give him the chance. And at the same time to return the favor.

For a couple of seconds Mallory just watched him approaching; then he stepped back into view, raised his own pistol, locking his left hand around his right wrist in the classic Weaver stance.

The man skidded to a halt the instant Mallory appeared, perhaps stunned by the realization that the man he'd just tried to shoot was also armed. He again lifted his pistol.

Mallory didn't wait, just took careful aim and fired the moment the man stopped moving.

He had always been a good shot, and his bullet took the Dominican squarely in the stomach. The Italian staggered backward a couple of steps, the pistol falling from his grip, and then crashed heavily to the ground, letting out a piercing shriek of pain as he did so.

The two men carrying the wooden box glanced back over their shoulders, but continued on their way.

Mallory swung the heavy church door shut and slammed the bolt into place, just in case another of the Dominicans decided to come and try his luck. Then he bent down and picked up the ejected cartridge case—he didn't dare leave that behind him, just in case the police managed to find both him and the weapon—and ran back inside, to see Robin kneeling beside the injured rector.

"He's still alive," she said as he approached, "but in a lot of pain. And there's nothing we can do about that. What happened out there? I heard more shots."

"The Dominicans are now one man short," Mallory said, "and that means we have to get out of here right now, before the cops turn up. Otherwise, we'll really be in the shit."

And as he said that, they both heard the sound of another shot outside the church.

"They can't get in," he said. "I've bolted the door on the inside."

Mallory led the way, the pistol back in his hand, just in case. At the door, Robin slowly released the bolt, making as little noise as she could, then pulled the door open just far enough for Mallory to see outside.

"I think it's all clear," he said, stepping through the narrow gap and looking around the churchyard. "In fact, I'm pretty certain they've gone, because they've cleaned up after themselves."

"What do you mean?" Robin asked.

Mallory pointed at the unmoving figure lying on the grass, a ghastly red halo around his head.

"That's the Dominican I shot," he explained, "but I only wounded him and now he's clearly dead. Not only that, but his pistol has gone as well. That's what I meant by them clearing up after themselves."

"So, that last shot we heard," Robin said, but didn't finish the sentence.

"Exactly. One of them came back, executed the wounded man, and took his weapon, just to make sure that he couldn't talk to the police or anyone else. They did exactly the same thing in your apartment in Dartmouth right back at the start of all this."

There was nothing else they could do there, either for the wounded rector or for themselves. What they had to do was get as far away from what was now an obvious crime scene as soon as they could.

Mallory led the way out of the church tower, leaving the door open behind them, and they jogged along the path, past the dead body of the Dominican, and out of the gate. As soon as they reached the road, they slowed to a brisk walk and immediately turned off into a side street, because they could hear the distant sound of an approaching siren. The vehicle was probably already at the village limits.

"I hope that's an ambulance, not a patrol car," Mallory said, as they slowed to a gentle stroll. "I feel guilty about Unwin. I really hope he makes it."

"You didn't shoot him," Robin snapped, her eyes clouding with tears.

"No, but if we hadn't been there talking to him, the church would probably have been locked and he'd have been somewhere else and out of harm's way. That's what I mean."

About a minute later the noise of the siren died away, and with a roar from its engine an ambulance, lights blazing, swept past the end of the lane, heading straight for the church.

"What did you tell them when you dialed triple nine?"

"Just that a man had been shot in the church at Templecombe. And I left the phone off the hook so that they could confirm the location that way if they misheard me or anything."

"Good," Mallory said, glancing back. "Now let's get out of here."

The village was quite small—Mallory thought that the population was round about 1,500 people—and they only saw a few dozen of them as they made their way back to the road where Mallory had parked the Porsche. The local residents clearly seemed to have been attracted by the unusual noise of the sirens echoing around the village, as they were all either looking at or actually walking toward the church, where the ambulance had been joined by at least two police cars that they had both heard and seen.

And although he and Robin were doing their best to blend in with the scenery and not attract any unwanted attention, Mallory was keenly aware that he had a totally illegal loaded pistol stuck into the waistband of his jeans under his jacket, and even a rudimentary test of his hands would prove beyond doubt that he had fired that weapon or another firearm. So as well as keeping a lookout for the Dominican enforcers, they both knew only too well that they needed to stay away from the British police.

"If a police car stops anywhere near us," Mallory said,

as they both heard the sound of another siren approaching the village at speed, "we separate. You've got nothing incriminating on you, and you've done nothing wrong, so there's no legal reason why you should be detained. But if they stop me, then I am in trouble, because there's no way I can talk myself out of jail this time."

Robin shook her head decisively.

"I'll stick with you," she insisted.

"You won't," Mallory replied. "If you're with me, then the official view of the Thin Blue Line will be that you're an accessory before and after the fact, as they describe it, and so whatever mud gets slung at me will stick to you as well. And, frankly, you'd be a lot more use to me walking around outside the local police station, sorting out a sharp legal eagle to help me, than sitting in the same police station in the cell next door to mine. So if it looks as if we're attracting even the slightest sign of any official interest, you have to just walk away. If you don't, then I'll make a run for it anyway and that will ensure they chase me and leave you alone."

The expression on Robin's face showed that she didn't like it, but she did nod her reluctant agreement.

In any event, none of it mattered, because they reached the car without seeing a police vehicle anywhere near them, or any sign of the Dominicans. And this time, when Mallory unlocked the doors of the Porsche using the remote control, Robin held out her hand for the key.

"Just in case," she said firmly, dropping into the driving seat and starting the engine. "In this car, I can lose the Dominicans and any number of local rozzers, unless they put a chopper up after us. But let's hope I don't need to," she added.

"We should be okay," Mallory said. "I was involved in a few incidents like this when I was in the force, and I can almost guarantee that they won't be looking for anybody at the moment. Whenever somebody is wounded by an attacker, with a knife or a gun or whatever, their first priority is always to get the victim to hospital as quickly as possible, and only when that's been done will they start to take a proper look at the crime scene itself and try to work out what actually happened. Once they're satisfied about the probable sequence of events, they'll start doing house-to-house inquiries, appealing for witnesses and all that kind of thing. And by the time they start doing that, we could be in another county, or even in another country."

Robin was driving the Porsche in a general northerly direction away from Templecombe, traveling as fast as the road conditions allowed. When she saw signs ahead for the junction with the A303, she slowed down and glanced at Mallory.

"So, where are we going now?" she asked. "Back to the same hotel?"

"There's not really much point in doing that," he replied. "We checked out this morning, and all our stuff's with us in this car, so we can go wherever we like."

"Right," Robin replied, steering the Cayman to join the eastbound carriageway of the A303 toward Wincanton. "But that doesn't really answer the question, does it?" She sounded peeved. And almost resigned. "We still need to decide where we're going next and, even more importantly, what we're going to do next. Do we just give up, or do we go back to the drawing board and take another look at the clues we've uncovered so far? Because the one thing we definitely know right now is that we read that last one completely wrongly. The rear of the wooden panel was very obviously unmarked, and as far as I can see that pretty much means it's the end of the trail. There was nothing for us to find 'behind the eyes.' There might have been something on the wood a couple of hundred years ago before the Victorians got their hands on it, or maybe a piece of Latin text carved into some cupboard in the church, but whatever was there must have been swept away during the renovations."

"If it was a carving, if it was something chiseled into the stone of the church, it might still be there somewhere, just covered over with plaster or whatever," Mallory pointed out, "but that's exactly the same as it not being there at all, unless we could somehow identify the precise spot where the carving was done, and I have no idea how we could do that. Let's hope we missed something, or we read that last clue wrongly."

They batted the subject back and forth between them for the next few minutes, but reached no useful conclusion.

"Okay," Mallory said. "This isn't exactly a plan, but it's an idea. I still think the encrypted text was quite clear about Templecombe and the Head. That is where we were supposed to go. So why don't we find another hotel in this general area and stay there tonight? We can go over the stuff we decrypted again and look at it really closely. And if anything jumps out at us, we can go back there tomorrow or the next day, once the police presence has ended or at least diminished, and have another look around."

"I can pretty much guarantee that we won't be the only ones at the church if we do that," Robin said. "The shooting in the building will attract all the local ghouls and the sensation seekers. It'll probably be standing room only."

Mallory grinned at her.

"You're probably right," he agreed. "But that might actually help us. We could lose ourselves in the crowd and have a good snoop around without looking any different to everybody else there."

"We still need to lose ourselves," Robin said. "The biggest place around here is Warminster, so let's head over there and find somewhere to stay."

Mallory fell silent as Robin drove past Mere and headed toward the A360, the road that would take them north to Warminster. In his mind, he replayed, again and again, the violent events of the day, wondering if he should have acted differently, and decided eventually that he had done the right thing. The shooting of the rector was a despicable act by any standard, and he could think of no good reason why he shouldn't have visited the same level of injury in retribution. An eye for an eye, an appropriately biblical sense of justice.

Then he mentally switched his attention to the—as it turned out—abortive investigation. And a sudden realization dawned on him. Something that made such obvious sense that he was simply amazed that it hadn't occurred to either of them before. Something that he absolutely knew would have been blindingly obvious to the Templars as well.

And then he started to laugh.

36

"Over there. That'll do," Toscanelli instructed from the passenger seat of the leading car, pointing ahead, and the driver immediately touched the brake pedal and moved the indicator stalk, giving an obvious warning to the driver of the car behind of his intentions.

The two cars containing the Dominicans, their number now reduced by one because of what had happened in Templecombe, pulled to a halt in a lay-by—in reality nothing more than the wide triangular-shaped end of a little-used farm track—and all the men climbed out.

Toscanelli issued a brief instruction, and a few moments later they were standing around in a rough semi-circle looking at the glass-fronted wooden display case that held the enigmatic Templecombe Head.

"It's ugly," one of the men said. "The face, I mean."

"It may be," Toscanelli agreed, "but if our experts in

Rome are right, this painting holds the key to the lost treasure and the vast wealth of the cursed Templars. And we managed to snatch it away before Jessop and Mallory could get their hands on it."

"It's a shame about Salvatori," another of the men said, slowly and deliberately.

"He did the right thing," Toscanelli said, staring at him. "He did just as Vitale ordered. As soon as he recognized Mallory he opened fire at him. But neither he nor I expected the Englishman to be armed. He shot Salvatori and then bolted the church door. Once he did that, there was no way I could get inside and finish them off. That door was massive and it would have withstood almost any assault—that was what it was designed to do by the medieval carpenters who built it. So I had no choice. This is supposed to be a covert operation, and I was certain the British police were already on their way. Salvatori was badly wounded, and would probably have died even if we could have got him to a hospital. But we couldn't do that, for obvious reasons. Our instructions were quite clear about contact with the British authorities. We couldn't move Salvatori, so I did the only thing I could to ensure that he wouldn't talk. If it had been me who'd been shot by Mallory, I would have expected one of you to do the same to me."

The Dominican who'd made the comment didn't appear entirely convinced by Toscanelli's obvious justification for his actions, but looked away. Men who accompanied Toscanelli on missions tended to have a really short shelf life, as had been demonstrated on several occasions in the past.

"Right. Get it open. The information we need is on the back."

Two of the Italians produced screwdrivers and pliers and set to work opening up the wooden case. It didn't take long. The box had been designed to support and display an interesting curio on a church wall, not protect the contents from a determined attempt to open it. Within a few minutes, the case was open, and they could extract the ancient wooden panel bearing the image of the un-identified man's face.

"Turn it over," Toscanelli said, taking a compact digital camera from his pocket to record whatever information the reverse of the panel contained.

The two men who'd pulled the panel out of the box obeyed him, and rested the panel against the side of the car.

For a few moments there was complete silence. Then one of the Dominicans laughed briefly before lapsing into silence again.

The reverse of the panel was devoid of any markings whatsoever, exactly as George Unwin had told Robin and Mallory. In fact, there were a few marks and blemishes, just as there always were on any piece of wood, but nothing that in any way resembled letters, numbers, or recognizable shapes.

Toscanelli stared fixedly at it, almost as if he was daring some hidden message to somehow manifest itself, then shook his head and tucked the camera away again.

"And Salvatori died for *this*?"

He turned to look at the man who'd spoken.

"Be quiet," he snapped. "Let me look at it closely."

He stepped forward and bent to look at the panel, running the tips of his fingers over the wood, just in case there were any indentations that could form a part of a clue or message that was invisible to the naked eye. But he found nothing.

"This doesn't make sense," he muttered. "Everything pointed to this as the location of the next clue we needed to follow. I must talk to Vitale, and find out what he wants us to do now."

He produced his mobile and took three pictures of the blank reverse of the panel, and one of the painted face, and then used the phone's Internet connection to send them to the duty officer in Rome. He knew that Vitale was expecting to see the images as soon as possible, and guessed that he would have them displayed on his computer monitor within a matter of minutes.

Less than two minutes later, Toscanelli's mobile rang.

"I'm not impressed with this, Toscanelli," Vitale said, the tension in his voice obvious. "And I'm a lot less impressed that you left a dead man behind you at Templecombe."

"How did you know?"

"We have tertiaries everywhere," Vitale snapped. "Who was it?"

"Salvatori. He had no identification on his body and I removed his weapon. We had no option but to leave him. Mallory was carrying a pistol, which we hadn't expected, and shot him in the stomach. All I could do was finish him off."

"Just as you've done in the past. Several times," Vitale reminded him. "Who shot the rector? I know about that as well, and the only good news is that he will probably recover, so at least there isn't a murder hunt in progress for him as well as for Salvatori's killer."

"That was Salvatori."

"Poetic justice, I suppose. And now the panel turns out to be blank, unless you know something I don't."

"I don't," Toscanelli admitted. "We can see no signs of any writing or carvings or anything else on it. But we can ship it out to Rome today and let our experts examine it."

"Don't bother," Vitale instructed. "If you can see nothing on the panel, there's probably nothing there to see. The Templars were sophisticated for their time, but the chances of their being able to use invisible ink or something to inscribe a clue on the panel, a clue that would endure for over seven hundred years, are nil. If they put something on it, you'd be able to see it. That means we must have interpreted the clue wrongly, so we'll have to look at the decryption and translation again."

"So, what do you want us to do now?"

"Until we can work out what went wrong, nothing. Change your hire cars, just in case anyone saw you in them, and find somewhere to stay within about fifty kilometers of Templecombe. That part of the clue seemed clear enough, so the information we need has to be hidden there somewhere. It's now just a matter of working out where you should be looking next. Do not execute Mallory or Jessop, just in case they eventually lead us to the clue we need to follow."

"And the painted wooden panel?" Toscanelli asked.

"It's an important religious artwork and a small part of the history of Christianity, so treat it with the proper amount of care and respect. I gather it was displayed in a case, so put it back inside it, and then leave it somewhere near the village, so that it will look as if the thieves changed their minds about stealing it. But do not go back into Templecombe itself until I give you your new orders. The place will be full of British police for the next day or two at least while they clean up the mess you left there."

37

Warminster, Wiltshire

"I'm glad you think something is funny about all this," Robin said, as they entered the southern outskirts of Warminster.

"It's not funny, exactly," Mallory replied, "more a bit surprising that there's something that now seems so obvious to me that we both missed."

"Okay, I'll buy it. What, exactly, is obvious and what did we miss?"

"Just look back at the clues we've found so far. In fact, not the clues themselves but the mediums used to carry them. The parchment hidden away in that book safe. The images concealed in the metal scrollwork of those wooden chests. And then the sheet of vellum hidden in the false bottom of another medieval wooden chest."

"So what?"

"They were all chosen to last the centuries either by

virtue of their own strength or by being hidden inside secure containers. And neither of those criteria apply to the Templecombe Head. That was just a face painted on a piece of wood that was apparently kept somewhere in the village, but with no obvious effort made to protect it. At any time over the centuries somebody might have decided to break it up and use the wood for something else, or even chop it up for firewood. Knowing what we do about the Templars, I don't believe they would have entrusted a vital piece of information to something so potentially fragile and ephemeral, not to mention unprotected."

Robin nodded.

"That does make sense," she conceded. "So, do you mean we misread the clue completely, and we're actually in the wrong place?"

"No," Mallory said. "I think we were in exactly the right place when we went to Templecombe, but we were looking at the wrong thing when we got there. I think what we're trying to interpret is almost like a double clue. We worked out that the location had to include the word *Temple* or *Templar* in its name, because of the phrase 'the settlement named for us,' but that would still have left a lot of potential candidates. When we added in the other phrase, 'behind the eyes,' that pointed us straight to Templecombe, because as far as I know that's the only Templar establishment that still survives where there's a face, or a head. To me, nothing else makes sense."

"You mean, that's the double clue or whatever you called it?" Robin asked.

Mallory shook his head.

"No. I think the double clue is 'behind the eyes.' The first interpretation just confirmed that we should be looking at Templecombe, but the second meaning is actually telling us where to look. And it isn't at the Templecombe Head."

"It isn't? Then where should we be looking?"

"We've been thinking laterally, assuming that the phrase meant to look behind the Head, on the reverse of the painted face, but what I think we should be doing is taking the meaning of the expression quite literally. We need to look 'behind the eyes.' Not behind the face painted on the wooden panel, but somewhere much more substantial. What do you find 'behind the eyes'?"

"You've lost me," Robin said.

"No, I haven't. Just think literally. Behind your eyes and behind my eyes is exactly the same thing—the skull. Somewhere in or near the church at Templecombe there must be a carving of a skull or perhaps even a full skeleton, and when we find it I think we'll also find what we're looking for."

Robin said nothing for a few seconds, then nodded.

"That does make sense," she said, "in a strange kind of way. And you're right. A stone carving—I assume that's what you're talking about—would last a whole lot longer than a painting on a piece of wood. But do you actually know if there is anything like that back in Templecombe?"

"No, but skulls and skeletons have always been quite common motifs on gravestones and in churches, so I'd be quite surprised if we didn't find one, maybe even a few of them, at the church. But if we go back there and find nothing, then obviously this is something else that I've guessed wrong."

On the southern outskirts of Warminster, they picked a small hotel with a car park that was behind the main building and screened from passing traffic by thick hedges. Robin parked the car in the farthest corner, out of sight from the road; then they carried their bags into the building and booked a double room on the first floor.

Mallory put their bags on the bed and then washed his hands and forearms thoroughly in the bathroom sink to try to remove all traces of cordite from his skin, to get rid of the indisputable evidence that would prove he had fired a pistol. Then he cleaned and reloaded the weapon itself before tucking it away in his computer bag. Because of what had happened that day, he was determined that the Browning had to remain out of sight but close at hand.

38

Templecombe, Somerset

The following morning they drove back to Templecombe and again parked in a quiet lane on the outskirts of the village, where the Porsche Cayman would, they hoped, be less likely to attract attention and be remembered by anyone.

They strolled hand in hand through the village, making toward the church, trying to look like any other young couple out to enjoy the fine weather. Over one shoulder Mallory had slung a rucksack, newly purchased at a camping store in Warminster, inside which was what he hoped was a useful selection of tools—a hammer, a folding metal shovel that apparently had military aspirations because it had been sold as a "trenching tool," a short jimmy, a large screwdriver, and the like—also bought that morning. They hadn't known what to expect, so Mallory had suggested they come prepared. In one of the side pockets of the rucksack, hidden underneath a pair of heavy-duty gloves, was the Browning, invisible on a casual inspection but still accessible in a few moments if the need arose. They both hoped it wouldn't.

"Nearly there," Robin said, as the gray tower came into view around a corner. "What do we do if the place is stuffed to the rafters with police and forensics teams?"

"We do just what the song says—we walk on by. Then we find a café or somewhere we can get a drink or even a late breakfast, and come back later when hopefully they'll have gone. But let's wait and see. They might already have finished."

They hadn't.

When Robin and Mallory reached the end of the churchyard, they saw a uniformed constable standing just inside the gate behind a couple of strands of blue-and-white police tape that barred the entrance. Beyond the constable, a line of hunched figures was visible, moving slowly across the short-cropped grass of the churchyard. The dead body of the Dominican enforcer had obviously already been removed, probably the previous day.

"They're doing a fingertip search," Mallory murmured as they approached, "and it looks like they've nearly finished, because they're getting close to the wall around the churchyard. They're probably looking for cartridge cases or bullets, any bits of evidence they might be missing from the shooting."

It was obvious that they wouldn't be able to get into the churchyard, far less the church, until the search was complete, so they just walked past the uniformed sentinel and continued down the road. They didn't find a café, but the local pub already had its doors open and a sign outside promised coffee, so they walked in and sat down. When the barman appeared from whatever back room he'd been in, Mallory ordered two coffees and a couple of wrapped muffins. They weren't the best they'd ever tasted, but the coffee was hot, and that was more important.

About an hour later, they walked out of the building and back toward the church, and this time the searchers were nowhere in sight. The police constable was just removing the lengths of tape, scrunching them up and putting them into a black garbage sack. As he strode away, the sack in his hand, Mallory led the way into the churchyard.

They walked across to the door set into the base of the tower, but as they'd both expected it was locked.

"I wonder how Unwin is," Robin said, as they turned away.

"With a bit of luck he'll make it. He was probably on the operating table within about two hours of being shot, so that would give him a good chance of survival. With wounds like that, time really is of the essence."

"I'm slightly surprised there aren't any ghouls snapping pictures and rubbernecking about the place. At least we'll be able to have a good look around without being interrupted. What about getting inside the church, though? Isn't that a more likely location for this skull thing you think we need to find?"

"Not necessarily. Churches, like every other kind of structure, occasionally need repair or renovation, even though the fabric of the building will usually remain the same, and I'm sure the Templars would have known that. But graves are only very rarely touched, because they are the last resting places of friends and family members. So I hope we're more likely to find what we want out here, rather than inside the church."

At some time in the past the area in front of the tower had obviously been used as a graveyard, as was confirmed by a number of ancient upright gravestones and what looked like the tops of some underground crypts that projected above the grass.

Mallory gestured at the nearest of the old stones.

"Let's make a start here," he said.

His prediction was right: there were a lot of gravestones that included the shape of a skull, often with crossed leg bones as well in a kind of pale imitation of the classic pirate flag. Each time they saw anything like that, they stopped and examined both the front and back of the gravestone carefully, but saw nothing that seemed in any way helpful to their quest.

"Let's have a look at the crypts, or whatever these stone structures are," Mallory suggested, sounding both hot and frustrated. "They might be a more likely location anyway, because they're obviously a lot bigger than a standing tombstone. There's more space on them to hide a clue."

They walked over to one of the biggest, half-buried in the grass of the churchyard and lying in front of the gray stone tower. That yielded nothing that looked even slightly like the shape of a skull, nor did the raised burial chamber that lay even closer to the church and to the right of the tower itself.

"There are a few more over on the far side of the church," Robin said, "though this is beginning to look like a bit of a wild-goose chase to me."

They walked over toward the other small crypts she'd indicated, and began to examine each of them just as carefully as they'd inspected the standing tombstones. But, again, although several of them bore weathered carvings that resembled skulls, and in a couple of cases complete skeletons, none of the crypts yielded anything else. They found no anomalous markings that could have been construed as a piece of text or anything else even slightly helpful to their quest.

And then Robin spotted something that looked slightly out of place, or at least unusual. At one end of a half-buried crypt she noticed a carving. In fact, really just the outline of a carving, because the stone was badly weathered.

"Does that shape look even faintly familiar to you?" she asked. "There, on the end of that crypt."

Mallory looked where she was pointing, and shook his head.

"Not really, no. It's certainly not a skull."

"I know that," Robin replied, somewhat testily. "But we are looking for a Templar tomb, or at least a tomb that dates from the time when the Templars owned this area, aren't we?"

"Yes, obviously."

"Well," she said, pointing at the shape she'd seen, "I know that's not a skull, but it does look to me like a carving of a horse, and there are definitely two people riding on it. And that is one of the classic Templar motifs. So at least we know this stone is the right kind of age."

"True enough."

They walked over to the stone crypt and knelt down to examine it more closely.

The carved shape was more or less in the center of the end panel of the tomb, and appeared almost to be framed by two carved diagonal shapes that ran from the upper corners of the stone down toward the ground, almost like an uncompleted letter *V*. Where they reached ground level they terminated in the top of a curved object that looked immediately familiar to both of them. And the lumpy but rounded upper ends of the diagonal shapes more or less confirmed it.

"I know what this looks like," Mallory said, his voice tinged with excitement.

"So do I," Robin agreed. "We're looking at the top half of a carving of two crossed thigh bones, and my guess is that the curved shape that's almost buried in the ground is the upper part of a skull. It's a skull and crossbones, in fact."

"That pretty much confirms the link with the Templars."

"It does? How?" Robin sounded surprised.

"It goes back to Jacques de Molay. There's a story that when he was burned alive in Paris as a relapsed heretic—meaning somebody who'd confessed under torture to whatever his interrogators wanted, but then recanted his confession once the torture stopped—his thigh bones and skull were pulled out of the ashes of the pyre by three

Knights Templar, and then became something of a symbol of the order, usually surmounted by a skull. As we know, the skull and crossbones later came to be used by pirates on their flag, the Jolly Roger, but the origins of it do seem to date back to the early part of the fourteenth century. In fact, almost every pirate had his own version of the flag, but the skull-and-bones symbol was a part of virtually every one. Mind you, there's another story, that the bones of de Molay and Geoffroi de Charney, who was executed alongside the Grand Master, were collected by King Philip's men after the execution, ground up, and then tossed into the river Seine. In reality, nobody knows what happened."

"Didn't Jacques de Molay curse the pope and the French king when he was executed, and they both died within the year?"

Mallory shook his head.

"That's a myth. It's true that both of the men who were responsible for the ending of the Templar order did die within a year, but that specific story of the curse wasn't recorded anywhere until something like two or three hundred years later—I can't remember exactly when—which almost certainly means it was made up to fit the facts. According to an eyewitness to the execution, Jacques de Molay did claim that God would avenge their deaths, but that was all."

Mallory stood up straight, glanced around, but saw nobody anywhere near the churchyard. He slipped the rucksack off his shoulder, opened it, and took out the collapsible shovel. He snapped the handle into place and again checked that they were unobserved. The solid bulk of the church meant that there were only a couple of places where a passerby could see them at all.

"Keep your eyes open," he said. "I'm going to do a bit of unauthorized gardening, so yell out if anyone starts taking an interest."

He rammed the blade of the shovel into the grass a few inches clear of the rounded shape they could see and levered up the turf to expose the earth beneath it. Then he drove the blade down into the ground and started shifting the earth itself. The soil was hard packed, but largely free of stones, which would have made the task that much more difficult, and within a couple of minutes Mallory had cleared most of the earth from the carved shape, which they could now clearly see was a skull.

"There's a brush in my bag," he said. "Could you pass it to me, please?"

Robin rooted around and then handed Mallory a two-inch brush with stiff bristles.

Kneeling down beside the hole he'd made, he quickly used the brush to clear the last traces of the soil from the carved-stone skull. Then he bent even farther forward to examine it closely.

"Can you see anything?" Robin asked, peering over his shoulder.

"I'm not sure. The stone is very discolored from being covered with earth for so long."

"Any writing or anything like that?"

"Not as far as I can tell, no. But there is— No, hang on a minute. That's a bit odd."

"What is?"

"It's the skull. The shape of it, I mean."

"You're not making sense," Robin said irritably. "Tell me what you mean."

"The skull," Mallory said again. "It's kind of rounded. Most skulls are more elongated in shape."

"So?" Robin asked, an even greater edge to her voice. "So what?"

"It looks like there's a line around it. As if the skull had been carved as a separate unit and then attached to the stone. But I don't know why that would have been done. I would have expected the carving to be all one piece."

"Is that all?"

Mallory sat back on his haunches and shook his head.

"I think it is. No text, no inscription. Nothing useful, as far as I can see. Maybe we're in the wrong place, or in the right place looking at the wrong thing."

"Or maybe you're missing the obvious."

"What?"

"There's a very obvious reason why the shape of the skull would be circular rather than elongated. And why there might be a line around it."

Mallory had no idea where she was going with that.

"What do you mean?"

"According to the text we've translated, the text that has brought us this far, somewhere here there's supposed to be this license or permission or whatever it is. That's not the kind of thing that could be carved into a piece of stone. Or at least I don't think it is. I think we should be looking for a container of some sort. So do you think that the skull could be a lid or cover, something that you could just lever off? And that there could be a cavity behind it?"

Mallory leaned forward again and looked closely at the carving, and used the brush to clean it as much as he could.

"Maybe," he said. "It is a distinct line, with no breaks that I can see. It's definitely worth a try."

He turned back to Robin, who had already anticipated what he would most probably need and was offering him the jimmy and the heavy screwdriver, holding one in each hand.

"Choose your weapon," she said.

Mallory picked the jimmy, because its curved shape would allow him—he hoped—to insert the point of the tool behind the edge of the carved-stone skull and then use the curve as a lever against the edge of the crypt to shift the stone.

He slid the point in, rammed his closed fist against the other end of the tool a few times to try to seat it as firmly as he could, then applied pressure to attempt to lever out the carved stone. For a few seconds, nothing happened, and then there was a sharp crack and the jimmy slammed into the stone of the crypt.

"Is that it?" Robin asked eagerly, leaning forward to see what had happened.

Mallory looked down into the opening he had created and shook his head.

"No. All that's happened is a sliver of stone from the carved skull has cracked off. I don't know if we're going to be able to shift this or not without a lot more digging.

I really need to be able to apply pressure all round the skull, to ease it out slowly. The only good news is that you were right—the skull is definitely an insert, not an integral part of the crypt. Where that piece of stone cracked off I can see the join quite easily."

He positioned the jimmy a few inches farther around the skull and prepared to apply pressure once more, but then Robin stopped him.

"What?" he asked.

"I don't think it pulls out," she said, "or not like that, anyway."

She pointed at the skull.

"See how deep the eye sockets are? The holes go inches down into the stone, and the skull is completely circular. I don't think you lever the skull off to free it. I think you turn it, and probably when it was placed there originally the Templars or whoever stuck a piece of wood or something into each eye socket to give them something to grip hold of so they could turn it easily."

Again, Mallory was grateful for Robin's sharp eyes and almost instant grasp of a situation.

He hadn't got any suitable lengths of wood—or any wood at all, in fact—but what he had got was a pair of heavy-duty pliers with rubber-covered handles. He took the tool out of his rucksack, opened the jaws wide, and then drove the handles as deep as he could into the stone eye sockets. Then he picked up the jimmy again, inserted the end of it between the handles of the pliers, and tried to turn the head using this makeshift combination.

It was awkward work, because he had to use one hand

to keep the pliers firmly in place while turning the jimmy with his other hand. And, just as with his first effort at levering the stone skull out, nothing happened.

"Try going the other way," Robin suggested. "Clockwise rather than anticlockwise. As soon as you see any movement, we'll know which way you have to turn it."

Mallory changed the position of the jimmy and again applied a turning force to the carved stone. And this time there was movement. Barely perceptible, and accompanied by the unmistakable sound of stone moving against stone, but movement nonetheless.

"That's the right way," Robin said, "but just be careful. You know how much the Templars—or at least the people who left this trail for us to follow—liked their booby traps. Don't, for God's sake, just sit there in front of it any longer."

That was undeniably good advice. Every time Robin and Mallory had stumbled across one of the ancient Templar secrets, they had also had to contend with some kind of lethal defense mechanism. And they had no reason to suppose that this Templar relic would behave any differently.

Mallory stood up and changed position completely so that he was beside the end of the crypt and leaning down and over it to remove the carved stone. That made it even more difficult to hold the pliers in place while he used the jimmy, but slowly, a fraction of an inch at a time, the stone skull began to rotate.

When it had turned through about twenty degrees, it became noticeably easier to rotate, and Mallory removed the pliers and placed the jimmy to one side. He opened up his rucksack again, this time the side pocket, and pulled out the pair of heavy work gloves.

"They should provide some protection if the stone's coated with poison or something like that."

Robin looked doubtful.

"In our experience so far, the Templar booby traps have tended to be violent and mechanical," she said. "I don't think they believed in using anything quite as subtle as poison. So just be careful."

"I will. And you keep well clear while I do this."

Mallory shifted position so that he was almost lying on the top of the crypt, leaning down to shift the stone with his gloved hands at full stretch. Before he did anything else, he checked that Robin was still well out of danger, standing a few feet behind him and to one side of the ancient stone structure.

"Here goes," he said.

He gripped the skull as firmly as he could with the gloves, and continued rotating it steadily in a clockwise direction.

It began moving even more easily, and then, quite suddenly, the stone was torn out of his hands by some unseen force, and the whole crypt vibrated as a hidden mechanism did its deadly work.

39

Somerset

Marco Toscanelli normally did precisely what Silvio Vitale told him to, working on the very sound basis that if he did so his life expectancy was likely to be significantly longer than if he disobeyed the man in charge of the organization.

But just occasionally he "interpreted" his orders in a way that allowed for a certain amount of flexibility. On that day, his particular concern was that Mallory and Jessop might return to Templecombe well before Vitale expected. In fact, they might even turn up there while the police were still investigating the crime scene. And if that happened, they might well discover whatever the real clue was in the village.

The experts in Rome had deduced that "behind the eyes" was most probably a reference to the reverse of the painted wooden panel known as the Templecombe Head, and they'd clearly been wrong about that. Mallory and Jessop—or certainly Mallory—had probably known that, because he or they were already inside the church, presumably talking to the vicar or whoever he was, the little man who'd tried to stop them from taking the relic and been shot for his pains, when Toscanelli's men had appeared. And if they had known that the panel didn't hold the answer, it was at least possible that they might work out where the answer actually was. If they did that, it would be a disaster and the Dominicans would once again be reduced to playing catch-up, following the English couple instead of leading the race.

So it was essential, in Toscanelli's view, that he get some eyes on the ground in Templecombe sooner rather than later.

Vitale had specifically ordered him not to return to the village until the British police had left the area. That, Toscanelli knew, was intended as a blanket command meaning that all of the group should stay away, but he hadn't specifically said that. So when he told three of the team to get in their car and drive back to Templecombe, he rationalized that he was bending the rules rather than actually breaking them.

The instructions he gave them were very specific.

"Lucca, you are to stay in the car at all times, just in case you need to get out of there in a hurry. You two, Mario and Michele, are to find yourselves vantage points in the village where you can watch out for Mallory and Jessop. If you see them, just watch them."

"I thought Vitale had issued a kill order against them?"

"He had, but it's been temporarily rescinded because the wooden panel didn't contain the information our experts thought it would. So for now we just let them live in case they lead us to what we're looking for. But if they do find it while you're watching them, the moment you're certain—and I do mean completely certain—that they have cracked it, all bets are off and you can take them out.

"But before you do that, you call me and tell me what you've seen."

40

Templecombe, Somerset

Mallory rolled off the top of the crypt when the entire structure shuddered, throwing himself backward and—he hoped—out of danger.

"Are you okay?" Robin asked.

"Yes. I just thought moving would be marginally safer than staying still," Mallory replied. "So, what happened?"

"Let's find out."

They walked around to the end of the crypt and looked down. The carved-stone skull was lying on its side about eighteen inches away from the hole where it had been placed some seven hundred years earlier, but that wasn't what attracted their immediate attention.

Projecting over three feet out of the circular hole in the end of the crypt was a lance. Usually such weapons consisted of an iron or steel head with a double-edged blade attached to a wooden shaft. This one was different.

The head, the business end, of the weapon was metal, but so was the rest of it, making it unusually heavy and almost indestructible in the largely airless interior of the crypt. The only sign of its age was a light sprinkling of rust on the surface of the iron. Obviously removing the carved skull had triggered an ancient mechanism that included a powerful spring that had driven the metal lance out of the hole in the end wall of the crypt.

"If I'd still been sitting there," Mallory said, and shook his head, "I'd have ended up as a kebab."

"I know," Robin said quietly. "Is it safe now, do you think?"

"Probably."

But just as a precaution, he picked up the jimmy, climbed back onto the stone top of the crypt, looped the end of the tool around the shaft of the spear, and tugged it a few times. Nothing happened. The metal spear was locked rigidly into the fired position, as far as he could tell.

"I think that's it," he said. "Somebody who didn't know about the possibility of a booby trap would be dead, which was the intention. Let's see what we have here."

The base of the carved skull was circular, as they had expected, but had a couple of broad grooves cut around its circumference. A glance into the hole in the crypt showed that these had mated with corresponding lands carved into the stone interior: a simple but effective locking system.

Robin turned the skull upside down and looked at it.

"It's not solid stone," she said, her voice rising with excitement. "There's a cavity inside the skull and there's something hidden in it."

Her slim hand reached down toward the hollow interior, but almost immediately she stopped.

"Bad idea," she said. "There could be some sort of nasty lurking in there as well."

Mallory passed her the pliers, and she used them to probe inside and grip whatever had been concealed within the hollow skull. But as she glanced at the small leather-covered package she had retrieved, before she slipped it into her bag to examine later, she noticed something else.

Both the base of the skull and the stone around the circular hole in the end of the crypt bore lines of tiny neatly chiseled letters.

"That has to be the next clue," Robin said, pulling out her mobile phone and taking a series of pictures of what she had spotted, ensuring she got at least three photographs of each section of the text.

Mallory did the same, with both his digital camera and his mobile, because the more records they had of it, the better. Then he put his hands around the shaft of the spear and tried to push it back inside the crypt, but it simply wouldn't budge. Whatever mechanism had been tripped to release the weapon had obviously also locked it in place.

"We're going to have to leave it like this," Mallory said. "I can't shift it."

"That's irritating," Robin replied, "because that means those bloody Dominicans will be able to read the text the same as us, so the race is still on."

And as she spoke, a shot rang out, the sound of the gun firing occurring at the same instant that the bullet plowed into the top of the crypt, sending stone chips flying in all directions.

Thirty seconds earlier Mario Donatu had ended a call to Toscanelli, explaining exactly what he had just seen taking place in the churchyard, everything from Mallory's initial removal of the section of turf to the triggering of the hidden booby trap and the way the targets had taken pictures of the stone skull and the end of the crypt. That, Toscanelli had agreed, almost certainly meant that the English couple had located the next clue. And that, inevitably, meant that their lives were expendable from that moment onward.

Mario's only mistake had been to fire his first shot at them from over forty yards away, much too far for accurate pistol shooting.

Realistically the maximum accurate range of most semiautomatic pistols, including Mario's Beretta, is about thirty yards. Beyond that, the short barrels of these weapons, barrels to which the sights aren't attached, mean that accurate shot placement is difficult even for an expert. Revolvers are much more accurate because of their design, but aren't as common in military or law enforcement roles because of their slow firing and reload rate and the limited number of rounds they hold. In most firefights, the more rounds, the better, and the high-capacity magazine and the instant reload facility of an automatic pistol usually outweigh all other considerations.

His second shot was closer, but not much, and by then his targets were no longer in sight.

*   *   *

Mallory reacted instantly, diving behind the solid and demonstrably bulletproof stone of the crypt, but Robin actually got there first. Not only that, but she'd also somehow managed to grab Mallory's rucksack on her way down.

"I don't like being shot at," she said, reaching into the side pocket of the rucksack and pulling out the Browning Hi-Power.

She racked the slide back to chamber a round, clicked off the safety catch, and crawled to the end of the crypt. She risked a quick glance, looking for a target, and snapped off a single shot toward a black-haired figure wearing a dark suit and standing behind the boundary wall of the churchyard. He ducked out of sight, and she didn't even bother to see where her shot had landed.

"I can only see one man," she said, "but my guess is that there are at least two of them, because I don't believe they'd send only one man here. So we need to get out of this place before we're caught in the cross fire with nowhere to go but into a couple of body bags."

"Can't argue with that," Mallory said. "If we can get across to the wall of the church, we'll be out of sight from where he's standing. Give me the pistol and I'll make sure he keeps his head down while you run for it."

"I'm a better shot than you are," Robin said. "You go."

"No chance. And at this range, accuracy really doesn't matter."

Robin didn't respond for a moment. Then she looked at Mallory.

"Let's confuse him with a moving target. In fact, with

two moving targets. We'll go together. Duck and dive while you're running, obviously."

Mallory nodded, then grabbed the rucksack. All that was left in it was a handful of tools.

"I'll throw this, just as a distraction. Then we go," he said.

Robin nodded, then eased herself up until she could shoot over the top of the crypt. Immediately she glimpsed a dark shape just coming into view above the stone boundary wall—the head and right arm of the gunman—and pulled the trigger.

At the same instant, Mallory heaved the rucksack toward the churchyard wall as hard as he could, hoping to make the gunman's attention waver for the brief few seconds they'd need to reach safety behind the solid walls of the old Templar church.

Then they were both up and running, running for their lives.

It was a distance of only about twenty yards between the crypt and the end wall of the church, but to Mallory, jinking from side to side as he ran and keeping well clear of Robin to give the gunman two widely separated targets to engage, it felt like a mile.

Robin was doing the same, following an erratic path and switching her attention from the ground in front of her to the lurking danger behind the churchyard wall. She saw the figure stand up and take aim at them as they ran, and immediately fired two quick shots toward him, barely even taking the time to point the pistol accurately, just trying to make the Dominican keep his head down.

The man fired one shot in answer, and neither of them had any idea where the bullet went, but it didn't hit them, and that was all that mattered.

"We're not out of the woods yet," Mallory said. "You're probably right. There'll be at least two of them here, so we need to get to the car and get out of here as quickly as we can."

The gunman was out of sight, completely hidden by the bulk of the church, but they had no doubt that he was already on the move, probably running around the outside of the building to try to cut them off.

They paused for a matter of seconds, deciding which way they needed to go to avoid the gunman behind them and trying to second-guess where the other Dominican was likely to be waiting in ambush for them.

"Not the gate," Mallory said urgently, pointing across the churchyard. "The wall over there only looks about four feet high. We can easily get over that. And that'll protect our backs."

They ran again, both taking frequent glances over their shoulders as they checked for danger from behind, as well as looking ahead to try to spot any sign of a second gunman. They reached the wall, both slightly out of breath, and Robin immediately handed Mallory the Browning, butt first.

"Cocked, safety catch off," she snapped.

A range officer would have had a field day at such an unsafe practice, but right then neither of them cared, and the reliable Browning mechanism meant that an accidental discharge was highly unlikely. It would take a deliberate pull on the trigger to fire the Hi-Power.

Mallory spun round to place his back against the wall and took the pistol in both hands to cover the area behind them, his finger on the trigger as he scanned the normally peaceful grassy churchyard.

Beside him, Robin scrambled lithely over the wall and dropped down onto the other side, where the ground level was slightly lower.

"Give me the pistol," she said.

Mallory repeated her action, but clicked on the safety catch as a precaution.

"Safety on," he said.

While Robin looked warily back toward the church, the direction from which they had come, Mallory climbed over the wall and stepped down beside her.

"Which way now?" Robin asked.

"Down that lane," Mallory said, pointing over to his left. "I think that'll take us in the right direction."

They both took a final glance into the churchyard, but saw no sign of the man who'd fired at them.

"Maybe one of your shots hit him," Mallory suggested.

"No bloody chance," Robin replied. "I was just trying to keep his head down. I doubt if any of my bullets got within ten feet of him."

But whether or not that particular Dominican was still in the land of the living became a purely academic question a few seconds later.

41

Templecombe, Somerset

When they turned into the lane, Mallory slightly in front of Robin, they came face-to-face with another of the enforcers from Rome, who was jogging straight toward them, his pistol in his right hand. Presumably he had heard the sound of the gunshots from around the church and had decided to investigate.

He immediately swung his weapon to point at Mallory, clearly believing that of the two people he was the more dangerous, as a man.

Mallory thought he could actually see the whitening as the man's finger tightened on the trigger of his Beretta, but the shot that rang out came from beside him, not in front, as Robin pulled the Browning from behind her handbag, which had completely hidden it from view, and neatly put a round from the pistol through the Dominican's right shoulder. He staggered backward with a yell of pain, dropping his own pistol and clutching at his wounded shoulder.

"Wrong guess," she said to him with a smile as Mallory bent down to pick up the man's weapon. "The female is always deadlier than the male. You'll probably remember that from now on."

"That's if Marco Toscanelli doesn't decide to blow your head off because you're wounded," Mallory added, as he and Robin left him lying on the ground and ran quickly down the narrow lane that they were hoping would take them back to the part of the village where they'd parked the car that morning.

When they reached the first bend in the lane, they heard an angry shout from behind them, and then another gunshot. But this bullet missed them by an even larger margin than before, at least thirty feet, slamming harmlessly into the wall of an adjacent building.

"We're pretty much out of range now," Mallory said as they rounded the bend, "and now that we outnumber them two to one and have got twice as many weapons as them, I don't think they'll try and follow us."

Once they'd covered another hundred yards or so, they slowed to a walk, and both Mallory and Robin tucked the pistols away out of sight. Robin put the Beretta into her purse, because it was the smaller of the two, while Mallory tucked the Browning into the rear waistband of his trousers, under his jacket.

They saw no one else as they made their way back to the Porsche. Or, to be absolutely accurate, they saw quite a lot of people wandering around different parts of the village, just as you would expect to see in any village in Britain on most days of the week, but they saw no one whom they considered to be a threat. Many of the pedestrians, as on the previous day, seemed to be heading in the general direction of the church, no doubt attracted by, and curious about, the repeated gunshots.

Robin and Mallory almost reached the car when they heard the first sirens, heading straight toward them. Standing on the street didn't seem the brightest of ideas, just in case the dash cam in the police car recorded decent images of their faces, so they took a side road that ran almost parallel to the street they wanted, and stayed on that, out of sight of the traffic, until the noise diminished behind them.

Robin said she'd drive, just in case they needed to put some distance between themselves and the Dominicans, assuming that the Italian enforcers spotted their car as they left Templecombe. She sat in the driver's seat and turned the key in the ignition, and the engine started with a dull rumble.

But before she moved off, she reached into her handbag and removed the small leather-bound packet she had pulled out of the hollow stone skull.

"Just take a look at that, will you?" she said. "The leather felt to me as if it was in pretty good condition, so hopefully whatever's inside it will be as well."

Mallory nodded, but didn't do more than glance at the object before slipping it into his jacket pocket.

"I'll wait until we get well clear of this place," he said. "I don't want to be sitting here with my head down, looking at it, if some Dominican steps out of the hedgerow and aims his pistol at us."

He took out the Browning, checked that it was cocked and ready to fire but with the safety catch on, then placed the weapon on his lap, where it would be immediately available if he needed to use it.

Robin kept the speed right down to well below the legal limit until she reached the derestriction sign at the village boundary, and then gave the car its head.

Six minutes, and five miles, later she nodded to Mallory.

"There hasn't been another car behind us for the last three miles," she said, "so I think we're well clear of them. If they didn't make themselves scarce when the police cars arrived, they're probably arguing with our guardians of law and order right now. But either way, I don't think we need worry about them for the moment."

"That was a good shot," Mallory said. "I presume you were aiming to wound him, not kill him."

"I've taken the lives of remarkably few creatures since I arrived on this planet," she replied, "and I'd quite like to keep it that way. I don't hunt and I don't shoot animals or birds, and I never have. I grant you that these Dominicans are among the least attractive specimens of the human race that I've ever encountered, but I would still rather they walked, or least staggered, away from any encounter with us. So, the short answer is, yes, I was aiming to wound him. His right shoulder was the obvious target, because he was clearly right-handed and that pistol was aimed straight at you. Hitting him there pretty much guaranteed that he wouldn't be able to pull the trigger."

Mallory nodded.

"Well, thanks," he said. "Rather than look at this thing on the move," he added, taking the leather-covered object out of his pocket, "why don't we find a parking spot, or even a café or pub with a car park, where we can look at it together?"

Just under ten minutes later, Robin steered the Porsche onto the forecourt of a roadside café, and parked the vehicle out of sight behind a large white Transit van emblazoned with the name of a firm of jobbing builders. Inside the building, Mallory organized drinks and a small plate of sandwiches, then sat down opposite Robin at the corner table she had selected.

"I could really do with something like a stiff gin and tonic," Robin said, looking with uninterest at the alleged cappuccino Mallory placed in front of her, "but I suppose this will have to do for the moment."

There were only half a dozen other customers in the café, and they could talk relatively freely. Once they'd demolished the sandwiches—neither of them had eaten anything, apart from a muffin each in the Templecombe pub, since breakfast at the hotel that morning, and everything that had gone on had given them both an appetite—Mallory took the leather packet out of his pocket and put it on the table between them.

It was about six inches long, a couple of inches wide, and roughly circular in cross section, the leather sewn together at both ends and along the length of the object, to form a kind of purse or case. Mallory hefted it in his hand, feeling its weight.

"It almost feels empty," he said. "If it isn't, then whatever is inside it doesn't weigh much at all. My guess is that we might be looking at yet another piece of parchment that we'll have to decipher and then translate."

"Well, we'll see in a minute. Have you got something to cut the binding?"

Mallory pulled out a small multitool from his pocket and opened up the knife blade. It was sharp—he'd never seen the point of having a knife with a blunt blade—and in a matter of seconds he had sliced through the thin leather strips that held the object closed along its long side. With Robin watching closely, he then repeated the operation at each end, removing all of the lengths of leather from the holes and putting them to one side.

"You don't think there's likely to be anything dangerous inside it, do you?" Robin asked.

"If you mean something mechanical," Mallory replied, "then the answer is definitely no. It's far too light for anything like that. That doesn't mean it's completely harmless, though. Toxins and poisons were big business in the Middle Ages, and I'm quite sure that the Templars would have had access to all the most sophisticated and dangerous substances available at that time. But I very much doubt if there's anything to worry us in this. This object was protected by that spear device in the crypt, just as the original piece of parchment was concealed inside that book safe with the antitheft device built in, but once we'd circumvented that, the parchment was harmless. And in any case, I very much doubt if any poison would still be viable after seven-hundred-odd years."

"Okay, then. Why don't you go for it?"

On the table there was a stainless steel pot containing a selection of cutlery, and before Mallory did anything else, he removed half a dozen knives, the heaviest objects in the pot. He placed the steel pot on the end of the leather to hold it down, then used the blades of the knives to maneuver the package open, slowly unrolling it to reveal the contents.

It was exactly as he had expected. The only thing inside the leather pouch was a small piece of parchment that had been rolled into a cylinder and around which the protective leather had been sewn.

"I told you," Mallory said. "We're obviously back on the decryption-and-translation trail yet again."

"Actually," Robin said, "I'm not absolutely sure that we are." She picked up one of the knives and aimed the point at a part of the parchment where the writing was clearly legible. "I don't know what this is yet," she added, "but what it isn't is *scriptio continua*, which is what we've seen on all the other bits of parchment we've recovered. In fact, there are a lot of words on this that I can see and translate immediately. This isn't a ciphertext. This is a piece of plaintext Latin, and that does seem rather odd."

That stumped them both for a few moments, and then Mallory remembered the word that had bothered Robin when they'd been doing the previous decryption.

"If it's in plaintext," he suggested tentatively, "do you think this could be that license or permission which the other text mentioned?"

"That's not a bad thought. The Latin word was *licentiam*, if I remember rightly, and it really didn't make sense in the context we were looking at."

"But if it was some kind of permission, then you would expect it to be written in plain language—Latin, in this case—because presumably the document would have to be offered or shown to officials or somebody, and they wouldn't be able to accept an encrypted document. So, what does it say?"

"I can't translate it now," Robin replied. "I'll need access to an online dictionary, so we'll have to wait until we're back at the hotel."

"Then let's head over there right now."

42

Somerset

"Tell me again exactly what you saw," Toscanelli ordered.

He had arrived at the outskirts of the village about twenty minutes after the shooting had started, and had met Mario and Lucca on a quiet road with a couple of convenient parking areas beside it.

"They must have guessed there was a booby trap in the crypt," Mario said for the third time, "because Mallory climbed onto the top of it before he loosened the stone skull. When it came free, that iron spear was forced out of the structure and locked in place. I tried moving it afterward, before the police arrived, but I couldn't shift it."

"I know what *you* did," Toscanelli snapped, "but I only want to know what *they* did."

"Once they'd triggered the booby trap, they examined the skull."

"You told me the skull was hollow. Did you see them take anything out of it?"

"No. It was the woman who checked the skull, presumably just to see how it had been fitted into the hole, but then they both took a series of photographs of the base of the skull and around the hole in the crypt. It was obvious to me that they'd found an inscription of some sort, as I told you on the phone. You gave me permission to shoot them, but unfortunately I missed."

"You missed," Toscanelli repeated. "I'm surrounded by idiots. You had two sitting targets, neither of them aware that you were watching, and you still managed to miss both of them."

"I didn't miss by much," Mario protested.

That wasn't the right thing to say, obviously.

"You still missed." Toscanelli raised his voice almost to a shout. "Then Michele meets them on the other side of the church, and gets shot himself for his trouble. And you failed to finish him off when you found him, so he's now talking to the British police, or he will be as soon as they've managed to dig the bullet out of his shoulder. It's a complete shambles, and Vitale will not be impressed with your performance."

Or, Toscanelli knew, with his own conduct, but he certainly wasn't going to say that. With a bit of luck, he'd be able to spin the story so that it would appear Lucca, Mario, and Michele had acted on their own initiative in going back to the village, against Vitale's and Toscanelli's direct orders, and had screwed up.

"Absolutely the only thing you did right was duplicate

the photographs you saw Mallory and Jessop taking, so at least we can send copies of those back to Rome. We passed a café offering free Wi-Fi a few miles back, so we'll get those images on their way within a few minutes. Then we'll just have to wait until our people have decoded the inscriptions before we know where Mallory and Jessop are heading. And once we do, we'll bring this whole sorry matter to a permanent end."

43

Somerset

"We were right," Robin said a couple of hours later. "This is plaintext Latin and it is a kind of license. Well, maybe not exactly a license but more a sort of Templar passport."

They'd returned to the hotel without incident, gone immediately to the bar to allow Robin to down a couple of long gin and tonics, Mallory sticking to coffee just in case they had to drive anywhere, and then climbed up the staircase to their room. Ever since, Robin had been working on the new piece of parchment, putting together the most accurate translation she could manage.

"I've never heard of a Templar passport," Mallory said.

"Well, that is what this looks like. There are a couple of telling phrases. One requests that all authorities, secular and religious—this is my translation of it, but it is what the Latin means—should allow the bearer to travel with 'such goods and valuables as he may possess,' and another one says he should be permitted to pass 'without let or hindrance upon his way.' That's pretty similar to a phrase you'll find in a modern British passport. It also specifically identifies the bearer as a member of the Knights Templar and states that he is engaged upon the official business of the order, is acting on behalf of the Grand Master, and answers to no authority save the pope himself. The document was issued over the signature of Jacques de Molay as the Grand Master, and 'whosoever may succeed him in that post,' and in the name of Pope Clement V. It's dated 10 August 1307. The final sentence states that the document and all its permissions and conditions will remain valid in perpetuity, and the authority to use the passport— for want of a better word—and to hold and dispose of the goods entrusted to the bearer is to pass from him to his firstborn heir 'until the ultimate generation.'"

"Primogeniture," Mallory said, nodding. "The right of the firstborn male child to inherit the wealth of the family, just twisted slightly because in this case it didn't relate to familial wealth, but to the assets of the Templar order. At the time, that would have been an incredibly powerful piece of parchment. Basically the holder could go anywhere and do anything, without reference to anybody else. And the date is obviously significant. By August 1307 the Templars would have known their order was doomed and facing ruin at the hands of Philip the Fair of France. So, although it doesn't explicitly say so, that document obviously must have been given to the member of the order who organized the transfer of the treasure of the Templars out of France. He would have been in charge of the small fleet of ships that sailed from Honfleur, and a whole train of wagons, accompanied by a bodyguard of armed and armored knights in France and in whatever country the Templar fleet made landfall. He would definitely have needed that document to allow him to cross borders and avoid being detained by local troops or even questioned by officials. And nobody wanted to annoy the Knights Templar, or go against the wishes of the pope, so it would probably have worked very well."

Robin nodded. Mallory's interpretation exactly matched what she thought.

"And of course this does tie up with the reference we found earlier, about de Molay entrusting this man with a specific document that he was to keep safe, to *conservare et salvare in perpetuum*, meaning to 'protect and save for all eternity.' The other odd thing about it," she went on, "is that the word *puer* is used again to refer to the possessor of this document. If you recall, we found that on the sheet of vellum you pulled out of the secret compartment in the wooden chest we recovered from that cave in Switzerland."

"I remember," Mallory said. "He was the fourth member of the order summoned by de Molay to that meeting in August 1307, when the writing was already on the wall as far as the Templars were concerned."

"Exactly. The text on the vellum describes de Molay as spending some hours with that person after the meeting had concluded. When you consider that, along with this passport thing we've found, it does suggest that our interpretation of who that fourth person was is probably wrong. We thought that *puer* could mean a servant or retainer or maybe a lay member of the Templar order, but this passport or whatever you want to call it was just too powerful to have ever been entrusted to anyone who wasn't a full member, a genuine Templar knight."

"But I thought the vellum text stated that three knights were summoned to the meeting by de Molay, along with this other person. Surely, if he'd also been a knight, the text would have described four knights being summoned."

"Precisely. So, that almost certainly means that our first translation and interpretation of this man's status was wrong, because *puer* does have another, rather different meaning that seems to me to be more likely to be correct."

"And what's that?" Mallory asked.

"Son," Robin replied. "The Latin word *puer* could also translate as a young man or a son. I think in August 1307 Jacques de Molay was organizing the removal of the treasure and assets of the Knights Templar order and entrusting the entire operation to the one person he was completely certain he could rely on absolutely—his son."

Mallory looked as startled as he felt. Then he nodded slowly.

"That does make sense," he said after a few moments. "The rules were quite simple. The Templar order didn't grant knighthoods, so you had to be a knight in your own right before you could join. You were also required to be single, either unmarried or a widower, but of course that did allow people who had been married, and who had had children, to join. So it's quite possible that de Molay had a son. There was nothing in the rules of the order that would have forbidden it."

"And that does rather enhance the significance of these two parchments, especially the second one."

When they'd unrolled the document in the hotel bedroom, they'd found that it wasn't one piece of parchment, as they'd thought, but two, one wrapped around the other.

"What was on the second one?" Mallory asked. "You haven't told me yet."

"Two things," Robin replied crisply. "First of all there's an inventory, a list of chests and their contents, which doesn't mean a lot to me because although it's another piece of plaintext, they've used a kind of shorthand to describe the assets and their values. But there are direct mentions of both gold and silver, so I think it's clear it's referring to the real, tangible wealth of the Templars."

"We've thought we've been here before," Mallory said. "Are you sure?"

Robin nodded.

"Pretty sure, yes. There is one oddity, though. As well as listing the contents of these various chests and boxes, the document also refers to the 'treasure' of the order as if it's something different to their material wealth, something separate. It's also referred to as the 'proof,' which I don't understand at all, unless the Latin word had a different meaning back then. And this parchment does state specifically that this proof, whatever it is, was hidden under the 'stone that is not as it seems,' virtually the same phrase as the one we deciphered before."

"Working that out is probably a bit academic unless we can locate the treasure," Mallory pointed out. "Hopefully, if we do locate it, it'll probably be quite obvious what the document refers to."

Robin nodded.

"Of course, knowing what the treasure consists of is one thing. It's interesting, but not helpful, as you might say. But the second piece of information on the parchment seems to be the route the treasure was supposed to take. Or a partial route, at least. There's a list of the most important Templar establishments in France, starting with Paris, as you would expect, and a couple of sentences explaining how their assets were to be collected and then transported to Honfleur and embarked on the ships of the Templar fleet. Again, that's just a confirmation of the text we decrypted earlier."

"So, does it say where the ships were to take the assets? That's the really big question."

"And the really big answer is no," Robin replied. "The other text we deciphered talked about the *insulae ad aquilonem*, the islands of the north, and this mentions the order's 'friends in the north,' but again it's not specific. Oddly enough, bearing in mind the codes and ciphers we've been faced with, I don't think the writer was being deliberately obtuse or trying to be misleading. It's more as if he expected that the reader would know exactly whom he was referring to by that phrase, so he didn't need to be explicit about it. Or that's my impression, anyway."

"So, the bottom line, unless I've missed something," Mallory said, "is that neither of the documents we found at Templecombe really tells us anything useful. We don't even know what country we should be looking in. Was there anything definitive in the text carved into the wall of the crypt itself? I saw you looking at the pictures earlier."

"I'd almost forgotten about that," she admitted. "I really just checked that the images were clear enough to let us read the letters. Let's take a look at it right now."

Working together, they carefully transcribed the carved letters from the images on Robin's camera—checking them against the pictures Mallory had taken—onto a couple of sheets of paper. When they'd finished, they checked it again, just to make absolutely sure that every letter was right, and then started working out the encryption system.

That didn't take anything like as long as they'd been expecting. In fact, after only about ten minutes Robin put down her pencil and looked at Mallory.

"I'm not sure I believe this," she said, "but unless I've got it completely wrong, this is a really simple Atbash cipher, just using the reversed alphabet but with a five-letter shift to the right."

"You're not wrong, obviously," Mallory replied, pointing at the sheets she'd been writing on, "because it's working. Even I can tell that the decryption is producing Latin words."

"But why, after all the complex decryptions we've had to sort out to get this far, is this one so simple?"

"Maybe because we're at the end—or at least we think we're near the end—of the trail. Or maybe it's got something to do with those two plaintext parchments. Perhaps the earlier stuff was deliberately made difficult to ensure that only a Templar knight or someone who knew a lot about the order would be able to decrypt it. But because we've got this far we've passed the test or something. The reason doesn't really matter. All we actually need to do is read the plaintext and see where that leads us."

Robin nodded and looked back at the translation she'd done. She checked a few of the words against the online Latin-to-English dictionary she was using, and made a couple of minor corrections as a result, then wrote out a fair copy—it wasn't a long piece of text—and slid it over so Mallory could read it.

He eagerly scanned the few lines that Robin had produced, then looked across at her.

"Is this it?" he asked. "It's not what you might call comprehensive, is it?"

He looked again at the text, running the tip of his forefinger along each line, making sure that he didn't miss anything.

"About the only concrete piece of information I can see here is that the final resting place of the stuff taken from the Templar properties in France and elsewhere was near a temple in the north, which is extremely nonspecific. It doesn't even say which country it's in."

"Hang on a minute," Robin said. "I just thought of something."

She took the sheet of paper back from Mallory, put a line through the word *a*, and replaced it with the word *the*.

"I know that's only a small change," she said, "but we've got so little to work with that every word needs to be right. Does that help?"

"Possibly," Mallory replied cautiously, "if you are certain about it," he added.

Robin nodded.

"That noun clearly needs the definite article," she confirmed.

"Then that might be a good lead. The word *temple* was obviously closely associated with the Knights Templar, both because of their origins, in the way they got their name, and also because it was a monastic order. They were warrior monks, and every Templar establishment had a church or chapel of some sort, though it wasn't normally referred to as a temple. Lots of them are still standing today, places like the Temple Church in London, and there are quite a few round churches dotted around the country that are Templar in origin. But if we *are* talking about the British Isles, there's one location that does fit the bill exactly: Temple, in Midlothian."

"I've heard something about that place," Robin said. "Wasn't it the main Templar stronghold in Scotland?"

"It was, yes. And it's worth remembering that the majority of the arrests of the Knights Templar took place in France. The rulers of most other countries were extremely reluctant to move against the order, either because they didn't believe what the Templars were accused of, or because they were so deep in hock to the order that they didn't want to rock the boat. As far as I recall, hardly any of the Templars in Scotland were even arrested, far less tortured or burned at the stake. In fact," he added, "at some point they were given land in Scotland, and they had a really good relationship with the Scottish ruling house."

"I see where you're going with that," Robin said. "You could quite easily argue that the expression 'the islands of the north' could refer to the British Isles, bearing in mind that the Templars' main stronghold was in France and their normal theater of operations was the Mediterranean. And it's also possible, from what you've said, that the Scottish ruling house could be the people referred to in the parchment as 'our friends in the north.' That does all make sense," she finished.

Mallory nodded.

"You could well be right," he agreed. "It's also worth bearing in mind that the Scots might have been grateful to the Templars because of their military prowess. It's never been proven historically, but there is a persistent story about the Battle of Bannockburn in 1314. When the English troops were clearly gaining the upper hand, a new force of unknown men, thought to be Templars and all clearly very experienced warriors, appeared on the battlefield and quickly turned the tide in favor of the Scottish forces. The identity—and even the existence—of these troops has never been confirmed, but the Templars had been the most powerful fighting force in Europe until 1307, just seven years earlier, so if a group of them had made it to Scotland, and that country had given them shelter, it's certainly conceivable that there could be some truth in the story."

"But wasn't there some prohibition against Templars killing Christians?" Robin asked.

"Yes, and the order was also forbidden from fighting in nationalist wars. But after the way the Templars had been utterly betrayed by both the king of France and the pope, I doubt very much if those prohibitions would have meant anything to them. They would have been fighting for their survival, and my guess is that they'd have bent the rules to suit the situation, or just ignored them altogether."

Mallory looked back at the translation Robin had given him.

"But this doesn't actually say that the ultimate destination of the Templar treasure was Temple, does it?"

"No. What it refers to is an underground chamber that I think was a part of an existing cave system. It might have been something that the Templars modified and enlarged, but the basic structure was already in place. That's how I read it, anyway. The bits I really don't understand are the two sentences that follow that one. The first one seems to be referring to a place that hadn't yet been built at the time this parchment was prepared. There's this enigmatic phrase about a building that would 'give thanks and honor for those who came before and remind those who would follow.' And the next one is even more obtuse. That says, 'From the sacred mound seek beyond the battlefield for the open and closed door,' and I really have no idea what either of these two mean."

"Join the club," Mallory said. "But what we do know, if that translation's right, is that this trail or quest or whatever you want to call it ends somewhere near Temple, so at least we more or less know where we have to go next. Scotland's a long way, so the sooner we get going, the better. Let's pack our stuff now and get on the road. We'll find somewhere to stay on the road."

Twenty minutes later, Mallory put the last of their bags—as usual, they were traveling light—in the front trunk of the Porsche Cayman and pushed the lid closed.

He started the engine and programmed the satnav for the middle of the main road in the village of Temple— about seven miles southeast of the center of Edinburgh— glanced across at Robin to make sure she had her seat belt done up, then drove slowly out of the hotel car park.

44

Midlothian, Scotland

Temple, when they reached it the following afternoon, proved to be something of a disappointment, because it had almost vanished and had a tiny population—only just over two hundred people, according to a website Robin had consulted when she was a passenger in the car. Seven hundred years of wear and tear and the usual ravages of time had reduced the once-important Templar stronghold to nothing more than a tiny village, not even marked on some maps.

They'd been swapping over all the way up to Scotland, each driving for a couple of hours before pulling over for a drink or a toilet stop, and they had spent the previous night in a small pub just off the main A1 trunk road. They'd also stopped a couple of times that day for a snack meal, and Mallory was behind the wheel for the last leg.

"It doesn't look like there's much here," he said, pulling the car off the road.

They got out of the vehicle and looked around but saw nothing that appeared to be either helpful or even interesting.

"The translation didn't say that this was the location," Robin reminded him, accessing the Internet on her smartphone, "only that it was somewhere near here."

"Good, because it looks to me as if there's even less to Temple than meets the eye."

"And that, my dear, is where you're wrong. I suppose I should have checked the place out properly before we got here, but I didn't. In fact, there's a lot of interesting stuff about Temple, and especially about the Templars. What's more important is that it seems to confirm what we thought."

"Tell me," Mallory said.

"Well, starting at the beginning, the Templar order was formed in about 1119 in Jerusalem, and as we know for the first nine years they did almost nothing, because they were believed to be excavating under the Temple Mount. Certainly they weren't patrolling the roads around Jerusalem and protecting the pilgrims, which is what they were supposed to be doing. And then, suspiciously quickly, the order was recognized by the Catholic Church and then by the pope."

"We know all that," Mallory pointed out.

"I know. But what *I* didn't know was that in 1128, the same year that the order was recognized at the Council of Troyes, it was also recognized by David I of Scotland. Hugues de Payens, the founder of the Knights Templar and the same man who had persuaded King Baldwin II of Jerusalem to accommodate the Templars in the Al-Aqsa Mosque on the Temple Mount, met with the Scottish king and also managed to convince him to support the new order. In fact, David didn't just support and recognize the Templars; he also gave them the 'Chapelrie' and Manor of Balantrodach. That's an old Scottish name that translates as the 'stead of the warrior,' and the land includes what is now Temple. In fact, the name Balantrodach was still used for the village until the end of the sixteenth century. In 1618 it was formally renamed Temple after the old chapel that was still in use at the time."

"I didn't know that, either," Mallory said. "Reading between the lines, that is a kind of confirmation that the Templars did find something buried inside the Temple Mount, something that frightened the religious establishment. Otherwise, I doubt if King David would even have agreed to see him. But to both recognize the order and hand over a tract of land to the Templars suggests that whatever Hugues de Payens said to David or maybe showed him must have impressed or concerned the king enough to make him agree to whatever the Templars wanted."

"Exactly. Anyway, there was already a settlement here when the Templars moved in, and this became their main headquarters and preceptory for the whole of Scotland. They built high walls around their buildings, a church with the round tower that was typical of Templar religious architecture, a cloister, and a mill, and—now, this is interesting—they also started tunneling works here in Temple. But before you get too excited about that, this particular tunnel was intended to mine coal, not hide treasure."

"But that was in the twelfth century, presumably," Mallory said, "not the early part of the fourteenth. If the mines were no longer in operation by that later date, they could possibly have used the old mine workings as a repository. It's worth looking at, anyway. Anything else?"

Robin scanned the screen of her mobile again.

"There is a church here," she said, "called the Old Temple Kirk, which gave the village its name. It's a ruin, with just the walls left standing. According to some sources it dates from the twelfth century, but most people think it's more likely fourteenth, after the Templars were purged."

"Why?"

"Because it's a fairly conventional design, with none of the usual Templar architecture, and there's some late Gothic tracery on one of the window arches, which suggests a later date. On the gable end there's an inscription that might help date it, though this bit's extremely tenuous, in my opinion. The inscription reads 'VAESEC MUHM.' That's not a known abbreviation for any standard Latin phrase, as far as I know, but it's been tentatively translated as *Vienne Sacrum Concilium Militibus Johannis Hierosolymitani Melitensbus.* And in English that means 'the Sacred Council of Vienne, to the Knights of Saint John of Jerusalem and Malta.' As I said, really tenuous, bearing in mind that the abbreviation doesn't even come close to matching the initial letters of the phrase it supposedly represents.

"But if that deduction and translation are right, and if that inscription was carved when the church was built, rather than added sometime after the event, then the church dates to the period after the Knights Templar were purged. In 1312, because of what had happened in France, the Templar order in Scotland and England was suppressed and all the property handed over to the *Sovrano Militare Ordine Ospedaliero di San Giovanni di Gerusalemme di Rodi e di Malta*, the Sovereign Military Hospitaller Order of Saint John of Jerusalem of Rhodes and of Malta, better known as the Knights of Saint John or just the Hospitallers. There's also a suggestion that in Scotland the Templars weren't abolished, but instead merged with the Hospitallers and the joint order simply acquired a new name: the Order of Saint John and the Temple. Bearing in mind the good relationship the Templars had enjoyed with the Scottish crown, that does make sense. That way, the Scots could be seen to be obeying the instruction of the pope to dissolve the order, while actually doing nothing of the sort and letting them continue to exist, just in a slightly different form."

Robin hopped onto another website, then glanced again at Mallory.

"There's one other thing, though. I'm not sure if it's either true or relevant. In 2006 a couple of amateur historians, I suppose you could call them, found what looked like a small headstone at Temple, presumably in or near the ruined church. When it was examined, it was found to have a barely visible but unusual design on it. There's a possibility that it could be a thing called a baculus, a kind of stylized carving of the Templar *croix pattée*. If so, that could be the symbol of office for a Templar knight. As I say, probably not relevant, because the Templar presence here was well established, but interesting all the same. And that," she added, "is more or less it as far as Temple is concerned."

Mallory nodded and looked up the road to the small main street of the village.

"Interesting though all that is," he said, "I don't think we're much further forward. I just hope we can do a bit more research on that parchment before we pick a place to start digging. Scotland's a bloody big place and what we're looking for is probably quite small."

Robin nodded.

"I'm not too sure that there's much more direct research we can do. There was little enough text to work with. I think we need to do a bit of lateral thinking."

"Like what?"

"If my interpretation is correct, wherever the Templars stashed their loot was an existing cave system, or a part of one, or maybe an ancient tunnel. Or maybe, as we were talking about earlier, the old coal mine that they started excavating soon after they arrived here. So perhaps we should try and find a geological map of the region and see if there are any underground spaces marked. That might give us a good starting point."

"Good thinking," Mallory said, opening the car door. "We won't find anything around here, but there are bound to be specialist bookshops in Edinburgh. We'll find a hotel somewhere in the city, get a room, and then go exploring. How does that sound?"

"Like a plan," Robin said, "which is very unlike you.

And, oddly enough, it actually sounds sensible and might even work. So let's go."

They booked into a large chain hotel near the junction of the M8 motorway with the City of Edinburgh Bypass, basing their selection more on its location, anonymity, and ease of access to fast roads and the metro system than on the advertised merits of the hotel itself. Finding bookshops was not a problem, once they'd taken the metro from the Edinburgh Park stop into the city center, because they were spoiled for choice, and although what they were looking for was fairly specialized, they returned to the hotel after a couple of hours with three topographical charts that covered most of the area to the south of Edinburgh. More importantly, all three maps included the area immediately around the village of Temple.

Back in their double room, Mallory opened up his laptop and logged on to the hotel's Wi-Fi network so that they could check whatever information they gleaned from the maps. Then he spread out the biggest of the three maps on the foot of the bed, and they both bent forward to study the details.

It was immediately obvious that caverns and cave systems weren't exactly rare in the region, and a number of different ones were marked on the map, though none, as far as they could see, was very near Temple.

"That village is only a starting point," Robin reminded Mallory, "not necessarily the final location. The way I read the text on the parchment, the Templar treasure was loaded onto their fleet of ships at Honfleur. If we assume that Britain was their destination, maybe some of the other details will start to make more sense. The parchment states that the vessels first made landfall on what it calls 'the island at the wide river mouth,' which is both specific and general, because we don't know which river it means. There are probably dozens of rivers and islands that it could refer to. But the next sentence might help clarify it, because that says they sailed 'from the river to the river.' I think that means the ships sailed up one main river and then traveled along a tributary."

While Robin was talking, Mallory leaned over to the desk and typed a search string into Google. When the results page appeared, he scanned down it, then double-clicked on one particular result. He read the first part of the text and nodded.

"That could be a reference to Temple," he said. "According to this website, there's a persistent legend that directly relates to the Templar establishment there. There's a rhyme about the Templar treasure being buried between the oak tree and the elm tree, which is obviously not much help, because I'd be really surprised if either tree could still be standing seven hundred years later. And even if we could somehow work out the precise location of those two trees, that would still only give us a vague idea about where the treasure might have been buried."

"I don't see the link to Temple," Robin said.

"That's this next bit. There's a prevalent legend in France about the end of the Knights Templar—and we have to at least give this some credence, as the French arm was the most powerful part of the Templar establishment—

which claims that the treasure *was* taken to Britain, and that does link up to what you've just been saying. According to this story, the ships of the Templar fleet first landed on the Isle of May."

Robin immediately turned her attention to one of the maps, which showed the Firth of Forth, the major estuary that lay to the north of Edinburgh and speared deep into Scotland.

"I think that counts as a wide river," she said. "At its widest point, it's about fifteen miles from north to south, and the Isle of May is a bit north of the centerline of the river at the mouth. So, what does the French legend say happened after that? And do we have to visit the island?"

"No, we don't. According to this story from France, the ships sailed on from the Isle of May and along another river to their planned destination. You said the parchment claimed that the fleet sailed 'from the river to the river.' If the Templar ships sailed up the estuary from the Isle of May, the first river they would have met on the southern side, and which certainly counts as a river in a river, is the Esk. And the river Esk follows a more or less straight line all the way south from the coast at Musselburgh through Dalkeith and on to Temple itself."

Robin traced the path of the river on the map in front of her with her fingertip, and then nodded agreement. When she looked up at Mallory, her eyes were shining with excitement.

"Things really are starting to fall into place," she said. "The stories about the treasure being buried at Temple, and the French legend tying up so well with the information we've got from that piece of parchment—I think we're onto something here. I mean *really* onto something."

Mallory nodded.

"I hope we are. I wonder if the river Esk is navigable all the way up to Temple. I mean, if it is, then maybe the Templars built rafts or something to haul the treasure chests upriver. Obviously they'd be going against the flow, but that might have been easier than off-loading them and taking everything overland."

"I don't think they did that," Robin said, "because here's a sentence about the resident members of the order meeting the fleet somewhere—the location isn't specified—and supervising the transfer of the chests to a large number of wagons drawn by horses and oxen. They then provided an escort for the caravan to the end of the journey. Anyway, it looks as if the treasure arrived in Scotland in August or September 1307, and if these various stories and legends are correct, and what they say is borne out by the text on the parchment, it was stored in a stronghold in Temple or somewhere nearby while this cave or tunnel was being prepared to receive it. So, that means, logically, that it definitely has to be somewhere fairly close by. Otherwise a different storage area would have been chosen, somewhere much closer to the treasure's final destination."

"That's a lot of assumptions," Mallory said, "and lots of guesses. But that's all we have, so let's make the best of it."

45

Midlothian, Scotland

"I didn't expect to see you here, Silvio," Marco Toscanelli said, shaking hands with Vitale as he walked into the arrivals hall at Edinburgh Airport.

"You've screwed up so often, Toscanelli, that I decided the only way to ensure this mission would end the way it should was to come here and supervise it myself. Have there been any other developments?"

Toscanelli shook his head as he led Vitale out to the hire car on the road outside the building, the engine idling and with another member of the team behind the wheel. As soon as they approached the vehicle, the driver climbed out nimbly. Vitale had only brought a carry-on bag, and he gave it to the driver—Mario—to put in the trunk, then climbed into the backseat, being joined a moment later by Toscanelli.

"Nothing else has happened since I last called you,"

Toscanelli said. "The hidden text carved into the stone of the crypt at Templecombe was encrypted, obviously, but it was only a very simple Atbash cipher, and we deciphered it ourselves even before our experts in Rome sent us their decryption."

"And then you came up here." Vitale was stating the obvious.

"Yes. The reference to Temple seemed unambiguous, and we assumed this would be where Mallory and Jessop were heading."

"At least you got that right," Vitale said. "Through our contacts here I can confirm that Mallory's car was detected on a number of traffic cameras as he drove north. Jessop was confirmed as being in the car with him. The first sighting was in a town called Warminster, which is where we presume they were staying when they visited Templecombe, and then we had another dozen or so sightings. When it was clear that they were probably heading for the same place you were, I decided to fly over here as well. I'm waiting for confirmation of further sightings now that they're presumably in this area."

"What are your orders regarding them?"

"The kill order is rescinded for the moment. You were far too precipitous at Templecombe. I agree that the carved inscription was probably the last clue, but it's fairly nonspecific. It gets us as far as Temple, but it doesn't tell us exactly where the heretics concealed the treasure. I've told you before that those two are a quantum leap ahead of you when it comes to deduction and logical thinking, Toscanelli, and for the moment they're more valuable to us alive."

Toscanelli glanced forward and saw Mario smirking in the rearview mirror.

"So, what do you want us to do?"

"As soon as we get confirmation of where they are, we must follow them. Once they have led us to the hidden vault used by the Templars, they will become expendable."

"You don't think we can find it from the translation of the carved text?"

"I doubt it. There's not enough information to go on. I know you had a man watching what they did in the churchyard at Templecombe, but I still think there might have been something concealed inside the carved-stone skull, something that Mallory or Jessop removed and which might provide the final piece of information they— and we—need to locate the vault. I saw the photographs Mario took of the base of the skull, and that cavity was an obvious place to hide something."

"Mario saw nothing to suggest either of them removed anything."

Vitale snorted dismissively.

"Mario," he said, "you've been listening to what we've been saying. Can you swear they *didn't* take anything out of the skull?"

"No, of course not. I was watching as carefully as I could, but they were moving around and sometimes I found myself looking at their backs. They could have done something like that, and I wouldn't have seen it. That was what I reported."

"Exactly. So, first we find them. Then we follow them, and we only kill them when this mission has ended to my entire satisfaction."

46

Midlothian, Scotland

"I've been thinking," Mallory said after a light lunch the following day.

"I don't like the sound of that," Robin replied.

They were lying fully clothed on the large double bed in their hotel room, their heads on the pillows as they stared up at the ceiling. Robin was tucked comfortably into Mallory's left armpit, the maps discarded on the floor at the foot of the bed. In fact, they'd both been thinking, but largely lost in their own thoughts, which had inevitably been centered on the one question to which neither of them had an answer: Where had the Templar hoard been hidden?

Robin's idea about using topographical maps had seemed like a good idea, but there were just so many possible locations—natural caverns, man-made tunnels, mine shafts, and the like in the area—that it was impossible to decide where to even start looking.

"We're missing something, obviously," Mallory said, "and by that I don't mean that we don't know where to go next. I think it's a bit more basic than that. I've been thinking about that line in the decrypted text about a building that wasn't even constructed when the text was written but would somehow 'give thanks and honor for those who came before and remind those who would follow.' And I'm just wondering if that's a kind of oblique reference to what's perhaps the most famous building ever to be associated with the Knights Templar, despite having been built almost a century and a half after the order ceased to exist."

"Rosslyn," Robin said immediately. "That is where you mean, isn't it? Funnily enough, I was thinking about that as well, but I didn't say anything because I've always thought it's a bit of a cliché. And, as you just said, the Templars ceased to exist in 1312, and they didn't start building Rosslyn until 1456. Even I know that."

"Cliché or not," Mallory said, rolling over slightly so that he could look at Robin, "that does seem to fit the bill, and explain the expression we found on the parchment. The imagery inside the chapel is bizarre and in some parts inexplicable, including carvings of things that look remarkably like corn on the cob, but which were unknown in Europe at the time. Plus, there are a couple of images definitely associated with the Templars, like the Agnus Dei, the 'Lamb of God,' which was used as a Templar seal and symbol, especially in southern France, and even what's been interpreted as a stylized sculpture of the classic Templar image of two knights riding on a single horse. The chapel is owned by the St. Clair family, and at the center of the St. Clairs' engrailed cross symbol is what looks very much like a Templar *croix pattée*. There's clear evidence that the chapel was designed using sacred geometry, and it's also been claimed that it was modeled on the layout of the Temple of Solomon, another clear link to the Templars. The obvious problem with that is that nobody knows for sure exactly what the Temple of Solomon looked like, far less what its detailed layout was, so that's a claim that can't be either proven or disproven."

"But if your damned shaky deduction is right, then that's pretty much it as far as this quest is concerned, because unless the Rosslyn trustees have changed their minds in the last few weeks there's no possibility of us doing any excavation there. They don't let anyone excavate anywhere near the building."

Mallory nodded.

"That's one way of looking at it," he agreed. "And if the Templars dug a hole and buried their treasure and then the St. Clairs built Rosslyn Chapel on top of it, then I would absolutely agree with you."

"But," Robin said.

"But what?"

"There was definitely a 'but' coming at the end of that last sentence."

"Oh, yes. Right. All I was going to say was that there's another way of looking at it. If we've got this right, the Templars buried their assets somewhere in this area in 1307, getting everything they could carry out of France before Philip's men started hammering on the doors of their preceptories and commanderies on Friday, the thirteenth of October. Even if it took them two or three months to get their vault finished, they would probably have had the chests stowed away safely by the end of that year. And because of what had happened in France, they would have known that the Templars were finished, at least in the short term. But I'm also certain they hoped that at some time in the future the order would rise again, like the mythical phoenix, from the quite literal ashes of the bodies of the knights burned at the stake, and so they would have wanted to keep their assets safe."

"So, what are you saying?"

"I don't know yet. I'm just thinking out loud, I suppose. But there is that other phrase we decrypted—the 'friends in the north'—and I'm wondering if that could possibly be the missing link. If we assume that our guess is right, and that Rosslyn Chapel is the building that was constructed later to honor the Templars, then it would make sense that the St. Clair family might well qualify as being these anonymous 'friends.' In fact, it's difficult to come to any other conclusion. The chapel is clearly linked with the Templar order, because of what you can see inside the place today, and only a family or group friendly to the order would erect such a building, especially a century and a half after the Templars were purged. So the St. Clairs must not only have been linked to the Templars, but were also very probably entrusted with keeping the secret of the treasure safe. Possibly they even used Templar funds to erect Rosslyn. Some of the gravestones there are carved with what look very much like Templar effigies."

"Okay." Robin nodded. "Do you know much about the family?"

"Not a lot, no. So let's ask the oracle—Google—what he knows."

"She," Robin said.

"What?"

"Google is obviously female, because she knows everything."

"Yeah, right," Mallory said.

Fifteen minutes later, using their two laptops, they'd both seen more or less everything publicly available about the St. Clair family. Rosslyn Chapel was the brainchild of Sir William St. Clair, at that time probably the richest and most powerful nobleman in Scotland, though he never lived to see the building finished. There was apparently even some doubt about exactly where his wealth came from, which might be a kind of confirmation that the St. Clairs were entrusted with the Templar treasure and were able to use at least some of it for their own purposes.

"I don't know if you can read anything into this," Robin said, looking at one particular website, "but Sir William St. Clair was known to disapprove of the use of torture on prisoners, at a time in history when that was the norm. Do you think that could have been just his personal feeling about it, or was he influenced by his knowledge of what the Knights Templar had suffered in the torture chambers of the Dominicans?"

Mallory looked interested.

"It might be an indication that we're on the right track," he said, "but it obviously doesn't prove anything.

Now, this is the basic information about the chapel. Work began on it in 1456, and originally it was intended to be just one part of a much larger, cross-shaped building containing a central tower. The chapel took almost forty years to construct, but Sir William died in 1483, before it was completed. His son, Sir Oliver St. Clair, completed the chapel, but for whatever reason the remainder of the structure was never built."

"Sir William intended the chapel to be the final resting place of all the St. Clairs," Robin said, picking up the story, "and to start the ball rolling, so to speak, he exhumed and transferred the corpses of many of his illustrious ancestors from their tombs to the chapel to be buried in a large vault under the floor. That vault—or maybe those vaults, because it's not clear if it's just a single chamber or several different ones—is supposed to extend the whole length of the chapel. These reburials included his grandfather Prince Henry St. Clair of Orkney, widely known as the Navigator, who was reputed to have led an expedition across the Atlantic to America about a century before Columbus set out to find a westerly route to the Spice Islands and found the Caribbean instead. Columbus, of course, never even saw the North American continent. If Prince Henry did make that voyage, then that would at least help explain the carvings of corncobs found in Rosslyn Chapel, because he could have seen the plant growing in America and might even have brought some back with him."

"This is something else that's interesting," Mallory said, pointing at an image of a male figure on the screen of his laptop. "This character was another of Sir William's ancestors who had their last rest disturbed when their bodies were hauled over to Rosslyn for reburial in the vault. He's Sir Henry St. Clair, Baron of Rosslyn, who was killed fighting for the Scots at the Battle of Bannock-burn in 1314, that same conflict that a force of Knights Templar was supposed to have been involved in, on the side of the Scottish army. According to this, the vault holds some twenty bodies, most of them buried wearing full armor, and it's supposed to be so dry down there that a report from 1663 states that even after being interred there for eighty-odd years, the corpses appeared as fresh as if they'd just died."

"Slightly creepy," Robin remarked, "and weird if it's true."

He and Robin read on further.

"You know that Freemasons often claim that they are the lineal—or at least the spiritual—descendants of the Templars?" Mallory asked.

"Tell me about it. My father was a Master Mason, but I've never been convinced that there's any link between the two apart from wishful thinking."

"You may be wrong there. Look at this, because I don't think it's a coincidence. We've worked out that it's more than possible the St. Clairs were the 'friends in the north' of the Knights Templar and ended up as the guardians of their treasure, because they were so deeply involved with the order. But the same family, the St. Clairs, were also the hereditary Grand Masters of Scottish Freemasonry since at least 1600. However you look at it, that does seem to me to establish a probable spiritual link between the Templars and Masons. Not that it's important as far as we're concerned, but it is interesting."

Robin nodded and looked back at her laptop.

"The chapel's suffered a lot through the years," she said. "Look at this list. The interior was smashed up and vandalized during the Reformation. Then it was used as a stable for Cromwell's forces in 1650, and ransacked again by a mob in 1688. It wasn't until the early part of the eighteenth century that anyone got around to protecting it and started a restoration project, and not until 1862 that it was rededicated as a place of worship. And then the Victorians got their hands on it and did a lot of work inside the chapel, putting in stained-glass windows and making other improvements. I think the real trick would be finding which bits of it are original and how much resulted from the later restorations."

"Then I think it's lucky we don't need to. I think what's important is the position of the chapel, rather than what's inside it. If the St. Clair family members were the Templars' 'friends in the north,' then it would make sense for them to construct the chapel that would honor the order fairly close to where the treasure was concealed."

"Are you sure about that?" Robin asked doubtfully.

"No, but at least it's a starting point. I'm going to take another look at those topographical maps and see if there are any natural caverns or anything marked near Rosslyn Chapel."

"There's certainly one," Robin said, a few minutes later, still using her laptop, "but it's of no help to us. There was an echo-sounding survey using ground-penetrating radar, that kind of thing, carried out around the chapel a few years ago, and apparently that showed a large chamber lying to the north of the building, beyond its boundary walls. Nobody has any idea what that might be, though I suppose the obvious conclusion might be that it's a part of the St. Clair family burial vaults. But to get inside it, you'd either have to dig straight down into it, which the trustees would never allow, or try and find a way into it from within the chapel itself, and that wouldn't work for exactly the same reason. Have you found anything?"

"Frankly, no, but I have got an idea. You remember that other phrase that seemed to make no sense to us, the one about the sacred mound?"

"Er, yes," Robin replied, opening up a folder on her laptop. "The translation I came up with was 'from the sacred mound seek beyond the battlefield for the open and closed door,' and I still have no clue what that's supposed to mean."

"This may not be correct, but I was thinking about the 'sacred mound.' This does all seem to have something to do with Rosslyn Chapel, and the author of the parchment text obviously knew that at some point in the future a building was going to be constructed to both honor the Templars and remind people about them. The chapel is built on a hill—part of the ridge, in fact, overlooking Roslin Glen and the Esk River valley—and like a lot of high ground, there's at least a possibility that the site was considered sacred or to have some religious importance. I can't find any proof of that, but it's certainly possible.

What I'm wondering, really, is whether the site of Rosslyn Chapel could be the 'sacred mound' that's referred to. What do you think?"

Robin looked at the location on the maps.

"It might be, I suppose," she said, "but of course the only thing marked on these maps is the chapel itself. There's no indication whether or not there was an earlier religious building or anything else at that location. But even if we assume it was the 'sacred mound,' I don't see how that actually helps us."

"Well, it might." Mallory sounded tentative as he explained what he was thinking. "I was just looking at a website that deals with the history of the area, and it turns out that in February 1303 there was a battle—the Battle of Roslin, the name spelled differently—that took place only about half a mile up to the north of the present site of Rosslyn Chapel. So, if that interpretation is correct, and the high ground that the chapel is standing on is the 'sacred mound,' and that's the right battlefield, then we are supposed to be looking for a door that's both open and closed somewhere beyond it, and presumably in the same direction."

"Fine," Robin said. "And now I suppose you're going to amaze me with your explanation of exactly what the text means by a door that can be open and closed at the same time."

She looked at him expectantly, and Mallory smiled at her.

"I don't think that since we met I've amazed you about anything," he said, "and I'm not entirely sure that I'm going to start now. But I did have a thought about it. We know how fond the Templars were of using caverns and underground passages. Let's face it: we've seen enough of them in the last few weeks, and the treasure that we're looking for was almost certainly buried underground. Or, rather, stored in a cave or tunnel. At first glance, there's no way that any door could be both open and closed, but we know that many of the phrases we've deciphered are obscure until you grasp their true meaning, and perhaps this is another one. So I don't think we're looking for a door in the conventional sense, not a door as a lump of wood or metal and fitted with hinges and a lock inside a frame. I'm wondering if the open door is the entrance to a cave, the doorway to get inside, if you see what I mean, and it's closed because the entrance is blocked with rocks or something. That could more or less explain the expression. It's an opening that's also closed."

"Sort of, I suppose. But that only helps if you know of a cave entrance somewhere up to the north of Rosslyn Chapel that's been blocked by stones."

Mallory nodded.

"I know, and there actually is one," he said. "There are a couple of problems with it, but it does seem to me to be a contender."

"Where is it?"

"About four or five miles to the northeast of the chapel. It's a place you can visit, and it's become something of a tourist attraction, because it's another one of those locations that has a somewhat peculiar and definitely mysterious history. It's called Gilmerton Cove," he finished.

47

Midlothian, Scotland

"They're definitely in Edinburgh," Vitale announced, ending the call he'd just taken on his mobile phone. "There were two traffic camera sightings as their vehicle approached the city and another one on the bypass, all three of them yesterday. And now we even know where they're staying."

The Dominicans had booked rooms in a hotel near Penicuik, to the south of Edinburgh, quite close to the city and with easy access to the network of fast roads in the area.

He opened a typical tourist map—long on colors and adverts and short on detail—on the table and pointed.

"Mallory used his credit card here, in this hotel, yesterday afternoon. That wasn't a good idea, but he may have had no choice. Some of the larger hotels insist on authorizing a card even if the final bill will be settled in cash, just in case the guest absconds or something. What-ever the reason, that's what he did, and the chances are that they're still there, so that's where you'll go now. I want all of you out there, in two cars. I will remain here and await your reports."

Toscanelli nodded.

"And your orders?"

"Follow them when they leave, obviously. Mallory's car is very distinctive, so find it in the hotel car park and then put a tracker on it."

Vitale opened his briefcase and took out two black boxes, each smaller than a matchbox.

"You've used these before," he said. "Link their output to the tracking software on your mobile phones—I mean all of you, so that there is plenty of redundancy—and make sure that all of you keep your phones switched on and fully charged. If you haven't got chargers that work off the car systems, make sure you buy some before you reach the hotel. Most garages sell them. One phone in each car is to be on charge all the time. The trackers use mobile phone technology, so as long as Mallory's car is within range of a cellular tower you will be able to keep out of sight but still track it accurately."

He handed one tracker to Toscanelli, and the other to Mario.

"You are to call me when you reach the hotel and have located Mallory's car. Once you have done that, at least one car is to remain close enough to the target vehicle to allow continuous observation of it. You are to call me again when you have placed both trackers on the target car, and again the moment you see either Mallory or Jessop, with a report on what they're doing."

"You're sure you want both trackers on the same car?" Toscanelli asked.

"Yes," Vitale replied shortly. "It is essential that we find out where they are going, and I'm not prepared to risk a single tracker falling off the car or starting to malfunction or being spotted by Mallory. That's why you'll be positioning both of them, obviously choosing different places on the vehicle and placing them out of sight."

"And then what do we do?" Toscanelli asked.

"You keep following them, and then call me again the moment they stop, even if they are apparently just going into a café or restaurant. You are not under any circumstances to approach them. I will decide what action we are to take, and when we are to take it. Now get going."

48

"What, exactly, is Gilmerton Cove? It sounds like a tiny little village on some rocky coast, all whitewashed houses and steep streets, a few yachts bobbing at anchor in the bay, seagulls wheeling overhead, a fishing boat in the distance, all that kind of thing."

"Very poetic," Mallory said. "Unfortunately it's absolutely nothing like that. First of all, it's inland, some distance from the sea in a suburb of Edinburgh about four miles from the city center, and it's under, rather than in, a small mining town named Watson. As in Sherlock Holmes. More importantly, it's the entrance to an extensive cave system, though there's almost nothing known about its origins. There's a vague official version of its history, which is that in 1719 a blacksmith named George Patterson excavated it from the local sandstone bedrock, and it took him five years to create the whole complex.

The problem with this tale is that the cave system is big, really big, and it's really unlikely to have just been the work of one man, even if he did nothing but tunnel his way through the rock every day. And presumably he would have had to do a bit of blacksmithing as well, just to earn a living."

"So, who did build it?"

Mallory shrugged his shoulders.

"The short answer is that nobody knows," he replied. "It's certainly been there for hundreds of years, and quite probably some bits of it may have started out as natural caverns and tunnels that were then enlarged and reshaped for different purposes, and not just by George Patterson. What it consists of is a series of hand-carved chambers, rooms, and passageways. In plan, it's built around a main corridor about forty feet long, with six main rooms and two entrances. The rooms themselves are somewhat bizarre, because all the furniture is built in and carved from the natural rock. In all, the cave system extends to over a thousand square feet, and it's located about ten feet below the present street level.

"What records there are suggest that the main rooms were in use up to about two hundred and fifty years ago, which was when George Patterson lived there, but after he died the place was apparently abandoned, at least as a full-time residence. It might have had some quasireligious functions, because one of the slabs in there has had a circular hole cut into it. The slab is called the 'punch bowl,' but what it resembles more than anything else is a baptismal font. It is known that the cave also functioned as a convenient and secret location for different types of illegal activities, including whiskey distilling and smuggling. For part of the time it was even used as a brothel, and presumably they took beds and bedding down there for that, because it wouldn't have been a lot of fun doing that sort of stuff on cold, bare rock, especially on the sharp, pointy bits."

"You old romantic, you," Robin said.

"Not really. There was an investigation there in 1897 in an attempt to uncover its history, but this didn't actually discover very much at all. There was a lot of graffiti carved into the walls, but about all this confirmed was a connection to the Masons, because the only shape that appeared with any degree of frequency was the classic Masonic symbol of the square and compasses. According to legend, in past centuries it had been used as a meeting place for members of the Knights Templar order and the Freemasons, which I suppose was borne out by the graffiti, and more recently it was a meeting place and no doubt a secret location for all sorts of interesting activities by members of the Hellfire Club.

"There was a modern investigation as well, carried out in 2002, with the same intention, and that did produce a bit more historical data, though the actual origins and purpose of Gilmerton Cove are still a mystery. The most obvious fact that this survey did manage to establish was that George Patterson did not build the place—though he almost certainly modified and changed bits of it—because it appears that the cave system had been used as a refuge by the Covenanters at least a century earlier."

"The Covenanters? I've heard of them, I think. Just remind me."

"This is from one particular website, because I didn't know anything much about them, either. According to this, they were a group that opposed the way that the Stuart kings were trying to interfere in the Scottish church in the mid-seventeenth century, opposition that resulted in a national covenant. The Scottish royal household couldn't tolerate what they saw as this seditious rebellion, and so the Covenanters were hunted down like animals by the royal armies. This was a grim time in Scottish history, with thousands of them being killed and far more than that made homeless. This period became known as the Killing Times, and in their attempts to avoid being slaughtered, many of the Covenanters hid out in the countryside or in the various cave systems dotted around Scotland, including places like Gilmerton Cove. There's a monument to them near Oxgangs, to the southwest of the city center and just north of the Edinburgh Bypass. Not too far from here, actually."

"Okay," Robin said, somewhat impatiently. "All jolly interesting stuff, but what's the relevance to Rosslyn and the lost treasure of the Templars?"

"I was coming to that. The other thing that the 2002 investigation found was a doorway in one of the rooms, a doorway that was special for two reasons. First, it was completely blocked by stones, masonry, and rubble, and there's no easy way of shifting any of it because it goes under a roadway and if it's moved there's a real chance the road could collapse. That was what I was thinking could possibly be the door that's both open and closed. But the most interesting thing about it is that the blocked doorway and the tunnel that is believed to lie behind it appear to point directly toward Rosslyn Chapel, which is less than five miles away."

"Does it, now? And has anyone suggested that whatever lies beyond the blockage could be the Templar treasure?"

Mallory nodded, then shook his head.

"Not exactly that, or not specifically, no, but a few people have come out of the woodwork to claim that the Holy Grail is hidden in the tunnel, apparently brought to Scotland by the Knights Templar, and that the Grail was the relic they recovered from the hidden chambers under the Temple Mount in Jerusalem. So, yes, there's supposed to be a form of treasure there but not the one that we're looking for. That idea has been raised a few times, but nothing has been done about it for several reasons. First, nobody's come up with any compelling evidence that there's anything at all beyond the pile of masonry apart from another empty room, not even necessarily a tunnel at all. And, even if there was, shoring up the roadway to allow the stones and rocks to be removed and the tunnel to be opened up would be a really expensive and quite difficult civil engineering project for all sorts of reasons. To do it at all would also require official permission, and there's no real likelihood of such permission ever being granted, at least not without cast-iron proof that the Grail—or something else of equal historical or commercial value—is actually hidden somewhere in the tunnel. And that isn't ever going to happen, for obvious reasons."

"So, we have a possible tunnel leading from this Gilmerton Cove place toward Rosslyn Chapel. We don't know if it goes all the way from one to the other, and it might only be ten feet long. It's also a tunnel we can't get into at either end. And, even if we could get into it, we have no idea if there's anything inside it or not. Is that a fair summary of the situation?"

"Yes. And no," Mallory said with a grin. "Because as far as I can see, there is a tunnel there and it's certainly not just ten feet long," he added.

He picked up one of the topographical maps, folded it so that they were only looking at the area between Gilmerton Cove and Rosslyn Chapel, and then pointed.

"See these faint lines?" he asked.

"I see a lot of lines. Which ones do you mean?"

"These dotted ones. They all show the location of underground voids. I presume that at some time there was a seismic survey done because of the caves that formed naturally in this area, and, more importantly, all the mining operations that took place here in the past, which would have resulted in abandoned tunnels and workings. Voids can be a problem, obviously, because you can get sinkholes appearing suddenly, and if one of those developed under a house, the whole thing could vanish into it. It wasn't a complete survey, but there are enough marks to show that there is a tunnel that runs from Gilmerton Cove out into the countryside toward Rosslyn Chapel.

There are breaks in the marks, but it makes sense that it's actually a continuous underground space rather than a whole series of separate underground voids, because it does seem to follow a fairly straight line."

Robin studied the marks he was indicating.

"I see what you mean," she said, "but there's one obvious problem. Even if there is a tunnel running between Gilmerton Cove and Rosslyn Chapel, we still can't get into it at either end, unless I've missed something, so we're no further forward."

"That's because you're not thinking laterally," Mallory said. "To get into a tunnel you don't necessarily have to use either end. If you know the route the tunnel takes— which thanks to these maps I think we do—you can cut your way into it almost anywhere, because according to this topo chart, it's not a tunnel through rock, or not for the whole length, anyway. We identify a place where it's definitely man-made rather than natural, and then all we have to do is to dig down until we reach the roof, and hack our way inside."

"That sounds easy if you say it quickly," Robin said. "I have a feeling the reality might be a whole lot different."

49

Midlothian, Scotland

What they couldn't do, quite obviously, was just pick a spot at random and start digging. They needed to be absolutely sure that they were in the right place, and to do that Mallory knew they'd have to spend quite some time with the topographical maps, studying the entire length of the tunnel, or those sections where it was marked, to try to find the right place to break into it. They would need the smallest possible depth of earth above the tunnel roof, and that was something they would have to deduce by looking at the contour lines on the map. They would also have to find a place out in the countryside, somewhere quiet where they wouldn't be disturbed, because they clearly couldn't start excavating in someone's back garden or a farmer's field.

"We're going to have to check this, recheck it, and then check it again," Mallory said, "and that's going to take us all afternoon and probably most of the evening as well."

"I know. That's obvious. So what?"

"All I was going to suggest was that it might be worth going into Edinburgh now and buying the stuff we need—all the equipment, I mean—so that when we do locate the best spot we'll be able to get in the car and drive out there right away."

"That's not a bad idea," Robin said. "And I could certainly do with a break."

Mallory jotted down a rough list of what he thought they would need; then they left the hotel and walked the short distance to the metro station for the ride into the center of Edinburgh. It took them a little while, but eventually they found an old-fashioned hardware shop, one of those places that seemed to sell everything from screws and nails up to concrete mixers and industrial space heaters.

The things they needed were fairly obvious, the two biggest and heaviest items being a pickax and a shovel, but when they left the shop the heavy-duty canvas bag Mallory had bought was bulging at the seams with the weight and bulk of the club hammer, selection of masonry chisels, two jimmies, heavy-duty gloves, climbing rope, earth anchors, powerful torches with spare batteries, and all the other equipment. In fact, the bag was so heavy that after he'd paid the bill, Mallory spent even more money purchasing a collapsible trolley that was sturdy enough to carry everything, including the pickax.

They took the metro back to the hotel and transferred everything from the trolley and the bag into the luggage compartments in the Porsche. Most of the smaller items fitted in the front compartment, and Mallory squeezed the shovel, pickax, and folded trolley into the space behind the seats.

Their preparations completed for the physical work to come, they returned to their hotel room to resume their study of the maps.

From his seat in the back of the hired Audi sedan, Toscanelli muttered to himself as he watched the English couple tucking a selection of tools into the luggage compartment of the Cayman. They were so close that he could be on them, and killing them, in less than ten seconds. But he knew perfectly well that if he did that Vitale would order his own execution the moment he heard about it, and his own death would likely be both protracted and a virtual symphony of agony. When it came to inflicting astonishingly painful revenge on anyone, Silvio Vitale really was in a class of his own.

"What are they doing now?" Vitale asked, his voice emanating from the small speaker on Toscanelli's mobile.

"Putting away all the tools they bought in Edinburgh," Toscanelli replied. "In the car, I mean."

He hadn't risked being a part of the surveillance team himself, in case Mallory or Jessop recognized him, but two of his men had followed them into Edinburgh and from shop to shop until they had made their purchases, and had then dogged their footsteps all the way back to the hotel.

"Are they going anywhere in the car?"

"Just a moment. They've opened one of the car doors, and they're putting the last couple of large tools into the vehicle through the rear hatch. Now they've closed the door and Mallory's just locked the car. And they're heading back into the hotel."

"It might be a bit late for them to go off and start digging somewhere this afternoon," Vitale said, "but we can't take a chance. All of you stay on watch until it gets dark. Then both vehicles are to return to the hotel. If nothing else happens today, I will want surveillance to be mounted against them tomorrow morning from six, so ensure you all get a good sleep tonight."

"I think this is probably our best bet," Mallory said, drawing a rough circle around one particular part of the topographical map. "As far as I can see from this, the land isn't used or developed. There are no buildings anywhere within about a quarter of a mile, and no footpaths, either. But the road runs past it on the other side of this stand of trees, and that's only about a hundred yards away, so we won't have too far to lug everything."

"I'm really more interested in the tunnel," Robin said. "I'm definitely following your lead on this, but are you sure that we're not going to have to dig about a dozen feet or more straight down and then find we're looking at solid sandstone, with no way of getting through it unless we bring in a pneumatic drill?"

Mallory shook his head.

"It's very difficult to be certain," he said, "but I've been studying the blasted contour lines on these maps until I've virtually gone cross-eyed. That place is in a kind of dip near the base of a small hill, and all three topo-graphical maps quite clearly show a subterranean void right below the spot I've marked. As far as I can tell without actually going out there and digging a hole, that's where the tunnel roof has to be closest to the surface. What I can't tell, for obvious reasons, is whether or not that's a section of man-made tunnel, rather than being a natural cave in the bedrock. But what I do know is that if the markings on these topographical maps are accurate—and they should be—that particular void seems to have quite straight sides, which does suggest it's not a natural feature."

He indicated another area on the same map, but some distance away from the point he'd marked.

"If you look here, about a mile or so north, the void is shown as having different widths and the path it follows is a long way from being straight. So that looks to me far more like a cavern or a long fissure in the rock. I'm hop-ing that what we've deduced is correct, and that when we dig down to the tunnel roof we'll be confronted by worked stones and not a mass of solid bedrock. But real-istically, there's no way of telling. I've looked at the whole length of the tunnel on the maps, and I've located two other places that seem to be possible access points, just in case the first spot doesn't work."

"All we can do is hope," Robin said. "Hope that you're right about where we should start digging. And more importantly hope that if—or when—we get into the tun-nel, we don't find that it's full of spiderwebs and dead rats and nothing else, and that everything we've been through has been for nothing. That would really piss me off."

"Me, too. Anyway, we'll know soon enough. Let's try and get out there early tomorrow morning. The sooner we do this, the sooner we'll know if we've just been wasting our time."

50

Midlothian, Scotland

Mallory braked the Porsche to a stop a few minutes after nine the following morning and switched off the engine. He'd seen a convenient pull-off, just about big enough for a single car, only about fifty yards from the place he'd wanted to park. For a minute or so, they sat there, listening to the ticking sounds of the cooling engine and the almost complete silence of the woodland outside the car through the open windows.

"Time's a-passing," Robin said. "Let's do this."

Mallory nodded, raised the windows, and stepped out of the car. In a few minutes he'd opened up the rear hatch, replaced the tools in the canvas bag, and strapped it to the trolley, the pickax and shovel lashed on top. There was no traffic on the road, and not even the distant sound of a car engine. The silence was almost complete.

He locked the Cayman and they walked across the

fairly narrow road, Mallory pulling the trolley, and stepped into the field on the other side, the land sloping down and away from the road. The ground was slightly damp underfoot, the result of a couple of hours of light drizzling rain the previous afternoon, but that morning the sun was already shining, still low on the eastern horizon behind them.

Robin was carrying the maps, two folded up in one of the pockets of her waterproof jacket—they'd come dressed for the conditions they expected to encounter during the day, both above- and belowground—and the other in her hand, opened to the area Mallory had decided to explore.

Once they'd cleared the narrow strip of woodland they stopped so they could orient themselves. Mallory had spent quite a long time identifying landmarks that should be visible from the target location, and marking the appropriate bearings of them on the map, so that they would be able to confirm precisely where they should start digging.

He took out a pocket compass that he'd bought in Edinburgh the previous afternoon at a camping and outdoor store and flipped up the cover as he looked around them.

"Okay," he said, "we're still at least fifty yards from where we need to be, I reckon, but I'll just check we're basically in the right place."

He aimed the compass toward a road junction over to the west and noted the bearing, then did the same thing with a distinctive house about half a mile to the north. Then he closed the compass and took hold of the handle of the trolley again and walked forward about twenty yards.

Then he took out his mobile phone and opened the mapping application. The other thing he'd done, as a final check, was to note the latitude and longitude coordinates of the spot he wanted to find from the map. The application—as usual—took several seconds to respond, and longer still before it locked onto enough GPS satellites to confirm his location on the ground. When it finally did so, he was able to pinpoint his position.

"We keep going straight ahead," he said, pointing. "When we reach that clump of bushes I'll check again, but the spot I chose is right in front of us."

The next time he stopped, one of the bearings was spot-on, but they had to move a few yards farther north until the second one lined up exactly. There was a third landmark he'd identified on the map, but it was invisible behind a distant wood, and a fourth that for some reason he couldn't identify against the backdrop of the urban development to the north, so he had to rely on just the two that he could see, but they should be enough. He made a last check of the GPS system on his phone, then nodded.

"This is it," he said, lowering the trolley to the ground so that he could remove the tools from the bag.

He released the top of it, reached inside, and took out the gloves. Then he removed his waterproof jacket, picked up the shovel and pickax, walked a couple of paces farther down the gentle slope, and stopped. He checked that Robin was well out of the way, then swung the pickax in a short arc, driving the point deep into the soil. Perhaps because of the rain, the soil was comparatively soft, and he was able to make quite quick progress. The pickax broke up the soil, and after every half dozen or so swings he dropped the tool on the ground, picked up the shovel, and lifted the loose earth out of the hole he'd created, tossing it to one side.

To begin with, he tried to dig straight down, but he quickly realized that wasn't going to work. The hole needed to be fairly wide, because ultimately he was hoping that both he and Robin would be able to climb down into it in order to lower themselves into the tunnel. So he began widening the hole at the same time as he dug downward, aiming to end up with a roughly square vertical shaft, each side about three feet long.

"I don't know if this is good news or not," he said, after a few minutes, "but what I've been shifting here is just earth. There are almost no stones or rocks in it. And it's quite easy work."

"Good," Robin replied, "because I'm going to take my turn when you get tired. I'm just as strong as you are."

Mallory didn't doubt that, but he really didn't want Robin to have to get involved in the strictly physical stuff. He was enough of a gentleman that he didn't like the idea of a woman working at anything like digging a hole in a Scottish hillside.

Just under a quarter of a mile away, at the edge of a small copse of trees, Silvio Vitale and Marco Toscanelli lay on the ground side by side and watched the operation, using powerful binoculars.

Following the Porsche through the early-morning traffic had been perfectly straightforward, thanks to the two trackers, which meant that neither of the pursuing vehicles had needed to get within sight of the Cayman at any point. They had been able to rely on the electronic link between the trackers and their mobile phones to follow the vehicle accurately but at a safe distance. Once the trackers confirmed that the Porsche had stopped, the Dominicans had been able to park their own vehicles reasonably close to the location but out of sight and then find a vantage point to observe their quarry.

"They've obviously found something," Toscanelli said. "I can order my men to kill them right now."

The other Dominicans had already moved up to within about a hundred yards of where Mallory and Jessop were excavating the hole, and were waiting for instructions, their mobile phones set for silent operation and to vibrate only when a call was received.

"As far as I can see, Toscanelli, they haven't found anything yet. They're just digging a hole. It will be time to move when they lift something out of it. Unless you want to go over there and dig the hole yourself, of course? As I told you before," Vitale added, his voice cold and hard, "I will decide what we do and when we do it. So, if you have nothing meaningful to contribute, just shut up and watch. This could be a very long day, and we'll be doing nothing until I'm absolutely certain what the situation is."

Although the day was still cool, the digging was hot and sweaty work, and within about twenty minutes Mallory had stripped off his shirt and handed it to Robin.

"That's better," he said.

"Better for you, maybe," she replied, "but less so for me, because I've got to watch your half-naked body grunting and sweating, and one of the Chippendales you're not. Mind you," she added, "I've never found the male body desperately attractive, with all sorts of bits and pieces dangling and swaying in the wind, but yours isn't that bad. Just make sure you keep your trousers on. Otherwise, I might die laughing."

"Thanks for that, I think," Mallory said, swinging the pickax again.

Just over a quarter of an hour later, by which time he was standing in the hole as he dug farther down into the earth, the tip of the blade of the pickax hit stone, jarring Mallory's arms, and the impact making a very distinct noise.

"That sounds hopeful," Robin exclaimed, stepping over to the side of the hole Mallory had excavated and staring down into it. "That wasn't just a loose stone, I take it?"

Mallory shook his head.

"Definitely not. Whatever it is, it's pretty solid. Of course, it could just be bedrock, but I'll see in a few moments."

He put the pickax to one side and picked up the shovel, using it to lift the earth away from that part of the hole and then scraping the blade across the hard surface he had encountered. Then he leaned the shovel against the side of the hole and looked up at Robin.

"Strike one," he said, sounding irritated. "What I think I've found is one of the Pentland Hills or whatever this collection of uplands is called. This is definitely bedrock, not man-made."

"Bugger," Robin said, with feeling.

Mallory passed her the pickax and the shovel and climbed out of the hole he'd dug, then shoveled most of the soil back inside it.

"Do you need to do that?" Robin asked.

"Probably not, but I don't like leaving a mess."

Inevitably he ended up with a small mound of earth rather than a flat surface. Robin pointed at it.

"I suppose that proves the old saying that you can never put back into a hole everything you've dug out of it," she remarked. "So, where to now?"

"There are two other spots that we identified as possible sites from the map, so we'll try both of those."

"And if you hit rock on both of those, we just call it a day?"

"Unless you've got any bright ideas," Mallory replied, "we'll have to."

Vitale gestured at the distant scene as he and Toscanelli watched Mallory and Jessop walk away from the patch of grass on the hillside back toward the spot where their car was parked.

"That is precisely why we are only watching them," he said. "Neither you nor I have any idea exactly what clue or clues they are following, and if I'd adopted your suggestion and had them killed half an hour ago, we would have lost the only lead we have to the location of the treasure. Trying to persuade them to tell us what they know would be prolonged, messy, and with no guarantee of success. This way, we just let them run. They will do all the work for us, and we will simply step in at the last moment, relieve them of whatever they find, and then eliminate them. Contact the others and tell them to head back to the cars. We'll follow them to wherever they're going next."

51

Midlothian, Scotland

The second location was about a quarter of a mile from the first, and Mallory was back in the saddle, so to speak, pickax in his hand, in well under ten minutes. He again used the map, his compass, and the mapping application on his mobile phone to confirm that he was in exactly the right spot, and then he started digging.

His interpretation of the contour lines on the topographical maps had suggested that the underground void marked in that location was probably deeper underground than he had expected at the first place, but in fact the point of his pick hit stone only about four feet down. And this time, when he used the shovel to clear away the soil, it was immediately obvious that he had not struck bedrock.

"I can see oblong blocks of stone," he said, the excitement in his voice obvious, "so unless this is some other kind of underground structure, I think I'm standing on the roof of the tunnel built by the Templars."

"Do not," Robin instructed, "fanny about. Get some of those blocks shifted so we can see what we're looking at."

Mallory nodded, but before he did anything else he levered himself up and out of the hole and opened up the canvas bag of tools and equipment.

"I think the important thing to remember," he said, "is the expression 'the roof of the tunnel,' so the first thing I'm going to do is attach a rope to the trunk of that tree over there and then wrap the other end around me, so that if the roof gives way when I start removing stones, it won't take me with it."

"Good thinking. Do you want me to tie it for you?"

"You're probably better at it than I am," Mallory said, "but as it's my neck that'll be broken if I fall, I'd rather do it myself. Then if the bottom does fall out of my world, I'll only have myself to blame."

"Fair enough. I'll fish out some hammers and crowbars and stuff for your demolition job."

Mallory wrapped the end of the climbing rope around the tree. In fact, he wrapped it twice around the tree and then tied it using a clove hitch and two half hitches, a totally secure knot that he knew would neither slip nor loosen. Then he walked back to the hole, estimated its depth by eye, added a couple of feet for good measure, and then tied the rope around his own waist using a bowline.

"They both look secure," Robin said, walking back from the tree trunk where she'd inspected the rope and looking critically at the knot Mallory had just tied. "Anything I can do at the moment?"

"Just pass me the tools once I'm back in the hole," he replied, and lowered himself into it. "I'll try using a crowbar first."

The spade was still in the hole, and before he did anything else Mallory cleared all of the soil away from the layer of stones that now formed the bottom of his small excavation. What was revealed was not fine masonry, by any stretch of imagination. The stones were all about the same size and shape, each about a foot long and eight inches wide, but the tops had been left rough and unfinished.

"I suppose they didn't bother about what the outside of the tunnel looked like," Robin said, "because the structure was obviously going to be buried once they'd finished it."

Mallory nodded, then jammed the end of the crowbar into the cement layer between two of the stones, working the tip of the tool in and sideways to provide a surface that he could lever against. He put pressure on the stone as soon as he was able to do so, but with no result whatsoever: as far as he could tell, the stone didn't move at all.

"It might not look very pretty," he said, glancing up at Robin, "but they built this to last."

"The other problem we've got," she replied, "is that you'll probably find the stones are tapered, so the lower surface will be smaller than the surface you're looking at. I think you'll have to shift all the cement or whatever it is from around one of the stones before you'll be able to move it. And once you've levered that one out, there's a pretty good chance that some of the stones around it will fall straight to the floor of the tunnel, so it might be a good idea if you weren't standing on them when that happens, rope or no rope."

"That kind of was my plan," Mallory said, kneeling down and chipping away at the exposed cement that marked the boundaries between the individual stones. "This stone is more or less in the middle, so I'll try and shift this one. I'll also need that long-bladed screwdriver to shift all of the cement."

The cement or mortar that the tunnel builders had used was hard and brittle with age, and much of it came away in chunks. Mallory worked his way methodically around the stone, using the screwdriver and the end of the crowbar, and after a few minutes he could see that the stone was moving very slightly in response to what he was doing.

"Just a suggestion," Robin said, "but you might find that if you shift all the cement the stone might actually drop further down into the cavity, and you'll have to do the whole thing all over again with a different stone."

"So you think I should try and lift it out right now? Yes, that does make sense."

Mallory rammed the straight end of the crowbar into the gap he had opened up at one end of the stone and levered as hard as he could. With a protesting squeal, the stone shifted perhaps half an inch. He kept the pressure on, trying to lever the end of the stone out of the tunnel roof. Once it had lifted, he held it in place with the end of the screwdriver while he changed the position of the crowbar to increase the leverage. And slowly, painfully slowly, that single stone began to emerge from the roof of the tunnel.

With a final shove of the crowbar, the end of the stone came clear. Again, Mallory slid the screwdriver blade under the stone to stop it from falling back, then changed position and grabbed at the block with both hands to lift it clear. As he did so, he reeled backward slightly as a waft of foul, musty air reached him.

"What is it?" Robin asked.

"I just got a whiff of seven-hundred-year-old air," Mallory replied, struggling with the weight of the stone, "and it's not the nicest thing I've ever encountered. It smells as if something died down there a long time ago."

"It's probably just the result of no ventilation for the better part of a millennium. Now, be careful with that," Robin said, reaching out to take part of the weight of the stone as Mallory lifted it clear of the hole.

Slightly unexpectedly, although now deprived of a measure of support, the other stones showed no immediate signs of moving.

"I've only removed one stone," Mallory said, "so each of those left still has support on three sides. That's probably why they've not fallen yet."

He took the crowbar again and began the same process of shifting the cement from around the end of one of the stones that bordered the hole, then applied leverage to the same end of the stone. Almost immediately, the heavy stone shifted, but before Mallory could lift it out of position, it simply fell into the darkness of the tunnel to land with a dull and heavy thud somewhere below. And that was immediately followed by four other stones that tumbled from the roof and into the tunnel.

Mallory carefully stepped back onto what he hoped was firmer ground, tossing the crowbar and screwdriver out of the hole as he did so. Then he used the rope and clambered out and onto the grassy slope, Robin grabbing his arm as he emerged.

"We're going to have to be careful going down there," Mallory said. "One of those stones could kill you if it fell on your head."

Before they did anything else, Mallory retied the bowline around his chest, shortening the length of the rope as he did so to prevent himself from falling, then resumed his position in the hole and stamped as hard as he could on the remaining stones, both to increase the size of the hole and, more importantly, to try to dislodge any that might be loose and likely to fall. Two more stones tumbled out of position, but as far as he could tell the others were still securely in place.

"Right," he said. "Now we can find out what—if anything—is down there."

The vantage point Vitale had found didn't offer anything like as clear a view as the previous one, because the site where the English couple was now working was partially screened by bushes and vegetation, so he was unable to see everything that was going on. As before, the other Dominican enforcers under his command had moved closer to the location to be ready when the order to kill or capture Mallory and Jessop was given. It was possible that some of the men had a better view of the site, but Vitale had forbidden them to talk or use their mobiles for fear of alerting their quarry. Instead, he had rationalized, he thought he could see enough of the location to be able to tell whether the two people he had been following for so long had actually found what they were looking for. Or if this place, just like the first spot they had investigated, would yield nothing to their digging.

Through the partial screen of bushes he could see both of them moving around, but his view was sufficiently obstructed that he couldn't tell exactly what they were doing. That didn't bother him, for one very simple reason: he knew that Mallory and Jessop had driven to the site in Mallory's Porsche Cayman, and if their quest was going to be successful, that was completely the wrong vehicle to be using. If they did discover the long-lost treasure of the Knights Templar, at the very least they would need a large van to haul it away. Possibly more than one van.

So, from Vitale's point of view, he didn't need to keep the two of them under constant observation. All he had to do was wait until they had found what they were looking for, then kill them and make his own arrangements for the removal of the treasure.

"I've lost sight of them," Toscanelli said.

Vitale resumed his scan of the digging site through his binoculars and came to the same conclusion.

"Perhaps they're both in the hole, digging deeper," he suggested, "and that's why we can't see them."

But after three more minutes, Vitale was beginning to worry.

"Call one of your men," he instructed, "and tell him to confirm that their car is still in place. And pass me that map."

As Toscanelli held a brief conversation with the Dominican who had the clearest view of the place where the Porsche was parked, Vitale studied the appropriate section of the topographical map they had brought with them.

"The car hasn't moved," Toscanelli said, ending the call, "and Carlo cannot see the digging site from where he is."

"Wait," Vitale snapped, his entire concentration directed at the map in front of him.

After another few seconds, he nodded and turned to his companion.

"I know where they are and why we can't see them," he said. "I should have realized earlier."

"I don't understand."

Vitale pointed to two faint parallel dotted lines marked on the map.

"That's where they are. That's a tunnel, and they must have dug their way into it through the roof. And if this map is correct, that same tunnel runs all the way over to Rosslyn Chapel. There have been lots of stories and legends about what may be concealed in hidden chambers below the building, and for a number of reasons this part of Scotland is one of the most likely locations for the lost treasure."

"So they may well have found it?"

Vitale nodded.

"They wouldn't have gone to all the trouble of digging their way into the tunnel unless they were reasonably certain that they were close to it. And according to this map, that tunnel is the only possible way to get into the chambers under Rosslyn Chapel. This really is the end of the quest."

"So we need to get into the tunnel after them, as quickly as possible," Toscanelli said.

Vitale smiled bleakly.

"There's no hurry," he said. "Mallory and Jessop are caught like rats in a trap, and they're not going anywhere. Tell your men to get over to the place where they were digging and to wait for us there. It's time to finish this once and for all."

Mallory had checked the security of the rope knotted around the trunk of the nearby tree, then tossed the end of the rope into the hole in the roof of the tunnel. That was going to be their way into—and more importantly their way out of—the tunnel, and because they were going to be climbing up and down it, they needed to take as little equipment with them as possible. Torches and spare batteries were obviously essential, and Mallory took only a small crowbar with him to open any chests or anything else that they found. Apart from that, they each had a paper mask to cover their mouths and noses to keep out the dust that they expected to find in the tunnel, and a plastic helmet that might stop them from being brained if a stone fell from the roof.

"What about the pistols?" Robin asked.

They still had the Browning Hi-Power and the Beretta that Mallory had taken from the wounded Dominican back in Templecombe near the church.

"I think all we're likely to encounter down there are a handful of dead rats and some very old spiderwebs, so I doubt if we'll need them. The Browning pistol is in the Porsche, under the driver's seat."

"Okay. Your choice. Now let's go."

Mallory went first, dropping the crowbar into the tunnel before climbing down the rope, hand over hand, until he was able to stand up. He stumbled slightly over one of the fallen stones, then switched on his torch and checked his surroundings.

The tunnel was about eight feet wide and ten feet high at the apex, the roof curving down to meet the walls. The interior surfaces of the stones were much smoother than the outsides, the masonry finished properly and professionally. The stones were dark brown, almost black, in color, and in the light from his torch Mallory could see a number of wall-mounted metal sconces, clearly designed to hold burning brands that would illuminate the space, in both directions, up and down the tunnel. And apart from those, and the half dozen or so heavy stones lying on the floor beside him, the tunnel appeared to be completely empty.

He slid the fallen stones away from the point where the end of the rope lay on the ground, to prevent Robin from tripping on any of them, then waited for her to follow him down the rope.

"So, what we seem to have here," she said when she, too, was standing on the floor of the tunnel, "is a whole lot of nothing."

"That's not too surprising," Mallory said mildly, "bearing in mind that the tunnel's over four miles long. If it was full of treasure, that'd be enough to pay off the American national debt with plenty left over. My guess is that the treasure, assuming that it still exists, will be in a chamber near one end or the other of this tunnel, and most likely somewhere near Rosslyn Chapel."

"Then we'd better get moving. From what I remember of the map, we're just over a mile from that end."

They had no idea how long they would be underground, and although they had spare batteries for the torches it obviously made sense to conserve them, so Robin kept hers switched off and they headed down the tunnel toward Rosslyn, their way illuminated by the light of only Mallory's torch. Once they'd moved well away from the hole they had carved through the tunnel roof, he switched off the torch for a few moments. The blackness was total, not even the faintest glimmer of light showing anywhere.

Robin shivered involuntarily.

"I wouldn't want to be down here without a light," she said.

"It's like the old expression," Mallory replied, turning on the torch again. "It's as black as the Earl of Hell's waistcoat. Which might be quite appropriate, bearing in mind we're now quite deep underground, I think."

The tunnel was largely featureless, very dark brown stones forming the walls and roof, though in places it ran through what was obviously a natural cavern or part of a cave, where the stones were replaced by bedrock still bearing the marks of chisels and hammers wielded centuries earlier. But the floor was consistent: flagstones apparently cut from the same dark rock that had been used to fabricate the tunnel itself, and that provided a level and even surface to walk along.

There were cobwebs, large gray masses covered in dust, that clung to their faces and hands as they pushed past them, but the spiders themselves had obviously been dead for hundreds of years. They didn't even see any rats, or any live ones, though the occasional collection of small bones on the tunnel floor shone white in the torchlight. But that was all they saw, at least until they'd been walking for almost twenty minutes, by which time Mallory calculated they'd covered almost a mile and had to be getting quite close to Rosslyn.

For the most part, the tunnel had been fairly straight, with only the occasional gentle bend, but they were then confronted by a more serpentine section of the tunnel, bending left, then right at irregular intervals.

And then, as they walked around a gentle bend in the tunnel, they saw something in front of them that defied belief.

They came to a sudden and involuntary halt and simply stared at what was illuminated by the powerful beam of Mallory's torch. He could actually feel the hairs rising on the back of his neck, and his body suddenly felt cold with fear.

52

"You were right," Toscanelli said, peering down into the rough-sided hole that Mallory had cut in the Scottish hillside. "That's obviously a part of a tunnel system."

Vitale nodded, then stepped to one side.

"It looks like it's over two meters to the tunnel floor, and I'm too old to start clambering up and down ropes. You," he said, turning to one of the Dominicans, "take a car and find me a ladder from somewhere. Buy one or steal one—I don't care—but just get back here with it as soon as you can."

The man nodded obediently and trotted away.

"So, what do we do now?" Toscanelli asked. "Just sit here and wait?"

"That's exactly what we do. The only way into or out of that tunnel is through the hole that's right in front of us, so Mallory and Jessop aren't going anywhere. As soon as we have a ladder, we'll get down there after them and finish the job."

The man Vitale had dispatched returned in only about fifteen minutes, much faster than any of them had expected.

"There's a farm only just up the road," he explained, lowering a rigid aluminum ladder, about ten feet long, to the ground. "I saw this leaning against a building in the yard as I drove past. There was nobody about, so I stopped and put it in the car."

"It's about three meters long," Toscanelli pointed out. "How did it fit?"

"I opened the passenger-door window and the rear window diagonally opposite, and it fitted quite neatly from one side of the car to the other."

"It doesn't matter how he got it," Vitale said impatiently. "It's only important that he *did* get it. Lower it into the tunnel so that we can end this. Make sure you've all got torches and batteries," he added.

The ladder made everything very easy, and in less than three minutes the entire group had climbed down it to stand on the tunnel floor.

Then Vitale had an idea.

"Carlo, climb back up the ladder, untie that length of rope from the tree, and bring it down here. When you've done that, we'll lower the ladder into the tunnel out of sight of the hole above us. We don't want to be disturbed."

That took only a couple of minutes.

"So, which way do we go?" Toscanelli asked.

"Both," Vitale replied. "We don't know what final clue Mallory and Jessop deciphered, so we don't know which way their path will have taken them. So we split up. You two"—he pointed at two of the Dominicans—"head northeast, and the rest of us will go toward Rosslyn Chapel, because I think that's most likely the right way."

"And your orders if we find the English couple?" one of the men asked.

"Subdue them if possible. If not, kill the man but keep the woman alive, just in case she knows anything useful to us. All of you, use your torches sparingly," Vitale ordered, "and try to keep the noise down. I don't want them to know we are in here with them until the last possible moment."

The two groups split, torches sporadically illuminating the walls and floor of the tunnel as they separated.

"What the hell is that?" Mallory muttered. "It's bloody creepy."

More or less in the center of the tunnel and perhaps sixty yards in front of them was a faint white object defaced by a dark marking, apparently suspended in midair.

"I have no idea," Robin said, "and we aren't going to find out if we just stand here. But I agree it does look pretty weird."

"That's weird, too," Mallory added, as the light from his torch illuminated the roof of the tunnel in front of them, "though actually that does make sense of something I spotted a few seconds ago."

"What?" Robin demanded.

"I'll tell you later. Let's find out what this is first."

They stepped forward, moving cautiously, Mallory keeping the beam of his torch pointed straight at the mysterious object. The shape became clearer with every yard that they advanced.

And then, at almost the same moment, they both recognized the object for what it was.

"It's a man," Robin said incredulously. "But that's impossible."

Sitting squarely in their path, almost blocking it, was unmistakably a human figure, but not just any human figure.

"It might be impossible," Mallory agreed, "but that is the figure of a man, without a doubt. A man from the distant past, by the looks of him."

In the light from the torch they could now identify the white object they'd seen as a surcoat, emblazoned with the red *croix pattée* of the Templars. Around it was the glint of chain mail and armor, and above it the horizontal eye slits of a battle helmet. What they seemed to be facing was a fully armored knight of the Templar order.

"This can't be," Robin said, her step faltering as they got closer.

"Whoever it is," Mallory said with a confidence that he wasn't entirely sure he felt, "he's been dead a long time. He can't be any danger to us now."

The closer they approached, the more they could see, and in moments it was obvious that their initial conclusion was correct.

Sitting in the center of the tunnel on a heavy wooden

chair was the dead body, just skin and bone, of a Templar knight in full battle order, his war sword resting across his lap, his shield leaning against the side of his body, his left hand—now little more than a cluster of bones with a few patches of mummified tissue clinging to them—gripping it. The corpse was held in place on the chair with a leather strap around his torso to keep him upright, and another, much thinner strap supporting his helmet. From a distance—as they could both confirm—he had looked alive. Alive and alert. A knight very obviously on guard.

"A fell guardian indeed," Mallory whispered. "A knight left here to guard the Templar wealth for all eternity."

He handed Robin his torch, then picked up the battle sword and eased the blade out of the scabbard. The ancient steel of the weapon glittered in the torchlight.

"This looks almost like new," he said. "Even the leather of the scabbard feels as if it was oiled recently, and there's no rust that I can see on the shield or the helmet. The constant temperature and lack of humidity down here must have acted to preserve everything really well."

"Do you think they tied him here when he was still alive?" Jessop asked, her eyes fixed on the eye slits of the helmet, almost as if she was expecting to see some sign of life there.

"I doubt it. It's difficult to tell, but he looks to me like he was an old man, and I guess that after he died his body was then dressed in his battle armor and secured to the chair."

They studied the ancient body in the torchlight for a few moments; then Mallory shook his head.

"I can well imagine that he would probably have spooked any local treasure hunters who found their way into the tunnel. Imagine coming across him when the only light you have is a flickering wooden torch. Let's face it: he stopped us in our tracks."

"My heart's still pounding," Robin said. "But at least we now know two things. First, this tunnel was obviously built by the Knights Templar, because otherwise the guardian would not be here. And the other thing is that I think the treasure is still here." She pointed behind the silent watcher in his wooden chair and shone the beam of her torch in that direction.

Mallory looked where the beam had come to rest, and against one side of the tunnel he saw a large lumpy shape, some kind of a tattered black cloth concealing whatever was underneath it. To one side of the shape, mounted horizontally on a couple of stone pegs in the wall, was another Templar battle sword.

"That really could be what we've been looking for," he said, and quickly strode over to it.

He bent down, took hold of the corner of the cloth, and slowly, with infinite care, peeled it back to reveal a collection of ancient wooden boxes bound with ornamented metal bands.

For a few moments, neither of them spoke. They both just stared at what, if they had followed the clues correctly, was the lost treasure of the Knights Templar. A hoard of precious metals and jewels and other assets that in the medieval period had a value greater than the national treasury of most European countries. In the twenty-first century, its value, based on its intrinsic worth as bullion and precious stones, would be virtually incalculable, and perhaps significantly higher still for its historic importance.

"This has to be it," Mallory said quietly, "but there's definitely something missing. And why is there a second sword?"

"Forget the sword. What do you think is missing?"

Mallory gestured at the pile of chests in front of them.

"Look at these boxes. I'm a long way from being an expert on anything, and especially things to do with the sea. But I do know that according to the best available information we have, the Templar fleet that sailed from Honfleur in the autumn of 1307, allegedly carrying the bulk of the treasure of the order, numbered about eighteen ships. They weren't big vessels, but they certainly had seagoing capability and were big enough to weather Mediterranean storms and to sail the coast of the Atlantic Ocean. We also know that they were obviously carrying passengers as well as cargo, but this"—he pointed again at the boxes in front of them—"just isn't enough."

"I see what you mean," Robin said. "Even though these boxes and chests are bound to be heavy because of what's in them, what we're looking at here could probably have been carried by two ships, maybe by three at the most. So, where's the rest of it?"

"Maybe there was a second hiding place somewhere else," Mallory suggested, "and maybe there's a clue somewhere in this lot that could lead us to it."

"Or maybe there isn't," Robin said, staring at the wall behind the chests, and then pointing at it. "Just take that sword and touch the stone with the end of it."

Mallory had no idea what she meant, but he obediently lifted the Templar battle sword off the stone pegs, pulled the blade from the scabbard, and extended the point toward the black wall that rose up behind the pile of chests.

Then something totally unexpected happened. Instead of the metallic sound of the blade touching stone, the point seemed almost to sink into it, and the whole wall seemed to ripple slightly. And then Mallory realized what Robin had seen and that he had missed.

"That's not a stone wall," he said. "That's another black cloth, and it's concealing an opening in the wall. Maybe these chests wouldn't fit inside that chamber, and the rest of the Templar treasure is stored in there."

Mallory started to resheathe the battle sword, then stopped, his attention drawn to the shape of the blade near the point.

"That's odd," he said, showing it to Robin. "The blade of this sword is an unusual shape. The blades of most medieval swords followed exactly the same pattern. The edges of the blade were parallel almost to the tip of the weapon and the blade often had a central groove running down the center of each side, as this one does. That was known as a fuller, and was intended to lighten the blade and make it easier to handle in battle. Near the tip of the blade that changed to a central ridge that provided added strength where the metal was at its thinnest. But on this blade the central ridge is present on only one side, and on the other the fuller extends all the way to the point, so in cross section it looks a bit like a flattened letter *V.* I've never seen that before. I wonder if that was a unique Templar design."

Mallory walked back to the body of the seated knight, lifted the sword off his lap, and drew the blade out of the scabbard.

"No," he said. "This is the traditional pattern, with the central ridge extending down each side of the blade to the tip."

"Does it matter?" Robin asked.

"Probably not," Mallory admitted. He replaced that sword in its original position, across the thighs of the long-dead knight, and walked back to where she was standing. "It's just unusual, and that could well mean that the sword is special. It's probably not important. But the other thing that puzzles me is the way the sword was hanging. Usually a sword was hung vertically, point downward, from a pair of pegs that fitted either side of the scabbard so that the weight of the sword rested on the cross guard, the steel bar between the handle and the blade. That way, it was ready for immediate use and because most of the weight was in the blade it was a very safe way of storing it. I can't help thinking that because the sword was positioned horizontally, with the blade pointing toward the far end of the tunnel, near Rosslyn Chapel, it must be significant in some way."

He picked up the second sword, slid the blade back into the scabbard, and leaned it against one of the iron-bound chests. Then he stretched out his hand toward the chest directly in front of him and ran his fingertips over the ancient wood and polished metal.

But then he stopped abruptly and drew back.

"You've remembered the Templar booby traps," Robin suggested.

"No, it's not that," Mallory said. "Listen."

"I can hear footsteps," she said after a moment, her face pale in the darkness. "Faint footsteps."

"And not just one pair. We need to get out of here if we can. Or hide if we can't."

"Is it the bloody Dominicans, or just somebody who saw the hole you made and decided to explore?"

"I'll give you three guesses. Sound travels well in tunnel systems. I can also hear faint voices, and I think they're speaking Italian."

Mallory picked up the Templar battle sword again, and the black cloth that had concealed the chests.

Robin covered the glass of the torch with her fingers to reduce the amount of light it was emitting, and they moved as quickly and quietly as they could beyond the pile of chests and deeper into the tunnel. But only about fifty yards farther on they came to a dead stop because the tunnel in front of them was completely blocked by a rockfall, either accidental and caused by the geography of the area or, perhaps more likely, brought down deliberately to seal off that end of the tunnel.

"We have to go back," Robin whispered. "I saw a crevice in the rock. It might lead to a side passage, or at least be somewhere we can hide."

In fact, it was rather more than a crevice. She led the way into a short side tunnel that appeared to be a natural feature of the cave system. It was reasonably wide to begin with, and the opening meandered some distance deeper into the bedrock, becoming more narrow and restricted as it did so. It didn't appear to have ever been used in the past, as the floor was heavily ridged and uneven, and if it had been a storage area or employed for some other purpose, then logically the Templars or whoever had occupied the site would have tried to flatten it out.

There were a number of fissures in the rock on both sides of the cave, most of them only a couple of feet or so deep, but one of them was more like a side passage and extended for at least twenty feet. Inside, there were numerous cracks and crevices, and the narrow opening at the very end of the passage was just wide enough for both of them to slide into it and get out of sight.

"The cloth," Robin whispered. "Now I know why you picked it up."

"Black stone, black cloth," Mallory replied. "I thought we could maybe hide under it somewhere. But this will work better, I hope."

He positioned the cloth across the opening of the fissure behind them, wedging it into place with the Templar sword and making sure that neither of them was touching it. If it was going to function as a hiding place, the cloth had to remain completely motionless to anyone looking into the side passage.

"That should look like the back wall of the opening if

anyone comes in there," he said. "I just wish I'd brought the Browning," he added quietly. "I'd feel a whole lot better with a gun in my hand."

And as the sound of footsteps grew appreciably louder, they both shrank as far back into the crevice as they could.

Then all they could do was wait. And hope.

53

The group of Dominicans, Toscanelli leading the way, his pistol in his hand, and with Vitale a few paces behind, stopped abruptly as they rounded the final bend and, just like Mallory and Jessop, were confronted by the sight of something that made no sense. But they paused only momentarily, then strode on, each man apart from Vitale himself carrying a pistol, and confident that they could take care of anything they found in front of them.

A few seconds later, they stood in a loose circle around the long-dead Templar knight.

"The last of the heretics," Vitale said dismissively. "A pathetic attempt to scare people away."

"But at least it means we're in the right place," Toscanelli pointed out. "The Templar treasure that we seek must be somewhere nearby."

"And what about the English couple?" Carlo said. "We

know they have at least two pistols, because of what happened at Templecombe. They could be waiting for us in ambush anywhere down here."

His remark prompted an immediate reaction: all the Dominicans were carrying torches, and all of them, including Vitale, switched them on, the beams stabbing into the darkness as they looked around them for any sign of danger.

"We have no idea where they are," Vitale reminded the men. "They could be anywhere in this tunnel system. Spread out and check this end of the tunnel. When you've done that, we'll try and find the treasure."

Searching for one person armed with a pistol in a dark and unfamiliar space is invariably unpleasant, always dangerous, and potentially fatal. Looking for two armed people more than doubles the danger and greatly increases the chance of stumbling into an ambush or a cross fire. So although the enforcers were dedicated to their cause and each was holding a weapon, the search proceeded noticeably slowly. Apart from anything else, each of the men knew perfectly well that the torch he was holding in his left hand made him an immediate target for anyone waiting in the darkness ahead. The only piece of good news was that with the exception of the long-dead Templar knight sitting for eternity in his wooden chair and the pile of boxes positioned behind and to one side of him, the tunnel itself appeared to be largely empty.

While Vitale remained safely out of danger—he hoped—near the corpse and the chair, the other men spread out and made their way steadily down the tunnel. As they advanced, they shone their torches into the various crevices and fissures in the rock, but saw nothing to alert them. In a few minutes, they reached the rockfall that sealed off the tunnel and turned back the way they'd come.

"They obviously can't have gone beyond that," Toscanelli said. "So if they're here at all, they must have hidden somewhere behind us. Check out all the openings we've passed so far."

That was potentially a much more dangerous operation. In the comparatively open space of the tunnel there would at least have been a chance that they could see their quarry before he or she opened fire, but in the close confines of the rocky crevices this would not be true.

"Take it slowly. One man to enter each space while two others cover him from the tunnel," Toscanelli ordered. "Be quite certain of your target before you open fire, and remember that we are surrounded by rock, so there will be ricochets. Now get on with it."

Behind the heavy black cloth that Mallory had draped over the narrow cavity in which they were standing, all he and Robin could do was listen and keep as silent and motionless as possible.

They had heard the sounds of footsteps approaching their hiding place, then seen a brief flash of illumination as one of the Dominicans shone his torch into the crevice, but then the footsteps receded.

"They're searching the tunnel," Mallory whispered, his mouth right beside Robin's ear, as the sound of heavy treads diminished.

"They'll get as far as the rockfall, and then they'll come back," she replied, equally quietly.

"You can depend on that."

They heard a male voice obviously speaking Italian, and equally obviously issuing instructions, and then the noise of the footsteps of several people began to increase once again.

Mallory put his arm around Robin's shoulders and squeezed.

"We'll get through this," he said, his voice barely audible, "and I think I love you."

"I know you do," she whispered in reply. "And you do pick your moments, don't you?"

Moments later, they both saw the unmistakable loom of light through the dense black material as at least two torch beams were shone into the opening. Then a third torchlight appeared and they heard heavy footsteps on the rocky floor as one of the Dominicans stepped into the side passage.

The cloth was too thick for them to see what was happening outside their hiding place, but the changing intensity of the light told the tale anyway: a man was obviously shining his torch around the space, looking for any sign of them.

The beam passed over the draped cloth three or four times, but never stayed focused on that spot, presumably because Mallory had been right: the black cloth looked remarkably similar to the black rock that surrounded it.

They heard snatches of conversation that meant nothing to either of them, as they spoke no Italian, and then, to their unspoken relief, the lights disappeared and the sounds of voices and footsteps receded down the tunnel.

"I presume you didn't find them," Vitale said, when Toscanelli and the other men stopped beside him.

"No," Toscanelli replied. "The tunnel is blocked by a rockfall a few dozen meters farther on, so they didn't get out that way, and we've checked all the side passages and cracks in the rock, and there's no sign of them. They probably went the other way down the tunnel once they got inside it."

In the torchlight, Vitale looked and sounded profoundly unconvinced, but there was nothing else he could say. He had expected Mallory and Jessop to head toward the southwestern end of the tunnel, but if they hadn't, then that certainly gave his men time to check the wooden chests piled against the tunnel wall.

"You might have missed them and they could still be hiding somewhere here," he said, "so keep your eyes open. Now check those boxes. You all know what we're looking for."

Toscanelli moved over to the side of the tunnel opposite the pile of wooden chests, a position from which he could see in both directions up and down the tunnel as well as watch his men investigate the boxes.

"Be careful when you open each one," Vitale warned them. "Remember that we've already encountered a number of Templar booby traps. Some of those chests might incorporate defensive mechanisms, so when you open the lids, make sure you're standing behind or beside the boxes, not in front of them."

*   *   *

In the crevice at the end of the short side passage, Mallory and Robin stood still and silent, worried that their hiding place had been spotted, and that if they emerged from behind the sheet of cloth, they might find themselves looking down the barrels of a couple of pistols held by two Dominicans. From the tunnel, they could hear the sounds of heavy objects being moved—presumably the Dominicans were removing some of the chests from the pile and then opening them up—accompanied by the almost constant chatter of Italian male voices.

But that wasn't all. Occasionally they both heard a metallic clatter, followed in each case by raised and obviously excited voices. And despite not understanding the language, it also became obvious to them both that one man was very much in charge. A cold and commanding voice, quite different to Toscanelli's, belonged to the man who was clearly directing operations.

It was also apparent that something had happened that their pursuers hadn't expected. The raised voice of an angry man sounds very much the same no matter what language he's speaking, and several of the Dominicans were obviously getting annoyed. For what reason, Mallory couldn't guess, but the tones of the voices he could hear left him in no doubt that something had gone wrong.

Maybe the chests were empty and they hadn't found the bullion and jewels that they had been expecting to recover. Perhaps it was yet another deception by the Templars, and the boxes were full of rocks or something else of no value whatsoever. Whatever the cause, the raised voices were not what Mallory had expected to hear.

And then, in a long sentence obviously spoken by the leader of the group, he picked out one single word in Italian that he did know. He couldn't remember where he'd learned it, but he was quite certain of its meaning. And that made no sense, either, in the context of where they were and what was happening.

He heard another brief sentence, uttered by the same voice, then the sound of footsteps receding down the tunnel and back toward the hole he had cut through the roof of it.

Mallory waited until the silence around them was complete, and then slowly and with infinite care he pulled back the edge of the black cloth just far enough to allow him to look across the stone chamber.

His eyes were well-adjusted to the darkness because of the length of time they had been down there, but he could see absolutely nothing. The blackness was total.

For a few seconds he did nothing, just concentrated all his attention on trying to discover if there was anyone else in the chamber with him and Robin. He heard nothing. No sound of movement or breathing.

He took his torch, extended his arm to one side of his body as far as he could, then flicked on the light and immediately turned it off again. That brief flash, almost like from the flashgun on a camera, allowed him to confirm what he had hoped: the chamber was empty. And, he believed, the torch had been illuminated for such a short time that the Italians farther down the tunnel would not have seen it.

"They've gone," he said quietly. "I think we can move."

"Thank God for that. All my joints feel as if they've locked solid."

Mallory wrapped his fingers around the glass at the end of the torch to reduce the amount of light it would emit to little more than a glow, then switched it on and cautiously led the way out of the rocky chamber. At the entrance, he paused and listened, the torch switched off again, in case his deduction was wrong and the Dominicans had left an ambush behind them. But he saw and heard nothing.

He stepped out into the tunnel and, still using the minimum amount of light he could, he looked at the pile of chests.

And what he saw made even less sense of the word he had not only clearly heard but also clearly understood.

About a dozen of the medieval wooden chests stood open on the floor of the tunnel. Seven of them had incorporated defense mechanisms within their lids, because each of those open chests exhibited some kind of an extended steel blade, some individual but most double, that had obviously been triggered when the lid was lifted. But the absence of any blood or bodies showed that the Dominicans had learned from the hard lessons of the past, and had opened each of the chests by either standing behind it or making sure they were out of range of the defense mechanism when the lid was raised.

"I don't understand this," Robin said, looking at the chests.

Within each of the open boxes, below the triggered antitheft devices, the dull yellow of incorruptible, eternal gold shone in the light of the torch. Each chest was full almost to the brim with a literal fortune: chalices, cups, goblets, plates, knives, coins, and bars of gold, interspersed with the occasional object fashioned from silver. Without the slightest shadow of a doubt, they were looking at part of the lost treasure of the Knights Templar order.

"They've just opened roughly a dozen chests and then walked away," Robin went on. "You'd expect them to take some of the boxes or the contents with them, but as far as I can see they haven't. And even if they've just gone off to organize a van or a lorry to haul this away, I would have thought they'd have left an armed guard here, just to protect what they've found."

"You're absolutely right," Mallory said, "but I have a theory about that, based on one single word that I heard and understood."

"I didn't think you spoke Italian."

"I don't, but I do recognize the odd word or two. You heard their raised voices just before they left this end of the tunnel? One man was doing all the shouting, and he was obviously the one in charge. One of the last sentences he uttered contained the Italian word *chincaglieria*, and that was the word I recognized."

"Which means what?" Robin demanded.

"It translates as 'trinkets,' meaning ornamental objects of no particular value."

She didn't respond for a moment; then she shook her head.

"That makes no sense, either. I'm no expert on gold and silver objects, but I don't doubt for even a second that what we're looking at here is the real thing. This isn't some kind of Templar trick. Those boxes genuinely are full of gold and silver objects, worth a king's ransom, so why would that Dominican refer to the contents as trinkets? Are you sure that you heard the word correctly?"

"As sure as I can be, yes. But actually, this does make a kind of sense. If you remember, some of the text we decrypted referred to the treasure of the order, but also to the assets, as if these were two different things, not just two different ways of referring to the same thing. I think what we've found here are the assets, the working capital and financial wealth of the order."

"Then what the hell is the treasure?"

"I do have one idea about that. More to the point, I think the Dominicans opened up these boxes hoping to find one very specific object, and when they didn't the man in charge of them dismissed all of this vast wealth as a collection of mere trinkets, because in his eyes that's exactly what it is. I think the Dominicans are after something very different, and they've probably all gone off to try to find it."

"And I suppose you know what it is, and where it's hidden?"

Mallory smiled at Robin in the darkness.

"Actually, I *have* got a good idea about the answers to both those questions. And if I'm right we'll definitely need this sword."

54

"When all this is over," Robin said, as they made their way quickly and quietly back along the tunnel, "you can spend an evening explaining to me exactly what you meant when you said you thought you loved me, preferably over a candlelit gourmet dinner in a Michelin-starred restaurant attached to a decent hotel with the biggest and most comfortable beds available. I'm not the kind of girl likely to be satisfied by a muttered expression of devotion while she's hiding under a bit of dirty old cloth in a cave and expecting to be shot at any moment."

"When all this is over," Mallory replied, "not only will I be glad to do that, but hopefully I'll be able to *afford* to do that."

"I think you'll find a way to pay for it. But in the meantime, what's the thing with this sword?"

Mallory was clutching the second Templar battle sword,

the one that had been hanging on the wall near the end of the tunnel.

"I think the sword means something, because of the strange shape of the end of the blade. More accurately, I think the end of the blade might function as a key to something. Remember the book safe that started all this?"

The trail they had been following for what seemed so long had begun when Robin had found an old piece of parchment in a medieval book safe that had arrived in her shop as a part of a job lot of old books she'd purchased. When she opened it, she triggered an ancient antitheft device that had forced two rows of sharpened spikes out of the safe, obviously intended to seriously injure anyone who forced it open. Fortunately she'd been using a long-handled screwdriver at the time, and although it was a shock when the booby trap was actuated, none of the spikes had even touched her.

"I'm not likely to forget it," she replied. "And you worked out that the 'key' that would open the safe without driving spikes through your hands was the blade of a particular dagger. So do you think we're looking for something similar? Some chest or box that needs the blade of that sword to be inserted to open it?"

"More or less, yes, but probably not a box, because that would have been forced open by somebody centuries ago. I think we're looking for something much more subtle and less obvious than that."

"And where is it?"

"The sword was mounted on the wall with the blade pointing toward the blocked-off end of the tunnel. That was quite deliberate, and I think that's a fairly clear indication that whatever the sword blade is designed to open lies in that direction, on the other side of the rockfall."

"Does that mean you've got to go and dig another hole so we can get into the tunnel on the other side of the blockage?"

"I hope not," Mallory said. "I think it's simpler than that. As far as we could tell from the topographical maps, this tunnel seems to run all the way from Gilmerton Cove to Rosslyn Chapel. We cut into the tunnel roof just over a mile from the chapel, by my rough calculations, and we walked about a mile underground. So I think the Templar treasure and the end of the tunnel are really close to the chapel, perhaps even underneath it. So I don't think the sword was necessarily pointing toward the last few yards of the tunnel, the bit we couldn't get into, but more likely toward Rosslyn Chapel itself."

"So is that where we're going?"

"That's where we're going," Mallory confirmed.

He turned off the torch when he saw a dim glow ahead of them in the tunnel.

"I hope that's light coming into the tunnel through the hole and not the torchlight from a Dominican reception committee."

It wasn't a reception committee, but when they reached the opening in the roof, they both saw at once that the rope they'd used to climb down had disappeared. The Dominicans had obviously removed it.

"That's a bit of a bugger," Mallory said, "but it's not a problem. The roof of the tunnel is only about nine feet high at this side. There's another rope in the car, and I can boost you up so you can get out and go and fetch it."

He put the sword safely to one side, handed her the car keys, then leaned back against the wall of the tunnel, bent his knees, and laced his hands together. Robin put her left foot into his cupped hands. As soon as she did so, Mallory straightened up and then lifted his hands as high as he could, up to chest level, boosting Robin high enough that she could easily scramble out of the hole.

"Okay?" he asked.

"We won't need the rope," Robin said in reply. "Keep out of the way," she added.

Moments later, Mallory saw why as the end of a rigid aluminum ladder appeared. Robin lowered it down into the tunnel.

"It was just lying here on the grass a few feet away," Robin explained as Mallory quickly climbed up it to join her. "Presumably the Dominicans brought it with them."

"I'm glad they did," he replied. "I've never been very good at rope climbing. Right, let's go."

They jogged up the slope to where Mallory had parked the Porsche. He opened the car, slid the sword into the space behind the seats, then sat down and started the engine. It was only about a mile and a half to Rosslyn Chapel on the twisty country road, and he stopped the car in the largely empty parking lot reserved for visitors.

"I'll take the sword with us," he said. "There don't seem to be that many people here today, and hopefully we can find what we're looking for quickly and without attracting too much attention."

There were a few visitors inside the chapel, standing in small groups or as individuals, looking at the bizarre decorations, but it was largely empty. The word *chapel* usually conjures up images of a fairly small place of worship, but Rosslyn was big. They both stopped after they'd taken a few paces inside and just looked around them.

"I have no idea where we should even start," Mallory said.

"Hang on a minute. I've just remembered something. The translation we did of that text on the parchment said that the wealth of the order was in one place, but that the 'treasure' was 'beneath the stone which is not as it seems' or something like that."

Mallory shrugged.

"As far as I can see, apart from the pews and one or two other bits in here, everything is made of stone," he pointed out. "So which particular one do you think we should be looking at?"

"Now, that is a bloody good question. I have no idea."

"Nor me," Mallory said. "Let's split up and just walk around the place to see if anything strikes us."

They each did a complete circuit of the chapel in opposite directions, looking carefully at every single piece of stonework that could possibly suggest some kind of double meaning, which obviously excluded the walls of the building because a wall was, ultimately, just a wall. They met each other again near the entrance, neither of them having spotted anything that seemed vaguely hopeful.

But Robin had found something, though it was nothing directly to do with their search. On a pew near the back of the chapel she'd picked up a discarded guide to Rosslyn, and when Mallory walked up to her, she was flicking through the pages, hoping for inspiration.

And then, strangely enough, she found it. Or, at least, she found a photograph and a half page of text that identified something that just possibly might have been what they were searching for.

"This could be it," she said. "That pillar over there. If this guidebook is right, that does seem to fit the bill, more or less."

"What is it?"

"That's the Prince's Pillar, better known as the Apprentice Pillar," she said.

"I've heard of that," Mallory said. "Something to do with a murder, isn't it?"

"Yes. Now, if this is right, then it means that at least one of the documents we translated had to have been written after Rosslyn was built, because the story of the killing goes right back to the time when the chapel was being constructed. According to the legend, one of the master masons employed in building the chapel was given a model of a pillar of extremely complex and sophisticated design, and was told to reproduce it in the chapel itself.

"The mason decided that it would be so difficult to manufacture it that he first needed to go and see and measure the original, which was in some building in Europe, possibly in Rome. So he went off to look at the original pillar. But while he was away his apprentice took the model and constructed the pillar that we see in front of us today. When his master returned from his travels, he was both stunned and furious when he saw the finished work, and when he was told that it was his own apprentice who'd fabricated it, he picked up his mallet and killed the apprentice on the spot. That's why it's now known as the Apprentice Pillar, though until roughly the end of the seventeenth century it was known as the Prince's Pillar."

"But that's only a legend," Mallory said. "It's the kind of story that could have been made up at any time in the past. Is there any historical basis for it?"

"According to some sources, the legend only dates from the eighteenth century, but actually a number of things do support the idea that the murder actually happened. Far from being an eighteenth-century legend, there's a written version of the same story recorded by a man named Thomas Kirk in 1677. But more significantly there are a number of references to the need to 'reconcile Rosslyn,' which is kind of church-speak and means that the building had to be cleansed because of some act of violence that had taken place within it. There's also evidence that the chapel was reconsecrated sometime after it had been built. And that is something that wouldn't normally be done unless something extremely unpleasant had happened in the building."

"Right, so maybe the story is true and the murder did take place. But I still don't see why you think that's what we should be looking at."

"Well, it's just my own interpretation," Robin said, "but the object we're trying to find is 'the stone which is not as it seems,' and this pillar was built by an apprentice because his master didn't think he could do it without extra help, without viewing the original. And what that obviously means is that the apprentice was by far a better mason than the man he was serving, so you could argue that the Apprentice Pillar should really be called the Master Pillar. So this particular piece of stone has arguably been misnamed, and so it could be described as a stone that is not as it seems. But if you've got any better ideas, I'd be really happy to listen to them."

Mallory shook his head.

"No," he said. "What you said does make perfect sense, so let's take a look at it."

The pillar was very obviously a structure of solid stone, the top helping to support the roof and the base resting on the stone-flagged floor. There was clearly no way of moving it, or of getting into whatever crypt or chamber might lie below the floor of the chapel, the space where they'd deduced that the supposed "treasure" was meant to be hidden.

They both examined the pillar very closely, looking for any kind of catch or lever that might allow it to be moved, but there was nothing visible. Absolutely the only mark of any kind on it, apart from the rows of complex carvings, was on the base, a thin line of slightly discolored stone about an inch or so long.

Mallory crouched down and looked at it, scratching at the stone with his thumbnail.

"This mark seems to be much softer than the stone surrounding it," he said. "I wonder if that could be it." He glanced up at Robin. "It's all old and worn, obviously, but that mark does look a bit like the strange V-shaped cross section at the end of the blade of the sword."

"Well, don't just sit there thinking and talking about it. You're carrying the sword, so why don't you try it?"

Mallory stood up and glanced around the chapel, but it seemed to be deserted for the moment, the visitors they'd seen when they arrived having left the building.

He grasped the handle of the Templar sword and pulled the weapon out of its scabbard. Then he rested the point of the blade on the discolored line on the stone and pushed down and inward. With remarkably little resistance, the blade of the heavy sword slid three or four inches into the stone.

"I thought that shape looked like the cross section of this blade," he muttered.

He pushed it just a little farther. Then they both heard a faint click, and the lowest section of the Apprentice Pillar moved very slightly.

They crouched down side by side, seized the edges of the stone, and swung it sideways. The stone opened on some kind of hidden hinge, and directly below the base of the pillar was a wooden box, about a foot square.

Eagerly, Mallory reached into the cavity, grasped it with both hands, and lifted it out to place it on the floor of the chapel. He gently brushed the dust of the ages from it, and then they both stared at what they'd found. On the ornate wooden lid was a small carved panel, something like an escutcheon, and on that was an inscription in a language they hadn't expected to see.

"That looks a bit like Hebrew," Mallory said. "I had a holiday in Jerusalem once," he added.

"Funnily enough, this isn't really a total surprise to me," Jessop replied, "because this is now making sense. In fact, it started to make sense to me back in that blasted tunnel when the Dominicans walked away from the Templars' chests and all that bullion and other stuff. And as a bit of a confirmation, I can read a little Hebrew."

"What does it say?"

"This inscription is a name, *Yeshuah ben Yusef ben Heli*, or 'Joshua, son of Joseph, son of Heli,'" Jessop said.

Then she took hold of the edge of the lid of the wooden box, turned it away from both Mallory and herself, just in case there was an antitheft device built into the lid, and slowly opened it. Nothing happened, except that the lid lifted jerkily, the old hinges obviously in need of some lubrication.

Inside, nestling on what was originally a bed of fabric but was now rotted and virtually disintegrated, was a human head, wisps of hair and patches of flesh still clinging to it.

She closed the lid again and looked at Mallory.

"That must be Baphomet," he said in answer to her unspoken question. "The disembodied head that was supposed to be worshipped by the Templars. But what does the inscription mean? I know it's a name, a person's name, but that's all."

"This is the real treasure of the Knights Templar," she said. "When the Dominican inquisitors were torturing the information they wanted out of the knights of the order, they were asking the wrong questions, or maybe listening to the wrong answers. One of the accusations leveled at the Templars was that they denied Christ, but that's not the whole story. At that time, a lot of societies in Europe practiced a kind of cult of the head, worshipping the head or the skull of an important man who'd died maybe centuries earlier. I think you're right: what we have in this box is Baphomet, the most sacred of all the Templar possessions. In fact, this really is the treasure of the order. The Hebrew inscription tells you exactly who this head once belonged to. At the time he was alive, people knew him as 'Joshua, son of Joseph, son of Heli,' but today the whole world knows him just as Jesus Christ.

"In this wooden box is the head of Jesus, and because the Templars knew that they owned the actual head of Jesus Christ, they also knew absolutely that he was not divine, and that there could have been no Resurrection. So they weren't denying Christ—they were just denying his supposed divinity, and they worshipped him in their own way as one of the most important religious leaders in history. They knew that he was only a prophet, not the son of God."

"Bravo, Jessop," a coldly harsh voice said.

Mallory and Jessop looked up to see two heavily built men dressed entirely in black standing just inside the door of the chapel, only a few feet away from them. They immediately recognized the man who hadn't spoken as the Dominican Marco Toscanelli, the man who'd confronted them before, in Devon, Cyprus, and later in Switzerland, but they'd never seen the other man before.

Two other Dominicans of similar build and dressed all in black were advancing toward them.

"You've done our work for us," Toscanelli said, a cruel smile on his face.

Mallory took a half pace backward and drew the Templar battle sword from the slot in the base of the Apprentice Pillar and brandished it in front of him. One of the men grabbed at him and he swung the sword in a vicious arc. The sharpened tip of the weapon cut across the man's stomach, slicing open his shirt and carving a furrow across his flesh as, for the first time in over seven hundred years, a Templar sword drew blood in combat.

The man gasped with the pain and shrank back, clutching at his abdomen, as Mallory swung the weapon again, threatening both him and the man close beside him.

Toscanelli took out a pistol and aimed it at Mallory, but the man who'd spoken, presumably the leader, raised his hand to restrain him.

"Wait," he said. "We should be grateful to these two for what they've done. They found the treasure for us."

"The Hounds of the Lord again," Robin Jessop said. "Dominican Black Friars, still pursuing the Templars after the better part of a millennium? Still acting as inquisitors, are you?"

The leader inclined his head in agreement.

"Not so much pursuing the Templars as making sure that their heresy doesn't damage the Mother Church. And of course collecting all their assets to hand over to the rightful owners, the Knights Hospitaller. Once we've removed all those chests from the tunnel, our work here will be done."

Robin pointed down at the wooden box.

"But that's not a heresy, is it? What's in that box is a truth that you daren't risk ever becoming known, because it proves conclusively that the Resurrection never happened, and that fact alone could be enough to destroy Christianity completely."

Again the leader nodded.

"What's considered a heresy depends entirely on where and when you're standing," he said. "The church has got very used to bending and shading the truth over the centuries, but the fear that the Templar treasure, the real treasure, would surface one day has always been there. Now we can walk out of here with that box and that will be the end of it. We'll ensure it isn't destroyed, of course. The relic is far too important for that. We'll just find a home for it in the darkest recesses of the Vatican Secret Archives, where nobody will ever find it. Now, step back and do not interfere."

With Toscanelli's pistol pointing at them, there was nothing Mallory or Jessop could do except obey his order.

The uninjured Dominican bent down in front of them, picked up the wooden box, and rejoined his companions by the door, the injured man stumbling along behind him. The leader of the Dominicans gestured for the two of them to leave the chapel with the relic, and for a minute or so nobody else moved.

"Now it's time for you to die," the black-clad figure stated.

"Why? You've got what you came for," Mallory said.

The Dominican looked slightly surprised at this remark.

"Don't be so stupid. You both know far too much to be allowed to live," he said. "You know the truth of what we've been searching for, and for that reason alone you obviously have to die. And, of course, you've both been a thorn in the side of my organization ever since this quest began. Toscanelli here has been looking forward to this moment for weeks. It's just a shame that we don't have time to allow him to execute you both in a leisurely fashion— I know he'd prefer that, to take his time over your deaths— so it will at least be quick. Good-bye."

55

But before Toscanelli had even brought his pistol up to aim, Robin reached into her pocket and in one fluid movement took out the Beretta they'd liberated from the wounded Dominican at Templecombe and fired two quick shots across the chapel and straight at Toscanelli.

The first bullet missed, slamming into the stone wall directly behind him, but the second caught him in either the shoulder or the upper part of his right arm. He dropped his own pistol, clutching at his wound, and as Robin took a couple of steps closer to them, shortening the distance, both Toscanelli and the other man turned and ran out of the building, the pistol lying forgotten on the floor.

"I didn't know you had a pistol with you," Mallory said, "but I'm glad you had."

"It was under the passenger seat in the Porsche. I picked

it up and put it in my pocket on the way over to the chapel, just in case we hadn't seen the last of the Dominicans."

Mallory walked across the chapel, picked up the discarded Beretta pistol, and put it in his own pocket.

"We seem to be collecting quite an armory on this job," he said. "Just as well you didn't kill him. Otherwise, I suppose they'd have had to cleanse and reconsecrate the chapel again."

At that moment the door of the chapel swung open and a large group of tourists entered, accompanied by a guide, all of them looking slightly perplexed.

"We heard two explosions," the guide said to Mallory, walking over to him, "and they sounded as if they came from inside here. What happened?"

Mallory looked at him blankly.

"Explosions? In here? We didn't hear anything. Are you sure it wasn't just thunder or something outside the building?"

The guide shook his head, clearly still puzzled, then turned back to the group he was shepherding. The new arrivals started to spread out, looking in every part of the building.

Mallory walked back over to the Apprentice Pillar, swung the stone panel back into position, and picked up the Templar battle sword.

"We need to get back to the tunnel," he said, "before those bloody Dominicans take everything."

They left the building cautiously, checking that the Dominicans weren't lying in wait for them outside, then retraced their steps to the car. Mallory powered up the narrow road to the place he'd parked before and plucked the Browning pistol from under the driver's seat before he got out of the car, grabbing the Templar sword as he did so. Then they headed back across the field to the hole he had dug through the roof of the tunnel.

"Are you sure this makes sense?" Robin asked. "There are two of us, and we've each got a pistol. In fact, you've got two of them plus a medieval sword, for some reason. I don't know how many Dominicans are down there, but I'd guess there are at least half a dozen of them, and they'll all be armed. We're outnumbered and outgunned, so what exactly are we going to be able to do to stop them?"

"I've got an idea about that," Mallory said, "because I saw something down in the tunnel that should help us."

They climbed down the aluminum ladder into the darkness, and within a few minutes they could hear activity ahead of them, and the unmistakable sound of voices speaking Italian. It was obviously the Dominicans, and they had no doubt that the Italians were closing up the opened boxes of bullion and preparing to take away the lost wealth of the Knights Templar.

Sitting in the Audi sedan about fifty yards beyond where Mallory had stopped the Porsche, the injured Dominican nursed the horizontal slash across his stomach caused by the Templar sword. His companion had applied rudimentary first aid—basically a thick pad held in place by a bandage wrapped around him to compress the wound, slow the bleeding, and prevent his intestines from falling out—before he'd left him to return to the tunnel. Another of the Dominicans had been sent off in the other car to hire a large van to transport the wooden chests. The injured man didn't know that Toscanelli had also been wounded. But in his case, the bullet had only ripped through the skin of his biceps muscle, and once he had had it roughly bandaged he had gone back down into the tunnel with the other men.

And at that moment, as the Dominican hugged his stomach and moaned in pain, he saw the man who had caused his injury walking quickly across the field toward the tunnel, the Englishwoman beside him. Unbelievably they were both quite obviously unhurt. He watched them descend the ladder into the tunnel.

For a few seconds, after they'd both vanished from sight, he tried to make sense of what he'd seen. He'd assumed that Mallory and Jessop would have been dealt with at the chapel. When he'd left the building, Toscanelli had been about to execute them both. What had gone wrong?

In a few moments, his indecision passed. Something clearly wasn't right, and it was just possible that the English couple could interfere with the removal of the Templar assets from the tunnel. But there was something he could do about that. He hoped.

Grunting with pain, the Dominican eased himself across the seat and pushed open the car door. For some reason, he didn't find standing up quite as difficult or as painful as he had expected. He checked that his pistol was in his pocket and fully loaded; then he pushed the car door closed and began walking unsteadily across the field to where he could see the top of the ladder sticking out of the hole in the roof of the tunnel.

*   *   *

"So, what do we do now?" Robin Jessop asked, in a soft voice. "We can't stop them."

They had reached a point in the tunnel system from which they could just see the ghostly figure of the long-dead Templar knight sitting in his wooden chair. Mallory was certain that the attention of the Dominicans would be firmly focused on the task at hand, and he quietly led Robin a few yards farther down the tunnel.

Shading the lens of his torch with his hand again, he aimed the beam toward the roof.

"What do you see?" he whispered.

"A lot of heavy round boulders and metal bars," Robin replied, equally quietly. "So what?"

"So, we can't stop the Dominicans," Mallory agreed, "but I think the Templars probably can. This is one last trap right here that we can trigger."

There was a sudden shout, a cry of alarm, from the far end of the tunnel, and in an instant the beams from three torches swung away from the pile of wooden chests and speared down the tunnel in the direction of Mallory and Robin.

"Run!" Mallory instructed, as two shots rang out from the Dominicans, the bullets singing and ricocheting off the old stone walls that surrounded them.

He pulled out the Browning, but even as he turned to fire, Robin stepped beside him and loosed off four rapid shots.

"I'll keep them back," she snapped. "You just trip the

booby trap. You'd better hope that it still works. Otherwise, we're in trouble."

They both turned and ran back down the tunnel, the way they had come, random shots and ricochets pursuing them as the Dominicans tried to gun them down.

Mallory flicked on his torch, running the beam down the side of the tunnel, looking for the object he had seen when they had first walked that way: the thing that looked like a sconce on the wall but actually wasn't.

As another volley of shots rang out, the Dominicans probably now aiming toward the loom of his torchlight, Mallory suddenly saw the heavy metal bar he was looking for, sticking out of the wall at an angle, the dark steel discolored by a pattern of rusty patches. It was probably about eight feet off the ground.

He didn't just pull the bar downward; as he ran he handed the torch to Robin, then jumped up and grabbed it with both hands, letting his body weight pull the lever down. For one sickening instant, nothing seemed to happen. Then the lever jerked in his hands and traveled downward until it was at a right angle to the vertical wall.

For perhaps two seconds after Mallory released the bar, the only sounds in the tunnel were the shouts of the Dominicans and the volley of shots coming from behind him. But then he and Robin heard a deeper and much louder bang as something heavy moved against some other massive object.

Mallory grabbed Robin by the hand and they both started running, as hard as they could, back toward the opening in the tunnel.

And then the last Templar booby trap, cunningly designed and constructed by a group of men who had known exactly what they were doing, was activated after lying dormant and waiting for some seven hundred years. Metal catches linked to heavy chains were snapped open, hinged steel bars swung downward, and hundreds of tons of boulders, their edges painstakingly rounded to ensure that they would not jam the mechanism, rumbled down from the hollow chambers built into the roof of the tunnel.

In just seconds, with a noise like a thousand simultaneous thunderstorms, the banging and crashing echoing from the walls, the boulders smashed to the floor, one upon another, until the entire tunnel was completely sealed by the huge rockfall.

As the noise finally ceased, Mallory and Robin slowed their headlong flight and then turned to look back down the tunnel.

Of the Dominicans, there was no sign. They had probably been too far back to be crushed by the falling rocks, but they were now, without any doubt, imprisoned at the end of the tunnel along with the enormous wealth of the Knights Templar.

"The Templars seem to have been quite good at this kind of thing," Mallory said. "That's three birds with one stone," he added, coughing in the cloud of dust thrown up by the rockfall. "It keeps the Dominicans away from us. It also keeps them here on the site where they can be arrested, and makes sure that they can't steal anything. Now we can call the police and organize a rescue party. An armed rescue party, obviously."

They both took a last look down the tunnel, then continued walking.

"Well, at least we'll show a profit on this little adventure," Robin said, as they walked back down the tunnel toward open air and the ladder thoughtfully provided by the Dominicans. "The gold in the tunnel must be worth tens of millions of pounds at least, just as bullion, and probably a lot more because of its historical importance. It's a bit of a shame that we'll have to declare it a treasure trove, and that means we'll probably never see any of it again, except as an exhibit in some museum."

They reached the ladder and Robin started to climb up it.

But as her head emerged above ground level, a shot rang out and she tumbled back down the ladder to land in a crumpled heap beside Mallory on the tunnel floor.

56

The Dominican had waited only to positively identify the person climbing up the ladder as the woman Jessop before he had fired. He'd heard both the sound of gunshots and then the thunderous rumble a few minutes earlier, and had guessed that the English couple had probably had something to do with what was quite obviously a rockfall. There might have been nothing he could do now to help his companions, but at least he could take his revenge on the English couple in the name of the Dominican order.

He wasn't entirely sure that he'd hit Jessop, though the complete absence of sound from the tunnel suggested that he probably had. In fact, it suggested he'd probably killed her, because if she'd just been wounded, he would have expected to hear—and he would have enjoyed listening to—her cries of pain.

And he still didn't know where Mallory was.

He waited a few more seconds, then began walking slowly and carefully toward the aluminum ladder, his pistol held ready in one hand in front of him, while his other hand pressed gently on the dressing over his stomach.

When Robin had fallen limply and clearly out of control down the ladder, Mallory had rushed forward, fearing the worst because of the shot he'd heard. But when he reached her, she rolled over, stood up, and pulled him away from the opening and deeper into the tunnel.

"Are you okay?" Mallory demanded.

"Yes. That bloody Dominican you slashed with the sword is up there waving a pistol about. When he shot at me it was a hell of a shock because I didn't expect to see anybody at all, and I missed my footing on the ladder. That's why I fell. I'll be a bit bruised for a while, but that's all."

"Right. I'll take care of him."

"No, you won't," Robin said firmly. "He shot at me, so he's mine."

"Okay, if that's what you want, but could I just suggest something?"

The wounded Dominican was about ten feet from the ladder when he saw something that made no immediate sense. From the dark opening in the tunnel a Templar battle sword suddenly appeared in the air, turning end over end as it rose high into the sky. The sight was so unexpected that he simply couldn't take his eyes off it, and it was only as he turned away from the tunnel entrance to see the sword slam, point down, into the grassy surface of the field about twenty feet away that he realized he had been duped.

He turned back to the aluminum ladder, raising his pistol to aim as he did so, but the woman Jessop was already there, standing on the ladder with the upper part of her torso out of the tunnel and her own pistol pointing steadily at him.

He muttered a curse as he squeezed the trigger, but he knew it was already too late.

As two bullets slammed into his body, knocking him backward, his last conscious thought was about the word that the woman had said in the instant before she pulled the trigger. His command of the English language was reasonably good, and he found the word almost as insulting as the bullets that tore the life from his body.

The word was *amateur*.

There was nothing they could do for the Dominican who had tried to kill Robin, so they left his body where it was and headed back to the car. Mallory would make all the calls and be on-site when the police and the rescue teams arrived. But because Robin had fired her pistol four times in total, and because there was a dead man, shot by her, lying in the field, it was vitally important that she get out of the way and leave the scene as soon as possible.

They decided to drive back to the hotel, where Robin could shower and give her hands a good scrub to try to remove the cordite, and where they would also pack the three pistols away in one of their bags.

They also decided that once she'd done all that, Robin

would check out of the hotel, hire a car, and then take a room in an entirely different hotel some distance away, just to ensure that there was no easy way for the police to question her for at least a couple of days, by which time any test administered to her hands would reveal no traces of cordite.

"Are you okay?" Mallory asked, as he drove away from the site and back toward the hotel. "About killing that Dominican, I mean."

"Yes. That was completely justified, in my opinion. I'm sure I'll suffer the odd nightmare over it for the next few weeks, but really, I'm fine. I'm quite tough, you know."

"I do know that," Mallory replied, resting his hand on her thigh. "You've proved it often enough."

After a few minutes, Robin returned to the topic she'd started talking about earlier.

"So, I'm sure we should get something out of this," she said, "some reward for what we've found—all the incredible wealth of the Knights Templar—but I suppose we probably won't be able to keep any of it."

"We might," Mallory replied, "because of the unusual circumstances. The rules of treasure troves basically depend on two things: whether the object was lost or hidden deliberately, and whether or not there was an intention to return to recover it. In this case, we know who hid it—the Knights Templar, led by Jacques de Molay—and we also know that they meant to retrieve it one day. And that means you can argue that it's still owned by the Templar order."

"But the Templars don't exist any longer," Jessop objected.

"True, but not necessarily relevant. One of the rules of the order was celibacy," Mallory replied, in an apparent non sequitur, "but as we talked about before, many of the knights joined the Templars not as young men but later in life, when they might have already been married and fathered children. One of them was Jacques de Molay himself. There are probably hints in the historical record that he had a male child, and we know from what we've discovered—that word *puer*, for starters—that he had a son, a man he was almost certainly grooming to enter the order as a knight and who perhaps would even end up following in his father's footsteps, to become the next Grand Master. Philip the Fair put a stop to that, of course. But we've recovered a crucially important document during this quest."

Jessop nodded. "You mean the parchment we found in the Templar church at Templecombe?"

"Exactly. As we discovered, that was a kind of Templar passport," Mallory went on, "that would allow the bearer to pass freely with his goods. I looked carefully at it, and the bearer was very clearly the son of Jacques de Molay. He was the man entrusted by his father to spirit the treasure, the gold as well as Baphomet, out of the clutches of the French king. And obviously Jacques de Molay guessed that it would be a long time before the order rose again, if it ever did, and so there was one additional paragraph on that parchment. In it, in his role as the Grand Master and as a way of trying to safeguard everything that the order owned, de Molay passed on the ownership of all the Templar wealth to his son and, more importantly, to his son's offspring, down through the generations in perpetuity, obviously to try to achieve some kind of continuity."

"So what?"

"So, you remember I told you I was researching my family history? I was surprised when the main branch of my family tree shifted north to Scotland, and even more surprised when it jumped over to France a few centuries earlier, but I've checked it several times now, and the results are always the same. De Molay's son brought the treasure out of France, and transported it on to Scotland using the Templar fleet that sailed out of Honfleur. But to foil any attempts by the Dominicans or anyone else to seize it, when he arrived in Scotland he and his companions, the Templar knights charged with accompanying him and guarding the treasure, made sure that it was really well hidden. Then he must have built on the preparations that Jacques de Molay had already put in place in Cyprus at the castle of Saint Hilarion, and also worked with the Templars who'd escaped from France into Switzerland with the Templar Archive. They must have prepared and encrypted the clues that would lead to the final hiding place of the treasure, and he must have done his best to ensure that the trail and the meaning of the messages would be intelligible only to a fellow Templar. That was his intention, anyway.

"But the son of Jacques de Molay did something else as well. He changed his surname from de Molay to Mallay, and that, over the years, morphed into Mallory. Having done everything that he could to ensure that the Knights Templar order would have access to the assets if the order ever rose again, he also settled down in Scotland, got married, and had children in his new country. Jacques de Molay had stated and arranged that the succession would be through primogeniture, through the firstborn and through the male line, and the whole point about this is that that is what I am. I'm a direct lineal male descendant of the last Grand Master of the Knights Templar, firstborn all the way, and I can prove it.

"It'll be an epic legal struggle, I've no doubt," Mallory finished, "but I think I've got enough evidence to prove that everything that we found in that tunnel actually belongs to me."

"You mean you think you're the last of the Knights Templar?" Robin asked, a broad smile on her face.

"That's a bit of a stretch," Mallory admitted, "though I suppose I've got more right to call myself that than any of these idiots who prance around wearing funny clothes and pretending that they're modern-day Templars. And I'm certainly unique because I used a genuine Templar battle sword today in personal combat with an enemy. And kind of won the fight, I suppose. But I definitely wouldn't call myself a Templar, and certainly not a Templar knight. What I am really is just the beneficiary of the Knights Templar order.

"But however you look at it, that's one hell of an inheritance."

Author's Note

The Knights Templar

From its earliest days, the order of the Knights Templar didn't really make sense. Ostensibly, it was a group of nine warrior monks, all related by either blood or marriage, or both, to the founder, Hugues de Payens, and it had been formed in 1119 with the stated objective of protecting pilgrims on their journey to Jerusalem. Quite how a force so small could possibly guard the thousands of miles of pilgrim routes that ran across Europe, or even the dozens of miles within the Holy Land, was never explained.

They received permission from King Baldwin II of Jerusalem to establish their headquarters on the Temple Mount, and they were accommodated in the Al-Aqsa Mosque, then known in Latin as the *Templum Solomonis*, because it was believed to have been erected on the original site of Solomon's Temple. Indeed, their lodging was largely responsible for the official name the order adopted:

the *Pauperes commilitones Christi Templique Solomonici* or the "Poor Fellow-Soldiers of Christ and of the Temple of Solomon."

The very first thing the order of the Knights Templar did after its formation was spend an inordinate amount of time—nine years, in fact—digging into and under the Temple Mount in Jerusalem, apparently searching for something quite specific and obviously of great importance to them. Exactly what they were looking for has never been definitively established. Some researchers have suggested it was either a kind of monetary treasure— though this seems unlikely in view of the determined efforts made by the order to accumulate funds soon afterward— or more possibly a religious artifact, perhaps even the fabled "Baphomet," the sacred head or skull the members of the order were believed to venerate.

That these excavations took place is beyond doubt, as Templar relics were found in the hidden chambers under the Mount by Charles Warren during his sponsored dig there between 1867 and 1870. He later became Sir Charles Warren, the Commissioner of Police of the Metropolis, the head of the Metropolitan Police in London, and the man who famously failed to capture Jack the Ripper.

In 1129, the Templar order was officially sanctioned by the Catholic Church at the Council of Troyes and immediately began asking for donations of land or money, or both, and also for the sons of noble families to join the cause to fight the good fight. It was stated that the funds and assets would help provide protection for pilgrims and for the defense of Jerusalem, and by implication also assist the donor in securing a place in heaven.

Only a decade later, in 1139, Pope Innocent II issued the papal bull *Omne Datum Optimum*, which was by any standards an astonishing document. It exempted the Templars from having to obey any local laws and from the payment of any taxes. It was the ultimate get-out-of-jail-free card that allowed the Templars to go where they liked, to cross any border and to do whatever they wanted, subject only to the authority of the pope.

No other military or religious order, before or since, has received anything like this blanket freedom and privilege from the Vatican, and nobody has ever managed to explain how the Knights Templar, formed only twenty years earlier, achieved this. There is a strong argument to suggest that the pope was so terrified of some object the order possessed—and by implication something they found in Jerusalem in the hidden chambers under the Temple Mount—that he gave the Templars whatever they wanted. If that were the case, then what the order owned had to have been of enormous religious significance. The two obvious contenders are the Ark of the Covenant—which quite probably at one time was hidden at Chartres Cathedral in France, as is discussed in the second book of this trilogy, *The Templar Archive*—or something that had the potential to destroy the Catholic Church, like the severed head of Jesus Christ.

A papal bull, by the way, was a specific charter or letter issued by the pope, and the unusual name is derived from the lead seal known as a *bulla* that was attached to the document as a form of authentication.

From the outset, the concept of armed monks was criticized—how could a man of peace carry a sword?—but the order was legitimized by the influential Bernard of Clairvaux, a nephew of one of the original knights who wrote a long treatise called *De Laude Novae Militae* or "In Praise of the New Knighthood," which not only supported the Templars as a group, but also defended the idea of a military religious order by appealing to the long-held Christian beliefs of fighting a just war and the taking up of arms to protect both the innocent and the Church against attack. By his actions, Bernard endorsed the mission of the Templars, who thus became the first "warrior monks" of the Western world.

The Templars very quickly became established in Jerusalem and started to spread their influence well beyond the confines of the Holy Land. The order soon became, by far, the most powerful of all the medieval religious orders, and was actually far more wealthy than many rulers and even some nations, both because of the estates and other assets donated to it by its members and benefactors, and also from its continent-wide banking activities. Almost all the modern financial instruments with which we are familiar—checks, letters of credit, interest, bank charges, loans, mortgages, bearer bonds, and the like—were invented by the Templars in the medieval period.

The Templars' headquarters in Paris were established after they loaned a huge sum of money to King Louis VII of France in 1147. Unable to repay the order in cash, the king handed over extensive tracts of land in Paris, mostly in the eastern part of the Marais, where the Templars built one of their largest commanderies, the Paris Temple. Though the buildings are long gone, the names endure in the rue du Temple and the rue Vieille du Temple, and the Temple Metro station. There are other extant references to the order as well, including an autoroute rest area called the Aire du Fond de la Commanderie near Conchil-le-Temple, a large village formerly owned by the Templars in the Nord-Pas-de-Calais region of France.

Philip IV of France, known as Philip the Fair, was essentially bankrupt, financially and morally, as was his country, and when he ordered the arrest of all the members of the order of warrior monks and the confiscation of their assets in 1307, his motive was entirely mercenary: he wanted the Templar treasure, and extirpating the Templar "heresy"—essentially an invented crime against the Church—was the excuse he had decided to use to get it.

Or rather he didn't, because when his troops entered not only the Paris preceptory but also all the other Templar fortresses in France, there was almost no treasure to be found, and remarkably few members of the order either. Despite the blanket secrecy of Philip's campaign, news of his intentions had obviously leaked, and the order had made its own plans accordingly.

The Templar fleet, which sailed from Honfleur in late September, probably carried much of the treasure, most likely to Scotland, although Oak Island in Nova Scotia (the "Money Pit" that is discussed in this novel) has been suggested as an alternative destination. The remainder was most likely removed from the various fortresses and secreted elsewhere in France or in neighboring countries like Portugal. To date, not one single coin from the vast hoard is known to have been found anywhere.

The information given in this novel about the village of Temple, the route probably followed by the fleet from Honfleur, and the possibility that the lost treasure of the Templars may be hidden somewhere in the vicinity is entirely accurate, or as accurate as it is possible to be some seven hundred years after the event.

The Templecombe Head, the Mandylion, and the Shroud of Turin

The Templecombe Head is real and is as described in this novel. It was discovered during the Second World War by a woman named Molly Drew, who described the image as a face surrounded by brilliantly painted colors of red, blue, and green—colors that faded away almost to nothing when the local vicar popped the painting into his bath and scrubbed it with scouring powder, an unforgivable act of religious vandalism no matter what his motives. The earliest date for the oak on which the painting was created is 1280 AD, based on radiocarbon dating, and the style of the work is clearly medieval.

A number of theories have been put forward about both the subject and the purpose of the painting. The two leading contenders are Jesus Christ and John the Baptist as the subject, and it does appear likely that the original painting was owned by the Templars, may well have been on display in their local chapel at Templecombe, and may possibly have been an icon or idol that they would have venerated. One of the charges leveled against the Templars by their Dominican inquisitors was that they worshipped idols.

It has also been established that the Templars traded relics during their occupation of parts of the Holy Land, which might suggest that the painting is a copy of the Mandylion, also known as the Image of Edessa, the cloth that is claimed to have been miraculously imprinted with the face of Jesus Christ.

The Mandylion itself has been linked to the Shroud of Turin, the suggestion being that the Mandylion was simply the Shroud folded so as to only display the face of the figure, but this seems unlikely, as stories about the Mandylion were in circulation at least as early as the fifth century AD, and radiocarbon dating has positively confirmed that the Shroud of Turin is far more recent, dating from between 1260 and 1390. Various challenges to this date and to the radiocarbon testing procedures have been made, but none of them stands up to impartial scientific scrutiny. It is now well established that the Shroud is a very clever medieval forgery, though many people still dispute this for reasons of their own.

It's perhaps also worth mentioning that although the image of the man on the Shroud fits very well with other medieval representations of Jesus Christ, it bears no resemblance whatsoever to the very few near-contemporary descriptions of Him, lending obvious weight to the forgery hypothesis.

Celsus, for example, writing in the second century AD,

described Jesus as "ugly and small." Other near-contemporary sources are in broad agreement, suggesting that He was bald, short, perhaps only three cubits—about four feet six inches—tall, with a long face and a connate eyebrow (a monobrow in modern parlance), and possibly physically deformed, maybe even being a hunchback. It's been suggested that the taunt "Physician, heal thyself" was used because of some obvious deformity of His body. Tertullian stated that he had an "ignoble appearance" and that physically He was in "abject condition," while Irenaeus claimed that He was a "weak and inglorious man."

The Bible itself confirms this. There's only one reference to Jesus's physical appearance in the entire text, in Isaiah 53:2. This states that "He had no beauty or majesty to attract us to Him, nothing in His appearance that we should desire Him."

A kind of backlash against these descriptions began in the early Middle Ages when a variety of documents of either unknown or at least questionable origin began circulating. These described Jesus in the way that He is generally depicted today, as a tall, handsome, and almost-angelic figure, presumably driven by the argument that the alleged son of God had to appear almost godlike Himself. By the nineteenth century, Christ had acquired an almost Aryan appearance in the eyes of many Europeans, no doubt influenced by prevailing anti-Semitic attitudes, despite the obvious fact that, whatever He actually looked like, Jesus was definitely a Jew.

Why the Templecombe Head disappeared from the pages of history only to reappear in the middle of the twentieth century is unknown. It's been suggested that when the Templar order was suppressed at the start of the fourteenth century, the Head was hidden away for safe-keeping in a secular rather than in a religious building for fear that it would be confiscated as a result of the trials of the English Templars. It's also possible that the Head disappeared a couple of hundred years later, in the middle of the sixteenth century, when the order of the Hospital-lers, the successors to the Templars, was dissolved on the orders of King Henry VIII, the relic possibly again being hidden to avoid confiscation.

But the short answer is that nobody actually knows, and the origins of the Templecombe Head are as mysterious today as they were when it surfaced in the 1940s. The Head is usually on display in the church at Templecombe, but it does occasionally go traveling to be featured in exhibitions around Britain.

The Anglican Church of Saint Mary at Templecombe dates from the twelfth century and is a Grade II listed building. The appearance of the tower is exactly as described in this novel, and it does look much more like a part of a fortification than of a religious building.

Friday the Thirteenth

It's a myth that Friday the thirteenth is considered unlucky because that was the day—Friday, 13 October 1307—when the mass arrests of the Knights Templar Order took place. In fact, the thirteenth day of the month was already thought of as being somewhat unlucky well before the medieval period because it was the number after twelve.

Numerology has always been quite important in history, and twelve was thought to represent completeness: things like the twelve tribes of Israel, the twelve apostles, the twelve months of the year, and so on. But the number thirteen was both irregular and a prime number, and there was an old superstition that if there were thirteen guests at the table for a meal, one of them would die soon afterward. That might have had its origins in the last supper—Jesus plus the twelve disciples—but nobody's very sure.

Friday by itself has also been thought of as an unlucky day of the week. Christ was supposed to have been crucified on a Friday, and since at least the fourteenth century, it's been thought of as a bad day to begin a journey or start a new business venture or other project.

But although the thirteenth was thought to be unlucky for a couple of millennia, it was only in the very early part of the twentieth century that Friday was added to the date, and that quite possibly derived from a novel, of all things. In 1907, a book called *Friday the Thirteenth* was published. It was written by a man named Thomas Lawson, and the plot involved a crooked stockbroker who engineered a panic on Wall Street on Friday the thirteenth. Certainly, after 1907, there were plenty of references to that day and date as being unlucky, and almost none before that year.

Gilmerton Cove and Rosslyn Chapel

Gilmerton Cove is also real, and what is known of its history is precisely as described in this novel. There is indeed a doorway in the cave system—a doorway that clearly leads under a nearby road and from which the rubble cannot be moved for reasons of safety. It is also true that the space beyond that doorway appears to point almost directly to Rosslyn Chapel. Whether or not there actually is a tunnel that extends all the way between the two structures is unknown.

Rosslyn Chapel is also as described and does contain a number of anomalies, including carvings that look remarkably like corncobs, which were unknown in Europe until after the discovery of North America in the years following the voyages of Columbus, well after the chapel had been built. Columbus sailed on his first voyage in 1492 but never got near enough to North America to detect the continental landmass on that or any of his subsequent voyages. In fact, it was Giovanni Caboto—his Anglicized name being John Cabot—who first landed on the coast of North America in 1497, though the Vikings had certainly been there about half a millennium earlier. They had tried to settle on the continent but had been driven away because of violent clashes with the indigenous population, who of course greatly outnumbered them.

Various sources state that building Rosslyn Chapel began in 1446, but this is inaccurate. In 1446, permission was granted by Rome to construct the chapel, the Vatican having had a long reach in those days, but the actual construction only began in September 1456.

The story about the Apprentice Pillar is also accurate, at least in terms of the legend, which does appear to be based upon a real event—the killing of an apprentice mason by his master—though there is no suggestion that there is any kind of hidden cavity or chamber lying below the base of the pillar. However, fairly recent surveys, including the use of ground-penetrating radar, have demonstrated that there are underground cavities, presumably crypts or some other kind of chamber, lying below and around the chapel itself. To date, none of these has been excavated or explored.

The Crusades

The words "crusade" and "crusader" are derived from oaths sworn by fighting men. When the armies arrived in the Holy Land to combat the infidels, they were each given a cross to sew onto their clothing when they finally arrived in Jerusalem to mark the oath that they had taken. This was known as the "taking of the Cross," and the symbol itself as the *croix* or *crux*. The name "crusader" evolved from that and the entire operation then became known as a "crusade."

About the Author

James Becker spent more than twenty years in the Royal Navy's Fleet Air Arm. Throughout his career he was involved in covert operations in many of the world's hot spots, including Yemen, Russia, and Northern Ireland. He is the author of *The Templar Archive* and *The Lost Treasure of the Templars,* as well as the Chris Bronson novels, including *The Lost Testament* and *Echo of the Reich.* He has also written action-adventure novels under the name James Barrington, military novels as Max Adams, and novels exploring conspiracy theories as Jack Steel in the UK.

CONNECT ONLINE

james-becker.com

Ready to find
your next great read?

Let us help.

Visit prh.com/nextread

Penguin
Random
House